Sorry
For
Your
Loss

Georgia McVeigh grew up in the south-west of England, and studied English Literature at Newcastle University. She works as the in-house editor for a literary agency. In 2022, she completed the Faber Academy Writing A Novel course, where she developed the concept for *Sorry For Your Loss*. She currently lives in London.

Sorry For Your Loss

GEORGIA McVEIGH

CORVUS

Published in paperback in Great Britain in 2026 by Corvus,
an imprint of Atlantic Books Ltd.

1 2 3 4 5 6 7 8 9

A CIP catalogue record for this book is available from the British Library.

Paperback ISBN: 978 1 80546 448 8
E-book ISBN: 978 1 80546 449 5

Printed and bound by CPI (UK) Ltd, Croydon CR0 4YY

Corvus
An imprint of Atlantic Books Ltd
Ormond House
26–27 Boswell Street
London
WC1N 3JZ

www.atlantic-books.co.uk

Product safety EU representative: Authorised Rep Compliance Ltd., Ground Floor, 71 Lower Baggot Street, Dublin, D02 P593, Ireland. www.arccompliance.com

For Dom, without whom this book would not exist.

1

When I think back, I see chairs arranged in a circle. Small, hard and plastic, they come in a range of primary colours, blotches of forced brightness in the otherwise drab, depressing space. Lino floors with chewing gum trodden into nondescript discs, a battered corkboard bearing peeling posters. The room has only two windows. The view through the streaked, dirty glass is of the car park.

This room has an assortment of uses. Knitting clubs, the local playgroup, dodgeball. More often than not, the chairs remain stacked against the wall. Towers of clashing reds and blues packed away to create more space for these joyful activities.

As far as I know, the circular formation is unique to Tuesday evenings. Unique to our particular group. The circle, you see, is a symbol of many things. It represents beginnings, it represents endings. Our group, obviously, is more concerned with the latter.

I would have liked some ambient noise to mask my entry: the rustle of a coat perhaps, or the low rumble of voices. Instead, there is only the *whump* of the swing door settling behind me, the squeak of my rubber soles against the floor. Here, silent as the grave is not just an expression; it's a mantra.

Fiona purses her lips as I take my seat. I sense, rather than see, that she's glaring at me, so I take my time to shrug out of my coat and settle myself on the chair. I don't make a habit of being late, but we've played this game a few times. It's important, I've discovered, to keep Fiona on her toes.

Only when I have finished rubbing sanitiser into my hands does Fiona clear her throat and shuffle her papers with a self-importance that is astonishing for a woman whose greatest achievement is the death of her husband. The smell of rubbing alcohol is sharp in the air.

'Now that we're *all* here, let's make a start, shall we?'

I don't dislike Fiona. In many ways, I admire her tenacity. Not many people have the stomach to profit from other people's despair, yet she does it with an enthusiasm that borders on relish. She's got a strong nose for business, and the personality to boot. If it weren't anti-feminist, you'd likely describe her as a battleaxe, but it is, so I won't. There *is* a whisper of the Miss Trunchbull about her, though. All of which is why, today, I'm alarmed to see her ample bosom inflating in a way that might almost be described as flirtatious, a flush spreading into those already ruddy cheeks.

'You might notice,' she says in a sugary voice I've never heard before, 'that we have a new member joining us today.'

She points to a man on the other side of the circle. I can't believe I didn't notice him before. We don't often get new members, and it's always an exciting diversion from the usual order of play: tears and long, meandering monologues that most of us have heard fifteen times before. Personally, I like to mix it up a bit when I speak. Critical to keep your audience engaged.

The reason for Fiona's sickening personality shift is instantly obvious. He's *very* attractive. Even though he's sitting down, I can tell he's tall. There's a nice symmetry to his face, too, and he has a full head of hair (which, when a man has suffered a loss, is not a guarantee). If I weren't here under such tragic circumstances, I might even be tempted myself.

The man seems utterly unbothered by our scrutiny, which is not always the case. I like to think we can be quite intimidating as a pack, and there have been occasions when new members have crumbled under the weight of our unsmiling stares. We don't mess around here. This is a serious group for serious loss.

This man, however, raises his hand in an almost lazy acknowledgement of our attention. Bereavement suits him. The three-day-old stubble gives him a rugged, unruly quality, and his suit hangs from him in a way that only emphasises his lithe frame. I bet he's pure muscle underneath—

I stop myself there. It's easy to become carried away in these sorts of situations, and I must keep my mind on the matter at hand: Freddie.

'This is Jack.' Fiona says, and simpers. Christ, even her cleavage is flushed now.

'Hi Jack,' we chorus back in monotone, to show how sad and solemn we are. Fiona looks as though she'd quite like to ask us to do it once more, *with feeling.*

'Do you feel comfortable sharing who you've lost, Jack?'

He clears his throat: a gruff, deep rumble. God, he's good-looking. Rita's clocked it too, now. She's staring at him, sucking in her cheeks, making her look not unlike an odd, inverted hamster, but at least she had the foresight to put make-up on. I look like shit. I have, admittedly, let myself go somewhat in the last few months.

'Sure,' Jack says, and as a collective we sit up a little straighter. There's a certain presence to him that even the men in our group – Charlie and Matt – have picked up on. With a single word, he's commanded our attention in a way that's almost enviable. I study his body language. He's leaning forward slightly, as though he's drawing us into his confidence. His hands are clasped tightly in his lap for sincerity, his brows pulled together for seriousness. It's good. Very good. 'I'm here,' he continues, 'because I lost my wife, Alice. She died of cancer earlier this year. Sixth of June.'

It takes me a moment to compute what he's said. I'm so focused on the clarity of his delivery, the projection of his voice, that the date does not immediately register. But when it does, my heart gives a little leap of excitement.

'Did you say sixth of June?' The eagerness has leached into my voice – not a good look – and I tone it down instantly. 'Sorry.' I clear my throat. That's better. Duller, deader. 'It's just, that's the date I lost my partner, Freddie. Sixth of June, this year.'

Jack looks at me for the first time, and I experience a lurch of intense desire. 'I'm so sorry to hear that,' he says. Then he looks away again, and it feels like the sun has slipped behind a cloud.

'Thank you, *Iris*.' Fiona's dropped all pretence now. To be fair, I have broken a cardinal rule: that we do not, under any circumstances, interrupt another member when they're speaking. I glance at Jack. He's new. He won't know the difference.

Fiona tries to claw back her composure and fails miserably. 'That was very brave, Jack. Well done,' she says, with a chip of ice in her tone.

'I'm just going to do a little rundown of the way this particular bereavement group works, and then we'll go round in a circle and introduce ourselves. I'm Fiona and I'm the group leader. Any concerns, come straight to me, yes?' Back on familiar ground, she hits her stride again. She loves new members almost as much as I do.

Fiona lost her own husband ten years ago and, in the wake of his death, wrote a nearly successful self-help book, which she flogs to all new members like it's the much-anticipated new chapter of the Bible. She now turns a profit by giving talks about her healing process, and I am beginning to wonder if losing her husband isn't the best thing that ever happened to her.

'This is a safe space. I want you to be able to share your feelings, whatever they may be, in a non-judgemental way. It's important to note that we are a social bereavement group; this is not group therapy, nor is it purporting to be. The aim is to bring people who have suffered a loss together – but bear in mind that not everyone will have experienced the same type of loss as you. We just ask that you are patient: others' experience may differ from your own, but that doesn't make their feelings any less valid. Understood?' She says all of this very fast, as though she is the voiceover for a radio jingle and is trying to fit the terms and conditions into the designated eight-second time slot at the end.

Jack nods, and Fiona turns to me.

'Iris, since you were so keen to interject, you can start.'

It feels, suddenly, like a lot is resting on what I say next. For one thing, I'm a little put out by the success of Jack's introduction. He played it perfectly: a tough act to follow. For another, I need him to notice me again. That look he gave me: something long-dormant stirred. And that's without even touching on the elephant in the room. His wife, dying on the exact same day as Freddie. I mean, really. What are the chances? It's like it was meant to be.

So, obviously, what I say next is critical. I have just this one chance to impress him. To impress *upon* him that I am someone worth more than a fleeting glance.

I start by leaning forward. It's a good trick, one I'll bank for future use if this is a success. I wait until the shuffling of feet has ceased, until all eyes in the room are fixed on me. I emit a deep, laboured sigh. Just to remind everyone why we're here.

'I'm Iris.' Nailed it. The perfect combination of sorrow and fortitude. 'As I mentioned just now – sorry, Fiona – I lost my partner, Freddie on the same date. Sixth of June.' A small, wary chuckle. As though I can't believe the coincidence of it. Which, to be fair, I can't. Jack sits up straighter. I've got him on the line, now I just need to land the finish. 'What I *didn't* mention...' Pause for another, shaky breath to emphasise the aforementioned fortitude. 'Is that Freddie wasn't just my boyfriend. He was my fiancé. He'd asked me to marry him a few days before he died.'

Is there anything more tragic than a love cut short? It's sad to lose your wife, sure, but by that point all those little idiosyncrasies that you found so adorable at the beginning have begun to grate. But an engagement ended by an untimely death? That's peak tragedy. That's the death of hope itself.

The others clearly think so, too. Rita's hand is clamped over her mouth in shock. I think I see the glaze of tears in her eyes, though admittedly that's not entirely unusual for her. Jack's eyebrows have knitted together in sympathy. I take a risk then: I press my tongue hard to the roof of my mouth and give him my most winning smile. I haven't used it in nearly six months, but it's all coming back to me now. In response Jack gives me a small, uncertain smile, but at least he's still looking at me.

Only Fiona does not look entirely convinced.

'But… you're not wearing a ring?' she says. I don't appreciate the challenge in her tone.

'A ring is a patriarchal construct, Fiona. It feeds into the idea that a man owns a woman.'

But there was a ring.

And I would have worn it.

2

I try to keep thoughts of Freddie to a minimum. It's not that I don't care. I do. But it's distressing to dwell on just how close I came to happiness. To companionship. That feeling of having someone *there*. He always seemed to know when I'd had a long day, like we were connected by some invisible thread. He'd put a bracing hand on my shoulder, just to let me know he was there, or send a thoughtful message: *You OK?*

I'm painfully aware, however, that rehashing every peak and trough of the relationship is not conducive to moving on. That's how you slip into bitterness. And, on the whole, I'm adept at keeping memories of Freddie at bay. I keep busy and work hard. I avoid silence. When things get really tough, I clean.

It may not surprise you to hear that the one place I struggle with thoughts of Freddie is the grief group, though not for the reasons you might think. It's more of a pacing issue than any deep-buried emotion dredged up by someone else's melancholic speech. The truth is that bereavement groups are really quite slow. So slow, there have been occasions where I have no doubt the corpse of those they're mourning would get to the point faster.

And we are currently suffering through another painful silence from our least eloquent participant: Charlie. After my shock confession, it's an abrupt return to the mundane, and – judging by the distant expressions – not a particularly welcome one.

Tonight, though, it's not Freddie occupying my thoughts, but Jack. My little speech went down better than I could have predicted. Every so often, we catch eyes. Jack always looks away quickly, but not before I've clocked it. We are an hour into the session, and he has looked at me twenty times already. That's got to mean something.

The last time I felt excitement like this was at the start of my relationship with Freddie. I was languishing then, too, stuck in the hellish normality of daily life. Looking back, I think I was a bit lost. Floating through early adult-hood without point or purpose. Freddie changed that. He changed everything.

It's all coming back to me now, like a rusty cog slotting into place. The smile I gave Jack earlier was over the top. I won't make that mistake again. It's crucial I don't come across as too keen. *Take the game out of it, and they lose interest instantly.* A little nugget of advice that my brain has kept tucked away all these months, as though it knew I might need it again. Yes, it's all returning to me now.

I pretend not to notice Jack taking me in. I fight the urge to cover my hair. I haven't washed it for three days.

My roots are an abomination. I'll have to deal with them before next week. I straighten my spine, square my shoulders, rest my hands softly in my lap. I cock my head, gaze fixed firmly on Charlie, and pretend to be absorbed in his prevailing silence, which is no easy feat.

It never ceases to amaze me, the effect male attention can have. I feel more alive tonight than I have in weeks, though I appreciate this is probably the wrong forum to boast about vitality. Don't get me wrong, I don't condone wrapping one's entire sense of self around the male gaze, but we all know it feels good, even if it is taboo to admit it. It's nice, to be looked at again. Particularly when it's by someone like Jack. By someone like Freddie.

I was new to this game when I met Freddie. Stuck in a dead-end job I was desperate to leave and still smarting from the labels I'd been branded with at university four years before: strange, intense, loner. That last one hurt the most, because it implied complicity on my part. I'd begun to wonder if I really was the issue, before Freddie showed an interest in me. Then, I realised it was everyone else.

We met in a coffee shop. I spotted him instantly: he was the most attractive man in there; and I was not the only one to notice. The barista was giving him a strong side-eye, which, from what I'd observed, could work wonders on the unsuspecting male. I had to move fast, find a way to get his attention, and so, as I walked towards the counter, I stumbled slightly and grabbed for his arm to steady myself.

'Whoa,' he'd said. 'Careful. Are you OK?'

I'd blushed prettily (not something I can generally do on command, but everyone in the shop was staring at me) and looked up at him through my lashes. 'Yes. So sorry. I don't know what happened there.'

He smiled, and, though it was wide and open and honest, I thought I recognised something beneath: something sad, which he'd gone to great lengths to conceal. It chimed with something inside of me, too. 'I'm always half-asleep before I have my morning coffee, too,' he'd said.

He was kind like that. Willing to put himself in others' shoes. It was one of the things I loved most about him. I didn't tell him that I was only in the café to pass the time before a covert interview for a job that I hoped might raise my frightful prospects. That I thought coffee tasted like mud. 'Exactly,' I said, mirroring his easy, casual stance.

Always the gentleman, he allowed me to go ahead of him. I knew he was listening, so I ordered a cappuccino, but when I went to pay he slipped round me, tapped his card on the machine and winked. The rush of attraction was so strong, I can feel it even now.

'My good deed for the day,' he said. Men do love playing the hero.

Imagine my surprise, then, when I walked into the interview room – for a design job at a magazine publishing company – later that same morning, and he was sitting there. A coincidence too strange to be insignificant. I learned that – should I get the role – he would be my manager.

'Small world!' he'd said with a laugh when he saw me. Buoyed by his presence, I performed well in the interview, but I couldn't help but feel that our encounter in the coffee shop clinched it for me. They offered me the job on the spot, and I started a month later.

See? Told you the group often sends me on a jaunty trip down memory lane. We're wrapping up now. Jack sends one final glance in my direction. If I've played my cards right, he'll try to talk to me at the end, prompted by my staunch refusal to engage with him. It's a delicious thought, a game I know how to play well. Marcie's magazines taught me the rules: *to generate interest, play it cool. Let him come to you.* I hope I'm not too rusty conversationally. Flirtatious looks are one thing. Dialogue is quite another.

But Jack doesn't try to speak to me at the end. He's the first out of his chair, and he heads towards the exit without a second glance. I'm momentarily dumbstruck, staring after him, open-mouthed. I was sure I'd done it right. I'd gone by the book: stirring his interest, before appearing indifferent to his response. I set up the game flawlessly, laying the pieces carefully on the board, but now he's refusing to play.

It must have been my hair. It really is bad. Thin, greasy and brittle. I'll book an appointment with the hairdresser. *Then* we'll see if he can resist my charms.

I'm the last to leave. I pick up my coat, head through the door to the lobby, and catch sight of the signing-out book. Fiona tries to insist we sign in and out in accordance with health and safety regulations, but most of us don't bother. A small act of rebellion, two fingers to sadness. Jack doesn't know that, though.

I run my finger down the list and there he is. Right at the bottom. The hasty scrawl of a man in a hurry.

Jack Reynolds.

3

It's vital to move quickly in these scenarios, because they don't come along very often. The coincidence with the date is too significant to ignore: someone, somewhere, has given me a second chance at love, and I intend to grasp it with both hands. I pull out my phone as my bus winds its way through the quiet streets towards home. It doesn't take me long to find Jack's Facebook profile. Over a thousand friends and not a single mutual. A shame. A connection would have given us something else in common, but I'll have to work with what I've got. I don't add him, obviously – I'm not a creep – but I do scroll through the photos that are publicly accessible.

He comes from money, that much is clear. The tailored suit and clipped vowels could have told me that, but these pictures confirm it. They go back years, depicting a painful combination of Jack Wills shirts, rolling tobacco and grey tracksuit bottoms pulled low to accidentally on purpose reveal Calvin Klein underwear. Evidently, he likes a party. And women. There are many of him in his teenage years, clearly tanked on booze and God knows what else, with his arm draped round girls who all look the same: back-brushed blond hair, smudged eyeliner, white smiles that must have cost thousands.

To his credit, the profile looks as though it is now all but defunct. The last profile picture he uploaded was in 2012, which was a questionable time even for those of us who didn't attend fifty-thousand-pound-a-year boarding schools.

His Instagram profile, set to the highest level of privacy, reveals even less, though the thumbnail – a picture of him standing atop a cliff wearing hiking gear – suggests he has, at least, moved on from posing with champagne girls in seedy nightclubs. No sign of the wife. I don't know if that's a good or a bad thing.

I can't remember her name. I was so distracted by his flawless introduction that it went straight over my head. It started with an A, I know that. Anna, maybe. Alice? That was it.

A quick search for Alice Reynolds reveals nothing, and then the bus pulls in to my stop, and I have to jam my finger into the button several times and run for the exit before it pulls away again. On the pavement, I fumble for my hand sanitiser and apply it liberally, feeling sick. I try to block the thought of the germ-infested button. Only once the 99.9 per cent effective sanitiser has dried on my skin do I feel better and begin the walk home.

Home – for the next twelve hours only – is a flat on the ground floor of an imposing redbrick mansion block.

From the outside, you would be forgiven for thinking that I, too, had a charmed upbringing. You would be wrong. It may have been grand once – circa the Victorian era – but on the inside, its age shows. For the last six years, I have contended – daily – with weak water pressure from the ancient pipes, black mould in the bathroom, and my landlord, Barry, who 'pops his head round the door' most days – ostensibly to complete some maintenance task, though we both know it's in the hope of catching me in various states of undress.

It is not, therefore, a surprise to find him lurking in the entrance hall as I step through the front door. Any lingering sentimentality about my departure is quickly dispelled. Barry is one male whose gaze is not – and never will be – welcome.

When he sees me, Barry resumes what he believes to be his most casually alluring pose. He rests one hand on the doorframe to his own flat and sucks in his stomach, the furred bottom of which pokes out from beneath his stained T-shirt that is three sizes too small.

'S'not too late, you know.'

I'm not close enough to catch a whiff of his unique brand of halitosis, but I take a precautionary step back anyway.

'I'm good, Barry. Thanks, though.'

'We wouldn't have to go the whole way. We could work our way up. You can have the flat on a week-by-week basis. That's a good deal, right? An hour of fun for a week of free accommodation?'

It pains me to admit it, but I have given serious consideration to this proposal. Barry smells, picks his nose, and, I suspect – strongly – that the last time he washed his genitalia was three months ago, when he asked if he could use my shower due to a build-up of limescale in his own. To put it politely, the thought of his penis makes me want to projectile-vomit. So, I am stuck, as you might say, between a rock and a hard place. Because the alternative is nearly as horrifying as genital warts and three months' worth of smegma.

I've always prided myself on being a careful person, even to the point of fastidiousness. Grief blew that right out of the water. After Freddie's death and the unfortunate loss of my job, I became quite kamikaze about my prospects. I'd been working for five years by that point. In the absence of a social life, I'd built up quite a nice little nest egg. I'd hoped Freddie and I might use it as a deposit on a flat, but he was dead, and I was all alone. So, I didn't immediately try for another job. Instead, I chipped away at my egg until it was less ostrich, more quail. It was at that point I realised I was in trouble.

So, I did what any self-respecting young professional would do. I went to Barry with my tail between my legs, hoping he would take pity on a grieving woman. His kind 'offer' was the solution he came up with.

'I'm still fine, Barry. Thanks.'

He releases the breath that's been holding his stomach in. The T-shirt rides up another couple of inches in defeat. 'Staying with your mum, are you?'

I'd rather not think about it, so I nod tightly and hope he gets the hint. He doesn't.

'She live near here?'

If he thinks I am giving him even a clue as to my mother's address, then he really is delusional. 'No.'

'Will you come back and visit?'

'Probably not, Barry.' I deliver this in the tone of a doctor breaking the bad news to a terminally ill patient. 'Look after yourself, yeah?'

He approaches me for a hug, so I do a neat little sidestep, close the door in his face and stand with my back against it. When I hear his door close – with more force than is necessary – I flick on the light and turn to double-lock my own. Once I'm sure it's secure, I turn to survey the flat.

It is, to the casual observer, underwhelming. More so now it's been stripped of most of my possessions. A deep crack runs down the hallway from the kitchen to the bedroom. The ceiling in the living room sags ominously. A damp stain is spreading from the corner of the bathroom and mingling almost artistically with the creeping black mould in the centre of the room. To me, though, it's independence. Even the mould has become part of the furniture, though not through lack of trying on my part to remove it. It doesn't bother me as much as you might think. The house I grew up in looked more like a pigsty than a family home by the time I left. Perhaps because of that, I am anal to the point of obsessiveness about the cleanliness of my own flat. I hoover daily, wash my sheets twice a week, mop the floors and scrub the shower until the air is spiced with lemon and just a hint of bleach.

I need to be out of here in good time tomorrow, so I don't linger in the hallway. I've done most of the packing already, but I'm in a nostalgic mood, and there's one task I've been putting off since I made the decision to take my chances living with my mother over the mildly less desirable threat of contracting a vicious STD.

I keep Freddie's things in a shoebox at the bottom of the wardrobe. He'd have laughed to see me, handling it like an easily triggered bomb. It was weeks before I could even bring myself to look at it, many more before I was able to lift the lid on all the memories it contained. But I'm stronger now. I place it gingerly on the floor, wriggle the top free. My chest pangs. Inside, there is a tortoiseshell comb that still has little speckles of dandruff between each tooth, a pair of red plaid pyjama bottoms that I've never washed, the key to Freddie's flat. The necklace that always sends an eclectic cocktail of emotions zipping through me. Not all of them are positive, but grief will do that to you.

I lift the pyjamas to my nose, and there it is. That unique smell. Freddie's distinct, woody musk layered through the material.

He always looked so peaceful when he slept. Those long nights are some of my favourite memories of him. I loved watching him sleep. Those small, guttural exhales. Sometimes, I'd place my hand on his chest and feel such an intense rush of attraction I truly thought I'd never feel that way about another person. Tonight proved me wrong. It does happen, sometimes.

I inhale deeply one more time, then fold the pyjamas and place them back into the box. I close the lid, then place the box at the top of one of the three plastic containers I'm taking with me to Mum's. I sanitise.

And then, because the thought of my mother, and returning to that house, sends a shiver of revulsion up my spine, I distract myself by preparing Barry's leaving gift.

I spent, admittedly, more time than was healthy pondering this particular present. I pictured him, within two minutes of my departure, snuffling around the flat like a truffle pig, hunting for a stray pair of underwear he could bury his pockmarked nose into. I considered, seriously, leaving a decoy pair poking out from beneath the sofa, covered in all sorts of unsanitary substances. But my tastes run to the highbrow and, frankly, I wasn't sure that even some of my more deplorable ideas would be enough to put him off. I settled, instead, for a book.

I leave the copy of *Men Who Hate Women* by Laura Bates in the kitchen, where I know he will spot it. Lest he be in any doubt over the intended recipient, I've written a dedication on the flyleaf.

Barry
Thought you might get some use out of this.

Iris x

4

I was not, obviously, compos mentis at my birth, but I would imagine the look my mother is giving me now is not too dissimilar to the one she gave me when she first laid eyes on her wrinkled, scrunched newborn. Our first meeting was not, by all accounts, the joyous occasion that is written about in novels. Birth rarely is. This wasn't helped by the fact that there were two of us.

For nine months, my sister Marcie and I shared a womb. Squashed together in our amniotic fluid, we divided everything: every morsel of food was halved, every toxin from the illicit cigarettes Mum would sneak in the back garden divvied up between us. Marcie came out within twenty minutes of Mum going into labour: dark blond, easy smile already plastered to her pretty face. Forty hours later, after near-fatal complications, I emerged: black-haired, blue-tinged, with a head mis-shapen by the birth canal.

'They told me they'd never seen such an angry baby. Well, vocal, was the word they used. But I knew they meant angry. Couldn't shut you up,' Mum told me when I was eight. The words she refrained from saying sat heavy between us anyway: '*Not like your sister.*'

Mum was still covered in her own bodily fluids when she was handed the babies she'd birthed. Marcie had been cleaned up by that point. She was wearing a babygrow that had been gifted by my grandparents. A cashmere hat was placed delicately over her downy head. And I was naked. Still wrinkled from the birthing fluid and smeared with blood. In the picture my father took of the happy moment, Mum – looking exhausted – cradles a child in each arm. But it's Marcie she's staring at. Marcie who was the recipient of that unique, adoring motherly gaze. We'd divided everything up until that point, but now we'd emerged it was clear there was not enough love for the both of us.

Mum, who had never experienced that maternal ache for a child, fell hard and fast for Marcie. Prior to giving birth, she viewed babies with the sort of clinical apathy that Victorian doctors had towards women with hysteria: a necessary evil bestowed upon the female sex that – once begotten – was difficult to shift. Ironically, her choice to have us was one of the most rational decisions she ever made. Children were a non-negotiable for my father, and – like with most things he desired – she bent over backwards (perhaps literally in this case) to give it to him. She went above and beyond, as usual. Provided him with two for the price of one. She never did quite master the art of compromise.

So, she allowed her belly to balloon and her hormones to spike and counted every new stretchmark that appeared as the months passed. 'Thirty, Iris. You gave me thirty stretchmarks. Your father never looked at me the same way afterwards,' she told me when I was ten.

My father was a kind man who took an impressively hands-off approach towards child-rearing. Two, as it turned out, was a bit more than he'd bargained for. For the first three years, home was a chaotic mess of nappies and formula and sick and poo, and Dad took refuge in the office. I think he viewed himself as some sort of jovial, benevolent Santa Claus. A judicial figure, a connoisseur of punishment and reward, who appeared at the end of the evening to review the evidence presented by my mother and make a final judgement on whether we'd been naughty or nice. I can't help but feel that the ruling was never quite weighted in my favour.

I've often wondered what would have happened if I'd emerged first. How life might have turned out differently. Because there is another photo of Mum with her newborns. This one was tucked away in the back of a cupboard for years. It can't have been taken long after the first one, but the difference is stark. For one thing, Mum's looking at me. Her expression, laden with love when directed at Marcie, is now one of mild distaste. She could have pretended, I suppose, but I suspect her acting skills weren't up to par after two days of labour. Weakened, filthy and deflating like an old balloon as she was, her indifference towards this spare child was obvious.

It certainly is now.

'I nearly forgot you were coming!' She delivers this from the doorway with a casual flick of her hand.

I smile thinly in response, in the way you might at a child who has just told a blatant lie. It is blatant: the net curtain in her bedroom had twitched as I struggled down the street with my boxes and bags, and, unless she's found a man who can tolerate her frankly disgusting habits (unlikely), she's been watching for me. I don't bother to catch her out: it's too early for that, and I didn't sleep well last night.

She doesn't allow me in immediately. Her eye travels the length of me, lips lightly pursed. I've dressed down for the occasion: I'm wearing my oldest pair of joggers and – as much as it pained me – I didn't wash my hair last night, so it falls in lank, greasy curtains. She must be satisfied, because she gives a sharp nod of approval and steps back to allow me to pass her.

In the hallway, there's a brief moment of awkwardness. We both know how we *should* act, were this a traditional mother/daughter relationship, but that's not really our style. It's a question of whether we bother to pretend before slipping back into the familiar, serrated roles we're more comfortable with. Clearly – tediously – she feels we should. I have to stop myself from rolling my eyes as she steps forward and wraps her bony arms round my waist. I pat her stiffly on the protruding notches of her spine. She stinks of last night's indulgences: stale booze and too many cigarettes. I let go as quickly as is polite and wonder how she'd react if I applied my sanitiser. Probably best not to risk it.

'Well?' She steps back and bares her teeth in what I can only assume is her attempt at a smile. 'How does it feel to be home?'

Unlike her, I'm a brilliant actor, but I cannot find a single positive to focus on. It's disgusting. 'Home' (in heavily inverted commas) is a terraced house on a tree-lined street in Battersea. Bought by my parents thirty years ago, it still exhibits many of the decorative faux pas of the nineties, when the fast approach of Y2K – and the possibility of the world imploding – resulted in some questionable interior design decisions. I can only assume that the resurgence of net curtains was so that they would be able to make out the silhouette of the meteor hurtling towards the earth.

Unfortunately, it is clear that my mother has not had a change of heart towards either the décor or standard-practice hygiene and cleanliness in the six years since I last set foot in this house. Yellow nicotine stains dribble thin lines down the browning floral wallpaper. The threadbare runner on the stairs peels away to expose damp, rotting wood. Even the plastic orchid by the front door appears to have died a long and painful death. The air is thick with stale cigarette smoke.

I try not to indulge in self-pity – when you've experienced as much tragedy as I have, there's a very real risk of total submergence – but today is an exception. I allow myself a moment of longing for my lemon-scented flat. Even, briefly, for Barry, but I dispel that thought quickly.

'Did you do something new with the carpet?' I keep my voice light and point to the network of thread on the floor.

Mum's eyes narrow. 'You're forgetting, I *think*, who took you in in your hour of need.'

Annoyingly, she's right, and it would not do to piss her off too early. I duck my head – the picture of subservience. 'You're right, Mum. I'm sorry. I really appreciate it.' Smashed it. There's a lovely deep sincerity to my tone, which I must remember to use again.

She seems mollified, and finally the awkwardness of the initial reunion is over. Mum leads the way to the kitchen.

I thought the hallway was bad, but this is a total disgrace. It's a mess of plastics. Only one thin layer of dirty linoleum separates us from the foundations of the house. The surface of the tiny Formica table is mostly hidden beneath bills and shopping bags, though a small space has been cleared at one end for an overflowing ashtray, a chipped mug and a bottle of Tesco own-brand vodka. The counter surfaces aren't much better.

It's filthy. Visibly filthy. Doesn't even bother to pretend filthy. All I can think of are the millions of bacteria that must be crawling over every surface. I hover in the doorway and wonder if there's a way I can avoid touching anything. Mum bustles around the kitchen as though salmonella and E. coli and bacillus and H. pylori don't feature in her vocabulary. I dry-retch, quietly. I'm going to have to sit down. If I make a scene, it will rupture this uneasy pretence at peace, and it's too soon for that. I inch into the room, and perch on the very edge of the laminated wooden chair, watching her. The tap splutters with limescale, and I close my eyes and say a silent prayer to a God I don't believe in.

'So, tell me about how you're feeling about Frank,' she says, flicking on the kettle and lowering her voice conspiratorially. I'll give it to her: she's committed to the act.

'Frank?'

'Frank?' She reaches for the mugs above the sink. 'Or Freddie, that's it.'

I am so not in the mood to talk about Freddie with Mum. Don't get me wrong, he's my favourite subject when I feel strong enough, but not with her. Never with her. She wouldn't understand how it felt when he kissed me, how I came to rely on him with an intensity I didn't think possible. I wish I'd never told her about him. I pick at an old chip on the table. It's been there since we were children. I used to dig at it at teatime, try to widen it with my thumbnail. 'What do you want to know?'

This is entirely my fault. For the last six years, Mum and I have met for coffee every three months. I choose the place. Somewhere local, neutral, with at least two exits. Never, ever here. I'm not sure who decided that these rendezvous were a good idea considering we both usually leave in a mood that's worse than the one we arrived in, but she gets what she comes for (news on Dad) and I can pretend that someone in my family still cares about me. I told her about Freddie when our relationship was still budding, hardly able to keep the excitement from leaking into my tone. I am aware Mum thinks of me not unlike my university cohort did: that I'm odd. Fundamentally flawed. A natural loner. I'd thought – misguidedly – that mentioning a boyfriend might dispel some of these preconceived ideas.

'A boyfriend?' Her nostrils had flared. I'd thought she was going to laugh, and it made me want to claw at her face.

'Are you coping?' she asks now. She doesn't care, but, since we're doubling down on the charade, she might as well float the question. Usually, I love questions like these. Usually, I'd curl my hands into fists and press them hard into my eyes, as though I were stifling tears. I don't bother this time. Those sorts of displays never seem to work with her.

Freddie always thought I was too harsh on her. In my first week on the job, he sought me out in the small kitchen, ostensibly to check how I was settling in, but there was a charged undercurrent to the meeting. A slightly unprofessional eagerness about him. In how close he stood to me, in the way our hands brushed as we both reached for a mug at the same time. The slight flush that rose in his cheeks at the accidental contact. I was very aware of our sudden proximity, and I loved every moment of it.

He gathered himself, leaned against the counter, seemed to shake off the brief moment of electric awkwardness.

'And what's Iris's story, then? The unofficial version – not the one you gave in the interview.'

I loved that he was showing an interest in my life. He had a way of focusing totally on whomever he was speaking to. Of making you feel like you were the only person with a story worth hearing.

I wanted – no, I *needed* – to impress him. To be worthy of the way he was looking at me: like I was someone worth listening to. There was only one person I could think of who commanded respect like that. So, I borrowed one of her favourite tactics as I told my story. A slightly self-deprecating retelling, peppering the darker moments with light, so they bordered on amusing. I told him about my run-down flat and Barry, Dad leaving, and Mum's alcoholism. Our strained relationship.

'She sounds like a real character,' he'd replied.

'That's one word for it,' I said.

He'd passed a hand across his face, suddenly serious. 'Ah, but family's important though. They're all we've got, in the end.'

I sensed that there was something deeper layered beneath this statement, so I asked about his own family.

'It's just me and my parents. I had—' He broke off, took a breath. 'I had a brother. He died when we were small.'

I recalled the sadness that I'd seen in his eyes that day in the café and wondered if he'd seen the same reflected in my own. If he'd sensed that common grief, binding us

together even then. It made me even surer of our connection. And so, I told him about Marcie, pulse thudding in
my neck.

'God, Iris. I'm so sorry. No one really understands, do
they? What it's like. Not unless you've been through it.'

He reached out, touched me gently on the arm, and
I wondered if he knew how alone I sometimes felt. If he
felt the same. And I think he recognised, in that moment,
that he'd just found someone who might be able to change
that for us both.

Now, as Mum bustles around, I shrug. 'Mostly I just
try not to think of it.'

She places a mug of watery tea down in front of me. I
thank her, but I won't drink it. I can't even bring myself
to touch the mug.

Mum lowers herself into the seat opposite. She's just
over sixty, but it's the stiff movement of a much older
person. 'Losing a partner is the hardest thing I've ever
had to endure.'

I roll my eyes. Of course she brings it back to him.

'Freddie's dead, Mum. Dad moved to Surrey.'

She stiffens. Dad's departure – cowardly as it was – is
always a touchy subject.

'And your job?' Her voice is tight with annoyance. And
so, it begins.

'Still looking for something more permanent. I'm
working in a café for the time being.' I was vague when
Mum asked why I'd lost my job. I always got the sense
that she felt my grief for Freddie was somehow not quite

as acute as the grief she felt over losing my father. If I told her that I lost my job because Freddie's death made it impossible for me to function, I know she'd scoff. Think less of me.

'And how are you finding the café?'

I smile sweetly. 'Oh, you know. Pays the bills.'

'Well, it clearly doesn't.'

'It's an expression.'

'Right.'

A muscle tics in her jaw. She's holding back, and I know why. I have something she wants. It's the only reason she's let me stay. Sure enough, it's the next question she asks. She's so predictable it hurts.

'And how *is* your father?'

I stifle a sigh, and mentally prepare my speech. It's important not to give too much away. I don't know how long I'm going to be here, and I must eke the information out until I can find a living situation that doesn't pose a public health hazard. I'll just have to go over some stuff she already knows, adding a few embellishments here and there.

I take a deep breath and begin.

I tell her that Dad still lives in a modern (read ugly) three-bedroom house in Surrey. It is surrounded by a privet hedge that he trims with a handheld bush-trimmer every fourth Saturday in the summer months. It has an electric gate, which is something that his scandalously young wife insisted on, for the safety of their now decrepit and largely incontinent dog, Florence. The gate was also essential to keep their two daughters from running into the road, as young children are wont to do. They have two cars: one four-by-four – essential for navigating the treacherous roads of suburbia – and a saloon, which Dad uses to attend his bank clerk job when he doesn't cycle in. When he does cycle in, he makes jokes about being a MAMIL (a Middle-Aged-Man-In-Lycra), which attracted a polite smattering of laughter the first time he made it, but now the year is 2026 and cute acronyms died a death in the final years of the pandemic. He enjoys it all. He enjoys the treacherous mundanity of his new, small, boring life. So much so that he barely thinks about the wife and daughter he left behind.

I don't include that last bit, obviously. Every time I mention Dad, I dip my voice to the reverential whisper of the religious, and Mum closes her eyes and nods along as though every word is an epiphany.

'Did he ask about me?' she says. Her hangover is setting in. Sweat beads along her upper lip.

'Yes.' He didn't, but it's a nice touch that will keep her sweet.

'What did you say?'

'That I hadn't seen you for a while. I told him I was moving in with you, though, and I'd let him know if there was anything to report.'

She nods and I think I even see a flash of gratitude. Then, she ruins it all by leaning forward and grasping for the pack of cigarettes. She doesn't bother to ask if I mind, which I very much do. The flame shudders as she raises

the lighter towards her mouth, where a cigarette now
dangles from puckered lips.

And, since I am understandably more mindful of my
mortality than most, I excuse myself. Back in the hallway,
I empty the bottle of hand sanitiser into my palms.

5

I didn't have high hopes for my childhood bedroom. I wagered it would be better than the kitchen, likely on a par with the hall. What I wasn't prepared for, however, was the sweet, sickly, cloying smell of death. Though perhaps she thought I'd be used to it by now.

The source of the stench – a rat – did not sequester itself in a dignified corner to die, like most self-respecting creatures. No, this one expired in as flagrant a manner as possible: on my bed, tiny paws raised to the heavens like it was sending one final plea to the great beyond. It must've been there for quite some time. The fur is coming away from its leathery skin, which clings to its skeleton like latex stretched thin over fingers. Death doesn't bother me. I've seen two human bodies now, and over-exposure has stripped most corpses of their macabre mystery. But I don't feel comfortable sharing a bed with one.

Other than my tiny bedfellow, the room is exactly as I remember. Divided into two almost identical halves, with two identical beds, two identical bedside tables and two identical lamps. Everything is caked in dust. There are black rodent droppings over every surface, husks of insects suspended in torn spider webs and a thick blanket of flies on the windowsill. I expect they died trying to escape. I know the feeling.

On the other bed – *her* bed – something has been propped against the pillow. Something glossy, which reflects the dim light from the bare bulb. A photograph. God, I hope Mum hasn't turned this room into some sort of shrine. If she has, it hasn't been well maintained.

I pull my sleeve over my hand and pick up the photograph with the material, then hold it to the light. It's one of me and Marcie. I recognise it, vaguely. We can't have been more than thirteen. Marcie's got her arm flung casually round me, whereas I'm hunched in on myself, shoulders rounded, as though the attention was all too much. I'd drawn the puberty short straw: mousy hair greasy with sweat that fell in limp waves around my shiny face. Bushy, unshaped eyebrows. Next to her, I didn't stand a chance. She's radiant, even at that age. Even with the mouthful of braces, the smattering of spots. It's all coming back to me now. That day: the heat. The smell of garbage. Marcie had been given a disposable camera for our birthday, and she'd asked a passing dog-walker to take our photo. She was always so self-assured. So confident, even with strangers. My heart aches for the small child next to her. Always eclipsed by a brighter light.

I can feel myself sinking into melancholy, so I force myself to snap out of it. I should deal with the rat, really, but I can't face it yet. I'm feeling a bit overwhelmed. This is all a lot to take in. But it's important to maintain a sense of humour in the face of adversity, and even I can appreciate the irony of a germaphobe being forced to live in this cesspit.

I sit on the landing – I'll have to wash these clothes later anyway – and pull out my phone. No messages. Disappointing. Jack has not miraculously found my number and sent a message apologising for his abrupt departure yesterday, which would be the polite, gentlemanly thing to do, but no matter. I pull up his profile anyway, scroll through the public photos again. Nothing new. Nothing to sate my interest. I need more.

It might be time to use Sally.

Sally is one of my more successful investments. A divorced, middle-aged mother of two, she enjoys baking, crafting and taking hikes in the glorious British countryside. Periodically, she shares gratifying posts about finding love again, though – for the benefit of her ex-husband – she will occasionally write cryptic updates about how she 'had the best time last night', with a not so cryptic winky face tacked on to the end.

Sally is most frequently to be found online in the evening, between the hours of ten and midnight. Her current profile picture features a woman with greying hair. She sits in a run-down café, a small, fluffy dog in her arms. She's focusing on the weak-looking cup of coffee that has just been placed down in front of her, her face angled away from the camera, so that half of it is in shadow.

I log out of my own profile, and type Sally's email address and password into the login page. I'm greeted with a few prosaic updates from people I'm keeping tabs on. Rita's shared yet another insufferable post about heaven, no doubt in the hope that's where her dead father has ended up. Somehow, I doubt it. I might need to unfriend her soon: she seems to be losing her grip on reality, and these posts are becoming tedious.

But back to the task in hand. I type Jack's name into the search bar, and this time I don't hesitate. I click the 'Add Friend' button, and feel better instantly. In control. Purposeful. People, I've discovered, don't do well without something to work towards.

It buoys me enough to go back downstairs in search of cleaning products.

Mum's where I left her, another lit cigarette clenched between her fingers. It turns my stomach. Disgusting habit. I'll have to be quick. The cancer statistics for second-hand smoking are dismal.

She looks up as I enter, and I don't like her expression. There's something knowing, almost expectant about it. I clear my throat pointedly in the fuggy air.

'You've got rats.'

Her mouth twitches, but it's no laughing matter. 'At least I had something to keep me company,' she says.

'There's a dead one on my bed. Rotting. You should get someone in.'

She taps her cigarette against the edge of the mug, and I watch a pillar of ash tumble in. My stomach heaves again. 'Expensive. And it's *we*.'

'What?'

'You said *you've* got rats. You live here now too, don't you? You deal with it. Call someone if you like. I'm not paying for it.'

I stare at her, hoping my disbelief is evident. 'I can't afford it. You know that's why I'm here.'

She shrugs in response. There's something about the way she's watching me that makes me pause in my quest for cleaning products. Direct, unwavering. Like she's trying to provoke a reaction. I wonder if there's something I'm missing. Some small misstep I've made already.

Mentally, I retrace my steps through the house, searching for a reason for the knowing, steady look she's giving me. It hits me all at once. Of course. I can't believe I missed it. The photograph of Marcie and me, utterly untouched by the dust. Not a shrine at all, but a reminder. A reminder intended for me, and me alone. The picture was so clean it could have been placed there yesterday. It probably was.

Which means – a surge of outrage – that she must have seen the rat on my bed. That she did nothing about it. I won't let myself consider that she'd put it there herself.

So, that's how she's going to play it. She's laid down the gauntlet; but she forgets that I'm more than up for the challenge.

I start by ignoring her pointed look. I find a plastic bag and cleaning products under the sink. Token reminders of a once-clean house. On my way out, I turn and give her a sweet, girlish smile, like I'm a dutiful daughter and she's a doting mother.

Back upstairs, I book an appointment with the hair-dresser for the very next day.

6

My earliest memory is of Marcie bathed in a pool of golden light. It is one of those intangible recollections where you're never quite sure if you've conflated and warped it. Added details here and there to bolster a particular feeling or emotion.

It was our first day of primary school, so we can't have been more than five, but I distinctly remember the thrum of anxiety in my chest. Meeting new people. Understanding social dynamics. Marcie was bouncing off the walls at the promise of it all. That morning, Mum had dressed us in our new uniforms: pinafore dresses, chequered shirts neatly ironed underneath. The cheap material was scratchy against my skin. I looked at myself in the mirror and held out my hand as I'd seen my parents doing with new people.

'Hello,' I said, and the gesture felt awkward and alien. 'I'm Iris.'

When it was time to go, I gripped my new book bag so hard my hands grew sweaty.

Marcie ran ahead of us on the walk there. I hung back, a step or two behind Mum and Dad, and dragged my feet. Periodically, Dad checked over his shoulder for me. Mum's attention, as always, was on Marcie. She darted, sprite-like, between the trees, ebullient with excitement.

We walked through the park as an odd isosceles triangle, as though, even then, Marcie – detached from our little group as she was – was somehow distinct from our prosaic trio. The tree canopy in the early-September light threw strange shadows onto the concrete walkway. Marcie, at least twenty feet ahead of us, had stopped to wait, her whole body gyrating with impatience.

'Wait there,' Mum called to her. 'Don't go onto the road alone.'

Marcie huffed and, as she did, a ray of light broke free from the blanket of cloud. It hit her directly, soaking her in warmth. Her dark blond hair, so different from my own thin, dark locks, caught the light so she looked almost otherworldly. Ethereal. Beautiful, even at that age. Wisps of baby hair created a halo around her. Mum caught her breath, grabbed for Dad's arm, nodded towards her. They smiled at each other in a way they never seemed to for me. The ray disappeared. We caught up with Marcie, and she was forced to stick with us for the rest of the walk. At the school gates, Mum gave her a hug that was at least two seconds longer than mine. Dad patted us both genially on the shoulder. Equally. Like we were the same.

And then, it was just the two of us.

It's not always true what they say about twins: I didn't always know what Marcie was thinking, and she was usually oblivious to my emotions. But that day, she seemed to sense my nerves. Her small hand slipped into mine.

'Stick with me,' she'd whispered with a confidence that felt too old for her. I suppose, looking back, it was a confidence that came from always coming first. She'd never had to fight for her place in the family, whereas the trauma of my birth still hung over my every interaction with Mum. Dad tried to bridge the yawning chasm between us, but it had never been right. I craved the looks Mum directed at Marcie. The pride I'd see in her expression when Marcie excelled. The laughter when she told a boring joke. Even when Marcie was told off, it was done with smiling eyes.

When Marcie looked at me as we stood at the school gates, it was with a similar expression to the one Mum wore as she bandaged a cut. Pity. Marcie knew she was the favoured one, and she felt sorry for me. But I let her clasp my hand in hers anyway, and I was grateful – stupidly grateful – for the comfort. She didn't mention how it was still clammy from being clamped round my book bag. She led me through the cavernous hallways, into our new classroom, and she didn't let go, even when the teacher came over to greet us.

Marcie beamed at her, then introduced us to everyone in the vicinity.

'I'm Marcie, and this is my twin sister, Iris.'

It was that easy. I became popular by default, on the assumption that any sister of the wonderful, sweet, enigmatic Marcie Jones was someone worth being friends with.

The day passed mostly without incident. Marcie was swarmed by our new classmates, and she tried to include me at every turn. Being twins worked in our favour. We had that hint of the exotic about us, even if our looks could not have been more different. At the end of the day the teacher called us over to her, asked us questions about home and if we'd enjoyed our first day. I scuffed my foot against the carpet and allowed Marcie to answer for both of us. But as we were leaving, I looked up and saw the teacher's quizzical expression travel from Marcie to me. It was one I'd seen countless times before.

A look that could not quite comprehend how two such different personalities could have come from the same womb.

People claim all children are charming, but it's not true. I knew, even then, that I did not possess that special quality. That I was a mere moon reflecting her radiant light. Marcie carried that charm with her until the day she died.

7

I booked the appointment at a salon ten minutes from work. It's more upmarket than my usual place, and I can't really afford it, but Mum's bathroom – I take a deep breath just thinking about it – must be a breeding ground for at least fifty different species of mould. Plus, I've seen the photos of the girls on Jack's profile. Those dye jobs must be worth hundreds, and, if he's accustomed to the best, who am I to deny him?

I scroll absently through Jack's photos as the hairdresser – Tony – applies the dye in silence. Still no joy on the Sally front, but no one under the age of forty checks Facebook regularly, so I remain hopeful.

'New boyfriend, is it?' Tony peers hopefully over my shoulder and points to the screen in a painfully obvious attempt to claw back his tip. Truthfully, I couldn't afford to pay it anyway, but at least now I have an excuse.

Tony had wrinkled his nose when he first saw my poor, damaged hair and picked at the brittle strands.

'When was the last time you had *this* done?'

I'd glared at him in the mirror. 'My boyfriend died, so hair hasn't been top of my priority list, funnily enough.'

That shut him up. He broke his silence only once, to ask about colour, and I'd pulled out the picture of me and Marcie. Only a little creased from my pocket. 'That colour,' I'd said, pointing to her. 'As close as you can get.'

Now, I consider him in the mirror. I could maintain my dignified, sad silence, but his question has unlocked a delicious set of possibilities. 'Yes. We haven't been seeing each other long,' I say. Then, to remind him that I am still vulnerable, fresh off the back of tragedy: 'I'm dipping my toe in the dating pool. No one could ever replace Freddie, but I think there's something special about this one.'

'Must be new. He hasn't even added you as a friend yet,' he says with a chuckle that makes me want to singe him with the straightening irons. I need to get control of myself: my voice shakes with suppressed rage, '*He's* respectful of my grief.' And Tony finally appears to grasp – even if he doesn't fully understand – the gravity of my situation.

He wouldn't understand. Only those who have experienced *true* loss can know what it's like to lose the one person who anchors you to this world. Freddie understood that, perhaps even better than I did. He changed towards me after I told him about Marcie. What had started as harmless flirtation became something deeper, something more entrenched, as though our common loss bound us together. He checked up on me constantly – first about my work, though it was obviously a smokescreen for what he really wanted to ask. The questions about timelines and design choices were more and more frequently suffixed by enquiries into my wellbeing.

'How are you *really*?' he'd ask, and I'd touch a self-conscious hand to my hair – another tic I'd picked up from Marcie – and tell him I was fine, in a stoic sort of way.

It worked so well that, by the end of my second week there, he'd asked me on our very first date.

'Sorry. That you went through that,' Tony mumbles now. He looks suitably chastened, so I resume my stately silence. He opens his mouth only once more – half an hour later – as though he's going to attempt another conversation, but seems to think better of it. Luckily, the hairdryer puts paid to any further endeavours.

He may be an insensitive prick, but Tony's very good at his job. I twist my head as he holds the mirror up behind me. This is the closest I've ever got to that gorgeous golden colouring, and there's a lovely sheen to it that I can never seem to replicate myself.

I still don't leave him a tip though. He can think about what he's done and hopefully be more gracious to his next customer.

'You look amazing.' Mick says when I enter the café.

My new look is wasted on someone like him, but he's right, so I bestow on him a gracious smile. I'm so happy not even the prospect of an imminent five-hour shift in this ghastly place can dampen it. I don the my apron with positive flair, then remember what I need to do today, and tone it down a bit.

It's not busy, which is both a curse and a blessing.

A curse because there are fewer people to witness my transformation. My hair looks amazing, and Mick's lovely, but he's another one whose gaze doesn't set the pulse aflutter.

A blessing because it will give me the chance to bring Mick round to my cause, which I've been carefully formulating in my head since last night. It was the bathroom that clinched it. I cannot stay in that house for any longer than I absolutely must. But, in order to move out, I desperately need more shifts. That's where Mick comes in.

I lean against the counter just suggestively enough to make him look twice. When he does, I employ a look of utter desolation: I bite my lip, pull my eyebrows together and stare anxiously into the distance, as though all my worries are jostling for space in my prefrontal cortex.

It works just as well as I remember. Men are tediously predictable, and most can never seem to resist a damsel in distress. Mick, it turns out, is no exception. 'Are you OK, Iris? You look like you're miles away.'

I blink a few times, as though his voice has brought me back from the brink of some deeply distressing thought, then force a pained smile.

'I'm OK, Mick. Thanks.' God, I'm good. I'm wasted in this café. I sound distraught.

'Can I do anything to help?'

I'm about to land it. Better yet, I'm about to make Mick feel like it's his idea. He gets to feel like my knight in shining armour, I get what I want, and everyone's a winner. Or they would be.

Because, at the critical moment – the moment where I am about to summon my most distressing memory (which never fails to produce tears) and break down – the bell above the door tinkles.

I experience a wave of fury so intense I am momentarily light-headed with it. Appalling timing, all so some old biddy can buy a cup of weak instant coffee that she could have made just as well – probably better – at home. Whereas I might need to wait hours – even days – before this opportunity comes up again.

Maybe I'll spit in her drink. Add salt instead of sugar. But I look up and these thoughts are chased instantly from my mind. Because, as I wrestle with my rage and step up to the counter, I see it's not some old woman at all, but Jack. All the air is driven from my lungs. The rage evaporates instantly.

It's like I've manifested it: the hair, the casual internet stalking, the friend request. Like I've summoned him to me by directing all my waking thoughts his way. The chances of bumping into someone you like when you're looking this good are exceedingly slim, and I intend to make the most of it.

So, I do. I shift to the right, out from behind the counter, so I'm standing directly in the sunbeam currently shafting through the café window. Hoping it touches my hair to capture that celestial quality I always coveted. When Jack looks up and catches sight of me and my new, golden tresses, there's a delightful spark of recognition in his eye. In one long, delicious sweep, his eyes travel the length of me. Slowly, almost lazily and with just a hint of appreciation. *This* is what I've been missing. Every cell in my body is on fire.

He takes a step towards me. 'Iris, isn't it?' There is something about the way he rolls my name around his mouth. Like it's not the first time he's used it. Like he's familiar with me. I'd been certain that I'd failed at the group somehow, that my performance was not quite up to my usual exemplary standards, but now I'm not so sure. I have a brief, glorious mental image of Jack typing my name into a search bar. Hovering over the add friend button on my own profile. Just as I've done to his.

I don't allow any of this to show on my face. Instead, I cock my head to one side and pull my eyebrows together as though I'm trying to place him.

'Jack?' I say, like I'm testing it out. He smiles in response. He has a very nice smile. Straight, white teeth, offset against the remains of a summer tan. An unusual quality in the grief-stricken. Most of us avoid sunshine, as though the warmth on our skin might bring us slightly too close to something resembling happiness.

But I need to keep my head screwed on, can't let the excitement of this chance encounter derail me. This is a big moment, and I may be off to a strong start but I need to lodge myself right at the centre of his psyche. So he goes away and me and my sparkling conversational skills are all he can think of. I need something punchy. Something that aligns our common interests. Commonalities are what bind humans together, after all, the foundation for any strong relationship. That's what Marcie's magazines used to say, anyway.

'The other dead partner,' I say, as though the connection is only just dawning on me. 'What are the chances?' It's a risk – I don't want him to think I'm taking his wife's name in vain – but you only live once; and it's enough to trigger a reaction.

He takes a half-step backwards, narrows his eyes, then blurts a laugh. Bingo.

'Slim, I fear. Or at least I hope so. Dead partners are difficult to come by at our age.'

Good. This is very good. He's past the stage of crying every time he thinks of her, which bodes well for our future. God, that bit was tedious.

To show that I approve of his answer, I slip him a mischievous grin and lean against the counter in much the same way I did with Mick earlier. Mick is looking at me as though I've had a lobotomy, as though he cannot square the woman who was on the brink of a breakdown not two minutes ago with the flirtatious, playful specimen in front of him. It's a difficult balance to strike, but Jack's needs are greater. I'll deal with Mick later.

'Can I get you a coffee?' I twirl a strand of blond round my finger and watch Jack clock the action.

'New hair?' he asks, and I think that's approval in his tone.

'I fancied a change. I'm normally better at keeping on top of it, but after everything that's happened…' I tail off, sadly.

'Suits you.'

I look down, bashful, as though I wasn't aware of this fact.

There's a pause, during which I can tell he's still looking at me – appreciating me – though I keep my eyes on the floor. It's really quite dirty.

Jack clears his throat. 'I have a few minutes before my meeting. I'd love a cappuccino.'

'I'll bring it over.' This is not the sort of establishment that serves cappuccinos on a regular basis, but I'll do my best. I point to a table in the corner, next to an older woman sipping her coffee. A fluffy dog pants by her feet, and I wrinkle my nose. I hate dogs. Horrible, unhygienic creatures, not that I'd ever admit that to anyone.

I make Jack's coffee, then take it over to him. It's the most effort I've ever put into anything at this café. Jack looks wrong in this setting: ill-suited to the metal-legged chair, the tiny table. And yet, he seems at ease. He's stretched one leg so it juts from beneath the table, and his arm is resting on the plastic surface as he scrolls through his phone. Emails, from the looks of it. This is a man who is comfortable with his place in the world. Utterly unbothered by taking up space. He smiles at me as I set the coffee down in front of him.

'What brings you here?' I ask. A lame opener, but some small talk is necessary. Small talk leads to big talk.

'I have a client meeting round the corner, and a few minutes to kill.' According to his LinkedIn, Jack works for a property development firm in the City. He's a long way from the office. 'I'm pleased I was early now.' He smiles again, eyes dancing, and yet I think I catch something lurking beneath it. A familiar trace of sadness that makes my heart thud very hard. 'Do you have time to join me?' He gestures at the seat opposite. 'I'm not very good at being by myself these days. Too much time in my own company and I get a little too morose, if you know what I mean.'

I know exactly what he means – that's why I spend so much time cleaning – and yet I hesitate. I watched a baby vomit all over this chair two days ago, and the memory is lodged in my brain like a parasite. But Jack's worth it, so I take a fortifying breath, nod, and perch on the edge.

'I must say, I didn't have you pegged as a waitress.'

I like that he's given my profession enough thought to peg me as anything. I didn't have me pegged as a waitress either, but beggars can't be choosers. It became clear five minutes into my first shift here that hospitality is not for me. When I'd first begun applying to cafés and bars, I'd pictured myself in an establishment with distressed wooden floors, an enticing chalkboard, small tables arranged neatly on the pavement outside. Not laminated menus, metal napkin holders, knock-off bottles of red and brown sauce that crust round the lid. Bacteria-ridden children who stuff their fingers into every available crevice. Still, my options were thin on the ground, and I'm grateful to Mick for taking me on.

I'm not pleased Jack has seen me here. It would have been nice to maintain some mystery over my career, and there is nothing at all glamorous or alluring about this job. Were it up to me, I'd probably have made something up. Something that set me apart from the crowd. Something Marcie might have done. But that's not an option now.

'Oh, it's not permanent,' I say lightly. 'I'm looking for something a little more challenging. I was in magazine publishing – a designer for them, actually – but after everything...'

'I understand. It's hard, isn't it?' Jack says gently. 'Gets you when you're least expecting it.'

It does, but I was actually thinking about how that child in the corner needs to be restrained. It's waddling round like a malfunctioning Roomba, trousers round its ankles and nappy exposed. I nod anyway, and give myself a small shake like I am trying to dislodge some long-forgotten memory. I ensure Jack sees me throw the child a maternal look. Nothing more unnatural than a woman who doesn't like kids.

'Was it sudden?' he asks.

'Very. He was hit by a lorry.'

'Jesus. I'm so sorry.'

'Yes, it was difficult. More than difficult, really. Horrible to have someone taken away from you so abruptly. And he'd just proposed, of course.' I look wistfully at my left hand. It's important that Jack sees me as an equal in grief, and boyfriend doesn't quite cut it.

'I can't imagine. I thought I had it bad with the cancer.'

As much as I enjoy his sympathy, this is heading down a dangerously platonic path. Nothing unsexier than dead partners. I need to lighten the tone. 'Yes. It's funny to think that he might still be with us if only he'd been looking where he was going.'

It takes Jack a second to register what I've said, but when he does he sputters with laughter, and his eyes soften. 'I like that you don't take it all so seriously. Things are serious enough without surrounding yourself with misery, too. That's why it took me so long to go to the group. Don't see the point of a bunch of depressed people all in one room.'

I am very nearly derailed by the first few words of this statement. *He likes me*. Said in that casual, easy way of his as though it's hardly a big deal. I force myself to focus even as his words reverberate over and over again round my skull: the group, depressed people. *Ask follow-up questions, show an interest in what he's saying*. Another piece of advice borrowed from Marcie's magazines. I lean forward and meet his eye. Marcie noticed that men like it when you maintain eye contact as they speak: it appeals to their egos, makes them feel as though you are hanging on their every word. Like they're the most important person in the room. Which, in Jack's case, he is. 'What made you change your mind?' I ask.

'My mother, I guess. I tried therapy and hated it, and she was convinced that I wasn't coping. Threatened to move in if I didn't "take steps" to help myself.' He lifts his fingers into quotation marks. Evidently, his mother is more caring than mine. Must be nice. He really is the whole package: good-looking, well dressed, loving family, au fait with grief.

'I've just moved back in with my mum,' I say.

'How's that been? Are you close with her?'

I consider my answer carefully, remembering a similar conversation I had with Freddie in the kitchen just before I told him about Marcie. *Family's important*, he'd said, as though it was a universal conviction. 'Very. She's my best friend.' I lean further forward. 'I know what you mean about mothers being a bit overbearing, though. She's *always* checking up on me, making sure I'm eating enough. She basically forced me to move in after everything with Freddie. Didn't like the idea of me living alone.'

Jack nods. 'That's it. Exactly. Can't blame them, really, but I'm over thirty for Christ's sake.'

I give him Marcie's best smile, tongue pressed to the roof of my mouth. 'Well, any time you need some respite, you know where to come.' I pat the table, and instantly regret it. My sanitiser is under the counter. I curl my hand into a fist, picturing the bacteria breeding on my skin, travelling up my arm. I suppress a shudder and refocus on Jack.

His eyes are twinkling in the loveliest way. 'Thanks. I'll bear that in mind. What about your dad? Is he on the scene?'

I have a checklist that I refer back to sometimes. It's from an article I found on Google back when Freddie and I were first getting to know each other. It was titled 'How To Tell If He's Into You', and it contained a veritable treasure trove of information that I pored over, logging each salient point for later. One of them mentions effort in conversations: constant questions that keep the dialogue afloat. Freddie was excellent at that. It seems that Jack is, too.

I cast my eyes down again – partly to hide my pleasure at this sudden epiphany, and partly to suggest the question has brought up a memory I'd rather not relive, which is not entirely untrue. The thought of Dad always gives rise to complex feelings I'm not equipped to unpick. Easier to lie. 'Sadly not. He died when I was about seventeen.'

'I'm sorry. My father's dead too. If it's any consolation.'

I must have a sixth sense for these things, stumbling into another similarity without even having to try. 'Recently?' I ask.

His hand curls on the table. 'A couple of months after Alice, actually.'

Mere months ago, yet he did not mention him at the group. I sense there's more to this story than he's letting on, but Jack's demeanour – so easy and relaxed thirty seconds ago – has shifted, and I don't push. That's the thing about me: I'm tactful to a fault. 'I'm sorry. That's awful.' I wonder if now might be the time to take his hand. To close the gap – both physical and metaphorical – between us, bolstered by my checklist and the fact that

Jack – with his eye contact, questions, body language – is ticking off many of the items.

But I don't want to come across as too forward on our first meeting outside the group, and I'm trying to maintain my slightly aloof air. It's always tricky finding the balance at this stage. I fix my face instead, drawing my eyebrows together in concern, mouth downturned. It's a look Mick is very good at, actually, and one I borrow liberally.

'Don't be. We didn't get on,' he says shortly. 'Though I have to say I have begun to feel like something of a bad omen. You need to be careful around me.' Interesting. Where a minute ago his face was set, now his eyes are soft, playful. It feels *almost* like flirting.

So, I respond in kind. I look up at him through my lashes. 'I'll take my chances.'

The next pause is thick with promise, and I allow the seconds to tick down without breaking it, allowing my words the space to breathe. The implication to settle. And then, I press my advantage. I'm ad-libbing now, but I know, somehow, that it's the right question to ask. 'Have you' – a brief look at the floor, as though I'm aware my next question is a touch transgressive. *Don't be too forward. Allow him to come to you* – 'ever considered moving on?'

I catch the way his eyes flick towards me. So subtle I could have missed it.

'I haven't yet, if that's what you mean. But if the right person came along...' He leaves the sentence hanging. I consider my response: too much too soon, and I might smash right through the delicate connection forming between us. But if I don't register my interest, he might think I'm still too caught up in thoughts of Freddie, which is categorically not the case. I'm ready. Only now am I realising just how ready I am. 'What about you?' he asks. 'I'm surprised you haven't been snapped up already.'

And there is no pussyfooting around it now. That was definitively an advance.

I shrug casually, though it goes against every one of my instincts, which are screaming at me to grin, lean over, kiss him even. I keep my eyes fixed on his as I respond. 'Same. If the right person came along.'

He swallows, and then there's a flash of something in his eyes. Something that looks almost like fear, as though something – or some*one* – has just crashed into his mind, short-circuiting the electricity between us. He swallows again.

'Well, Iris,' he says, and his voice is husky. This time, he doesn't meet my eye. 'This has been a very happy coincidence. I'll see you at the group on Tuesday, assuming I don't bump into you again before that.'

It is a monumental effort to maintain my calm expression. I can't believe that's it. After the intimacy – the suggestiveness – of the conversation, I'd expect some kind words of encouragement and a promise to look out for one another at the very least. Has he forgotten how circumstance brought us together? Partners taken from us too soon – on the same day, no less. The twist of fate that landed us in each other's laps. I make a fist, breathing heavily, as Jack pauses, his arm halfway into his coat sleeve. He closes his eyes briefly, like a priest might before doing something he knows he will have to ask forgiveness for later.

'Actually, perhaps it's best if we exchange numbers. Just so I can check you haven't succumbed to my curse, too.'

That's more like it. He *does* remember. I allow him the ghost of a smile as I tap my number into his phone.

'See you soon, Iris,' he says, and it feels like a promise.

I'm in such a good mood that, later that afternoon, I just come straight out and ask Mick for more shifts. It requires practically no dramatic effects at all. No cajoling, no tears.

To my surprise, Mick nods, smiling. 'It's nice to see you looking so happy. Of course. I'll amend the rota.'

8

I'm still feeling positive when I arrive home that evening. I don't bother to remove my shoes in the hallway – more dirt from outside is hardly going to make the difference, and I don't like the thought of my socks touching the floor. I go straight through to the kitchen in search of something to eat. I'm ravenous. This part always makes me hungry: the thrill of the chase, the first flicker of interest, the adrenaline that pounds through my veins. It was just like this with Freddie.

Freddie suggested our first date so casually I thought I'd misheard him. It was just over a week after I'd started, and we were in the kitchen together, discussing plans for the next month's edition of the magazine.

'What did you say?' I asked.

'Drinks at the pub round the corner on Friday. Only if you're free and keen, obviously,' he repeated. I noticed that he lowered his voice slightly, as though he was aware that he was crossing a professional boundary. As though he did not want our colleagues to overhear.

I touched the lobe of my ear, tried – and failed – to hide my grin. I didn't need to refer to any checklist for this. This was it. A sign he felt the same.

'I'd love to,' I said, and I didn't have to feign the breathiness to my voice. The slight catch of anxiety.

I'd never been on a date before, and it sent me into a spin of worry. I practised hard. Responses to possible questions he might ask, trawling through my memories of Marcie to ensure I said the right thing, maintained the correct tone. She was always so good at knowing exactly what to say.

Freddie and I had limited contact for the rest of the week, as though he was trying to throw our colleagues off the scent of any untoward relationship between us. We kept it strictly professional, our meetings brief and functional. But I kindled the knowledge of our date, and grew ever more anxious as Friday drew nearer.

I spent hours blow-drying my hair that morning, tonging it into the soft waves that Marcie had favoured. I could barely do my job that day, less so when I received a message from Freddie: *You still on for later?*

I risked a glance at him across the office, and – seeming to sense my gaze – he looked up, the question still on his face. I put my thumbs up over the bank of desks. I was sure I saw his face redden, just a little.

I don't have high hopes for the selection in the fridge. I've been trying to eat out of the house as much as possible – God knows what I might contract from the kitchen – but tonight I want to be here in case Jack messages. So that I can give him my full attention, when it comes. He must have finished his meeting by now. I allow myself a brief, glorious moment of remembering the intensity of his gaze; the way it made me feel. Like I was the only person who mattered in that tiny café. I picture him walking home, crafting a message in his head, waiting the appropriate length of time to send it. Games we must all play when in pursuit of something special.

It's so dim in the kitchen that at first I don't notice Mum in her usual seat at the table. Only when she speaks do I jump and swing round to face her. Her hair is greasy and unwashed, her face pallid. More pressingly, she looks enraged.

'What the fuck do you think you're playing at?'

I'm taken aback. The last couple of days have seen a fragile armistice settle between us, and I've grown used to the overly polite, stiff interactions we have whenever we accidentally encounter each other.

'What are you talking about?'

'What have you *done* to yourself?'

Her eyes sweep upwards. My hair. I've been so caught up with thoughts of Jack, I'd forgotten my fabulous new look. Whoops. I could've played this one better, eased her into it by softening the blow with news of Dad. I've shocked her, and – with her lifestyle – a heart attack is not beyond the realms of possibility. I'd rather not have her death on my conscience as well. I hold out my hands in a conciliatory gesture. If there was ever a time for subservience, it is now.

'I just thought I'd try something new.'

'You knew exactly what you were doing.' This is not good. Her voice has taken on that quiet fury that always spells danger.

'I spoke to Dad earlier,' I say quickly, and her mouth – open, and ready to spew a vicious vitriol – closes again. It takes her a while to collect herself. When she speaks, the words sound strangled.

'Sorry. It looks lovely.'

I bestow on her a kind, appreciative smile. 'Thanks, Mum.'

A pause as she wrestles with herself.

'So... your father?'

'Just a quick chat,' I say cheerfully. 'Mainly just complaining about the wife, you know how it is.' I lower my voice like I am letting her in on a big secret, knowing full well that my faux pas with the hair requires a grand gesture. 'Between you and me, I think they might be having problems.'

And there it is. A hungry flare in her eyes. If I'd been concerned that any leverage I had with Mum was waning, I'm not any more. She's still just as invested. Just as in love.

'It could just be a bad patch, of course.' Important to cover my back. Just in case.

'Of course,' she echoes. She sits, staring into space, as she processes this new information, then stands, mutters something about a shower – probably a good idea – and leaves the room.

I wait for her bedroom door to close before I go back to the kitchen to look for something to eat.

The encyclopaedia is waiting for me on my bed when I go upstairs. My good mood, which has been dissipating rapidly since I tried and failed to overcome my fear of the bacteria on Mum's disgusting kitchen surfaces, dips further. I'm starving, Jack hasn't messaged yet, and now this.

I recognise it instantly. Another reminder, placed right in the centre of the bed, where she's sure I'll see it. Punishment for my new hairstyle, I'm sure of it. Underhand tactics from her, but effective nonetheless.

The encyclopaedia is showing its age. The cover is faded, the paper thinner and more delicate than I remember. I pull my sleeve over my hand again and flip it open. There it is. Dad's messy scrawl across the flyleaf.

To my favourite little explorer. Stay curious.

I recall, with startling clarity, how his large finger would hover over a word as I struggled to pronounce it. None of us knew what was coming for us. We should have made the most of those times, but they slipped away, as everything does.

This book was the prelude to change. If only we'd known it, then. Perhaps things would have been different.

9

My relationship with Marcie changed one afternoon when we were eight. By then, I knew the natural order of things. Small fault lines had travelled down the centre of our perfect family, dividing us into two unequal halves. It was Mum and Marcie; Dad and me. You can guess who held the greater influence.

Perhaps that's not entirely fair. Mum did try harder with me in those days. At some point over the four years since we'd started primary school, Dad had set aside his role as our live-in peacekeeper and called her out for the flagrant favouritism she showed Marcie. Mum cried, relived the trauma of my birth and went to therapy. Things were better after that. More balanced, though she still reserved those special, love-laden looks for Marcie alone.

It made sense, I suppose. Marcie was free-spirited, outgoing and extroverted, which made her easy to love. I was not those things. I liked order. I liked routine. I liked to know when my next meal was coming and what it was. I liked to map out my days, and coordinate my toys, and learn about how things worked. I had a tendency to become fixated, could be obsessive in my interests.

This was useful for my relationship with Dad. He grew up a farmer's son, and never quite lost his affiliation with the natural world. It gave me the perfect in, so I pretended to love it too. I learned as much as I possibly could in my spare time: I learned the difference between a great tit and a blue tit; a woodlouse and a pill millipede; cow parsley and hemlock. And it worked. Dad was thrilled. He bought me a large encyclopaedia for my seventh birthday, and it quickly became my most treasured possession.

With a shared passion, we spent more time together. Sometimes, we'd take the train out of London on a Saturday morning and dig in the dirt beneath the large park trees and flip logs to watch insects and examine large mushrooms that sprawled like orange umbrellas from thick, moss-covered tree trunks. Dad always seemed so happy in these little pockets of time we stole together. He'd revel in the clarity of the air, drawing deep lungfuls of it as we got further and further away from the city. On the way home, he'd rest his large hand on my small shoulders, and I felt so important. These are memories I return to often. Looking back, those times were almost *too* perfect, the stillness before the storm.

I was excited when Dad said we'd be spending a week on his parents' farm. I didn't particularly care for my grandparents, who always frowned at me as though I was some complex puzzle too difficult to bother understanding. Conversely, they looked at Marcie as though she was some rare and beautiful butterfly. Nevertheless, the farm presented countless opportunities for Dad and me to spend time together. The night before we left, I packed my favourite wellington boots, closed my suitcase over my folded clothes and rested the encyclopaedia Dad gave me on top. I got into bed, willing sleep to come early, but Marcie was faffing around with her case, looking for her possessions that were scattered around the house, complaining about the journey and that she was tired and that she didn't want to spend a week in the countryside when all her friends would be in London.

'Mama,' she said, when Mum entered with a pile of her clothes over one arm. She called her *Mama* well into teenagerhood, and the pet name always preceded some request or demand. Even then, our lives revolved around Marcie's whims. 'Do we *have* to go? Can you and I not stay here, and Dad and Iris go? It'll be *boring*. There's nothing to do down there.'

Any normal parent would have told her to stop being so spoilt, but Mum was so far under her spell that she perched on the end of the bed and smoothed her golden hair away from her forehead. 'I know it's not what you'd like to be doing.' She lowered her voice. '*I* don't really want to go either, to be honest, but it's important to your father that we all go.'

'But what about Alicia's party? And Beth's invited us to hers for a sleepover. Iris might not want to go, but I do.'

'You can have them both over when we get back,' she said, and she stood to signal the end of the conversation.

This did not assuage Marcie's bad temper, which continued well into the drive down to Dorset. Mum tried to pull her out of it, but Marcie – unused to not getting her own way – was unusually quiet. She stared out of the window with her eyes narrowed, bottom lip jutting into a pout. I was quiet, too. I'd been on the receiving end of Marcie's barbed comments before and was always keen to avoid them when I could. Anticipation settled over me as the land grew scrubby and wild. So many opportunities for exploration.

We arrived at the farm in time for lunch. Marcie's nose wrinkled as soon as she opened the car door. The smell of dung was potent.

'They must be spreading manure,' Dad said, voice laced with excitement. Not even I could muster the enthusiasm to enjoy this particular agricultural practice, though I attempted to smile anyway.

Our grandparents greeted us at the car. If you were to picture a traditional British farmer and his wife, you would picture my grandparents. It was as though time hadn't touched them. Grandpa wore a tweed flat cap. Granny had an apron tied round her ample waist. Both are dead now, having succumbed not long after Marcie died. Natural causes, in their case.

'You've put on a few pounds.' Granny patted Dad's stomach affectionately. She reserved this sort of comment for Dad alone, and it was – I grew to understand – an expression of her adoration for him.

'Sarah,' she said, turning to Mum, voice hardening. 'You're looking well.' She didn't like Mum: the woman who lured her only child away to the excesses of the city. Mum gave a frosty smile and returned the compliment.

She turned, then, to Marcie, and her face lit up. 'There's my little rascal. Getting up to mischief as usual?'

Marcie, who had been standing just behind Mum and quietly but exaggeratedly retching at the smell for my benefit, straightened her back and fixed her best smile to her face. Her bad mood evaporated under Granny's fond stare.

'Mum got me this bracelet last week.' She held out her wrist for inspection. 'For getting into the netball team.'

'I heard about that, clever girl!' Granny said. I averted my eyes from her wrist as a thin thread of jealousy coiled in my stomach. The bracelet was beautiful. Delicate and silver, it suited Marcie's slender wrist, and made her look older than she was. It already had a charm hanging from it: a tiny netball.

'We can add more for each birthday,' Mum had said when she gave it to her. 'So that it's completely yours and unique.'

'I love it,' Marcie had said. I stood in the doorway, watching them, and realised that I loved it, too. Mum must have sensed my presence, because she turned. A flash of something that could have been guilt crossed her features.

'Iris!' she said. 'I didn't see you there. I was just giving your sister a belated birthday present. I didn't think you'd be interested in something so… girly. And since we got you the encyclopaedia…'

'It's OK. I love my encyclopaedia,' I said, wanting that bracelet badly.

'And there's Iris,' Granny said. I tried to ignore the way the enthusiasm in her voice waned. I mustered a smile, but it felt wrong and forced, as it always did when I sensed someone's energy change towards me. I waited for Granny to say something else: to comment on some special personality trait of mine; but she merely clapped her hands together and ushered us into the old farmhouse. Grandpa trailed behind us, stoic as ever.

The farmhouse was old and in desperate need of repair. Marcie and I always shared a room in the attic, where the groaning pipes made us throw our thin duvets over our heads in fright and the wallpaper peeled away in the top corner. I unpacked my bag while Granny prepared lunch downstairs, placing my neatly folded clothes into the old chest of drawers. Marcie threw her bag onto her bed and disappeared back downstairs. I couldn't wait to get outside. I'd already identified several fields that I could lure Dad into, but I knew I'd have to wait while he 'caught up' with his parents.

Downstairs was a hub of activity. Marcie had sat herself on the corner of the wooden work surface while

Granny sliced a loaf of bread, and was chattering away about school and her latest litany of achievements. Dad looked up when I entered the room and smiled at me.

'Iris is doing really well at school too, Mum. She's in line to win the science prize.'

Granny turned away from Marcie with a look of surprise. '*Are* you? That's brilliant, sweetheart,' she said, and she gave me a genuine smile. 'Here, do you want to help put this on the table? Then you can tell me all about it.'

She made me sit next to her at lunch. I told her in stilted sentences about my own school experience, but I was distracted by Marcie across the table. Her black mood seemed to have descended again. She stabbed at a piece of ham with her fork and left a pile of potatoes on the side of her plate. When Granny questioned her about the wasted food, she sniffed.

'I don't want to get fat,' she said, looking pointedly at Granny's ample bosom.

Grandpa roared with laughter. 'She's a precocious one, isn't she?' He chuckled. Granny made her do the washing up, which did little to improve her temper.

After lunch, the adults moved into the tiny sitting room and drank coffee. I hovered in the doorway, wondering when the best time to approach Dad was. He caught sight of me.

'Give me half an hour,' he mouthed.

'What are you doing?' Marcie appeared at my shoulder, and I jumped.

'Just waiting for Dad to be finished,' I said.

'I'll come outside with you.'

I looked at her sceptically. She hated the outdoors usually.

'You can show me what I've been missing,' she said, and she linked her arm through mine.

We ran up to the room together and pulled on our wellies. Marcie smiled at me as she shrugged into her coat, and I felt my chest warm. It had been a long time since she'd shown an interest in anything I was doing.

Though it was April, there was still a cold nip in the air, and the recent rainfall had turned the yard into sludge. I led the way, picking out the least muddy route I could find, in case the mire dissuaded Marcie from accompanying me. She didn't complain though. As we reached the field dotted with cows, she pointed things out and asked questions I was thrilled to answer.

We started at the hedgerow. I flipped logs and showed her the treasures underneath: the beetles and worms and nasty-looking orange centipedes that scuttled for cover as soon as the light hit them. We'd only been looking for five minutes when I noticed Marcie's attention waning.

'I was talking to Dad the other day,' she began slowly. 'He was telling me something really gross.'

I dropped the log I was peering under and looked at her, swallowing the small spark of jealousy that she and Dad had had a private conversation without me. 'What was it?'

'He was saying that sometimes worms live in cow pats. They help turn it into compost.' She looked at the cows grazing to our right. 'Told you it was gross.'

Secretly, I thought so too, but if Dad thought it was worth mentioning I was willing to set aside my true feelings. 'Shall we have a look?' I said and Marcie nodded. I found a large stick in the hedgerow, and we approached the cows slowly. Several fresh pancakes steamed in the cold air. As we drew nearer, Marcie close at my shoulder, hundreds of yellow flies took to the air. I held my breath and poked at the mass on the ground with the stick.

It happened in a split second. One moment I was on my feet, leaning over just enough to catch a glimpse of the writhing mass of worms. The next, there was a hard push at my shoulder, and I was tipping forward, straight towards it. I didn't have time to break my fall with my hands. I landed heavily on my shoulder and felt it spatter upwards, onto my face, into my mouth, which was open in surprise. I could feel the cool dampness seep through my jumper as I sputtered and tried to extract myself from the mess, which only made it worse. I tried to raise myself on my hand, and accidentally pressed it right into centre of the dung. I felt it squelch through my fingers and my stomach turned.

'Marcie Jones, you come here *right* now.' It was a tone I had never heard Mum use before, and certainly not with Marcie, but it rang out across the field with so much force even I quailed. I felt strong hands under my armpits as Dad lifted me from the cow pat. Mum had grabbed Marcie by her upper arm. Her jaw was set with anger. A few feet away, Grandpa and Granny stood, mouths ajar.

'You're OK,' Dad said softly. 'It's just a bit of muck. We'll get you cleaned up in no time.'

I realised I was shaking. I felt sullied. Disgusting. Betrayed. I stood with my arms at right angles to my body, spitting onto the grass. I thought I felt something – a worm perhaps – slither down my back, and then the tears came, and they did not stop.

'You will *never* behave like that again.' Mum was marching Marcie back towards the house, dragging her by the arm, voice carrying on the wind. 'In front of your grandparents too. Are you *trying* to embarrass me? You can forget about having your friends over next weekend, that's for sure.'

I waddled back to the house with Dad and his parents. They tried to make me feel better with vacuous comments – 'at least it wasn't dog or badger poo. That really stinks!' And, 'it'll wash out and you won't even know. I'll put the washing machine on as soon as we get in.' But they couldn't know how my skin itched, how it burned with the thought of those worms, and those flies. How it tasted: earthy, just a little bit bitter. I continued to spit until we reached the front door.

Dad offered to sit with me as I showered, but I shook my head and locked the door behind me. I stood under the weak, lukewarm water and scrubbed at my skin until it burned. Until it was red and raw. Still, I did not feel clean.

After my shower, I gave my soiled clothes to Granny and went to my room to change. Marcie was hunched on the side of the bed, shoulders shaking with tears. She glared at me, puffy-eyed.

'It was an *accident*, Iris. Tell them! This is so *unfair*. You know Mum's said I can't have anyone over for the rest of the holidays? It was only a joke. You found it funny, didn't you?'

Her tone was pleading. It was the first time she'd ever been the sole recipient of Mum's anger. The first time she'd been perceived as anything less than perfect.

I ignored her question, and instead spread a puzzle over the floorboards. I spent most of the rest of the week in that bedroom. Dad tried to tempt me outside again, but each time I shook my head vehemently and refused. Each time I finished the puzzle, I broke it up and started again. The encyclopaedia lay, deliberately forgotten, on my bedside table.

And, by the end of the week, it was as though nothing had ever happened. Marcie had managed to worm her way back into Mum's good graces, where she stayed until she died.

10

A grief group is not the right forum for someone with an aversion to bodily fluids. I've known this all along, but tonight it's particularly grating. Rita tears off a square of blue roll and blows her nose noisily. I feel my stomach turn and look away, but my gaze snags on Jack.

Jack: the man who took my number last week, promised to message, then failed miserably at this one simple task. It's as though our encounter meant nothing to him. As though he's forgotten the energy that crackled between us at the café, forgotten the coincidence that brought us together, so strange it feels like fate. Which – call me bigheaded – simply cannot have been the case.

He sits like a man who is totally at ease: legs spread just wide enough to ensure his comfort but not wide enough that he could be accused of manspreading. He is giving Rita – sobbing about her father – his full and undivided attention. This does nothing to brighten my mood. Rita is one of those women who manages to pull off the damsel in distress look effortlessly. She has that hint of the pathetic about her that men seem to go wild for. She dabs at her eyes with more delicacy than she usually uses during her frequent crying spells.

'Sorry. I'm so sorry. Look at me, not being able to keep it together. What must you think of me, Jack?' She gives a girlish, wet giggle that makes me want to shove the wad of kitchen roll straight down her throat. She's amped up the make-up this week, too: a garish red smear round her mouth, layers of mascara on her lashes, which she is currently fluttering in Jack's direction.

He shakes his head as though it's nothing, as though he understands completely, then reaches out and pats her on the arm. It's too much. Almost enough to make me spring from my chair, leap across the room and forcibly separate them. No, that wouldn't be enough. I'd grab Rita by her flimsy lace collar and drag her all the way out onto the street. Preferably into the path of a passing bus. I don't do this, obviously. I'm not mad. Instead, I look on with a benign smile, as though Jack's casual intimacy with Rita hasn't sent fury rippling through my veins.

'I'm just finding it hard to process. This was supposed to be the trip of a lifetime for them!' She collapses, predictably, into a wave of fresh sobs.

Rita's father did have an unfortunate end, to be fair. Still, if we're looking for silver linings, it makes a good story. He died falling from the deck of the yacht he'd hired to celebrate his recent retirement. He was – by all accounts – blind drunk when he slipped over the railings and out of sight, while his wife watched on with the sort of helplessness that borders on negligence. When they found him, three days later, he'd been nibbled at by the various inhabitants of the Caribbean Sea.

'His eyes were gone!' she'd wailed in her first session here, before we'd quite got the measure of her. When we still thought that her strangled cries were a product of the recentness of the event. It's been months now, and I can confirm, unfortunately, that they were not.

Since then, she's grappled rather tediously with the idea of another realm. It's not an altogether unusual reaction to bereavement – we've all wondered where our loved ones have ended up – but Rita does like to go the extra mile. She tones it down here, of course, perhaps aware that the incoherent musings she posts online would make her sound ridiculous in person. I added her (as Sally) on a whim, during one of those long, lonely evenings when I found myself pining for Freddie. For company. Her Facebook posts confirmed what I'd already begun to suspect: that she has utterly lost the plot.

Jack is still looking at Rita, sympathy etched on his face, and I realise I need to do something. To wipe that sappy expression away for good. Or, ideally, redivert it towards me.

I lean forward, tuck my hands into my lap, and apply my very own expression of deep worry for what Rita's going through.

'Rita,' I say, gently. 'You were saying the other day that you feel you can talk to your father? That you feel that since he's been gone, the barrier between us and…' I clear my throat delicately, 'The other side, I think you said, has become thinner. That you hear his voice in your head as though he's in the room with you? Perhaps it would help to talk to him, here? Voice your feelings. Pretend we're not here. This is a safe space.'

Rita narrows her eyes at me, no doubt thinking that she's already expressed those particular sentiments, in the rambling five-paragraph-long post that appeared on her page at four this morning. But no one here follows her, only Sally. The others shift, uncomfortably. I'm delighted to see that Jack's expression of concern for Rita's predicament now looks more like concern for her mental state.

'I— uh, I mean yes. I do feel like he's here, sometimes. Not in that way. Not like a paranormal way. Just that I *feel* him. Close to me. Just like a spirit, but not a spirit. Like his essence.' Oh, this is excellent: I've handed her the shovel, and she's dutifully digging away. Better yet, Jack is now leaning away from her.

His eyes flick to mine. He widens them, as if to share a conspiratorial look about Rita's madness, but I keep my face a blank page. I won't forgive his transgressions – both the message (or lack thereof) and the touch – so easily.

Fiona clears her throat. 'It's natural to feel a connection after death, of course, Rita,' she says, but the words don't quite have the authenticity she's aiming for. 'Does anyone else have anything to share?'

I'm surprised when Jack raises his hand. I'd expected one of the old guard – Matt, perhaps, who usually has *plenty* to say about his loss – so it makes for a pleasant diversion.

'I guess I've been thinking a lot over the last week about Alice, and the hold that losing her still has over my life,' he says, and I'm once again – reluctantly, this time – impressed by his delivery. The calmness of it suggests he has actually considered the words that are leaving his mouth, in stark juxtaposition to Rita's hysteria. 'She's all I've been able to think about for the last six months, but recently—' He breaks off and looks directly at me. Not Rita. Not Fiona. At *me*. 'Recently, I've begun to wonder what life will look like afterwards. If perhaps, there *is* a light at the end of the tunnel.'

Any frustration I'd been feeling towards Jack for his lack of communication evaporates instantly. Because I know – deep in my bones – that this is his apology. I'd been planning to play it cool, wanting to make it clear that such lack of regard for my time has consequences. But it's obvious now. He's been grappling with his feelings for me. And, though forgiveness is not my forte, in extenuating circumstances I can make an exception. I smile at him. I *knew* we had something special. I *knew* he felt it too.

It was just the same with Freddie, which is how I know this budding connection with Jack is so *right*.

On my first date with Freddie, I arrived at the pub vibrating with nerves. But when I pushed the door open,

I was greeted with a wall of noise and a few faces I recognised. It seemed as though a select group of people from the office had also decided they fancied a drink in the local pub.

Freddie was already there, talking to a tall man in the corner. He caught my eye as I came in, raised his eyebrows in apology for the unexpected turn of events. He beckoned me over and – ever gracious – acted as though the presence of our colleagues was part of the plan all along. He always was good at taking things in his stride.

I, on the other hand, had to do my level best not to look monumentally pissed off.

I forced a smile as he introduced me to the man he'd been talking to. 'My right-hand man, Greg,' he said, clapping him on the shoulder. 'Wouldn't know what to do without him.' I'd glimpsed Greg across the office floor before, often over at Freddie's desk. They had the sort of relationship I'd always coveted. An easy way that spoke of long hours spent in each other's company. More than a colleague. A friend. I stuck out my hand.

'I'm Iris,' I said, hardly able to keep the annoyance out of my tone. This was supposed to be *our* time together, and these people were eating into it. The man cocked his head at me, as though he'd picked up on my irritation. He took my hand anyway.

'Pleasure.'

Freddie kept the conversation going in our threesome, and, as the two men bantered, I was quiet, sullen. Finally, Greg seemed to pick up on my reluctance to engage, because he excused himself and then I had Freddie all to myself. I brightened instantly. But with an audience now, we had to be careful. We kept the conversation light in case anyone should overhear. We spoke about work to begin with, but I could sense that Freddie was frustrated at being limited to this. Eventually, he lowered his voice, moved closer and asked me more about Marcie. About how I'd found the immediate aftermath of her death, how I coped with it now. And though we couldn't act on the sudden closeness between us, the vulnerability of the conversation made it one of my most intimate encounters to date.

When the end of the session comes, I hang back, taking my time to gather my things. Jack's going to talk to me this time. His little speech made that clear. The room filters out, and I busy myself with my bag, packing and repacking it, until it's just the two of us left. I lift my gaze. Jack is staring at me. When our eyes meet, he holds his hands up in a pacifying gesture and crosses the circle towards me. 'I know, I know. I'm so sorry not to have messaged,' he says, and he does sound sorry.

I'd planned to give him the cold shoulder, but he deserves more than that after showing his hand in front of so many people. I tuck a strand of hair behind my ear. 'Don't worry. I know how busy things can get.'

He laughs. 'Partly. But it's not just that.' He pauses, huffs a sigh. 'I've thought about you a lot over the last week, and I'm very glad to see that you haven't succumbed to my curse, for what it's worth.'

I think of the hours and hours when he has dominated both my conscious and subconscious thoughts. So, it's not a lie when I say: 'I've thought about you, too.'

He moves closer still. I wonder if this is it. If this is the moment he is going to kiss me. Then, he ruins it all. 'It's all a bit confusing, isn't it?' he says, and I stare at him, not understanding. 'With Alice,' he clarifies. 'And Freddie.' Though Freddie's name sounds like a bit of an afterthought.

Truthfully, Freddie has never been further from my mind, but I nod anyway, hoping my frustration is not stamped across my face. 'Very confusing,' I echo.

He reaches out, gently touches the back of my hand. I want him to kiss me so much, but he pulls back, then rubs that same hand across his face. My skin where he touched me is on fire.

'Do you want to go for a drink?' I blurt, and I regret it the moment the words leave my mouth. It's not the play-it-cool approach that always worked so well for Marcie. Somewhere, deep in the back of my mind, her words echo. *It's the moment you think you've got them in the bag you need to be the most careful. They need to continue wanting you. Don't take the game out of it or they'll get bored.*

I want to tear the words back, even more so when Jack gives me a sad little smile.

'Ah, Iris, you're killing me. I would have loved that, but unfortunately my increasingly needy mother is calling this evening. She's obsessed with checking in on me. If I don't pick up, she'll get the police and the fire brigade and God knows who else to turn up at the door. But maybe next week?'

I hate rejection, perhaps more so than most. I put up with enough of it as a child. So, it is with a slight iciness that I reply: 'No worries. Possibly next week. I'll check my diary.' And just like that, Marcie's back.

There's a moment of awkwardness between us before Jack says, 'Cool. Look after yourself.' He half raises his hand, then turns towards the door.

I watch him walk out. I wait thirty seconds.

Then, I follow him into the night.

11

The verb 'to follow' is strange, isn't it? It's taken on a new meaning in this modern world. We follow social media pages, celebrities, colleagues and fathers' new wives. All that information at the touch of a button. A socially acceptable form of stalking – to such an extent, we've even reclaimed that verb, too. It's perfectly fine for someone to admit that they have spent long hours stalking an ex's Instagram, for instance.

What I can't understand, then, is why there is such a stigma attached to following someone in person. It's less revealing than the crap people put up about themselves on the internet, at any rate. I wouldn't be able to tell, for instance, from her walk alone, that Rita's sanity was hanging precariously in the balance, but there we are. That's the world we find ourselves in.

Jack walks with purpose: quickly, hunched against the cold. I've had to lengthen my stride to keep up, and am hopping between shadows, hanging back when he seems to be slowing down. This is not my first rodeo. There's an art to it. You have to be good at deciphering body language: watching for the slight stiffening of the shoulders that signifies they can sense another body behind them, the dipped head of someone lost in their phone, oblivious to their surroundings, the rummaging in a pocket for keys that suggests they're not entirely comfortable.

Jack displays none of these traits. He simply… walks. It's dull. There is something scintillating about knowing your very presence is putting someone on edge. Still, it's important to employ best practice, so I remain vigilant, occasionally daring myself to stray an inch too close. Just to keep the pulse aflutter.

I first learned these vital skills with Dad, after he left us. I'm not entirely sure why I followed him. Possibly out of some misguided sense of loyalty, not that he ever returned the favour. I was clumsier then. I knocked things over, was nearly caught several times. But it was on one of these excursions that I became aware of his new girlfriend, though the word 'girlfriend' always seems too young for someone with his portly stature and receding hairline. Mere months after my darling sister had left us, and he'd already moved on. Even by my standards it was callous. By Mum's, it was an act of savagery that nearly sent her to an ethanol-doused grave.

Jack hangs left and I pause, light on my feet. Marcie wasn't the only one who had ballet lessons, and, though I never had her knack for it, it's provided me with some essential skills. He turns into a smart street lined with Georgian townhouses. Plane trees cast sinister shadows on the pavement, like they're aware of me. Like they're beckoning me forward, encouraging me on.

This is the sort of postcode that us lowly lay people would never have cause to step foot in. It all clicks into place as he turns into an absurdly grand house midway along the street. The accent. The clear cut of him. The suits. The tan. It all screamed money from the start, but now it's confirmed. Moments like this are always jarring. My flat was nothing to write home about, but it was mine and it meant independence. Then, you see something like this, and you realise that whatever fragile delusion you had of success was just that: a delusion.

I watch as he lets himself in at the glossy black door. I didn't know front doors could be that shiny. It seems I have landed on my feet with Jack.

It was not quite such an instant love affair with Freddie's dingy flat. I saw it about a week after we kissed for the first time, and – as I took in the flat-roofed, squat building – I forced myself to take a deep breath and remember that he was worth it. When I saw the living room, I fumbled in my pocket for my sanitiser. The low-slung coffee table bore an ashtray overflowing with joint stubs. A single game controller was cast aside on the cracked, faux-leather sofa. A cluster of Chelsea Football Club mugs were balanced precariously on old pizza boxes. It was not, by any stretch of the imagination, the sleek flat I'd imagined him in. I'm not a snob, so I gritted my teeth and got on with it, but I did start making some grand plans for how I could gently encourage superior hygiene practices in Freddie.

It seems that won't be necessary with Jack. I can't believe that a man who lives in such an astonishing place *likes* me. Even if he did blow me off to take a call from his mother. I wait a respectable minute or two after the door closes behind him. No slamming here. It glides shut with a click. A light comes on in the downstairs window. Irritatingly, the bottom half is shuttered so I can't see in, but a low wall is closely wrapped round the house. In seconds, I'm balancing atop it, peering through the window and into Jack's life. Into the expansive living room.

Jack sits on a huge red sofa just beneath the window. It's angled so that his back is, thankfully, towards me, which gives me the opportunity to take in the room at large. It's the most elaborate sitting room I've ever seen: a dark-panelled room with brooding oil paintings lining the walls and red lampshades that afford the otherwise grand space an impression of cosiness.

Football flickers on the flatscreen TV in the corner. A common affliction of the male sex, so I won't hold it against him. Even Freddie liked football. Jack doesn't appear to be watching, however. His head is bowed so that I can make out the thick set of his neck, the small spring of baby hairs coiling at the base of his head. Over his shoulder, I can see his gaze is directed at the phone in his hand. Just being this close to him is stimulating. The thrill of proximity. Watching him in his natural habitat, unaware that he is being observed. His screen is visible from here. He's scrolling through social media. I press closer, balancing between the wall and the window, breath fogging the glass, pulse thudding in my ears.

He accepted Sally's friend request last night. It was a bittersweet moment, knowing he was on his phone, had accepted a middle-aged woman's request for his friendship, and yet still failed to message me: infinitely younger, and – I like to think – more attractive. Particularly with the hair. Still, it provided me with further insight into his life. Jack's entire youth was laid before me in pictures. It was all much the same, though I combed it with surgical precision. Boarding school, clubs, women, bars. In one family shot, posted by his sister, his father has his hand clamped tight over a teenage Jack's shoulder. Which might explain his strained reaction to my mention of him. Frustratingly, there was no sign of the wife. Clearly the millennial exodus from Facebook happened before they met.

The one interesting nugget of information that I did manage to glean was that Jack is in recovery. Two years ago, he'd posted something about being three years sober. It gained a bit of traction. One of the comments underneath praised him for his commitment to sobriety, and he'd replied, *I can't take all the credit. A has been a huge help*. A. Alice, presumably. A veritable Florence Nightingale to get him on the straight and narrow. It's no easy task, getting an addict to see the error of their ways. I should know.

As I watch, Jack's phone lights up with a call. *Mum*. The sting of rejection lessens. At least his excuse was honest. His demeanour changes instantly, even before he's lifted the phone to his ear. He tenses, a thick rope-like tendon lifting in his neck, a pre-emptive grimace across his face. Another feeling I can relate to, though not because mine is overbearing.

His head turns slightly as he speaks to her, so that he's in profile, his face set. His mouth moves so fast I can't make out the words, but I amuse myself by imagining him telling her about me. About my feminine virtues, my sleek blond hair, the zip of connection that travelled between us in the café and then again tonight. After I've exhausted that particular fantasy, it gets a bit boring, like watching a television on mute. I press my ear against the cool glass, but I can't make out any sound. After ten minutes or so, he gives a few tight nods, swallows, and hangs up.

He slumps back, navigates back to Facebook on his phone, types something in and pulls up a page. When I see what is on his screen, I realise that I have played my part very well, despite my blunder, my over-eagerness in asking him for a drink. Because he is looking at *my* profile – my personal profile. He clicks on my picture: from a couple of years ago now, when the faint lines that have started to appear round my eyes were less pronounced. I'm blond in this one, too. It's a selfie – no one ever takes photos of me – but I look good. He zooms in, then flicks to the next one. He does like me. So much so, he's doing exactly what I have spent a disproportionate amount of my own time doing. Stalking me on the internet. It sends a delicious thrill through me.

Once he's had his fill, he flicks off it. Opens his messages. I'm too far away to see what he's typing, but I watch him press send, and then my phone buzzes in my pocket.

Iris, as promised, sending you a message so you know I'm not dead. That would be boring for both of us. It was good to see you tonight. Perhaps we can get a drink after the next one. X

I wait the customary five minutes before I reply. Just to keep him on his toes.

I'll double-check my diary. Hope your mum didn't send the police over? Xx

Two kisses to make it very clear that I am also interested in him. Jack smiles when he reads my response, then chucks his phone to the side. He's playing the game too, I see.

I wait a few moments longer, but it's freezing cold, and – with contact firmly established – I feel confident enough to slink back into the night.

12

I always hate it when people reminisce about school as though it was the high point of their otherwise insipid lives. These are the people who enjoyed the fishbowl, the enforced hierarchy, the artificial semblance of power based not on merit but on those who fitted into the stringent parameters of what was deemed acceptable – and those who didn't. These are the people who look at their lives and wonder where it all went wrong. It's not rocket science. They peaked too early.

I have no doubt Marcie would have been one of these people. When I refused to tell Mum and Dad that my encounter with the cow pat was accidental, her punishment was swift and absolute. By the time we started upper school, she was my sister in name alone. I was responsible for a blemish on her character. For that, she could not forgive me.

Our first day at St John's – a small Catholic senior school that achieved a high Ofsted rating – couldn't have been more different to my experience with primary school. Marcie didn't slip her hand into mine. She walked three paces ahead of me and didn't acknowledge me at all.

This time, I trailed behind her into the classroom and watched her work her magic from afar. She was charming. She was beautiful. She adapted herself to whomever she was speaking with: a sympathetic hand on the arm if someone was sad, a witty remark to a boy who was already half in love with her. She blew into that school like a tornado, and – from the moment her dainty foot hit its hallowed hallways – Marcie Jones was worshipped like a deity.

By comparison, I shrank into myself and was largely ignored. Without Marcie to hold my hand, I quickly sank into oblivion. I spent a lot of time in the girls' bathroom, close to the sinks, scrubbing at the skin on my hands with the same vigour I used in the shower that day at the farm. I hadn't felt clean since.

On that first day, I walked into lunch alone. My skin crawled as I clocked the queue of people: the way they helped themselves to food with their bare hands, how they swiped at their running noses before handling serving spoons. I thought of the billions of bacteria that would have bred and multiplied by the time it was my turn, and felt bile rise in my throat. But people had joined the queue behind me, and I didn't want to make a spectacle of myself. So, I waited and watched as we inched closer to the food. The bread rolls were a no-go. People were handling those with their bare hands. The salad seemed like a safe option until I watched a boy cough as he was helping himself. By the time I reached the front, I had decided: I would stick with fruit I could peel.

I didn't bother to take a tray. I took an orange and a banana and considered ducking my head and eating in the safety of the bathroom. But no. I could do this. I scanned the seats available. Most people had found someone to sit with already. In the corner, Marcie sat at the centre of a large group, and I considered going over there, cashing in on our kinship, even if she was determined to ignore me. But as I started towards her, I noticed she was acting something out. She was holding her hands out in front of her, wringing them together and wrinkling her nose in an expression of exaggerated panic and disgust, before collapsing into giggles. She clocked me, clutching my orange and banana, and pointed. Several people turned to look. I felt my face burn.

I found a seat at a table with only one other person sitting at it. She was small, with glasses, and she looked as out of place as I felt. I nodded to her, then focused on ensuring neither my skin nor the fruit touched the table. I peeled the orange carefully, savouring each segment.

'Hey, are you Marcie's sister?'

I looked at her. She was staring at me, wide-eyed, and I wondered if perhaps I'd be alright. Maybe I didn't need Marcie. I straightened myself, looked at her properly, smiled. She was nice-looking, in a nerdy sort of way. I could see myself being friends with her. I could see myself being friends with anyone, at this point.

'Are you the one that fell in the cow pat? Did it really go in your mouth?' She leaned forward, her expression one of fascinated disgust. I could only stare at her as Marcie's betrayal pulsed through me. I knew she'd intended to ignore me. I didn't know she wanted to ensure my total annihilation.

'It was her fault,' I said, and I meant it to sound nonchalant, as though the memory didn't make my stomach curl in on itself, but there was a plaintive, whiney edge to it. 'She pushed me.'

The girl shrugged. 'Still gross.'

My appetite was gone. I stood abruptly, mumbled something about forgetting my bag and stumbled out of the dining hall.

Mum was waiting by the gates that evening. As soon as she saw her, Marcie was by my side, linking her arm through mine, playing her role to perfection. I resisted the urge to pull away from her: Mum would see and accuse me of being difficult.

'Well?' Mum said as we began the walk home. 'How was it?'

'So great, Mama,' Marcie gushed. 'We made loads of new friends, didn't we, Iris?'

I wondered what would happen if I told the truth. If I told Mum how I'd slumped by the sinks at lunchtime and eaten my fruit alone. If I told her how her favourite daughter had made my first day a misery. Marcie was looking at me as though she could read my mind. She raised an eyebrow, and I knew what it meant. That she could make my life a whole lot worse if she really wanted to. So, I gritted my teeth and smiled.

'Really great,' I echoed.

A new order was established. Marcie largely ignored me at school, and I grew used to a solitary existence. The teasing stopped after a while, when someone made a fool of themselves at a party, and I was grateful. Meanwhile, Marcie continued to collect friends like a politician running for the top job.

Now she'd established herself at school, something odd was happening at home. She was still horribly saccharine towards me when our parents were around, but in private – where she'd once sneered, and griped, and glared – she began to confide in me, like I was some empty vessel in which to keep all her secrets. I suppose, in a way, I was. If I ever told anyone what she'd told me, she had the power to ruin me.

I was now forced to endure nightly debriefs of her day. Who she hated, who annoyed her, who she fancied. This latter was something that gradually began to consume all her waking hours. Marcie, I was beginning to understand, was aggressively heteronormative, and fancied practically every single boy who crossed her path. Maddeningly, the boys who crossed her path almost always felt the same way about her.

She preened in front of the mirror as she spoke, pushing out her budding breasts, cocking her head, testing out a coquettish smile. And then, she began buying magazines.

She read article after article out loud, pausing every so often to look at me. 'You should listen to this bit, Iris. It might help you get a boyfriend.' Always said with a tone of voice that made it clear she thought the prospect impossible, irrespective of the advice. And though I hated myself for it, though I pretended with all my might to be disinterested, I listened as though she was divulging the secret to eternal life. I saw the way those boys looked at her – as though she was some rare new species, the only one of her kind – and I wanted that for myself. And when she left the room, I pored over those magazines and committed every word of advice to memory.

At first, the changes in Marcie were all physical. She said goodbye to her natural hair and dyed it a peroxide blond, because – according to one magazine – 'boys love a blonde'. She began wearing push-up bras. She went to the gym frequently and became slim enough to squeeze into the tightest of jeans. She wore crop tops that showed off her toned abdominals. She smiled with her tongue pressed against the roof of her mouth to define her jawline. She began chewing gum for the same reason.

And then, scarier still, she began to try on new personality traits. She learned how to dart glances across the classroom, with just enough frequency to indicate her interest. She learned how to master looking a little bit pathetic, which allowed the boys to step into the role of the hero. She would pretend to lose something, and they would scramble to help her find it. Once, she even used the bracelet.

She learned how to be confident around men, how to get what she wanted, how to ask them out. She developed new interests depending on who she was seeing at the time. It worked better than either of us could have anticipated. She was universally adored, by both boys and girls. The girls forgave her for stealing boys out from under them. The boys followed her with lovesick expressions. I never got the sense she truly liked any of them. What she craved was the attention, that feeling of being desired. It was a feeling I had never experienced.

But I gritted my teeth and said nothing as she emerged from each new relationship slightly altered. With each new skin, she was becoming someone I recognised less and less. It wasn't long before I realised I couldn't remember who she was underneath each of these different personalities.

13

On Thursday morning, Mum shocks both of us by rising early. The time between six and eight a.m. is usually my favourite. I like the quiet stillness of these hours: hearing the neighbours get up, alarms blaring faintly through the walls. Listening to the sound of their everyday mundanity: water gushing through shared pipes, the creak of their floorboards as they get ready for work; the quotidian rhythm of family life. After Marcie died, I would sometimes wish these faceless families would whisk me away with them. Anything was better than the blanket of grief that had fallen like an iron curtain over our house.

This sacred time has become more precious to me since I moved back here. When she's awake Mum hovers around like a disquieted ghost, glaring at my hair when she thinks I can't see her. I've stopped eating breakfast to minimise the risk of contracting some unsavoury disease, but I still like to sit in the kitchen in the mornings, for some variety. I disinfect everything beforehand, obviously, and give my laptop a thorough wipe afterwards. Mostly, she doesn't rise until noon, which gives me a good half-day of peace. Today is not one of those days.

I have just opened my laptop to Jack's profile when she walks into the kitchen. I've had to limit how much time I allow myself to spend on his respective profiles. It's not good to become too caught up in the fantasy and lose sight of the real-life man in front of me. I allow myself fifteen minutes each morning to click through my favourite of his photographs. My imagination can sometimes run a little wild. When Mum shuffles in, I slam the laptop closed. It's a sign of my exceptional self-control that I don't shout at her for interrupting.

We don't speak as she moves around the kitchen, though I'm hyperaware of her presence. I like to know where she is at all times, lest she spring some unpleasant trick on me, so I listen for the click of the toaster, the scrape of the knife, the clink of metal against ceramic. I'd rather not be in here, but to leave would show weakness, so I force myself to stay where I am. I open WhatsApp instead.

It is not plain sailing, once you've got that first little nibble of interest. Marcie was right in that regard. You must make yourself available, but not *too* available. Funny, but not funnier than them. Light, but with just enough genuine feeling to show that you are a functioning human being with *real depth*. I feel I've got it bang on the nose with each message I shoot off, but something's not working. Because Jack's responses arrive with such a lack of urgency that we might as well be using the traditional postal system. I can't understand it. It's almost as though he's forgotten those two precious moments we shared. I, for one, can think of little else.

He was last seen at one o'clock this morning. That was exactly two hours after my last message. I don't want to think the worst, but sometimes the doubts – the memories – make it difficult. I don't want to be one of those women who never trusts again after a betrayal, but sometimes I can't help the doubts that creep in. The questions. If Jack is not messaging me, who is he messaging?

I scroll back through our conversation. My last message was fun, a little flirty. Some comment on my day at the café: I told him about the children that came in that day, with just the right level of exasperation at their adorable antics. I asked him if he was ready for the weekend and what his plans were. Leaving myself just open enough for him to suggest a drink, if he was free.

He came online almost instantly, but the ticks remained grey. I swallowed my frustration and waited. So it has been for the last two days. Hours pass between messages. When his responses do come, they're effusive, and fun. There's just not enough of them. It's hard to maintain momentum when it feels as though I am communicating with a brick wall. And the doubts – the paranoia – really do start to stack up, if you allow them.

I've managed to discern much of his routine, through watching both the house and his 'last seen' on WhatsApp. What's it for, after all, if not to understand the rhythm of someone's life? He wakes between six and six thirty. He goes offline, presumably for his commute, then comes back on at around eight. He's on and off throughout the day – appearing more at lunchtime, then disappearing again for his commute home. I was waiting for him, despite the bitter cold outside, last night. I'd wrapped up warm, and I stood on the other side of the road, a large scarf wrapped round my face, my hood pulled up, as he trudged home in the dark. My heart rate sped up when I saw him. After he'd let himself in, I reinstated myself on the wall. It was boring, to say the least. He entered the sitting room an hour later, and pulled out his phone, but didn't message me back. It became too cold to wait. As I was on my way home, my phone pinged with a message. I managed to wait a whole hour before I replied. And now... this.

'You were out late last night.' I have been so engrossed in my phone, I barely noted Mum taking the seat in front of me. She takes a bite of toast. Crumbs cascade down her chin, littering the table. Disgusting. She looks – different somehow. Cleaner than normal, despite her porcine eating habits. She might even have washed her hair; it looks softer, less greasy. Almost disconcerting, if I wasn't so focused on Jack.

'I was visiting a friend,' I say.

She raises an eyebrow. She knows I have few of those. That makes two of us.

'I don't want you treating this like a guesthouse, Iris.'

'Not very welcoming for a guesthouse, is it?' I snap. I'm not sure where it comes from, this slip. Usually, I can maintain my composure better than this. Jack must be getting to me.

'Any news?'

I don't roll my eyes. Yet another example of my self-control. 'On what?'

She clears her throat lightly. 'Your father.'

Dad is so far from my mind, so unimportant compared with my current predicament, that irritation seeps into my tone again. 'I'm not keeping tabs on him twenty-four-seven, Mum. I'll let you know when I hear from him, OK?'

A very risky game, and one I'm not at all prepared for. Unfortunately she still has the power to turf me out, and, even with more shifts at the café, I am in no position to move out yet.

Mum sighs, a deep, mournful sound. Then, terrifyingly – horrifyingly – she leans forward and slumps onto the table. A sob erupts from somewhere between her arms. I'm not sure what to do – if I should get up and leave, or offer some empty words of comfort – so I do neither. I can only sit there, staring. I wish she wouldn't – I haven't seen her lose control like this for years, and I never quite got the hang of handling it then, either.

'I can't stop thinking about it,' she says. 'You being here. It's bringing it all back.'

'What are you talking about?'

'*Her.* Marcie.' Another sob.

Oh. And here I was, thinking she was about to produce another one of her cutting remarks. Her speciality, when aimed at me. I don't like thinking about those days. The days following Marcie's death. When Mum caved in on herself. When Dad left.

Everywhere we turned, there was another reminder. When her voice didn't drift from the shower in the mornings, when her shoes – two landmines – remained for weeks in the middle of the kitchen floor, where she'd last kicked them off.

When Mum retreated to her room and didn't emerge for days on end. I missed her.

So, one day, I mustered the courage to enter. It was dark, the heavy curtains drawn across the windows. I couldn't make her out immediately. When my eyes adjusted, I saw she was hunched over, sitting on the corner of the bed. She looked up.

'Is it really you?' Her voice was hoarse.

'Yes,' I whispered.

But as I drew closer, she reared backwards. 'Don't lie to me. Why are you lying? She's gone. She's never coming back. Where's Richard? I need Richard. I can't lose him, too.'

I was frightened by the madness in her eyes. It's still there, sometimes.

She doesn't say anything else. Just stays there, head bowed, shoulders shaking. And eventually, when it becomes too much to stand, I get up from the table.

'I need to get ready for work,' I say to her bowed head, but I'm not sure she hears me.

14

Jack works in a smart, glass-fronted building between London Bridge and the Shard. Thanks to Google, I've established the office hours. And with Street View, I've identified the ideal position to watch from: across the road, concealed enough that he won't spot me, but close enough that I can keep one eye trained on the entrance. I'm primed, ready to move at the first sign of him. Google, however, didn't give an accurate depiction of the throngs of people currently pouring out of every conceivable doorway. Five thirty p.m. on a Friday evening, and it's like standing in one of the seven circles of hell. I'm being buffeted from all angles. I don't often get things wrong, but I'm beginning to wonder if this was a mistake. It will be almost impossible to spot Jack from here.

There is also the very real risk that Jack might spot me before I spot him. It's a risk I'm willing to take. I've weighed up the pros and cons of this particular jaunt, and I've crafted a backstory should the need for one arise. I'm here meeting a friend. What a surprise to see him – yet another fateful coincidence! I had *no idea* that he worked in the City. Small world, and all that.

Plus, I can't deny that the thought of him spotting me in the crowd sends a small thrill of pleasure through me. I've done my hair specially – blow-dried so it falls in soft curls round my face. I look younger. Innocent.

It was so much easier with Freddie. Working together, I had access to his calendar. All it took was a few clicks, and his work day spanned before me in colourful little squares. I tried not to do it too often, of course. I respected his privacy. But when those first few niggling doubts about his fidelity began to creep in, I found it hard to resist.

With Jack, it's harder, which in some ways makes the whole affair more exhilarating. It has, however, necessitated my need to be here, right now, on this busy London street. Jack's WhatsApp habits have really begun to grate on me. He's left me no choice, really. What did he expect me to do with response times like that?

I push through the crowd so I'm closer to the door, sanitiser clutched firmly in my hand. I've applied it liberally, but there are too many people, and I have no idea where most of them have been. I'll need to scrub my skin in the shower later. I only hope this is worth it. The air smells like alcohol, with just a hint of promise.

I'm right by the door now. Someone knocks into me, and I whirl round and snarl, 'Watch where you're going.'

The malice in my voice causes the man – clearly drunk – to raise his hands. 'Sorry. No need to get so lairy about it.'

'My boyfriend just died, arsehole,' I say, and I ripple with pleasure as I watch his face crumple.

'I'm sorry. I am,' he says and backs away. I thrust my tongue into my lower lip at him, making as ugly an expression as I can, then turn back to the door. I'm in full view of the lobby now. It's expansive, smart. A few people are making their way through the turnstiles, none of them Jack. I can't have missed him. I've been here for an hour already. His status continues to go from online to last seen. I picture him sitting at his desk way above me, and wonder if he can sense that I'm here. I hope so. Like there's some invisible thread binding us together.

And then, suddenly, there he is. Walking through the lobby with three colleagues. Laughing, joking, jostling. My eyes snap instantly to the woman. She's walking too close to him, overly familiar. As I watch, she reaches out, touches his arm. So lightly, it could almost have been an accident, were it not for the fact that her hand goes straight to her hair after, tucking a stray strand behind her ear. It's the self-conscious gesture of a woman eager to be noticed. I can't blame her really. He's exceptionally attractive, and there is something about a widower that seems to drive women wild; but she's barking up the wrong tree. Jack is mine. And if she continues with these wanton displays of flirtatiousness, I will have to make that clear, in no uncertain terms.

But Jack – to his credit – doesn't reciprocate. He turns to say something to one of the other men, hanging back so she's left at the front of their small pack, walking alone. At least *he* has a sense of honour, of loyalty.

They're so close to the door now that they're going to pass right by me when they exit. I turn so I'm angled away from them, facing the street, and hear the door slide open behind me. They're so wrapped up in their conversation that they don't notice me. One of them brushes past so close it lifts the hairs on the back of my neck. I can smell the woman from here. Her perfume is too sweet. Sickening.

They begin to move as one, and I follow behind, always keeping at least two strangers between me and them. They're adept at navigating these crowds, and I'm at a disadvantage. I nearly lose them twice. After a few minutes, they turn off the main thoroughfare and towards a small pub at the end of a quiet road.

I hang back, watching from the corner. When they reach the door, Jack stands back, allows the woman to enter before him. A prickle of annoyance. They disappear inside, and I deem it safe enough to approach.

I peer through the mottled window, but it's packed inside, and I can't make them out. It's one of those old boozers that London used to be famous for. Old stable partitions carve the pub into segmented booths. Dark beams run along the low ceiling. It's dark, dingy. It looks dirty. I wrinkle my nose and wonder – for the umpteenth time today – if this is worth it.

Then, I think of the woman. How close she was to him. It's worth it. I need to remind him that I'm not just some faceless woman at the end of a phone. I enter through the very same door, though there's no one here to open it for *me*. I'm blasted with a wall of noise, hot air, the putrid scent of spilt beer. It's so crowded, I can't see them anywhere. I edge round a man towards the bar. I'm going to need a prop.

After some deliberation, I settle for a pint of beer. I don't like beer – it bloats me, and I dislike the way it lingers on the breath – but I don't intend to drink it. This is another tip I gleaned from Marcie. She discovered that men have an affinity for women who act like them. She was brilliant at it, put them at ease just enough to make them think she had an edge to her. Just enough to stop them from viewing her like she was somehow lesser, simply because she had better personal hygiene, no ugly appendage between her legs and no obsessive love of football or pints.

I pay for the beer, then stand with my arm against the bar, scanning the room. Still no sign. I tip a bit of the drink onto the floor, just to make it look convincing. It fizzes there for a second before seeping into the nasty carpet. A man to my left stares at me as though I'm insane. I ignore him.

And then, from behind me, 'Iris?'

This is it: my big moment. I gather myself, fixing an expression of charmed surprise, and swing round to face Jack. 'If I didn't know better, I'd say you were stalking me,' he says, and his eyes sparkle with amusement.

'I could say the same about you.' I keep my tone light, voice steady, but, truthfully, he takes my breath away. He looks adorably rumpled from his day in the office. Being this close to him again... it's intoxicating. 'Didn't you turn up at my work the other day?'

'Touché.' He grins. He looks genuinely thrilled that I'm here, which shouldn't be a surprise, but those ugly thoughts do have a way of making you doubt yourself. 'What brings you up this way?'

'I was meeting a friend.' It comes out so smoothly, I almost believe it myself. 'She had an emergency and had to shoot off. So, here I am.' I raise the beer.

He assesses my choice of drink, and his eyebrows lift with approval. Hook, line, sinker.

'Well, her loss is my gain,' he says, and he presses a warm hand to the small of my back. Something funny happens to my insides and my breath catches in my throat at the casual intimacy. 'I'm just here with some colleagues, but I don't suppose you want to grab dinner? They won't mind. We come here every Friday.'

I do my best to maintain my neutral expression, but it's very difficult with the fireworks exploding in my chest. A date. A real-life date.

'Dinner sounds good,' I say lightly, and Marcie would be proud of my composure. 'I'll just finish this.'

'Great. I'll go and let them know. Meet you outside?'

I nod. When he disappears back into the throng, I tip the remains of the pint onto the carpet, set the glass on the bar and head outside to wait.

15

My second date with Freddie was more success-ful than the first. He chose a quiet spot a few blocks away from the office. Somewhere he knew our colleagues didn't often frequent. Somewhere we would be safe from prying eyes. He'd sent the message the week before.

Can I buy you lunch next Thursday? ☺

I read it several times over, unable to stop the grin spreading across my face. We agreed on a time and, once again, I was sent into a complete tailspin of preparation. By the time Thursday rolled round, I was barely sleeping more than five hours a night.

I met him at the lifts, and we went down together. It felt like a bit of a risk, but if questioned we could say it was merely a manager taking the time to check in with his subordinate. There was something wonderfully transgres-sive about the secrecy of it all.

Our hands brushed a couple of times on the walk over. Each moment of contact caused my heart to skip erratically in my chest, though neither of us commented on the mounting tension.

Freddie had booked us a table by the window. I felt awkward as I sat down, half-wished that our colleagues *were* there, to assuage some of the pressure I felt. A strange sort of stage fright, I suppose. The pressure to perform, to be fun, and funny, and fey. To be just like her. I scrambled for something to say, but my mind had gone blank. Freddie seemed to sense my nerves, because he kept up a steady stream of chatter. Already, we were so in tune with one another that he was taking up the mantle when I failed.

We started with work, skirting around the deeper, more emotional subjects; neither of us was willing to venture into this territory without being sure of the other. He asked me how I was settling in, and what I thought of the office, and how I was finding the workload, but with each new question there was a blazing intensity to his eyes, as though he was hoping that I would read between the lines. Hoping that I would find the hidden meaning layered between his stale lines of questioning.

I wanted to tell him it was OK, that he didn't need to put on a front for me, but I couldn't find the right words, and Marcie's principal rule when dealing with men rang round my head, over and over: 'imgsrc*Never* make the first move,' she used to say. 'They have to be unsure of you, until they're not.'

The rest of the lunch continued in a similar vein, and I could tell that we were both frustrated. Unable to bridge the gap between professional and personal. I began to wonder if perhaps I'd read it wrong. And then, very distinctly, Freddie shifted in his seat, and his leg brushed against mine. And just like that, the ice melted.

I'm not a big drinker, for obvious reasons. I don't like feeling out of control. I hate the way my speech slows, and my limbs feel heavy, and the fact that I don't always think before I speak. I can count on one hand the number of times I've been drunk. It's how mistakes are made.

But when Jack scans the menu in the upmarket gastro-pub he's led me to, and asks if I'd like another pint, I nod. Just to maintain the veneer. I'll have to force it down. It's a lot of liquid to consume, and the taste will be horrible, but he's worth it. *This* is worth it.

This establishment is a lot nicer than the one we were just in. On the walk here, I subtly applied more hand sanitiser, rubbing it into my skin to try to rid myself of the unpleasant feel of the dirty glass in my hand. The small rivulet of beer that had snaked down my wrist as I poured it away.

'A pint for her, and I'll have a sparkling water,' Jack says with such authority that the waiter – a teenager with his hair pulled into a ponytail – gives a small, deferential bow more suited to a man twice Jack's age. It's attractive, the way he's taken control. A good sign. He knows what he wants and he's not afraid to ask for it. If only Freddie had been a bit more forthcoming at the beginning.

I try to mirror Jack's easy manner, but I'm very conscious of how high the stakes are. It's easy to maintain the charade for a few minutes of snatched conversation, but here I'm locked in for at least an hour. I'll allow him to take the lead. Maintain the illusion of control. *Eye contact is key, Iris. There's something very seductive about the eyes*, Marcie said once as she drew thick lines round her own, focus never straying from her reflection.

I place my elbows on the table, and meet his gaze. Marcie, by her own admission, was excellent on dates. She knew exactly what to ask, and when. When to lean forward, to press her advantage. When to pull back. Unfortunately for me, I was, obviously, never present, though when Marcie recounted them for me afterwards I hung off her every word, while pretending to be absorbed in something else. Now, I can't help but feel that it's *almost* like an interview. A chance to get a feel for compatibility, and longevity, and attraction. But a date is an escalation of an interview: a job lasts years at best, whereas a partner is for life. Unless you're careless, of course.

I decide to go with something benign, and, for lack of anything better to say, I ask a question I already know the answer to. 'You don't drink?'

He shakes his head. 'Had a bit of a problem with it, back in the day.'

I widen my eyes in feigned shock, careful that there's no judgement there – just a sympathetic smile as though I can't fathom how the enigmatic man in front of me could have succumbed to such a horrible illness. And I do understand how horrible it is. I've seen the other side of addiction – even tried to break the cycle. But you can only help someone who wants to be helped, and, though I tried hiding the bottles from Mum, she always found more.

'Well done. Can't have been easy.'

'Hardest thing I've ever done.' Jack leans back to allow the waiter to place our drinks down. 'But I'm glad. I was headed down a bad path. But what about you, Iris?' I love the way he says my name. I love how it sounds coming from his mouth. I'm easing into it now. Not an interview, just a conversation. 'Any skeletons in your closet I should know about?'

He smiles again. If only he knew.

If a man is interested in you, he'll want to know everything about you. He'll want to know what makes you tick. Another check on the list. This is a very positive sign.

I take a careful sip of my beer, suppress my grimace and swallow the bubble of air rising in my oesophagus. I'll have to play this one cautiously. Marcie requires careful navigation.

I make my voice so soft and feminine, the girl herself would have been proud. 'Well, I grew up in London. I was a twin. My sister, Marcie, died when we were seventeen.'

'Christ. I'm so sorry. The same year your dad died?'

Shit. I'd forgotten Dad was supposedly dead, but I don't let it throw me. I nod my head, a sad little jerk. 'Yes.

It's probably why my mum turned to alcohol at around the same time.'

I need to slow this down. I'm making myself sound like a charity case and, while *some* tragedy adds a little flair, too much and people avoid you like the plague. It's a hard line to walk. I should know. I nearly went overboard when playing this card with Freddie. But that was later.

'You poor thing.' Jack doesn't sound like he's put off. His eyes are soft with such sincerity – with such *sympathy* – I want to plunge on, if only to keep that look on his face. 'Mum still struggles with it, of course. She'll go through periods of sobriety, but she always seems to fall off again. It's good I'm staying there, actually. It helps to keep her on the straight and narrow.'

'It's not an easy thing to kick,' he says, and there's an edge to his voice that speaks of his own struggles.

I nod. 'She's my favourite person. I'd do anything for her. And family's important, after all.' An echo of Freddie's own words.

'You sound like a good daughter. That's a lot of responsibility for anyone to take on.'

I *could* sit here all evening, and allow him to shower me in compliments, but I'm aware that I have perhaps pushed a little too hard on my own misfortune. 'Seems like you're not the bad omen after all. Sister, dad, boyfriend. I'm coming up trumps.'

A small smile plays on the corner of his mouth. 'Very true. Don't suppose the family dog counts?'

'I'm afraid not.'

'Damn.' He leans forward. 'I really mean it though, Iris. I know I haven't known you long, but you're a special person. And you've been through a lot.'

You're a special person. It takes everything I have not to throw myself at him across the table. He thinks I'm special. Stand out. Someone worth taking note of. I lower my eyes: modesty is key. *No one likes a girl who's too full of herself*, Marcie had said, sounding entirely full of herself. 'That's kind of you to say. Anyone would have done the same.'

He shakes his head. 'They wouldn't.' He allows the words to sit for a second, then smiles again. 'Anyway, tell me about this man of yours. Freddie.' He holds a quick hand out. 'I mean, don't if you don't want to. I understand some people find it tricky. But I find it helps to talk about her. Alice.'

I'm not quite sure how to frame it. I like that he's showing an interest in Freddie, but it's a tricky subject to negotiate. I don't want him to think I'm not ready if I wax lyrical about Freddie's many attributes. He had so many lovely qualities. I'll go vague. Downplay it.

'We worked together. He was my boss, actually, so we had to keep the relationship quiet. He was charming and funny. Liked to be centre of attention.'

Jack smiles encouragingly. 'Good-looking?'

I laugh. 'In an unconventional way. Pretty questionable dress sense at times, but luckily he toned it down for the office.' I smile as I remember Freddie's novelty shirts, the ones he wore at the weekends. I liked that he didn't seem to care how he came across to others.

Jack looks down at his own outfit. The slightly creased white shirt, open at the collar. The suit trousers. 'I'm afraid I'm a bit more traditional than all that.'

Do I detect a hint of regret?

'I like traditional,' I say quickly, and he seems pleased.

'Anything you *don't* miss?' he asks.

It's an odd question. I think of the argument Freddie and I had just before he died. The accusations that we flung at one another. Accusations we've never been able to take back.

Usually, people only focus on the positives of those they've lost, like all the bad was wiped away the moment their heart stopped beating. But we're all multi-faceted. There's darkness in everyone. And I like that Jack seems to understand this. I wonder if the question comes from a place of jealousy. Not necessarily a bad thing. A bit of healthy competition never hurt anyone.

'I don't miss fighting with him. We had an argument just before he died. I regret that I didn't get the chance to say sorry,' I say, quietly.

Jack nods his head slowly. 'It's natural to feel like that, Iris. But fighting is a normal part of any relationship. You couldn't know what was going to happen. Fights are healthy.'

This is all becoming horribly morose and I don't like to think of that time if I can help it. I straighten my spine, re-establish eye contact. 'And what about you and Alice? What do you miss? Or what don't you miss?'

He's quiet for a moment, before he says, 'I miss so much. Having someone there all the time. Someone to come home to. Her cooking. As for what I don't miss...' A long pause. 'Nothing. She was as close to perfect as I think I'm going to get.'

It's trite, overly sweet, utterly unrealistic. No person is that perfect. Not even Freddie. I can't believe he's been crass enough to mention it in front of me. *Me*. The person he thinks is special, but apparently not perfect. I remove my hand from the table and curl it into a tight fist. I need to get a hold of myself, keep him talking.

'How did you meet?' The question has a gritty edge to it, but Jack doesn't seem to notice. He smiles to himself – at some memory, no doubt. Recalling the moment he met his *perfect* wife.

'At a mutual friend's party. It's a cliché, but I literally couldn't take my eyes off her. I worked up the courage all evening to go and speak to her. Drank way too much beforehand, which was par for the course for me back then. We had this instant connection, you know? We spent the rest of the night together. I was a bit worried I was coming on too strong – I tend to become a bit consumed by relationships – but she didn't seem to mind. She was – she became – everything to me.'

My nails are now digging into my palm so hard I'm sure I'm going to break the skin. But still, he ploughs on.

'We spent every day together after that. It was one of those whirlwinds where we just couldn't get enough of each other. She really helped me get it together. I was heading down a bad path, which is what happens when you get shipped off to boarding school aged eight. Your peers are your parents. And when your peers are experimenting… it normalises a lot of behaviour that's just not acceptable. I'm pretty sure most of the teachers knew about it, and turned a blind eye.' He takes a breath. 'But yeah. Alice was like a guardian angel, I suppose. She helped me turn everything around. Helped me get sober. She saw me at my worst and loved me anyway.'

Call me naive, but I hadn't given much thought to the dead wife up until now. If anything, I was grateful to her for dying when she did; bringing me and Jack together at the group. Giving me some light back into my life. But now? Envy blooms in the pit of my stomach.

'Well, she sounds like quite the saint.' I'm not sure where it comes from, but it leaves my mouth with hot, searing venom. Usually, my armour is pristine, but this small chink of darkness causes Jack's face to drop, then harden.

'I just mean' – I huff a laugh, but it sounds strained – 'that she sounds like a really lovely person.' I can't get the tone right. It sounds too high.

Jack's eyes have narrowed. I scramble for something to say, but my words sit heavy between us. The mood sours so suddenly, I don't have another chance to pull him back in.

It is a singularly British thing to struggle through something that no longer holds value, and that is exactly what Jack and I do. Conversation is painful. I try my best to generate more and more and more questions, but they feel forced. He doesn't ignore me. It's worse than that. He gives short, sharp answers that leave the silence blooming once more. When the waiter asks if we want pudding, he says no quickly and reaches for his wallet.

I've lost control of the situation. It doesn't happen very often, and I'm not quite sure how to deal with it. How to claw this back. And so, I do something reckless. I lean forward and grasp for Jack's hand with the sort of thoughtless desperation Marcie would have laughed at. It doesn't work. He jerks his hand away, looking at me with so much disdain I shrink back into my chair.

'I think you've misread this, Iris.' There's none of the playful, flirtatious tone now. 'I'm just not in the right place at the moment. I'll see you later.'

He stands, shrugs into his jacket and, without a single glance back, leaves me sitting by myself at the table.

16

The upside to Marcie's ever-changing façades was that she was almost too busy to notice me at school any more. At fourteen, we were both navigating the ups and downs of puberty, though she had somehow managed to avoid the plague of acne that peppered my cheeks and chin. She was barely at home at the weekends, juggling numerous dates with numerous suitors. She attended every party she was invited to and, when she was not necking some boy down a dodgy alley behind the chicken shop, she had plans to meet up with Jessica or Olivia or Helena. She wore heavy eye make-up that made her more intimidating than she already was. She took up smoking – a vile habit that would probably have killed her eventually, had she made it past seventeen.

But without her contempt school became a more pleasant place for me. One lunchbreak, she forgot herself to such an extent she smiled at me.

The thawing of our relations did not go unnoticed. Marcie liked to be looked at, and people liked looking at her. They noticed every tiny change in her appearance, every phrase she used was picked up and disseminated among our peers, every mannerism mimicked and honed to perfection. It was, sometimes, like being surrounded by a legion of Marcies. So, when she softened towards me, everyone else did, too.

A couple of years after we'd started at St John's, I found a small group of acquaintances, who were by no means popular but who I got along with just fine. It was a mutually beneficial relationship: they knew who I was and who I was related to, and I helped to raise their social standing that way. In turn, they made my days at school that little bit less lonely. I no longer dreaded walking the hallways. I had people to sit with at lunch. Despite this, I got the distinct impression they were never completely sure of me. They even seemed wary at times: they couldn't understand why I nipped to the bathroom after every lesson to wash my hands, nor why I produced my own sanitised Tupperware at lunch, filled with food I'd prepared myself.

I'd tell you their names, but there doesn't seem much point. They weren't around for long enough to matter. I had about six months of contentedness before Dad pulled me aside one evening and asked me a question that would, once again, drive a stake through mine and Marcie's relationship.

With Marcie out so much, I was able to form more of a relationship with my parents. I still caught Mum looking at me sometimes with a small divot between her brows, but Dad seemed keen to forge a new bond. I still refused to go on walks with him, but I allowed him to tell me about his latest discoveries, and found I enjoyed recalling my long-dormant knowledge of nature.

In the autumn term, we'd spend dark evenings discussing his findings, the encyclopaedia – in use once more – open between us. It was on one of these evenings that Dad cleared his throat, darted a glance towards the ceiling, where Mum was having a bath, and lowered his voice.

'I've been meaning to ask you about Marcie,' he said slowly, stiltedly, as though the next words out of his mouth would be rebellious. His eyes flicked towards the ceiling again. Clearly this was an original thought, not one sanctioned by Mum. I stiffened. I did not want him to ask whatever was coming next, but he plunged on regardless, oblivious to my anxiety.

I stared at an illustration of a stag beetle as he said, 'Do you think she's been going out too often? I'm a bit concerned she's' – he cleared his throat again – 'getting a bit of a reputation for herself.'

This was the sort of question that always made me uncomfortable. Because, in truth, I had heard rumours at school. You'd call it slut shaming now. Back then, it was the norm, when a girl's value was measured by her ability to hold out – not too much that it made her a prude, but just enough so as not to seem 'easy'. The rumours were the sort of salacious gossip that always surrounds someone like Marcie. Ill-advised attempts to topple her reign. She didn't care, not then. Not yet, anyway. She told me, privately, that the furthest she'd 'gone' was second base in a cupboard at Helena's party, but I saw it differently. The rumours marked a sea change. A suggestion that some of the allure of her was wearing off. Too much of a good thing, and all that. There were whispers about her losing her virginity, particularly transgressive within the parameters of a Catholic school.

I didn't know how to respond, so I remained silent for a good minute, wondering if I could get away with not answering at all. Dad leaned forward, placed his hand on my forearm. 'You can tell me,' he said softly. 'I know she hasn't always made things easy for you. I just want to know.'

I stared at him, taken aback. I hadn't realised that Dad was aware of the chokehold Marcie had over my life. I wondered, first, why he hadn't said something before. Why he had stood by as Marcie stamped herself all over my existence. And it was with this sense of injustice still thrumming through me that I began to talk. I told him what people had been saying about her, that she lied to them frequently about where she was going, that she smoked, and – I suspected – took drugs, too. With each sentence, the words seemed to gain momentum, until they took on a life of their own, tripping over each other in their haste to be spoken. I felt powerful and purged in that moment: like I was regaining some fundamental part of myself that I'd lost all those years ago.

But the words stopped flowing when I looked up and caught sight of Dad's expression. It was one of abject horror, and I knew I'd gone too far. My stomach lurched painfully, and I wanted to claw everything back, but what I'd said sat between us like a bomb.

Dad blinked once, twice, three times in quick succession. He seemed lost for words. He cleared his throat again.

'Dad,' I said, and there was a desperate edge to my tone. 'Please.'

'I can't not do anything with this information, Iris. Surely you understand that? I won't say it was you who told me, I promise.'

This was not a comforting assertion. She would know. She always knew. I'd gone into so much detail that it could only have come from me. Dad rose from his seat, the encyclopaedia forgotten. I grabbed for his arm, but he shook me off and left the room.

I sat, frozen, and listened to him mount the stairs. I heard the knock on the door to the bathroom. I heard the low rumble of voices, before Mum's became shrill. The door to the bathroom banged open.

'She could be lying!' she said as she crossed the hallway into their bedroom, bath forgotten. 'Did you ever think about that?'

'Come on, Sarah.' Dad sounded weary. 'You can't *not* have noticed how much she's been out.'

Their bedroom door closed behind them, and their voices became muffled. Cold dread pooled in my stomach. All I could do was wait.

I was granted one more day of peace. Marcie didn't come home that evening, despite several calls to her mobile, and even Mum had to admit that she was out of control. I saw her at school the next day, her mascara smudged under her eyes. She smiled at me again, unaware of what was waiting for her at home, and I couldn't bring myself to smile back. I averted my eyes and swallowed the nausea.

I dragged my feet all the way home. Marcie walked with me, last night's hangover seeping from her pores. 'Do you know why I got like a million missed calls from Mum and Dad last night? Did something happen?' she asked.

I squeaked a noncommittal reply, and ran to our room as soon as we were through the door. The shouting started two minutes later. I buried my head under my pillow, but I still heard a door slam and Marcie's voice ringing with panic, then anger. Five minutes later, she barged into the room.

'Why did you do it? Are you *trying* to ruin my life?' she said. 'I've been grounded indefinitely.'

I didn't reply. I closed my eyes and wished I was somewhere else. And then I felt Marcie's hand tangle in my hair. She wrenched my head backwards, so my neck was exposed. 'I said' – her teeth were gritted, her jaw jutting forward – 'are you trying to ruin my life?'

I think it must have been that question. The injustice of it. The flagrant hypocrisy. The utter obliviousness to how she'd treated me for the last few years. How she'd made my life miserable, and now she had the temerity to ask *me* if I was ruining *her* life. Something inside me snapped. I opened my eyes and forced myself to meet her gaze.

'Don't you ever put your hands on me again,' I said quietly. And there must have been something in my expression. Something that made her release me. Something that caused a flash of fear to cross her face. She tried to hide it. She shrugged, turned away, but I noticed her hand was shaking.

I sat up. For the very first time, I felt a small surge of power. It was intoxicating.

Marcie never did touch me again. She didn't wear make-up to school the next day. She wore her skirt at a normal length and her shirt buttoned in all the right places. She walked with her shoulders rounded, and her head ducked. People whispered about her in the corridors. They wondered what had happened to the vibrant, fun-loving girl, who was out every night. She did her schoolwork diligently. She seemed not to notice the boys who preened in front of her. Before long, they lost interest.

And with the change in her came a change in me. Without her critical gaze from across the room, I walked taller. I met people's eyes and spoke out in class and sat wherever I wanted at lunch.

My new acquaintances didn't seem to like this new version of me, or perhaps the change in Marcie's popularity meant I was no longer useful to them. Whatever it was, they shrank away from me in the corridors. I returned to my solitary existence.

The summer holidays rolled round. My parents were thrilled with the return of their golden child. She was welcomed back into the bosom of the family, and once again I became the outsider.

The days were long and hot and boring. My latest fixation was art. I found I was quite competent with a pencil. I spent hours perfecting my craft and learning about shading, colour theory and perspective.

And then school started again, and I prepared myself for the same old routine. Except it was not the same old routine. A new boy had joined our class. His name was Billy.

I fell in love with him instantly.

17

It could have gone better. There's no denying that. Evidently, I crossed a line by suggesting his dead wife was anything less than *perfect*, and that bothers me. I should have been smarter, played into the residual feelings that linger, and gushed over how wonderful she sounded, convincing him that I could be saintly and gracious about the woman who was my forebear. Evidently, Alice is still taking up a significant portion of his time and attention. A portion that could – should even – be transferring to me.

I'm shivering by the time I get home. I needed the walk. Needed to clear my head, try to come up with a plan. I considered going past Jack's house, but thought better of it. We could both do with a few hours to think.

I let myself in and go straight upstairs. Mum's awake – I saw the light on in her window on my approach – but I don't say hello, and she doesn't come out. She's left another gift on my pillow – an early drawing of mine. A fish. I don't have the time or the inclination to decipher what she means by it, so I ignore it, lie on my bed and open my phone. Jack's online again. I tap out a quick message: Thanks so much for dinner. I think maybe you got the wrong end of the stick re. the Alice thing. I didn't mean anything by it – she sounds lovely! I'd love to hear more about her. Hope you got home safely.

I don't have high hopes for the message – a hunch that is confirmed when the ticks go blue before Jack goes offline – but it's critical to start damage control early. And I *am* sorry. Sorry I allowed the mask to slip. It won't happen again. Not with him.

And then there's the wife. This paragon of virtue and grace and good will and kindness, who pulled him out of the rut he'd found himself in and positioned herself as his saviour. His guardian angel. It's little wonder he won't hear a word against her. She burrowed into his life like some – admittedly younger – Mother Teresa. Even in death, she clearly has her claws sunk so deep that Jack cannot – will not – hear a word against her. The good thing about claws, though, is that they must be trimmed eventually.

I cannot let this – her – be the end of something so promising. Something so good and fulfilling and perfect. He thinks – thought – I was special. I must make him think that again.

I google her again. I didn't really throw my weight behind it the first time, when she was a mere name on his lips, but now she's become a threat, and I need to find out more about her. Alice Reynolds is an annoyingly common name. There are hundreds of possible candi-dates, but none that seem to ring true to the woman he described. I don't know what it is that makes me so sure of this – perhaps it's that none of them look like what I've discovered is Jack's type (naturally expensive-looking) – but I come away from the search frustrated.

I'm beginning to wonder if I've played this all wrong. It's the first time in a long while that my carefully constructed persona hasn't worked for me, and I feel more than a little lost. I haven't felt this adrift since Freddie died.

All I can hope is that Jack will turn up at the group on Tuesday, take one look at me – with my lovely, blond hair that I take such good care of, the slightly overexaggerated make-up – and realise that he's made a huge mistake. Patience is not a strong suit of mine but, for him, I'd wait a lifetime.

Jack, however, doesn't come to the group on Tuesday. Fiona even delays the session for an unprecedented five minutes in his absence – and we all watch the clock tick down with a sense of impending doom. I swear there's a collective sigh of disappointment when Fiona gives her trademark phlegmy cough – a product of her twenty-a-day habit – that indicates we won't be waiting any longer. None of them are more disappointed than me.

I'd rested a lot on this meeting. I was well behaved over the weekend. I went to work and came straight home again. I ignored that deep, infernal tug towards Jack's house, and scrolled aimlessly through his profile over and over again, searching for something that might help me turn the tide on this unfortunate turn of events. But he's a different person now to the one he was in that profile. He's sober, for one thing. There was nothing – that I could see – that would bring him round to my cause.

I've sent him a few more messages. Small ones – just checking in – and he has staunchly ignored every single one. It's left me in a very bad mood indeed. I can't shake the niggling worry that I've messed up my chances.

Matt has the floor now. I can tell from the way he clenches and unclenches his fist that he is furious about something, and – to be fair – I can hardly blame him. I'd be angry, too, in his position. Incandescent, in fact.

Matt is here because his brother, Mark, died of a rare and aggressive type of prostate cancer. Matt was there through every appointment, ferrying him back and forth to the hospital in a truly heart-warming display of fraternal affection. It was only as Mark lay on his deathbed that he uttered the words that would change Matt's life for ever: *it's genetic*. Unsurprisingly, Matt harbours a not insignificant amount of resentment towards his dead brother for that revelation.

Matt mops at his head with a dirty handkerchief. His sanitary habits do leave a lot to be desired, but I suppose he's got more of an excuse than most. Still, just looking at that dirty rag makes me want to retch. He uses it for both his nose and his profuse sweating, and I can't help but think of the cross-contamination of bodily fluids, all coming together in one snotty mess. I rub my hands against my jeans, skin itching.

'My week's been bloody awful,' Matt says. 'That little fucker Mark left me everything in his will. I only found out on Friday. Nearly a million pounds! Which would be great, if most of it hadn't gone towards clearing his debt. There's only three hundred quid left. It's yet another kick in the teeth, that's what it is.'

It is not entirely clear why Mark chose to wait until his final few hours to reveal to Matt that there was a high chance the cancer was hereditary. I suspect there is more to the story than he is letting on, though Matt – in his capacity as a financial adviser – has hinted that he 'misguidedly' encouraged Mark into some dodgy invest-ments. Quite how much Mark lost is up for debate, though evidently we are not talking pennies. The will, I suspect, is intended as one final middle finger to his ailing brother.

Matt's prognosis is not good. Following Mark's revela-tion, he presented himself to the oncologist in a state of panic. A state that was only made worse when he was told – in no uncertain terms – that it was very bad news. Stage four. Perhaps, the oncologist suggested, they might have been able to do more if Matt had come to them sooner. He often uses especially colourful language when he recalls this particular facet of the story.

He tires easily these days. This little outburst is going to cost him – and sure enough he slumps back in his blue chair, looking spent.

Usually, I feel sorry for Matt. Mark's death means he doesn't even get a stab at revenge, and that's a sorry situation for anyone. Today, however, I'm not in the mood. All I want is for Matt to finish his little speech and it to be my turn. I'd interrupt, but we all know how Fiona takes to that.

When it becomes clear that his outburst is over, I raise my hand.

'Go ahead, Iris.'

I clear my throat. 'Firstly, I'm sorry, Matt.' Always good to start with sympathy, even if it's false. 'I can't imagine what a difficult situation that must be for you.'

He inclines his bald head – shining in the overhead lights – towards me.

'I've found the last few days quite tough.' Not a lie. 'A few things have brought up some... uncomfortable emotions, I guess you might say.' I take a deep breath. I'm going to need it, if I'm about to reveal this other, darker, sadder part to my journey with Freddie. 'Freddie and I didn't always have the easiest run of it. We had a few bumps in the road.' An understatement, if there ever was one. Another deep breath. My voice cracks, and it's not an act.

'The truth is, Freddie was involved with someone else... I don't think it was that serious, but it really drove a wedge between us. I found out about it, and we argued. And I think all those uncomfortable feelings have just been coming to the fore lately. I'm still angry about the betrayal, but I feel disloyal saying that. I still love him, but I'm hurting, not just from his death but from the deception.'

And there it is. The collective, sympathetic inhale from everyone in the room that suggests my words have met their mark. I don't like to think about those times, if I can help it, but it feels good to get it off my chest. I feel lighter, somehow.

'That must be incredibly difficult for you to process, Iris.' Fiona's voice is – amazingly – soft, and I allow her words to travel through me. To fill me up to the very brim, until even the Jack situation doesn't feel quite so serious. 'Grief isn't always a one-way street. There are often complicated emotions, regrets even, around those we loved. Nobody's perfect.'

A few people round the circle nod in solidarity, but Fiona's words hit me right at my core. I realise that she's right. Nobody *is* perfect; but Alice – to Jack – was as close as it came. And perhaps that's where I've been going wrong.

I shouldn't be sitting here spouting about Freddie. I must recalibrate my future without him in it. And that future – I'm more certain now than I ever have been – is Jack. I will find a way to get through to him. Even if it kills me.

The semblance of a plan starts to come together in my head.

18

Step one is establishing his whereabouts. As soon as the group is over, I'm out of my seat, and even Matt – in his weakened state – looks surprised that my tears have dried so fast. That my heartbreak over Freddie's infidelity has evaporated so quickly.

It's nice to work towards something again. This last week, when I'm not at work I've rattled around the house, avoiding Mum, and have felt more alone than ever. I barely have the energy to speak at work, and even Mick is getting frustrated with me, though he tries to hide it. Now, I'm charged with a new sense of vigour. Who knew Fiona's words would be just what I needed?

Jack's house looks the same bar one crucial difference. For the first time, the curtains are drawn across the window. Inconvenient, but not the end of the world.

I spend some time snooping around outside, looking for some sign that Jack is still in residence. I find it in the bins. A banana skin, still a gaudy yellow colour, stuffed right at the top of one of the bags.

I don't hang around after that. There doesn't seem much point with the curtains closed, and I've got what I came for. Evidence that Jack is still very much at home, and very much ignoring me. Ghosting is such a pedestrian punishment. I'm almost disappointed in him.

My phone pings with a notification on the walk home. My body has stopped reacting to the buzz of my phone – that thrill that used to come whenever a message from Jack arrived – but I pull it out anyway. It's just a Google alert for a new search result with the name Alice Reynolds attached. I check it, but I'm not expecting much since she is – obviously – dead. Perfect, but dead. Unsurprisingly, it's not her, or anyone who I imagine looks like her, so I put it away again.

Mum's house feels different when I step through the door. Some shift in the air that marks a change. An absence. Even from the hallway, I can tell she's not here. There's no creak overhead as she shifts across the floorboards. No bilious rattle of her breath. Just the lingering smell of cigarette smoke on the air, like her ghost still hovers, watching me.

I'm unsettled by it. Mum's world is even smaller than mine: she lost her job after Dad left and her dependence on alcohol began in earnest, and never bothered to get another one. She did well out of the divorce – though this was more, I suspect, due to lingering guilt from Dad than any particular skill from her layabout lawyer. She hasn't had to work since, and she's stingy with no perfect daughter to buy presents for. She receives one Sainsbury's delivery a week of canned goods, ice cream, oranges, vodka and cigarettes, and for anything else she pops to the local Tesco. The cashiers and I are the only people who know she exists. She has no friends. So, her absence feels significant.

I call up the stairs for her – just in case – but there's no response. My voice reverberates around the empty walls. Maybe she's died.

It's not beyond the realms of possibility that she's lying bloated and blue just beyond her door. Vodka and cigarettes are a famously unfortunate coupling. I doubt it, though. She's too noxious to go in such a banal way, without some final retribution aimed at reminding me what a disappointment I've been. Still, I can't deny the sympathy would be nice. I'd have a new story for group next week; it would be an entirely original performance. Plus, if Mum *had* died, Jack would have to talk to me.

It doesn't take long to conduct my search. I try every room in the house before I find myself standing outside her bedroom door. Even now, I'm not immune to the memories that come flooding forth. Memories of me hovering in this very spot, listening to the sounds of her breaking heart. When she decided, in no uncertain terms, that I simply couldn't replace the daughter she'd lost. It was a tough pill to swallow. Before that – before my relationship with Marcie went sour – we used to pile in here on a Sunday and read the comic strips that came in the papers.

I push the door open and wrinkle my nose. Her scent is everywhere. That nasty, slightly sweet smell of old, unwashed sheets. I reach into my back pocket for the sanitiser, and edge further into the room. If my room is a shrine to Marcie, then this one is a shrine to Dad. All these years, and a pair of his slippers are still tucked neatly beneath his side of the bed, his PJs folded on his pillow, a tray of his trinkets atop the dresser. So much respect for a man who didn't have the decency to even attempt to help her through her grief. I did. Or, at least, I tried.

Marcie's here, too. In the corner of the room is a cluster of photographs. Mum and Dad on their wedding day, looking adoring and entirely unsuspecting of the way their marriage would break down. There's a family photograph taken the year before Marcie died. I'm standing slightly apart from the rest of the family, who are clustered around the Christmas tree, smiling so widely they look like they might break with happiness. It's the only one of me here. There are two more of Marcie. A generic school photograph with a greyed-out background. She spent hours at the mirror that morning, applying liberal amounts of eyeliner. She looks sensational. I don't know what happened to mine. The other is a shot of her and Mum, arms flung round each other, beaming. They were so close. So happy in each other's company. I'm reminded, once again, of exactly where I stand in the pecking order of our little family unit.

I see it as I turn to leave. A glint of silver on Mum's bedside table. My pulse spikes. I thought I'd lost it. I haven't seen it in years. After Marcie died, I was sure I'd hidden it between my mattress and the bedframe, but, when I went back to check before I moved out years ago, it had gone. I looked for it, tore the room apart, but it was nowhere to be found. Mum's had it all along. I move to the bedside table, slip it into my pocket.

It's mine, now. Mum has no business with it.

19

Just like that, Billy consumed my every conscious thought, and even many of my unconscious ones. I'd been waiting for this moment for years – that special connection so often chronicled in novels and films. That connection Marcie claimed to have with every boy who crossed her path. Now, aged sixteen, here was my very own.

He was perfect. Tall and handsome, he had what Mum would call *presence*. The type of person that instantly draws all eyes in the room, whether they mean to or not. I had never wanted anything so badly in my life.

And so, what had promised to be the start of yet another boring school year gained a different focus altogether. I watched Billy at every opportunity – in class, and in sport, and in the library, and at lunch – and I grew to learn his routine. Without ever talking to him, I learned he preferred brown bread over white, blue biro over ink, football over athletics, white coffee over black. I learned – by eavesdropping on idle gossip – that he thought school was a waste of time, that he only came to use the art facilities. I learned that he felt painting was a form of self-expression, and I spent hours in the art block, poring over his creations in the hope of gleaning some small, secret nugget that would suggest he felt the same way about me. If it was there, I couldn't find it.

In fact – despite our best efforts – Billy didn't seem to take notice of any of the girls. He drifted between each class with the tortured, faraway expression of a misunderstood artist. So wrapped up in his own creative sphere, he failed to lift his head and take note of the twenty potential muses lining up for the privilege. For the first time in my life, I was gunning to be number one.

And yet, whenever I was around him – whenever I engineered an opportunity to talk to him – I found the words wouldn't come. My newfound confidence in the face of Marcie's strange subservience vanished whenever I opened my mouth. My body began to betray me: hot, red flushes that rose in my cheeks, trembling hands, forehead dotted with sweat. None of these highly embarrassing symptoms had been in Marcie's magazines. Since I lost the power of speech whenever I was in his vicinity, I realised I'd have to find another way. And then it came to me: my own art. But my drawings were rudimentary at best. I had a lot of work to do.

And so, I threw myself into my drawing with the sort of feverish passion you only hear of in articles about child prodigies. I used every waking hour testing out new techniques, spent everything I had on supplies, new pencils, different paper types. I stopped following Billy to the library and went straight home instead, where I hunched over our small, single desk as I drew and drew and drew.

I took my eye off the ball. I can admit it now. What happened next was, in part, due to my own negligence. I won't ever let it happen again.

For the best part of a year, Marcie had been a model student, a model daughter, a model classmate. She kept her head down, and worked hard, and kept a close group of sensible friends who preferred coffee dates to seedy warehouse raves. I thought she'd changed. It had been so long since I saw the 'real' Marcie that I became complacent. I thought this quieter, nicer, smarter, more natural (yet still astonishingly beautiful) version was who she was at her core. I forgot her moods. I pushed the incident at the farm far to the back of my mind. It was years ago now.

I've thought a lot about what must have been going on in Marcie's head during this fallow period. And the conclusion I've come to is this: Marcie understood better than I ever did that it takes twenty years to build a reputation, and only one misdeed to ruin it. So, when Mum and Dad pulled her to the side that evening and told her what I'd told them, she realised she was being talked about in all the wrong ways. She liked the attention, yes, but it had to be the right kind. She realised that the empire she'd painstakingly built up was beginning to crumble around her. People didn't know who she was any more.

Marcie's reputation was the most precious thing she had. And so, she rose like a phoenix from the ashes and set about trying to rectify her mistakes, and it worked. She was the exception to the rule. When she was spoken about now, it focused on her achievements, her kindness, her studiousness. Marcie defied all the odds. She rebuilt her reputation in a year alone. She no longer actively ignored me, but nor did she pull me close. She seemed, on the whole, entirely indifferent to me, even at home. It suited me just fine. I had bigger fish to fry.

I completed the drawing after six long weeks of working on it. I was thrilled: it captured him at his best. I'd pinpointed that often dreamy expression he wore, the slight pout, the rumpled hair. He would have to notice me now.

Giving it to him was another matter altogether. I was not nervous per se, but I knew I had to get it right, this first moment of contact. I practised what I'd say in the mirror: 'Hi Billy, I'm Iris. I thought you made an interesting subject, so I drew this of you. Hope you like it.' I perfected the casual tone, as though drawing pictures of people without them knowing was something I did every day.

But every time the opportunity arose to give it to him, I faltered, the words dying in my throat. I stowed the drawing in my bag each morning with a renewed sense of determination, but each evening, after another failed attempt, I concealed it back under the pile of books on the desk Marcie never used.

Eventually, one night, desperation prevailed. I turned to Marcie as we lay in the dark.

'If you wanted to give a boy you like a present, how would you do it?'

The words sounded too loud in the quiet room. We rarely spoke beyond over-polite, forced conversation at the dinner table.

She was so quiet I thought she'd fallen asleep.

Then, 'Who are you talking about? Who do you like?'

I should have foreseen this coming. 'No one,' I replied quickly. 'Hypothetically.'

'There's got to be *someone*. Otherwise you wouldn't ask the question.'

'It's for a friend.'

She was quiet again. I knew what she was thinking. I didn't have any friends. Not good ones. 'I'd probably,' she said after a long pause, 'just go up to him and do it. It's not hard.'

I lay for a long time staring into the dark. To me, it was the hardest thing in the world.

The next morning I dressed quickly, and left the room before Marcie woke. I didn't want to see her, filled as I was with the horrible sense that my question last night had made me vulnerable. It was only as we were halfway to school, bags slung over our shoulders, that I realised I had forgotten to pick up Billy's drawing. I thought about going back for it, but Marcie was in a good mood and I didn't want to sour it. She didn't bring up my question at all on the walk, and I wondered if this was yet another example of her growth. Her newfound maturity. I see now how wrong I was.

Her big move came after lunch. I sat in the corner of the school yard as I usually did, and watched Marcie break away from her gaggle of friends. She straightened her spine in a way I hadn't seen her do in months. In a way that always suggested she had her sights set on someone. And then – with a bolt of horror – I saw who she was making her way towards. Billy was sitting alone, just like me, except he never made it look awkward or uncomfortable.

He looked up as she approached. Marcie swung her golden hair over her shoulder and sat down next to him. Within two seconds, she had achieved what the rest of us could not. He laughed.

Then she reached down, extracted a roll of paper from her school bag. I knew what it was instantly, and the bottom of my stomach dropped out as Billy unrolled it. His eyes widened. He stared at it for a long time. His face split with a smile.

He pointed at her and there was a question in his gaze. She nodded modestly, tucked her hair behind her ear, and, in that moment, I knew she'd passed my work off as her own. Knew she was reaping my reward. And as she shuffled closer to him, arm brushing his, the dislike that always simmered in the pit of my stomach calcified into something darker.

The relationship developed fast after that. They became the most talked-about couple at school. They were all over each other like a rash. Like an infectious fungus.

'We're taking it slow,' I heard Marcie preach to a friend one breaktime. 'But' – she glanced at me, sitting in my usual spot in the corner of the yard – 'I think I might love him.'

I knew this was false. I waited for her to slip up like she had last time. To discard Billy like an empty crisp packet just as she'd done with all the other boys. I readied myself to collect the fragments of his broken heart. But the months dragged on, and they showed no sign of slowing down. I began to lose hope, hating her more with each passing day.

And, nine months after Marcie's big move, as though they could sense the growing discord between us, my parents suggested the trip to Cornwall. I think they thought it might bridge the gap between us. All I could think was that it was a whole week, where we'd have nothing to do except stew in our mutual dislike.

20

Mick's patience snaps on my very next shift. I can't muster any enthusiasm. This café is draining me of creativity. Any original thought. All I do, day in day out, is smile benignly at dirty children who I can barely bring myself to look at, make the same coffee orders for the same tedious people, scrub stains from tables while suppressing the urge to retch. And what do I get in return? A pitiful wage and ungrateful customers.

It's simply too much, particularly when I'm under so much strain from other aspects of my life. Jack. Mum's frequent absences. Freddie. That fucking house. It's all begun to crowd me in a way that is most unpleasant. I slam a coffee onto the counter so hard it spills right over. The exhausted mother for whom it was intended glares at me, but I ignore her and shove a wad of tissues in her direction so she can mop at the spill. I'm not doing it for her.

It is, apparently, the final straw. Mick grabs my arm and drags me into the back room in a blatant display of workplace harassment, but I can't be bothered to point it out.

I thought I'd become immune to the smell of bacon fat, but it's worse in here, right next to the tiny kitchen. Out front at least attempts were made to give the impression of cleanliness, but there's no need to keep the pretence up in this poky back room, where only the lowly employees are allowed to come. Sticky, thick grime has settled into every available orifice, between each page of the fat ledger book, which – judging by the figures – tells a sad story of the café's steady decline. I stand in the middle of the room, back straight, and try not to touch anything.

'What the hell's wrong with you?' Mick's eyes flash dangerously. I'd thought he was a well of patience, but clearly I have gone too far. Pushed him over the edge. 'It's like you've been a different person recently. I'm this close.' His thumb and forefinger are nearly touching. 'I don't understand,' he continues. 'You asked me for more shifts?'

He has a point, but that was before Jack started ignoring me. Before I realised that I was able to find exactly nothing about Alice online, despite the numerous hours I have spent trawling the internet. Because Alice, I have decided, is the key to all of this.

There is no time to dwell on her now, though. Mick is looking at me as though he barely recognises me. And, as much as I might like to, I can't afford to give up this job. Not if I want to leave Mum's. Which I very much do.

So, I summon tears. I grit my teeth, and slump against the desk, and force myself not to reach for my sanitiser.

I duck my head, round my shoulders, and allow them to shake with silent sobs. It's not long before the pretence becomes a reality, and the tears start to flow of their own accord.

Anger, frustration, confusion. It's all been simmering just beneath my surface for the past week. Jack's curtains are still closed. I've checked every night this week, but there's been no sign of movement. No flicker of interest. I've sent a couple more messages, but it's feeling increasingly like screaming into the void, and my patience – what little there was of it in the first place – is wearing thin.

Mick is by my side in seconds, just as I knew he would be. 'You poor thing. You've been through so much.' He rubs my upper arm, and it feels a little like a violation, so I shift slightly further away from him, and allow the tears to fall freely onto the desk. Hopefully, the salt will clear some of the bacteria.

I give a believable hiccup. 'I'm sorry. I know I haven't been on the best form recently. It's just… all been so difficult. All the memories of Freddie. I think being here just brings it all back. We met in a café, you know?'

Mick's eyebrows pull together. 'I didn't. I can understand how that might be difficult for you.'

I nod, a singularly sad gesture that conveys the depth of my grief. As though my head is too heavy for my body. 'And now,' I say. 'There's this new guy. You met him actually. He came in the other day. And I'm just so confused by all the feelings. He's not talking to me, I'm worried about him, and it's all just a mess.'

Mick smiles gently. 'I knew he liked you. He wouldn't stop looking at you. I thought I saw him outside the café the other day, but he didn't come in.'

I snap my head up. 'Did you? When?'

Mick removes his hand from my arm. Oh dear, I've confused him again with my capricious personality swings. It did come out more sharply than I intended, but I hope he chalks it up to emotion.

'A couple of weeks ago,' he says slowly. 'But I wasn't sure it was him, and, when I looked again, he was gone.'

I resist the urge to roll my eyes. Why is it that everyone in my life is so utterly incapable? 'Well anyway,' I plunge on, gritting my teeth. 'It's all been a bit much.'

'Listen.' His voice is gentle. 'If you like each other, it'll all be OK in the end.'

And therein lies the problem. Because I'm not sure if Jack *does* like me any more. I showed a side to myself that I rarely – with the exception of Mum – allow anyone to see. I ruined it, just by showing him a glimpse of myself.

Which is where Alice comes in. I tried every trick that I knew with Jack but, when the chips were down, it wasn't enough. I was audacious, and loud, bold and brash, flirtatious. I was Marcie. But it has become ever clearer that Marcie is not what he wants. What he wants is harder for me to emulate. What he wants is Alice.

'These things have a way of working themselves out. If he's not talking to you, is there someone you could reach out to, to check he's alright?' Mick says, patting me on the shoulder again, and – though his nails are rimmed with dirt – his words spark against something I hadn't previously thought of. Something that ignites a tiny nugget of hope in my chest. 'Why don't you go home?' Mick continues. 'Honestly, you're no use to me today. Offending all my best customers.'

I nod gratefully, give him a watery smile that I hope does not belie my mounting excitement. Going home is exactly what I need right now.

I sanitise as soon as I reach the street, then march home. My tears dry instantly. I don't detour past Jack's. There's only so much staring at the wrong side of a curtain one can do.

I let myself into Mum's ten minutes later, and head straight upstairs. She's not home again. That'll be the third time this week, but I don't have the time to dwell on her whereabouts. Because, to align myself with Alice, I will need to do more than simply combing the internet for mention of her. I need to speak to someone who actually knew her.

I need to speak to Jack's mother.

There are a few messages waiting for Sally when I log in to Facebook, but I ignore them and go straight to Jack's profile. I click on his friend list, type the name Reynolds into the search bar. There are a few, likely cousins, but only one woman of the right age with the right sort of *stature*. Catherine.

Sally won't work for these purposes, so I log out, and use Holly instead. I don't like using Holly if I can help it. She doesn't have quite the same level of benign inoffensiveness as Sally, whose achingly boring life can dupe even the most suspicious of stalkees. But she's too old for this. For what I need her for. So, Holly it is.

Holly is a little zanier. She's young and has several piercings, and a tattoo that travels up one side of her neck. She only came into the café once, and looked as though she'd stumbled in by accident. No doubt she'd expected something a little cooler, but – once inside – she ordered a coffee out of politeness and took a seat by the window.

In her profile picture, she's staring out of it, a wistful expression on her face. Like she wishes she hadn't come into this particular shithole. She's looking wonderfully arty; all credit to the photographer, of course. She was easy to create a backstory for: all poetry and tortured expression. A bit like Billy, actually. She's perfect for the task at hand.

I type Catherine's name into Facebook, add her as a friend, then compose my message.

> Hi Catherine, I hope you're well. I think we met a few years ago at Jack and Alice's wedding (I was a good friend of Alice's – at school with her). I don't want to trouble Jack with this, but me and a few old friends were hoping to pull something together of Alice to remember her by. Like a sort of digital photobook. I don't suppose you have anything you could share? Any memories? Voice notes? Photos/videos? Anything like that? We'll send you a copy too, of course, when it's ready. Thanks so much!

Perfect. Casual. Believable. Now I wait. It's going to be a tough one.

That done, I log back in to Sally's profile. There's a message from Tilly, rambling on about something or other. Some issue she's got with her husband, who is fifteen years older than her. Tilly is Sally's closest friend. A best friend adds to the veracity of Sally's profile, and she can always rely on Tilly to step up to the mark, commenting on each new post with an abundance of exclamation marks, liking every status update, sometimes posting something funny to Sally's timeline. Having someone *real* as a friend relieves the pressure on me to constantly generate believable content.

I keep Tilly sweet by listening to her insensitive complaints about her husband, though frankly it sounds as though she has it good. He's older than her, sure, and she does like to go into detail about his old-fashioned habits in the bedroom, but he sounds committed. Like he's a good father to their two children. Which, from experience, is not always a given.

She's a good distraction, though, so – to keep my mind off waiting for Catherine's response – I tap out a sympathetic reply and watch as those three dots bounce along the bottom of the screen.

21

Downstairs, the door clicks. Mum's home. I go out to meet her, encouraged by my message to Catherine. Usually, we avoid unnecessary interactions as though the other is contagious, but I'm in a better mood now and I can't deny Mum's recent absences have spiked my curiosity.

She doesn't see me instantly. I stand at the top of the stairs, watching her. She's unwinding her scarf from round her neck in the hallway. It's one I haven't seen before – a chunky knit – though I could have sworn she hasn't been shopping in years. Mostly, she keeps the same old, ratty items on rotation. The same faded jeans, jumpers stretched with age and peppered with moth holes. Stained T-shirts. When things were really bad, an old pair of Dad's pyjama bottoms.

Under her coat, which she hangs on the peg, she's wearing a bright red dress, cinched in the middle to show off her tiny waist. Another piece I've not seen before. Maybe she's met someone. Maybe I've given her too little credit, and she's spent the last few years squirrelled away in her room swiping on dating apps. I hope so. Anything to put her in a better way.

She must sense my presence, because she looks up as she's removing her coat.

'Where've you been?' I ask, leaning casually against the banister. She doesn't scare me as much as she used to. I stopped trying to make her love me years ago, and some of her power died with that impulse.

'Out,' she says, evidently not in the mood to talk, but I go downstairs anyway, and follow her through to the kitchen.

'Nice dress.'

She pats her hair. It's looking suspiciously clean. In the light, I can see she's wearing make-up.

'I thought it was time for a change. Can't be wearing the same old tatty stuff all the time.'

'It suits you,' I say generously. It does. I'd forgotten how pretty she could be. How like Marcie she looked. 'You should mix things up more often.'

'Thank you.' My flattery doesn't seem to be working. Her tone is clipped.

I take a seat at the table as she bustles around making tea. *Tea*. I check the time on my phone. It's five p.m. By this time, she'd usually be half a bottle deep. Something is definitely off. When she clocks me at the table, she sighs, then – reluctantly, I think – sits opposite.

'Was there something you wanted?' she asks. There's something off about her voice, too. It's too high, the question coming out too fast to be convincing. It feels performative, like she knows how she would usually act towards me, but for some reason she can't emulate her usual demeanour.

'No. Do I need a reason to want to spend time with my own mother?'

Her expression says that I very much do. We lapse into silence. I watch as she hunches over the table, scratching at something on the linoleum. It must be a man. I can't think of another reason for such a sudden shift in her. If I could find out who, it would balance the scales between us even further – give me more leverage, more time to find alternative accommodation. Because the truth is, my information on Dad is running thin on the ground.

'Is he nice?'

I ask it so casually I could be enquiring about the weather, but her hand stills on the table. I can't see what she's scratching at. She's got her other hand cupped round it, like a child trying to prevent another from copying her work.

'Who?' There's a definite quiver to her voice now. Sensing weakness, sensing *blood*, I lean forward.

'The man you're seeing.'

'What man?' Her eyes dart to the left, and a flush travels up her neck.

'Don't think I haven't noticed, Mum. You're out a lot these days. I'm glad for you. It's important you don't sit here, wasting away, surrounded by Dad's things.'

'You've been in my room.' Not a question, a statement. Her jaw juts defiantly, just like Marcie's used to.

'No more than you've been in mine.' I wonder if she's noticed the bracelet is missing. I put it where it belongs, in among the box of Freddie's things.

'I haven't. Been seeing anyone,' she says, but I don't believe her. 'I made a *vow*.'

God, this persistent allegiance to Dad is boring. 'A vow he broke the minute he left us. In sickness and in health, doesn't it go? I'd hardly say either of us were healthy.'

'Don't talk about that time. Please.' She swallows weakly. 'I'm not like you,' she says quietly.

'What's that supposed to mean?'

'Only that you've been going out just as much – more even – than I have. Don't think I haven't noticed.'

'I've been going to work?' I cock my head, keep my tone light. As though I have absolutely no idea what she's talking about.

'I didn't think cafés were open that late.'

'I've been seeing a friend.'

'A male friend?'

'Does it matter?'

'Well, given your partner died six months ago I'd say yes, it does.'

'I don't think Freddie would have wanted me to be single for ever, Mum. Not all of us go into self-imposed exile after a breakup.'

'All I'm saying is it can't have been that serious if you're already considering someone new.'

This is exactly the sort of poisonous comment that has eroded our relationship. The sort of thing that leaves a bad taste in my mouth, that sends anger zipping through my veins. She has no idea how serious Freddie and I were. Serious enough that he bought a ring and buried it, right at the bottom of his sock drawer. I stumbled upon it by accident when Freddie was out one evening. When I saw that little box, my heart leapt. I couldn't help myself: I opened it. A beautiful diamond set into a simple silver band. Not quite the right fit, but close enough.

I want to tell her about it, *prove* how serious we were, but Mum's not finished yet. 'You always were fickle,' she says, and there's a horrible, weary resignation in it.

'Meaning *what*?' If I was thinking straight, I'd do something to steer us off this path I've sent us down, but I'm not. We spend so long avoiding the past, and I want her to say it. To finally tell me what she really thinks.

But Mum only gathers herself and stays quiet, sipping at her tea with a dignity I'd thought had long deserted her.

'Shall I get you a drink?' The question drips with sarcasm, but she doesn't rise.

'Bit early for me.' Then, after a pause, 'Any word?'

I sigh heavily, remind myself what's at stake, and collect myself. 'Yes. I spoke to Dad yesterday.'

'And?'

I'm not quite sure what makes me say it. The implication that Freddie and I were not serious, perhaps. Or her calmness in the face of my rising anger. I come out with the lie before I can think it through. 'They're having problems. The wife's not attracted to him any more. Thinks he's too old. Divorce might be on the cards.' I don't use her name with Mum, if I can help it. It always elicits a cat-like hiss from her lips, as though it dredges up some animalistic instinct within her that is out of her control.

Mum's hand goes back to her hair. 'Are you sure?' And there's the emotion I've been looking for, except it's not aimed at me.

I shrug, a petulant child. 'Not a hundred per cent, but it doesn't sound good.'

'I should…' Mum swallows and gestures to the door. 'Go,' she finishes lamely, and she hurries out.

It is only after I hear her door close that I notice what she was carving into the table with her thumbnail. My sister's name is crudely written into the plastic, spiky and uneven. Just like Marcie was. And I know she has carved here what she wouldn't say to my face.

22

I wait until the very last minute to make my entrance. Once everyone's seated. Settled. Through the small window in the door, I watch Fiona checking the clock. No doubt wondering where I am. Matt shifts uncomfortably. He's looking worse this week: pale and drawn. Hannah – as always – has her hands folded in her lap and is staring straight ahead. Charlie looks as though he might be contemplating running into the road. Rita's wearing too much make-up, but it is, once again, in vain. Jack's not here. That's OK: I didn't expect him to be, and, honestly, if this is going to work, it's better he's not. These people, whether they know it or not, are my guinea pigs.

I fix a wide, open smile to my face and push through the door. 'I'm *so* sorry I'm a bit late,' I say, and I make my voice softer. I hoick my tote bag – another improvisation – up onto my shoulder and cross the room. It's filled with things I may need tonight: tissues, tampons, paracetamol. I hold an apologetic hand up in the air to Fiona.

'Sorry, Fiona. It won't happen again.'

She looks taken aback. Good. I'm going for different, and so far – judging by the shocked expressions around the room – it's working.

'It's alright, Iris,' she says, frowning, trying to collect herself. 'Just try and be here five minutes before the start next time.'

'Of course,' I say, nodding hard. 'Absolutely. I just lost track of time. I can be such a scatterbrain sometimes.' I release a girlish giggle that seems to derail Fiona once more.

'Right. Well then. Let's get started, shall we?' She casts one final look towards Jack's empty chair and begins. We run through the usuals: how this week has been (I tell them I've taken up baking sourdough – *'it's* so *therapeutic'*), whether anyone has anything to build on from last week (for this, I took a deep breath: *'I think I've come to realise that I need to have a different outlook. I should be grateful for the relationship Freddie and I had. Any other bumps weren't reflective of the love we shared.'*), before Fiona opens the floor.

Hannah sticks her hand in the air. It trembles slightly: she doesn't like being in the limelight, but she comes every week without fail. I could do with taking a few leaves out of her book, to be honest. She strikes me as the sort of character I could put to use: inoffensive, kind, meek.

She starts tremulously, 'I found a box of photos from when I was younger this week. And it just hit me. That I'm never going to see her again. It's all my fault.'

This statement isn't entirely untrue. She bears the responsibility, even if she wasn't driving the car that killed her mother. They were very close, had the sort of mother/daughter relationship that I've always half-coveted, half-feared. The sort of relationship where you tell each other *everything*. Hannah's father was not on the scene, which only drew them further together. Alas, it wasn't a relationship destined to last. Because with that level of closeness there comes a certain degree of expectation. And when – on the morning of the interview for the job Hannah was desperate for – her mother didn't ring to wish her good luck, Hannah threw her toys out the pram.

'I can't stop going over it. If I hadn't called her that day – if I hadn't got so *angry* – she wouldn't have been in the car to come and apologise. If she hadn't been thinking about me, maybe she would have been more focused on the road.'

She gives a loud sniffle, and I reach into my bag for the tissues. I lean over and hand her one.

'You're doing really well, Hannah,' I say, keeping my voice low and earnest. 'When I lost my father, I felt exactly the same. Well, not *exactly* the same, but I know what you're going through.'

These sorts of questions are something we must all grapple with. The dreaded *what ifs*. What if Freddie had simply stayed in the office a bit later the night he died, rather than running out? Could I have saved him, if I'd held him back to ask just one question? Was he still thinking about our argument when the lorry slammed into him? Perhaps. Perhaps not. It doesn't do to dwell on these things.

I rest a sympathetic hand on Hannah's back and rub slow circles. I don't like touching someone I don't know – particularly when I have no idea where she's been – but I grit my teeth and hope my face doesn't betray my discomfort. She's one of the least offensive people here, luckily. If it was Fiona or Matt, it would be a different story.

Fiona is watching my hand with a furrowed brow. Like she can't make sense of it. I ignore her. Hannah gives a delicate little hiccup that I quite like. I log it for later.

I've been logging a lot of things for later, since Catherine replied to my message. It came through in a chaotic flurry two agonising days after I sent it.

You are so sweet to get in touch, darling. What a lovely idea. I'm afraid I'm terrible with my phone. I can't figure out how to send you any photos.

I've never been able to do it. Such a pain!

I can send you some thoughts, if you'd like?

Such a darling girl.

I sat up, heart hammering. I replied, That's OK. Do just send them through if you figure it out. And yes – any thoughts/memories would be much appreciated.

There was a long pause. Then, three dots appeared at the bottom of the screen. I held my breath. After an agonising few minutes, where I pictured her with her glasses perched on the tip of her nose, stabbing at the screen with one finger, it appeared.

Well, I suppose my prevailing memories of Alice are all in the run-up to the wedding. We got to know her so well over that period: as you know, it was at our house in Dorset, and she spent a lot of time with us. Most people would be frantic leading up to the wedding. I know I was for mine. But she just had this manner about her. Like nothing fazed her. As you know, she was the sweetest, kindest girl. She'd have done anything for anyone. She had this quiet way about her. The night before the wedding, I was unbelievably stressed. And she just came up – the night before her wedding! – and asked if she could do anything for me. If there was anything she could help with to take the pressure off. I told her no, of course. But I can't tell you how much I appreciated it. I appreciated so much she did. She really helped Jack to get it together. She was always such a GIVER. She loved to cook. Said it was her love language. I was heartbroken when she died, after the battle with cancer, too. There aren't many truly good people in the world, but she was one of them. Does that help?

Well, as you can imagine, I was not thrilled by that. All this time, I'd been posturing as someone flirtatious. Someone confident, and loud. Someone like Marcie.

But Marcie was nothing like the person Catherine was describing at all.

It gave me something to work with. For that, I was grateful. And work I did. I didn't bother replying to Catherine's message. I'd got what I needed from her, and, unless she deigned to send some photos through – something I could model myself from – she was no longer useful. I closed my laptop and began to plan.

At the café the next day, I watched. I watched people come and go. I watched a woman tenderly stroking her boyfriend's cheek, her expression filled with such love, such warmth, that I filed it away. I watched a mother gently explain to her toddler why he could not go to the park. I liked her soft, low voice. How calming it was. I watched a girl reach into her bag and fish out a tampon to give to her friend. I absorbed all these niceties, these acts of kindness, and I knew what I had to do. I may not have Alice's photograph, but I could channel her personality.

I tried it with Mick first. I took him aside at the end of my shift and apologised profusely for my behaviour the other day. 'It wasn't like me,' I'd said, smiling widely – openly – at him. 'It won't happen again. I appreciate you, Mick, and everything you've done for me.'

His eyes had widened. I watched him soften in real time. It was electric.

'I appreciate *you*, Iris. We all have bad days, don't worry.'

It was tiring. I couldn't keep it up all the time. Not with Mum, who was flittering about the house like some irritating songbird after I broke the news of Dad's impending divorce – but I have honed it over the last week wherever possible. This – the group – was the final test.

I sit up on my chair and remove my hand from Hannah's back.

My next stop is Jack's house.

23

There is no sign of life on my approach. No twitch of the curtain – still drawn firmly across the window. No flicker of movement within. A distant scream of a siren, before it fades. The night is still. Perfect.

I reach for the large brass knocker on the door, and, for a second, I falter. It doesn't happen very often, but I am horribly aware of what rides on this. This is my moment. My make or break. I will have to put on the performance of a lifetime. I check my posture one more time, rounding my shoulders so I look weaker, more innocent, unthreatening.

The knocker booms inside the house. I can hear it echo and, out here, it cuts through the air like a gunshot. Silence. No rustle, no hurried footsteps. I try again, harder this time. If he's there – which I suspect, due to the chink of light I saw through the curtains, he is – I will make him come to the door. I won't wait any longer.

The sound echoes again. Three hard, efficient raps, which don't really fit with this new skin I've slipped on, but desperate times and all that.

This time, I think I hear a noise. A quiet click – a door perhaps. I recheck my posture, pull my brows together in an expression of deepest concern, clasp my hands anxiously in front of me. Footsteps. I'm sure of it. The sound of a chain being pulled back.

And then, there he is. Right in front of me, as though no time has passed at all. Except, it has. And it shows on Jack's face.

If he looked haggard the first time I saw him at the group, it's nothing on this. He looks as though he hasn't slept in a week. There are bulging purple bags under his eyes, deep lines etched across his forehead. For a moment, I forget the act altogether. I simply stare at him, open-mouthed.

A split second where he only blinks, as though he does not – cannot – register that I am here. On his doorstep. And then, we both come back to ourselves, and start to speak at once.

'I've been so worried –'

'Iris? What're you doing here?'

We break off. I allow the silence to stretch. Allow him to register my presence properly. His eyes are glassy. Unfocused. I ignore this. I look up at him through my lashes: not as I used to, which was brazen and unapologetic, but with a pretty innocence that I borrowed from the woman at the café. It worked so well, the way she did it. Her boyfriend's pupils dilated as she looked up at him. He'd pulled her into him, pressed a kiss to her forehead.

It doesn't have the same effect on Jack, who looks at me blankly, like he can't understand what I'm doing here.

'I've been so worried,' I say again, in that breathy, high voice. 'You didn't come to the group tonight. Or last week. And I just – I wanted to apologise in person.'

'How did you get my address?' I foresaw this question. An understandable one, given we never quite got past the dinner date stage.

'Well,' I say slowly, *slightly* apologetically. Sweetly embarrassed. It's a welcome change from Marcie's audaciousness. *This* new personality opens a whole new world of possibility. 'I actually looked in the signing-out book. I just – when you didn't come. People at the group are vulnerable. And I just… worried about you.'

'I'm fine,' he says gruffly. Doesn't question the fact that he didn't put his address in the signing-out book at all, though I doubt he's in a state to question anything at the moment. He smells, strongly, of alcohol, and his lips are stained red with wine. Tonight, that works in my favour.

I sense an opportunity. It was, after all, following a long night of drinking that Freddie kissed me for the first time.

On our second date – the lunch date where the brush of his leg against mine seemed to shatter the awkwardness that had blossomed suddenly between us – we finally moved away from discussing work.

He'd rubbed his hand over the back of his neck. 'There was something I wanted to chat to you about, actually,' he said, lowering his voice as though to take me into his confidence. Goosebumps raced across my skin. 'I've been feeling a bit… off, recently. It always happens around the anniversary of my brother's death. I don't feel like anyone in the office really understands. It was so long ago now, and when I tell them about it I can see them wondering why I'm still bothered all these years later.'

It was a moment of openness that still sends a thrill through me, even now. Because number one on my mental checklist of attraction was vulnerability. *He'll start opening up to you if he sees a future with you. He'll want to go deeper.*

I'd nodded, fighting to keep a straight face when all I wanted to do was grin. 'I understand. I feel it, too, around the anniversary of Marcie's death.' It was true. Every year, like my body was keeping score, I found myself becoming a little off. Sometimes, I'd do something to commemorate it, like apply overexaggerated eyeliner, or try out some of her more outrageous lines in the mirror.

And while that sadness in Freddie's eyes was genuine – I had no doubt about that – I couldn't shake the feeling that he was using this common ground as a way to get closer to me.

He'd smiled in relief. 'I *knew* you would. I can't tell you what a relief it is to have someone who understands what it's like.'

We realised, then, that our lunch hour had come to an end, bringing an abrupt close to the intimacy that had started to creep into the conversation. But Freddie did not let it lie there. That week, he sent several messages, checking in, and then, on Friday, he asked me out for another drink.

Two times in one week. I took it as a very good sign.

I was more than a little frustrated, therefore, to find he'd been in the pub for an hour or two prior to my arrival. *Greg* was sitting with him and both men were clearly well on their way to intoxication.

'Greg,' I said, in as dignified a manner as I could muster. 'I didn't know you'd be here.'

The man clearly had no sense of propriety, because he slapped his hand on the table and told me to grab myself a drink, join them. I did so, unwilling to pass up an opportunity to spend time with Freddie, though irritated that he'd so clearly crashed what could have been a lovely evening.

I sulked as they chatted, and occasionally Freddie would shoot me an apologetic look. They drank three more pints before Greg checked his watch and baulked. 'Fuck. She's going to be furious. I'd better go.'

He left, huffing and puffing about his long-suffering wife, and Freddie and I were alone. The atmosphere shifted instantly, becoming charged with promise. Again, we skirted around it, Freddie – evidently quite drunk now – telling me about his family, a little more about his brother.

'Dating's been hard, you know? I always feel like they recognise some sadness in me and want to try and fix me,' he said ruefully, toying with his glass. I knew he was telling me this for a reason. I liked the fact that he'd singled me out. It made me feel special.

Last orders were called at the bar, and Freddie sighed. He stumbled slightly as he rose to his feet, threw his jacket over his shoulder. 'We'd better get going,' he said.

Outside, he lit a cigarette, swaying on his feet. I stepped closer to him, bolstered by the knowledge that he saw something in me that others didn't. He blinked at me. We were very close now, breath mingling in the cool air. I tilted my head.

And despite the fact that he tasted like beer, it was – to date – the best kiss I have ever had.

'Can I come in?' I say, now, gently to Jack. 'I'd really like to explain what happened the other night at dinner. I've been feeling terrible about it. Eaten up with guilt.' I twist my face into an expression of utter wretchedness, as though the thought of that evening causes my skin to crawl with shame. It's not entirely off base.

He releases a long sigh, then stands back from the door with an air of defeat. Like he can't muster the strength to argue with me.

And so, I find myself entering the house of Jack Reynolds. The house of the man who has taken up more space than is probably healthy in my head.

It is every bit as wonderful as I pictured. Better even. It's huge, for one thing. The exterior doesn't do it justice. An imposing staircase rears upwards, right into the belly of the house. Ornate rugs cover the tile floor. A rich, spicy scent hangs low in the air: tuberose, I think. I catch sight of myself in the gilt, age-spotted mirror to the left. I need to tone down the excitement. It's plastered all over my face, still flushed from the cold.

Jack, stumbling, leads the way through to the room I have seen only from the outside. I'm hit first by the smell. The greasy scent of takeaway food, and a sour stench that I associate with Mum. Stagnant air. An unwashed body. Stale alcohol.

This fact is confirmed by the bottles that litter the coffee table. Beer, wine (expensive, from the looks of those labels), vodka. I wrinkle my nose, but the signs of Jack's relapse cause a frisson of excitement to trickle down my spine.

It seems I came at the perfect moment. It's almost like Alice is smiling down on me from above. She helped Jack out of it before, and I'll do the same now. I can step into her shoes and position myself exactly where I need to.

Jack still hasn't looked at me. He walks to the sofa, slumps into it, stares unseeingly at the television screen. It's playing some brain-rot reality show, but I manage to resist the urge to turn it off and instead take a tentative seat next to Jack. I'd planned on going straight in with the apology: short, to the point. I'd planned to prostrate myself before him, make up something about painful memories of Freddie that caused me to lash out, but having seen this I decide to change tack. I consider reaching for his hand, but – given his reaction to my previous attempt at contact – decide that it would be too much. I always try to learn from my mistakes.

'How are you, Jack?' I'm good at this, I realise. The bedside manner, gentle tone, soft expression. Perhaps I should consider a career in nursing.

Jack grunts in response, eyes glassy.

'I sense you might be struggling a bit.' This is the understatement of the century: it looks like he's had a raucous party for one. Glancing at the wreckage, I see the remnants of white powder, a dusting on the surface of the coffee table. Worse than I thought.

'I am a bit yeah,' he says in a tight voice, staring straight ahead. He reaches forward, tips the rest of a bottle of red wine into a dirty glass and knocks it back with the practised air of the hardened drinker.

'What can I do to help?'

He still won't look at me. I *need* him to look at me. I'm putting on the performance of my life, and he's just staring at that God-awful programme. But then, his lips become very thin, and I wonder – for a horrible moment – if he is about to shout at me. It is so much worse than that, though. Because his chin starts to wobble.

'She's gone.' A sloppy slur.

'Who is?' I ask, though I have a good idea, and I don't particularly like the direction this conversation is headed in.

'Alice. She's gone. She's never coming back.'

'Shh,' I say, and I make to pull him towards me. After a brief moment of resistance, he slackens, presses his head into my chest. I really hope he doesn't get snot on me. This is one of my best jumpers. I croon at him in the way the mother in the café crooned to her child. 'I'm here to help, Jack. It's all going to be alright. I'm here, now.'

I stroke his hair – oily after so long without a shower – and keep up a stream of encouraging words and noises. I'm not maternal by nature, but this comes easily to me. I'd do anything for Jack, if he'd only let me.

'Thank you.' His voice is muffled by my jumper, broken with sobs. 'Thank you, Iris. I'm sorry for being such a dick. I'm sorry for ignoring you. This… it's not often you find someone who shows up for you like this. Alice used to be that person for me. I didn't realise how much I missed it.'

He's still crying, and I rub slow circles on his shoulder, even as the euphoria spikes. I'm doing it right. I took the initiative, deduced what he needed from me, and I got it right. If that's not a sign that what we have is special, I'm not sure what is.

'I've been so confused. I like you, Iris, and that's… hard for me. I thought I'd never find anyone else.'

This is going better than I could possibly have hoped. Sometimes, it's important to change tack. Something Marcie knew all too well. He's falling for me. He thinks I'm special. *Me.*

'We'll find a way to get through this, Jack. Together.'

Although he doesn't speak, I feel him nod against my chest. We stay like that for a while, until the pattern of his breathing changes. He's asleep. How lovely, that he feels comfortable enough to fall asleep with me. It's a singularly vulnerable thing. I loved watching Freddie sleep, sharing the night with him. I inch out from under him, then shake him gently.

'Jack,' I say softly. 'Come on. I'll take you to bed.'

It takes some persuasion, but eventually he rises, and I steer him up the stairs. He grunts periodically to direct me through the house, and finally – and not without significant effort on my part – we arrive in the most beautiful bedroom I have ever seen. It's hard not to compare it with Freddie's grimy room. The stains on Freddie's carpet, compared with the plush spotlessness of this. The Ikea bed, compared with this huge antique four-poster. The gaming chair juxtaposed with this ornate dressing table, which feels like a distinctly feminine piece of furniture. My heart rate picks up as I see it. What secrets does it hold?

I lead Jack towards the bed. He's still stumbling, but he allows me to undress him. It is electrifying, being this close to him. Feeling his breath on my face. I resist the urge to run my hand across his chest. *Baby steps.* When he is down to his boxers, I pull back the covers and he slips in. He passes out instantly, and I stand and watch him for a while, before leaning down and kissing him tenderly on the forehead. I smooth his hair as a mother would a sick child, then turn to fold his clothes, which I then leave neatly on the chair in the corner. And though he's fast asleep, I find I don't feel quite so alone any more.

I don't want to risk rummaging through that dressing table while he's in the room, so I take one last look at him

– sleeping peacefully – switch out the lights, then make my way back downstairs.

I couldn't have planned this better if I tried. His current state means I have total, unfettered access to his house. A chance to find a picture of Alice at last, since his mother was so unhelpful.

But Alice is remarkably absent from the frames downstairs. I noticed it as soon as I walked into the living room; no sign of her at all. There *must* be one. A wedding photo at least. But I scour the living room from top to bottom – opening cupboards, eyes resting on an old, antique-looking chest – and find nothing.

I slip through the rest of the house like a shadow. The kitchen, the utility room, the dining room. Nothing. No sign of her at all. Which feels… odd. Particularly since Jack is still so caught up by her memory. I even slip back upstairs, open the guest rooms and poke my head in, but she's not there. She might as well not have existed at all.

24

The café is unusually busy when Jack turns up. I am serving one of our regulars – a brittle, demanding woman with an impressive aptitude for finding fault with everything – when he walks through the door, head bowed, cloaked in shame. The woman seems to sense the instant shift in my priorities: from delivering the limp, greasy bacon sandwich in my hand, to the handsome stranger who has just walked through the door.

'I might not be as attractive as him, love, but there's no need to make me starve for it.'

Usually, this sort of snippy comment would wrench more of a reaction from me. An accidental spillage as I passed her table, perhaps, or a marginal overcharge that I'd blame on our ancient tills if confronted.

Today, I allow it to wash over me. I've soaked up any negative energy this morning with the memory of last night's success. The intimacy of my encounter with Jack. His intoxicating gratitude. The sense that, finally, we are back on an even footing. That he still thinks – no, wholeheartedly believes – that I'm special.

Mick has noticed my sunnier disposition, too. I beamed at him as I donned my apron this morning, and he'd nodded his appreciation.

'That's the sort of attitude we're looking for, Iris,' he'd said.

Now, I'm frozen as Jack's eyes skim the busy tables before landing – finally – on me, plate still clutched in my suddenly sweaty palms.

'Iris,' he croaks. 'Can I speak to you?'

He looks terrible: in the place of yesterday's alcohol flush a nasty, green-tinged pallor, face puffy with over-indulgence. Yet, somehow, he's still the best-looking man I've ever laid eyes on, and I feel my own face flush with the memory of how close we were last night. So close our breath mingled as I unbuttoned his shirt. A seminal moment of intimacy that I have returned to again and again in painstaking detail, recalling how his hand landed on my shoulder as I helped him out of his trousers, the warmth and pressure as he squeezed his thanks.

'If it's cold when it gets to me, I'll need another one.' The woman breaks through the wall of memory, but I don't react. Only huff my apologies and place the plate carefully before her, ensuring Jack clocks my attentive-ness: the slight tilt to my head as I ask her if I can bring her any sauces, the docile, bovine smile as she demands mayonnaise without a word of thanks.

I'm grateful for the chance to collect myself. I nod to Jack that I'll be there in a second, and turn away towards the counter.

His appearance here is unexpected. I'd been sure he would message. I left a carefully penned note on the ottoman in the sitting room, imploring him to reach out should he need me. I hadn't expected it to be so soon, though. In person no less. I don't even need to mentally trawl the 'How To Tell If He's Into You' article. This speaks for itself.

Last night was exhausting, but worth it. I spent far too long at Jack's – first looking unsuccessfully for any crumbs of Alice and then cleaning up his mess from the last two weeks. It was worse than it had seemed. Broken bottles, wine on the carpet. Something that looked suspiciously like a little patch of vomit on the sofa. I scrubbed, and wiped, and disposed of it all and relished every second. Relished the thought of Jack coming down the next morning and seeing evidence of my presence. His guardian angel, come to pull him from the depths of the hell he'd found himself in.

I pressed hard on our similarities in the note:

Morning, hope you're not feeling too awful.
I hope you don't mind – I had a bit of a
clear-up. Here any time you need to talk.
Remember, I know what you're going through.
Perhaps better than most. X

I hoped it would remind him that we are in the same camp. Remind him what drew us together. The simple fact is this: we *are* the same. We have both lost someone very dear to us, and yet we found each other – a small chink of light in the darkness. That sort of connection is not to be sniffed at. It was just the same with Freddie. It's going to take more than a misunderstanding at a restaurant to drive us apart.

I return to the woman with the mayonnaise. She's wearing an oversized cardigan that I quite like the look of. I might get a cardigan. It feels like the sort of thing Alice would have worn. Every maternal figure in my life, barring my actual mother – the school nurses, even Fiona – have worn cardigans. Maybe I'll go and have a look for one this afternoon. It fits nicely with the aesthetic that I'm building in my head: a woman who is endearingly uncool, swathed in bangles, and oversized cardigans and possibly glasses. A woman I will have to become.

Finally, I turn towards Jack. We're too busy, really, for me to take a break, but Mick will understand that I am in pursuit of love, and nothing is so important as that. And if he doesn't, I'll turn on the waterworks.

Jack starts apologising as soon as I reach him, but I shush him and steer him towards one of the last empty tables, delighting in the easy contact with his arm. He sits heavily, head drifting into his hands.

'Iris, I'm so sorry that you saw me like that last night. I know it's a problem, and I've got to get a handle on it.

I'm so grateful you came over. It was the wake-up call I needed.'

He lifts his head like he's trying to gauge how the apology has landed. I consider, for one wild moment, utilising the power in this tiny move. Making him beg for my forgiveness, as I was tempted to do in the wake of that disastrous dinner. But I am bigger than that: I relax my face into a smile, brows pulled together in sympathy.

'Don't mention it. Honestly. I'm just pleased I could help.' Cool and calm, yet genuinely invested in his recovery.

'I'm going to start going to meetings again. I slipped up, but I need to take better care of myself. So that I can be better. For you,' he adds softly, and my stomach gives a delightful little swoop. 'Can we start over? Pretend last night – and the dinner – never happened?'

'Of course. Don't even mention it.'

'I don't know what I'd do without you, Iris.'

I don't either, but false displays of modesty are always a good idea when paid a compliment, so I adopt one of Marcie's later expressions: eyes lowered, bashful.

When I raise them again, I catch Mick flashing me an irritated look across the café. I don't want to risk his ire when we have so recently reached an armistice, so I press my hand on top of Jack's.

'We're really busy, so I should get back to work.' *Leave them wanting more.*

'Of course. I'm sorry I interrupted. I'll message you?'

He frames it as a question. I give him a genuine smile. 'I'd like that.'

He stands. 'I'm going to have a nap, then go to a meeting. Had to take a sick day today. This can't happen again. I *will* get it under control.'

'I know you will,' I say, ever supportive, and he presses a hand to my shoulder, just like last night.

'See you soon, Iris.'

For the rest of the day, I approach my job with such enthusiasm that Mick holds me back at the end of my shift.

'I don't know what's happened, but that's the fire I want to see every day, Iris. Well done.'

With his praise still ringing in my ears, I skip out. I buy myself a cardigan from TK Maxx, and slip it on to walk home in. It suits this new version of me well. My roots are growing out, too, and I'm considering changing to something different. Something that better represents who I am now. Mousy, perhaps. Or ashy. Unobtrusively sweet, just as I intend to be.

Mum eyes me suspiciously when I enter the house. It's alarming how much better she looks. Clear-eyed where Jack was misted. Her skin looks brighter too. No longer sallow and waxy. She's got some colour. Must be the new man. Or the news of Dad's divorce.

'What's got you in such a good mood?' she asks from the doorway of the sitting room.

'I'm just pleased to be here. Don't need a reason, do I?' I say, and, for her benefit, I give her one of my new, special smiles. She takes a small step backwards and her hand closes into a tight fist.

'Where have you been all these evenings, Iris?' There's a new intensity to her voice that I do not quite trust.

'Out. I told you.'

'Out where?'

'Do I have to run it past you every time I go out?'

'No, it's just –' She breaks off. I wonder if she was going to say she worries about me. First time for every-thing. 'Are you seeing someone? I thought I saw a man hovering around outside the house the other night. I wondered if he had anything to do with you.'

I stare at her, wondering if she has gone mad. Not impossible. It's not healthy, all that curtain-twitching. 'What are you talking about? What man?'

'I don't know. He was… hovering. He seemed suspicious.'

She needs to get out more. Everyone seems suspicious to someone whose only interaction with the outside world is a trip to the local Tesco.

'I'm sure everything's fine, Mum.'

Her voice hardens. 'So, are you seeing someone or not?'

I weigh my options. On one hand, I don't want Mum snooping in my affairs. That never ends well for anyone. But it would be nice to show off my new relationship, now things have taken such a significant upswing. Introduce the idea of him slowly, allow her to get used to it. I picture them meeting: Mum couldn't claim I was *odd* if she took in his charm, his class, his obvious adoration of me.

'I am,' I say finally.

'Where did you meet him?' Her voice is tight with some emotion I can't quite decipher. I don't like the way she's looking at me. Like she can see right through me. Right to my core.

'At the group I attend. The bereavement group.'

The other fist clenches now. 'That's tenacious, even for you. Who did he lose?'

I narrow my eyes, smile vanishing. 'His wife.'

She huffs a laugh that drips with derision. 'That's going to end well.'

'What do you mean?'

'Don't tell me you haven't thought about this. Men will do anything to avoid dealing with their emotions in a healthy way. Just look at your father – ran away, met someone new like Marcie didn't happen. He couldn't cope. Couldn't cope with any of it. He forgot what he had at home because that's where all the issues came from. You're nothing but a distraction for him, Iris. Regardless of whatever act you're putting on. If he's going to a grief group, it's because he's still pining for his wife.'

I only realise that I am clenching my fist when my nail slices into my palm. The words niggle like tiny parasites that burrow under my skin. I try to tell myself she's wrong. That she knows nothing about my relationship with Jack. But I think of the way his voice dipped reverentially when he talked about Alice, his reaction to my comment at the restaurant, and a thread of doubt plaits itself through my euphoria.

Mum must catch my expression, because she gives a nasty laugh. 'See? You know it, too. Trust me, Iris. You don't want to go there. You'll constantly be trying to live up to the memory of someone who you can't compete with.' She's quiet, contemplative. Then, she fixes me with a beady eye. 'This is classic you, you know? Always flaunting it for the boys. Obsessed with attention. It was just the same in Cornwall.'

25

We left for Cornwall in the first week of the summer holidays. Marcie and I packed in silence, fuelled by loathing. She kept up the pretence in front of our parents. I did not. Something inside me was broken beyond repair.

Mum and Dad tried to draw us into conversation on the way down. I stared pointedly out of the window as Marcie chattered away. I tried to tune her out, particularly when she spoke about Billy.

My parents liked him. She'd invited him over for dinner a couple of weeks before, and I'd absented myself from the table. I had to put up with them groping each other in the school hallways. I shouldn't have to endure it in my own home as well.

'It's a shame Iris didn't join us,' I heard Dad say when I slipped down the stairs for a glass of water after Billy had left.

There was a long pause. 'She's probably jealous,' Mum replied eventually. 'She's always struggled to make friends, let alone get a boyfriend.'

Dad gave a noncommittal grunt. 'Must be hard for her,' he said. 'To see Marcie so happy.'

'Well, she's not exactly hiding her mood, is she?'

Mum was right. I couldn't hide it. The darkness that enveloped me as I watched Marcie hand over my drawing had prevailed. I was no longer amenable. I found issue with everything.

The drive was long. Soon, concrete turned to hedges, then hedges to drystone walls. The sea appeared on the horizon. I remember feeling very small.

The hotel was run-down but nice enough. Naturally, Marcie and I were sharing a room. Always forced to share, even when there wasn't ever enough for two. I set my suitcase down on the purple-patterned carpet and began to unpack. Neatly, as I had all those years ago in our grandparents' attic. Marcie sat on the bed, texting. She hadn't silenced her phone. The incessant tapping noise set my teeth on edge.

We had lunch at the hotel. I picked at a soggy fish and chips and left most of it.

'I just don't know how I'm going to do a *week* away from him,' Marcie said to Mum.

'Do you want to come with me and see what's in the rockpools?' Dad turned to me, lowering his voice like we were co-conspirators. We were not co-conspirators. I no longer trusted him. Not after he betrayed me.

'No thanks.'

I was forced to accompany them down to the beach anyway. Marcie linked her arm through Mum's as we navigated the craggy coastal path. To our right, the cliff fell away into a steep drop. The sea stretched into the horizon. I could see the tiny white sail of a boat.

The beach was not as picturesque as Mum had made it sound. Seaweed tangled with blue plastic netting had washed onto the shingle. Mum spread four towels out. I sat on one and wished I'd brought a book, or something to signal that I wasn't keen to be drawn into conversation.

Dad went to look in the rockpools anyway. Mum and Marcie chatted about Billy. Each time they spoke his name, a small electric jolt travelled through me. Even after everything that had happened.

The boys arrived in the late afternoon. There were three of them. Tall, muscular, tanned, they carried that air of people who had never wanted for anything. They clocked Marcie instantly and flexed their sinewy muscles.

Marcie had seen them, too. I could tell from the way she adjusted herself. The way she subtly moved away from Mum so that she could no longer run her hand through her hair. She leaned back so that her stomach was flat and taut. Periodically, her eyes flicked towards the newcomers, who were playing with a frisbee not far from us.

As the sun bled orange, Mum got up to find Dad. The boys approached instantly. Marcie smiled with her tongue pressed to the roof of her mouth. Her jawline had never looked better.

Two of the three clamoured to take the towels next to her. The other – amazingly – did not seem drawn to her in quite the same way. He pointed to the space on the towel next to me. 'Can I sit there?'

I shrugged but moved aside for him anyway.

'Have you been here for long?' he asked.

I threw a rock towards the sea. 'We arrived this morning.'

'I love it down here. We come every summer.' He smiled contentedly, and I noticed he had a nice face. Kind eyes. A lovely smile. The thick black cloud that had been roiling inside me dissipated somewhat. I found myself smiling back.

Marcie glanced in our direction. A tiny line appeared between her brows. Her bottom lip jutted. I ignored her.

'What's your name?'

'Josh.'

'I'm Iris.' I held out my hand and he took it. It was large and warm. My stomach somersaulted.

It was easy to talk to Josh. He liked surfing and spoke at length about wave height. I found it didn't matter that I didn't understand what he was talking about. I liked listening to him. He went to a private school just outside of London. He made me feel normal.

When it was time to leave, he touched me again. Just lightly, on the arm. 'Can I get your number? Maybe we'll see you around later? I think we're having a bonfire down here.'

It was the first time a boy had ever asked for my number. Out of the corner of my eye, I saw Marcie's lower lip jut again. I straightened my back and smiled at him with my tongue pressed to the roof of my mouth. 'Of course,' I said, and I typed it into his phone.

I couldn't read Marcie's expression on the walk back up the hill, and I didn't bother asking. It was the first time someone had shown interest in me, and right in front of her, and it felt glorious.

She was not herself at dinner either. She was quiet. Sullen. I found myself taking up the mantle, talking for the first time in weeks.

Mum threw anxious glances across the table at her. 'It's OK,' she said. 'Maybe Billy can come with us on the next holiday? Would you like that?' Marcie shrugged.

I was tired by the time we retreated upstairs. Josh texted as we arrived back to our room. **Hey, it's Josh. We're going down to the beach now if you want to come?**

I started to reply, but Marcie caught me looking at my phone. 'Did he text?' she asked bluntly. I nodded. 'You're not thinking of *going,* are you? God, that's a bit desperate. You shouldn't make yourself seem too available.' And she turned her back on me. I did want to go. Badly. But her words had sown a seed of doubt.

I backspaced on my acceptance and typed **I can't tonight. But maybe see you tomorrow?**

He didn't reply.

I slept well for the first time in weeks, but, when I woke, Marcie was not in the twin bed across from me. I checked the loo. She wasn't there either. For some reason, the sight of those rumpled sheets sent a cold slug of dread through me. I felt them. They were cool to the touch.

She came into the room as I was stepping out of the shower. Her cheeks were pink, her hair mussed. She was dressed already.

'Where've you been?' I said, and it was the most direct question I'd aimed at her for a long time.

'Out. I went for a walk.'

'At seven in the morning?'

She shrugged. 'Couldn't sleep. What's it to you, anyway?'

I didn't reply. I dressed in silence, and we went down to breakfast as a pair, as though there wasn't a simmering chasm of mistrust and dislike between us.

I texted Josh after breakfast. He still hadn't replied to my message yesterday, and I felt yet another pang of unease that I couldn't identify. He didn't reply to this one, either.

I followed Marcie down to the beach again and we settled ourselves on towels. I'd brought my book this time, but I couldn't concentrate on the words. I kept an eye on the cliff path, hoping to see Josh picking his way down. Just after midday, he and his friends appeared, yawning. They jostled each other when they saw us, and came straight over. A hard knot of nerves formed in my stomach.

'Big night,' the tallest one said, elbowing Josh. 'How're you feeling this morning, Marcie?' He winked at her.

I sat up and looked between them. My stomach was tight.

'Pretty hungover,' Marcie replied.

'What?' My voice didn't sound like my own.

Marcie drew a line in the sand with her finger. 'I came down for the bonfire last night. You were asleep.'

'Did something happen?'

'Ask Josh.' The tall one winked again.

'What about Billy?' I said.

'Who's Billy?' Josh frowned.

'No one,' Marcie said.

'Marcie's boyfriend.' I stared at her. This was a new low, even for her. Fresh loathing boiled.

Marcie went red. 'It's not that serious.'

Before I knew what was happening, I was on my feet, strangled words whipping in the wind. 'Not serious? Are you joking? You've been all over each other for months.'

I couldn't stand to be in her presence for a second longer. I felt myself cracking. The darkness that had dissipated yesterday was creeping back in. I wanted to hurt her. I wanted to scratch at her eyes. I couldn't breathe. I gathered my towel, walked away, back towards the path.

'Don't worry,' I heard Marcie's soothing tone. 'She's always been jealous of me.'

The injustice choked me.

I couldn't settle. I paced our bedroom. I would ruin her, just as she had ruined me.

She appeared fifteen minutes later with fury flashing in her eyes. 'What the fuck did you do that for?'

I laughed in her face. She couldn't touch me now. 'Do what? Tell the truth? It's about time someone did, don't you think?'

'God you're predictable. You can't stand it, can you? You can't stand that I'm prettier than you, smarter than you, more popular than you. You can't stand that Mum and Dad like me more. Always so jealous, Iris. Always so predictable.'

'I'm not listening to this.' I gathered my things. I was shaking.

'That's right. Run away. Skulk in your little corner.'

'I'm not running away. I'm going to tell those boys the truth. About who you really are, underneath it all.'

She didn't have a chance to stop me before I slammed out of the room.

She caught up with me just as I reached the cliff path. I swung round. 'Just leave me the fuck alone!' I screamed, but my words were ripped away from me by the wind. Clouds were rolling in, thick and black. I felt a raindrop. 'Why can't you just let me have something for myself?'

I was at the path now. It carved a crevice in the rock to my left. The cliff face yawned to my right. Marcie took a step towards me. She was so close to the edge she disturbed a rock, which bounced all the way down. I thought about warning her, but the words wouldn't come.

'Because it's just so easy. You make it so easy to hate you. I know you still like Billy, even after all this time. But do you know what he told me the other day? He said he felt sorry for you. Even though he thinks you're weird. Even though you're too intense. He said he could sense your *tortured soul*. I told him he was giving you too much credit.'

It happened in the blink of an eye. I didn't think as
I took a step towards her, fury coursing through me.
As Marcie took a step back, wanting to put distance
between us.

She didn't have time to cry out.

In a scatter of loose shingle, Marcie was gone.

26

Jack's first message comes at the perfect time. How was the rest of your shift? Just went to my first meeting. Feeling better. Thanks again, Iris. Xx

I've worked myself into a bit of a state by the point it arrives, Mum's words reverberating around my brain like a noxious echo, so the message calms me. It proves she was wrong. I want to shove the phone in her face and show her those two kisses. I'd do just that if she was here, but she left the house an hour ago, slamming the door behind her. She doesn't understand the intricacies of my relationship with Jack. What she sees as a drawback – the dead wife, the lingering sentiment – *I* view as an opportunity.

I reread the message. Thanks again, Iris. I love gratitude. That indefinable contract that places him firmly in my debt. It calms me enough to focus on the matter at hand.

I sit in front of the mirror at our small desk and pull out my phone. I've saved a few looks that I want to try out with my hair. I googled 'librarian', because that's

200

what springs to mind whenever I think of Alice. It fits with the cardigan vibe, that slightly sanctimonious air that I associate with primary school teachers and other people who might be called 'do-gooders'. Unfortunately, it turns out that the prevailing hairstyle for librarians is a bob, and I'm just not willing to stoop to that level yet. So I saved some images of librarians with long hair, and now I try a French plait, which only highlights my too-large forehead, a low ponytail that doesn't look quite as sleek on me as it does on the woman in the photo, and keeping it loose, one side pulled slightly over my face. That one, I can just about cope with, but it doesn't give off the desired levels of attractiveness. Perhaps I'm barking up the wrong tree with hairstyles.

My phone buzzes with a message. It's Tilly, Sally's closest friend – strictly online, of course. Likely whining to Sally about some domestic issue or other, but I'm at a bit of a loose end, so I pick it up anyway. Occasionally – when I'm in a bad mood – I like to fuel discord in her relationship with her husband, just because I can.

Are you there?

Short. To the point. Very unlike her usual rambling messages. I frown and type back Yes.

Something awful has happened.

I wait, but there's no follow-up message. If she's attempting to build suspense, she's succeeding at nothing but making me irritated. After five minutes or so, I turn back to the mirror. My smile needs a bit of tweaking: it's too wide, which adds an unfortunate hint of madness to the whole look. I tone it down, then check my phone again. Nothing.

Downstairs, the door slams. Mum's home. She must still be in a mood; the house shakes with the impact. She should really learn to get her emotions under control. It's not an attractive look. Still, I'm keen to prove that her words earlier didn't affect me, so I skip down the stairs and find her at the kitchen table, cigarette clasped between her fingers.

'Tea? Something stronger?'

She doesn't reply, but I put the kettle on anyway. I bustle around and make an excellent show of just how fine I am. I take two mugs from the cupboard, sniff the milk. She doesn't speak, which is not altogether unusual, but there is something about her silence that feels off. Something about the rigidity of her spine, the way the cigarette burns and burns and burns and she doesn't lift it to her lips.

I strain the teabags and chuck them in the compost bin. Never let it be said that I don't care for the environment. It's only when I turn to face her, mugs in hand, that I realise something is seriously wrong. I barely looked at her earlier – better to avoid eye contact if you can help it – but I see now that she's sodden. It must be raining outside. Her hair hangs in limp strands, dripping onto the linoleum. Mascara bleeds down her face.

'What's happened?' I ask.

She's shaking, and at first I think it's with cold, but then I see her eyes. They stop me in my tracks. Black with fury. Sinister, deranged.

Maybe her new man called things off. History would suggest she doesn't take well to rejection. Like mother, like daughter. I start towards her, intending to rub the sympathetic circles on her back that worked so well with Hannah, but she rears away from me.

'Don't you dare touch me,' she says, and it occurs to me that perhaps her anger is not directed at a man at all, but at me. Her face certainly suggests that's the case. 'Were you ever going to tell me?'

'Tell you what?' I'm on the back foot here and I don't like it.

'Do you know where I've been, Iris?'

'No?'

'I went to visit your father.'

Up until this point, I'd been sure that – whatever transgression I had inadvertently committed – I would be able to talk my way out of it. Soothe her with news of Dad, and his wife's delinquency, tales of their horrible daughters. That's not an option now. There is no talking my way out of this one.

She plunges on, voice vibrating with fury. 'I thought it might have changed. You and your *scheming*. Do you know, I have absolutely no idea who you are? I'm your mother. I'm supposed to know *something* about the person I birthed, but you – it's like this blank space.'

Bit unfair. At least I've got a good sense of humour. I hold my hands out towards her and arrange my face so I look like I might be about to cry. 'Please calm down, Mum. It's not that big a deal.'

It's critical to defuse this situation as quickly as possible, make it out to be less serious than it is, and I go towards her again, but she raises her hand as though she is going to hit me.

'I know everything, Iris. I know you haven't spoken to him.'

'Who?' A last-ditch attempt at ignorance. But my acts have never worked with her.

'Don't play the innocent. You know I'm talking about your father. You've been lying to me for *years*. He told me he hasn't heard from you since he moved out. Yet you seem to know an awful lot about his life.'

She's got me there. She's right: I *haven't* spoken to him in years. Why would I? What use is he to me when he betrayed me to Marcie all those years ago, and again when he left me here with a woman who could barely hide her contempt for me? That's not to say I don't keep up with his news, though. I like to base my lies in truth, after all. It's how Sally was born.

Five years ago, a woman called Sally, using her newly established Facebook account, sent a friend request accompanied by a message. Hey Tilly, I hope you're well. I see you're also on my local Stitch and Bitch group! I've just moved to the area, and I'm looking to make new friends. Don't suppose you fancy meeting up at some point?

And for some reason — perhaps loneliness driven by the significant age gap between her and her husband — Tilly responded. What followed was a gradual getting to know each other, a thoughtful message exchange that revealed little bits of personal information until the pair progressed from strangers to firm friends.

They've become very close, though whenever Tilly suggests a meet-up Sally is sadly either visiting her ailing mother in Scotland or whisking herself away for a spa weekend in Europe. Which is probably for the best, because Tilly has her own busy life to contend with. She has two daughters, an ugly house in suburbia, and an old, incontinent dog called Florence. In a moment of wine-fuelled candour, Tilly opened up to Sally about her husband. The utter tragedy of his life. How he had twin girls, but one – the favourite – had a tragic accident. The remaining daughter still exists somewhere, though Tilly's never met her.

She'd once said, Does it make me a bad person to say I'm quite glad she's not in my life? It's hard enough raising my own girls. I don't want to take on someone else's. She has her mum, though that's not saying much. Total nutcase.

Fury rising, I'd replied, Not at all. Understandable.

Later that night, I'd scheduled my next coffee with Mum. We met the week after. 'She's got haemorrhoids,' I told her. 'Really bad ones. Dad told me normal treatment isn't working. She's about to have them ligated. You know, where they tie a rubber band around the lumps, and they drop off. Like a lamb's tail.'

Mum's eyes had gleamed.

Tilly had messaged soon after that, It's really weird. We got a package the other day that contained adult nappies and loads of toilet paper. There was no note!!! :S

Over the years, Tilly has proved to be a well of information. It's not, obviously, enjoyable for me to hear about my father's disgusting habits in the bedroom, but I accept the chaff in exchange for the wheat of the other insights she provides. The arrangement suits me well. It provides me with currency to use with Mum. She wouldn't have allowed me back into the house without it.

Now, Mum looks unhinged. Crazed with confusion, with anger.

It's all falling into place: the make-up, the sudden interest in personal hygiene, the hair. She wasn't seeing someone else at all, but still kindling a flame for my father. And when I mentioned the divorce... She's not so unlike me after all. She saw her opportunity and she took it.

'Do you know what a fool you've made of me? When I turned up at the door, believing they were separating? I've been watching the house, trying to find the right time to talk to him. I thought I could offer some support, and tonight I finally plucked up the courage. God, when he answered... I couldn't breathe, Iris. And then *she* appeared behind him.'

She: Tilly. Hard for Mum to experience that, I'm sure. *I* could barely stomach it, when I first saw Tilly in person, peeking through the window of their ugly house. She looked so *young*, so fresh-faced, juxtaposed with Mum's grief-lined features.

'That bitch had the audacity to look scared. Can you believe it? Threatened to call the police on the spot,' she continues. 'And he just stared at me, shaking his head.

I've never been more embarrassed in my life. And when I asked him about the divorce; when I told him it was what you'd told me, he said that you hadn't spoken in years. He feels bad about it – of course he does, he's a good man. But you were always so odd. So strange, and jealous, and *angry.*'

She closes her eyes, takes a breath as though preparing herself for something. 'You're the reason he left, you know?' she says, and the words find their mark. They hit me right in the chest.

'Is that what you've been telling yourself?' I spit. There's no pretence now. The words are hot, spewed with fury.

'I don't need to tell myself anything. It's the truth.' Her eyes flash. 'Do you think we don't know? Do you think it hasn't played on our minds from the moment it happened? She's dead because of *you.* If she wasn't so upset… if *you* hadn't upset her so much, arguing over nothing, she might still be here. She was *everything* to me, and you took that away from me.' Her lip curls now, and I see – for the first time – the depth of her disgust for me. 'Always so self-pitying and strange,' she sneers. 'And we just had to bring you home with us. We had to pretend to be this *normal* family when *you're* the reason she's gone, Iris. Your father knew it too. Hardly surprising he bolted at the first possible opportunity.'

I feel myself take a step away from her, as though my body is trying to put distance between me and her hateful words, even as they lodge themselves firmly at my core.

All this time... I'd known she thought me strange and rigid and impenetrable. I had not guessed at just how deep her fury – her disgust – for me ran.

But she isn't finished. She lifts her eyes to mine, and there is something black there – something that sends a shiver scuttling up my spine.

'Sometimes, I even wonder...'

She tails off, as though she cannot bring herself to speak the words into existence. But I think I know what she was going to say.

27

As quickly as it came on, all the fury seems to leave her. She slumps down against the wall, like her final sources of energy have been expended on this single interaction.

I can only stand there, staring at her, wondering how long she's kept this hatred bottled up inside. Wondering how I thought this relationship was ever salvageable.

And all at once, like all the anger she expelled had to find a new host to feed from, I feel it seep into me, filling me right to my brim until I am shaking with it. Marcie. It's always about her. The years of abuse, the years of feeling inadequate, the years of yearning for that special type of love that only ever seemed to be offered to Marcie, and she is *still*, somehow, the victim. For Mum, I will never be enough. I see that now.

I curl my lip as I watch her on the floor, her chest still heaving.

She's in trouble now, and she knows it. She is aware of the consequences for this afternoon's little accident. And

I can't even bring myself to feel bad about it. Not right now. Not after all she said.

Because there is a reason that Mum has relied so heavily on me for information all these years. A reason she has withdrawn from the world, refusing to see anyone beyond me and those cashiers at the supermarket.

Mum is more like me than she would care to admit. She, too, struggles to let things go. Something inside her broke on the day Dad left. Mired in grief for her daughter and her husband, she could not – she *would* not – accept that he had gone. And so, she began a campaign of harassment.

She started small, texting and calling at all hours of the day until he blocked her, unable to cope with her grief when his own was still so acute. So, she found his new address and turned up in person. When he refused to open the door for her, she screamed on the street outside. She called him a coward. She begged for him back. She said he was the last thing connecting her with her sanity. She was right. It wasn't long after that when she discovered he'd moved on. And you know what they say: hell hath no fury, and all that.

Things escalated quickly when she found Tilly's address. She posted threatening notes through the letter box. She howled on the street outside. The final straw was when she began slipping small, unsavoury 'gifts' through the door. The police were called. Eventually, a restraining order was put in place. My relationship with Dad up until that point had been minimal. After that, it was non-existent.

At that point, I was still optimistic enough to think that Mum and I could get by together. Join forces. I still held a small candle of hope that she might truly see me for the person I was, and not just an extension of the daughter she'd lost. And so, I began to lie. I pretended that Dad and I had a relationship. Small things, at first. Just what I judged he would be doing, in this shiny new life of his. And then, I got cleverer. Sally's friendship with Tilly added veracity, authenticity to my claims. I never went so far as to trigger Mum to go and see for herself, just made their relationship sound fractious enough to keep her happy. And then I mentioned the possible divorce. An overstep. That's on me.

She's rocking back and forth now, head in her hands. She looks so pathetic and small I almost find myself feeling sorry for her. Almost.

Then, she speaks. 'I want you gone. Tonight. I never want to see you again.'

It was the only possible outcome. Sooner than I expected, but an inevitable conclusion to this broken attempt at a relationship. I'm not sad to be leaving, but I wish I'd foreseen how quickly it would come about. Had a chance to get a contingency plan in place.

There is nothing more to be said, so I leave Mum in the hallway, and, as soon as I am back in my bedroom, my thoughts turn to Jack. The debt he owes me. It's time to call it in. Time for him to put his money where his mouth is.

My fingers are still shaking as I tap out a message.

Hi Jack, are you free for a call? I could use a friend. xx

Better to do it this way, so he can hear the rawness in my voice.

It takes him twenty minutes to respond. I use the time to pack, hoping he hasn't yet gone to bed, listening for the dull buzz of my phone against the sheets. Finally – finally – it comes.

Hi Iris, of course. I'm free now.

I snatch up the phone and call him immediately.

'Is everything OK?'

He sounds so concerned, I can't believe I ever doubted him. My voice wobbles as I begin to speak – no need for an act now. 'It's my mum. She's gone mad. She's blind drunk, says she wants me out of the house. I can't stay.' Then, to really hammer my point home. 'I'm worried that she might hurt me.'

'Fuck.' He's quiet for a moment. 'I'm so sorry, Iris. You poor thing. Is there anything I can do?'

'I'm sorry if this is a massive imposition, but I just wanted to ask if you might have somewhere for me to stay?'

There is a long pause. So long, I wonder if the line has gone dead. And then, 'Absolutely. Of course you can come. Shall I pick you up?'

'Yes please. If you're not busy. I can't tell you how much I appreciate it, Jack.' A small thrill plaits itself through my anger. It's as easy as that. Inadvertently, Mum has handed me everything I wanted. Finally, I am going to leave this house, and all its memories, behind, to live with a man who understands me, and everything I have been through. Who does not see me as *self-pitying* or *strange*. Who is so sure of our connection that he will allow me to move in even though we have only known each other a matter of weeks. That *means* something. A testament to the strength of our bond.

I finish packing with a renewed sense of purpose, throwing clothes haphazardly into my bag in a manner that is so far from my usual meticulous attention to detail that I wonder if I am getting ill.

At one point, Mum creeps past my door, moving softly across the floorboards. I freeze until I hear her door click shut. I won't say goodbye.

Jack arrives a little later than I expect, forty-five minutes after our call. I meet him at the door in case Mum should choose this moment to re-emerge. Who knows what further aspersions she would attempt to stain my character with.

When he sees me, he pulls me into a long hug, and, though I'm dry-eyed, I give a few convincing sobs into his chest and allow a small dribble of saliva to wet his shirt. Just to make it convincing.

When we pull apart, he smiles at me with such concern, my heart contracts with love. He insists on helping me with my bags and boxes, so I trail behind him to the car, rounding my shoulders as though I carry the weight of the world upon them. I take one final look at the house as he loads the car. Mum's curtain twitches. Apparently, old habits die hard. I resist aiming a sarcastic wave at the window, but only because Jack is here.

'I'm sorry I'm a bit late,' he says, as I climb into the leather seat beside him. 'I stopped on the way to get you these.' He reaches into the back and produces a bunch of daffodils. 'Thought they might cheer you up.'

It's not often that I'm rendered speechless but, as I open my mouth to thank him, the words don't come. I've never received flowers before. For all his many qualities, Freddie was not big into gifts. I'm mortified to find that real tears have sprung to my eyes.

'They're lovely. Thank you.' I mean every word.

'Do you want to talk about it?' he says gently, as he navigates the traffic.

I'd rather not ruin this moment with lies – and I *would* have to lie to him, reveal my relationship with Mum has never been as rosy as I'd made it out to be – so I shake my head.

He nods and is quiet. I can't take my eyes off the daffodils. They're wrapped in plastic, cheap probably, but they are the most beautiful things I've ever seen.

'Did something trigger it?'

My hand tightens on the cellophane. He is – it seems – going to insist on going there anyway. I think of the burning fury in her eyes as she told me about Dad, the wildness to her expression as she spoke of Marcie, and there's no doubt in my mind that she came as close to violence tonight as she ever has.

'Not really. She'd just drunk too much.'

'Do you think there's a chance of reconciliation between you?'

I consider how he might react if I answered in the negative: how his eyes might soften if I made much of how Mum has burned all her bridges now, how he might place a gentle hand on my arm if I positioned myself as the long-suffering daughter of a woman who never cared, but I stop myself as Freddie's words come back to me: *family's important... they're all we've got, in the end.*

And I suspect – just a hunch – that Alice would not have spewed abuse. Not on that fundamental relationship between mother and daughter. She was endlessly kind, endlessly forgiving.

'I'll give her a few days to cool off,' I say. 'It's good I'm out of the house for now. But yes, I hope so. I'm all she's got. I'd do anything for her.'

Jack nods, and we lapse into silence once more.

28

Jack's sympathy is like a drug. I find myself wanting more and more. He doesn't allow me to carry any of my bags and boxes, instead ushering me up the front path while he struggles behind me. 'You've been through enough today,' he says when I protest. 'Let's just get you inside.'

And so, clutching my daffodils, I find myself in Jack's front hall again, but with one crucial difference. This time, I'm here to stay. This time, I do not have to gorge myself on details with the hurried air of a visitor. I can luxuriate in it: take in the detail of the cornicing, the delicate floral wallpaper, the gleaming floor tiles.

But I cannot get carried away. It would be easy to get caught up in the glamour of it all and forget the terribly sad reason that brought me here. I check my posture, hunch so I am almost curling in on myself. It's the perfect setting for it. The hall is so large that I must look impossibly lost, impossibly small, standing right in the centre of the floor with the stairs rearing up behind me.

For his part, Jack appears to relish the role I've given him. This opportunity to step up: to be the knight in shining armour I so desperately need. *Men love to be needed*, after all. That's what Marcie always used to say. There is a nervous energy to him as he takes my coat, as he watches me digest my surroundings, like a little boy bouncing on the balls of his feet, desperate for approval.

I give it to him, making my voice soft, breathy. 'It's so beautiful.'

His open expression shutters slightly. 'Thank you. I can't take any credit for it. My parents did it up, and Alice added some bits here and there.'

'Your parents lived here?'

His lips tighten. 'They did. And my dad's dad before him, and so on.'

'Inherited?'

He rubs the back of his neck. 'Yup. It's a lot for one person.'

'Have you lived here long?'

He gives a mirthless laugh, then sighs heavily. 'I grew up between here and Dorset. I moved out in my early twenties, after uni, and then my father started the process of handing it over to me. Irrespective of whether I actually wanted to live here. It doesn't... it doesn't hold the best memories for me. But that's my lot, and I'm aware I sound horribly spoilt complaining about it.'

I move closer to him on instinct. He looks so bereft that I reach out and place my hand on his arm. It is so impulsive, it's like being here is causing Alice to rub off on me already, in a strange sort of osmosis. 'Sounds like I'm not the only one with difficult parents.'

He laughs, and the black cloud seems to shift. 'Very true. Well, you know where to come if you need any advice.'

'I'll bear it in mind.'

His eyes twinkle. 'Yes, do. Right, shall I show you where you're sleeping?'

Jack leads the way back up the staircase to a corridor lined with rooms – rooms I poked my head into briefly the other night, checking fruitlessly for photographs. I trail behind him, dragging my feet, wanting to take my time, to examine the old visitors book on the small table at the end of the corridor, the impossibly old artwork lining the walls.

Jack leads me to a bedroom adjacent to his. It's the smallest guest bedroom – a fact I know from my exploration – but I decide not to read too much into it. All being well, I won't be in here for very long. He hovers for a moment in the doorway: 'Can I get you anything? A tea, maybe?'

I'd like a chance to gather myself, so I give him an indulgent smile. 'Chamomile would be lovely. If you have it. It's been a long day.'

'Absolutely,' he says, and shuts the door quietly behind him.

Despite this being the smallest bedroom in the house, it's a world away from my dank, fly-infested room at Mum's. It's wonderfully clean. No dead rats to contend with here. I place the daffodils atop the dresser and sit at the end of the huge bed, on the starched white sheets. As a starting point, this will do nicely.

I unpack quickly. I take out Freddie's box of things and lay the items neatly across the dressing table. I deliberated over bringing them with me. I wasn't sure that Freddie had a place in this new future of mine, but the thought of leaving them behind caused my chest to pang uncomfortably. I push the pyjamas into a drawer. Afterwards, I go into the en suite and stare at the shower: the porcelain sparkling, the shower head wiped of limescale. I'm going to feel *clean* for the first time in weeks.

There is a knock at the door, and Jack enters carrying a cup of herbal tea and a vase, which he sets carefully on the dresser.

'I thought you might want this, too. For the flowers.'

'Thank you, Jack,' I say. He is so thoughtful. 'Honestly, I can't thank you enough for having me.'

'It's no problem.' He smiles, then rubs a hand over his face. 'Look, I'm so sorry but I have to be in work early tomorrow. Are you OK if I head to bed?'

'Of course,' I say, disappointed. I'd pictured us talking long into the night, finding yet more commonalities to bond over. But we have all the time in the world for that. 'Thanks again.'

When he's gone, I complete my nightly routine – in the shower, I scrub my hair until it squeaks, and use liberal amounts of the Aesop soap. I brush my teeth in the porcelain sink, and wrap a thick, fluffy towel round me. Afterwards, I put on my most alluring set of pyjamas. I spent more than I probably should have on them just after I met Freddie, though he never seemed to appreciate them.

After our first kiss, my relationship with Freddie progressed quickly. Like there was a magnetic field between us, we were drawn together, even when we should have been focusing on other things. We'd find ourselves sequestered in cosy corners of the office almost by accident, the air charged with tension. We'd sit close to one another during meetings, hands occasionally brushing under the table.

Within two weeks, I'd been to his house, borrowing his toothbrush in the absence of my own, relishing the thought of our DNA binding together on the bristles. I even took pleasure in his lumpy mattress, because it was *his*. I loved the intimacy of being in his space. Sometimes, I'd run my hand over his stuff, just because I could.

I took little items sometimes. Only things I did not think he'd miss. Things that proved – during the nights we didn't spend together – that we had something real. Something good. I'd lie in my own bed, staring at the ceiling, and press his pyjama bottoms to my nose, inhaling his scent.

It was the happiest I remember being. I was filled with a sense of completeness. Of finally finding my place in the world. And then Freddie had to go and ruin it all.

Once I have completed my routine, I settle into the large bed. It's so comfortable, I could sleep here and now, but I won't. I need to stay awake. Just for a while longer.

For an hour, I play on my phone, watching the minutes tick down. I message Tilly again. She's panicking now, asking if she should call the police – and, though I'm still angry with Mum, I do feel partially responsible. I manage to talk her down. I tell her it's the first breach of the restraining order in a long while. I encourage her to wait. If Mum turns up again, *then* she can go to the police. I know Mum won't do it again. She won't risk the embarrassment. My good deed for the day done, I scroll absentmindedly through my various social media profiles. I check Jack's again, just in case, but it's still dormant.

Finally, when I judge enough time has passed, I get up and leave my room. It's utterly still in the corridor. I press an ear to Jack's door. Silence. No rustle of movement to suggest he's still getting ready for bed. Perfect. I push the door gently and it gives with a click. It's very dark inside. He doesn't move when the light from the corridor floods into the room.

I pad over to the bed. 'Jack?' I whisper, forcing my voice to wobble. 'Do you mind if I sleep in here with you? I'm just… so upset about Mum.'

There is a long pause as I wait for him to come to, heart thrumming. Finally he blinks blearily. 'Of course.' And he rolls over to make room. I pull back the covers and slide in next to him. It is wonderfully intimate – we are wonderfully close – and my heart is beating so hard

I don't know if I'll be able to sleep. But at some point I must, because when I wake again in the early hours Jack's arm is across my body, and I think I feel a hardness pressing into my back.

29

I'm a little surprised by Jack's reaction the next morning, when he wakes to find me next to him in the bed. I'd expected *some* pushback, since he was half asleep when I crawled in beside him. Honestly, I'd worried he might be angry, and I've kept that memory of Marcie pushing me into the muck at my grandparents' farm simmering right at the apex of my mind since I woke up, should I need to call on it. But instead, when his eyes finally open, he smiles. In return, I give him the one I practised so hard in the mirror.

'How are you feeling?' he asks.

I don't want Mum to ruin this first morning in bed together, so I tell him I'm OK, then, to remind him of all I've suffered through, I say, 'I'm still trying to come to terms with it, I think. She was so *angry*, for no reason at all.'

'You've done everything you can for now. It's not easy to reason with an alcoholic.'

I give a sad little shrug. 'Maybe. I'll give it a couple of days and apologise.'

'*You* have nothing to apologise for. You've done nothing wrong, Iris.'

I wonder what I did to deserve such a kind, considerate man, who sees only the best in me. He's right. All I've ever tried to do is love her, and she's thrown it back in my face at every juncture.

'I hope you don't mind I ended up in here last night.' I use that bashful look again, a quick flick of the eyes downwards. Better, sometimes, to address the proverbial elephant in the room.

He's quiet for a moment. 'It was nice, actually,' he says. 'A bit of a surprise but, truthfully, I was going to ask you if you wanted to sleep in here. Then I worried it would seem presumptuous.'

If I wasn't in love with him before, I certainly am now.

He gets up then, and I watch him from the comfort of his large bed as he walks around the room, skin tingling with the intimacy of it all. I've imagined this scenario so many times. Fantasised about his morning routine in painstaking detail. Now, I am witnessing it.

As it turns out, Jack's morning routine is not so very different to anyone else's. He brushes his teeth in the en suite, shaves, has a shower. I listen to the water as I plump the pillows behind my head and arrange myself in a way that I hope looks sadly seductive for his return.

The shower lasts exactly six minutes. Six minutes where I arc my gaze around the room searching for some hint of *her*. This is the only room I wasn't able to search the other night, in case Jack should wake from his alcohol-induced slumber.

It's lined with cupboards: huge, floor-to-ceiling cupboards that make my fingers itch just to look at them. Almost as if they are sentient, beckoning me towards them with whispers of the secrets they contain. If this was the room that Alice and Jack shared, I am sure that there will be something of hers squirrelled away in here.

Jack enters from the en suite then, and I lie back, hoping I look pale, wan, perhaps a little ill. He smiles when he sees me, and I'm sure I see that protective flare in his eyes as he takes me in: so small and weak against these huge pillows. That masculine need to protect kicking in once more. He moves around the bedroom quietly – like he doesn't want to disturb me. He's bare-chested. A little on the thin side, but nothing that my nurturing can't fix. I'll have to learn to cook, get a roster of horribly wholesome recipes under my belt so I can nourish him. Catherine mentioned that cooking was Alice's love language, after all.

He dresses quickly, like he's overly conscious of his nakedness. I want to tell him not to worry, that it's nothing I haven't seen before, but decide that really does place me too firmly on the matronly end, and I'm treading a thin line between motherly and appealing as it is. He looks so handsome, all dressed up and ready for work. Before he leaves, he comes over and kisses me lightly on the cheek. 'Look after yourself today. Help yourself to anything in the fridge. I'll be back about seven.'

'Jack, I hate to ask,' I say, making my voice tremulous. 'But I don't suppose there are any clothes I might be able to borrow? I only had a chance to grab a few of my things at Mum's.' In truth, I grabbed everything I needed from that godforsaken house, but I am so close to Alice now I can almost smell her.

Jack's jaw tightens at the question, eyes flicking to the cupboard on the right.

'I have some shirts in the cupboard over there,' he says, gesturing to the one on the left. 'You're welcome to any of them.'

It's not the answer I was hoping for. I don't see the point in such blatant sentimentality after death. My box of Freddie's things is different. Each of those items holds a special meaning for me. But I only nod, thank him profusely once more.

I listen to Jack leave the house, then rise. When the door downstairs slams, I get up and take a moment to curl my toes into the thick carpet, stretching in the light streaming through the window. The whole day stretches before me.

I shower – to feel clean after all this time is a luxury I'll never take for granted again. I floss and brush my teeth. I make both my bed and Jack's. Then, back in his room, I begin my search afresh. I go straight for the dressing table, pulling open the drawers with an almost desperate force. And that is when I see the jewellery, glittering in the top right drawer. The first bit of evidence that Alice – that elusive presence – actually existed. That she was a real, living, breathing human being. Not just some warped memory that Jack has placed on a pedestal.

A diamond ring. Tangles of necklaces. Bangles that glitter in the light. All so beautiful my breath catches in my throat.

Naturally, I try the ring on first, on the third finger of my left hand. It's nearly a perfect fit, just like the one I discovered in Freddie's sock drawer. The one that changed everything.

I can still remember the first crack in our foundation. I'd been so sure that what we had was solid, that we were building towards a future together, that the first sign of fragmentation nearly pulled me apart completely. It was, as it so often is, a seemingly innocuous hiccup in our routine. He'd arrived in the office in a good mood – better than usual – and I wanted to be around his infectious energy, so I followed him through to the kitchen. He greeted me as he usually did: with a wide, open grin. An enquiry after my evening that was laced with feelings he couldn't voice in the office. He moved past me to get a mug and, as he did, I leaned closer so that I could catch a trace of that familiar musk – I'd missed it in the twelve hours we'd been apart – but I drew back like I'd been burned. Because it was a different smell that greeted me. A feminine sweetness that caught in my throat, causing a pit of nausea to yawn in my stomach.

'Everything OK?' he said, noticing the abrupt change in my demeanour. He always was so sensitive to my feelings.

Perhaps I should have said something then. Confronted him immediately. But the idea of losing him was too terrible to bear thinking about. I'd nodded mutely, feeling numb, and stumbled back to my chair.

I'm not afraid to admit I went a little mad in the days that followed. I started compulsively checking his calendar, but he never put personal appointments in there. I watched him more closely than ever, attuned to any slight shift in his routine. Sometimes, after work, I'd watch through the office window as he bundled himself into a waiting taxi that took him in the opposite direction to his flat. On these occasions, I'd wait for my phone to ping with a message from him. For him to provide some explanation about where he was going. It never came.

On the nights I stayed over, I'd wait for him to fall asleep, and silently comb his flat. I'd rummage, quietly, through his drawers in the dark, trying to find evidence of this other woman. For the first few weeks, there was nothing: no telltale hair tie thrown hastily on the bedside table. No thong in the washing basket or earring slipped between the sofa cushions. I wondered if perhaps I'd been imagining it. And then, late one evening, my fingers closed round a little velvet box at the bottom of his sock drawer. When I opened it, I felt as though my whole world was coming crashing down around me.

Now, I twist my hand. The diamond catches the light in a pleasing way. I wonder if this was Alice's engagement ring, or some other extravagance. A 'just because' present. Just because he has money. Just because she was the most important person in his life. I've always wanted to be *that* important to someone. That important to Jack. This diamond is twice the size of the one set into the band in Freddie's drawer. If it was Alice's engagement ring, it feels like an odd place to keep it, stuffed unceremoniously in a dressing table. I wonder if a doctor slipped it off her finger once she'd been pronounced dead. If Jack asked for it back as a reminder of the bond – the life commitment – they had made to each other. Or perhaps he simply deemed it too expensive to spend the rest of its life in the ground.

I take it off. It feels a bit seedy to wear it, even for me, but I take a mental inventory of the other items for later. I don't want to go in too hard too soon, but it might be that at some point I'll need to borrow something to remind Jack of my innate similarities to Alice. It's gratifying to know she hasn't been completely wiped off the face of the earth. That there is still material to draw from, if you know where to look.

I turn my attention to the cupboards next. Alice's cupboard is on the far side of the room, where Jack's eyes had flicked when I asked to borrow something to wear. I try not to read *too* much into his reaction. People do get very sentimental over the items left behind by those they loved.

The cupboard brims with clothes packed so tight they bulge outwards as soon as I open it. A rainbow of colour and material that causes my breath to catch. Generally, I take pride in my appearance. I realised – after Marcie's death – how important it was to come across in the right way. Particularly when I was no longer overshadowed by her extraordinary beauty. But this – this cornucopia of garments – is a whole new kettle of fish. A whole new level of wealth. I don't recognise half the labels.

I want it all instantly. I run my hand across the silks and denims and velvets and, as I do, a subtle scent is released into the air. The one I smelt before, downstairs. A floral, earthy scent. Tuberose.

'What are you doing?'

It's not often that someone manages to sneak up on me, but I'm so distracted by the cupboard I didn't hear her approach. I jump, violently, clutching at the clothes and dislodging many of them from their hangers. They fall in a crumpled heap by my feet, releasing more of that distinctive perfume.

The speaker is an older woman with greying hair and a frosty smile. I turn on the charm offensive, aware that I've been caught with my hand in the proverbial cookie jar.

'Hello!' A bright, light voice that I hope puts her in mind of sunshine, and bunny rabbits and rainbows, and distracts from my evident snooping. 'I didn't see you there.' I press a hand to my chest, emphasising my weak constitution. 'I was just looking for somewhere to put my things.'

Her mouth sets into a hard line. 'Jack told me that you were sleeping next door.'

I fix a puzzled look on my face. 'Did he? I was in here last night.'

'I see.' Judgement is etched into every line on her face.

'Sorry, can I help you?'

'I'm Martha. The housekeeper.' Still unsmiling.

Of course Jack has a housekeeper. An archaic role that should have died out with the late Victorians, though the upper classes are famously hopeless at looking after themselves. I can, I realise, use this to my advantage. Because, if the literature is correct, housekeepers possess a wealth of knowledge about the families they work for. Knowledge that could be useful. I stride towards her, hand outstretched. 'I'm Iris. Lovely to meet you. Jack's told me so much about you.'

If she thinks this an odd statement, she gives no indication other than a slight lift of her brow. 'If you need somewhere to put your things, I'll move those.' She gestures towards the wardrobe.

'Oh, please don't worry,' I say quickly. I don't want her to move these clothes. Not when I can learn so much from them: the sort of person Alice was, where she went, what she did. Not when I might be able to *wear* them. 'I can have a look in the room next door. I'm sure there's space there. I just thought I'd… check.'

A poor excuse – even to my own ears – but thankfully she gives a sharp nod and decides not to press the issue. I don't relax my stance. It's all too easy to slip up if you prematurely assume the threat has dissipated.

'So, how long have you worked here?' I ask airily.

'Coming up on thirty-five years.'

'Gosh, that's a long time. Must know everything about the Reynoldses.'

I turn, smiling sweetly, to see her eyes narrow. 'You do come to know a lot about the family, yes.'

I think of what Jack said about this house holding bad memories for him. 'I'm sure. What were his parents like?'

'They were always very kind to me.' Her tone is just clipped enough to signal the end of this particular line of questioning, and I decide not to push her. A tricky customer: I sense she'll be hard to dupe. I give her an indulgent smile.

'I'm sure. How wonderful to have been in the same job for so long.' As suspected, her face does not soften, so I make my exit. 'Anyway, I've got some bits to sort in my room. But it was *so* lovely to meet you, Martha. Let's have a cup of tea together soon.'

I leave her standing in the middle of Jack's bedroom, and retreat to the one allotted to me. After five minutes or so – five minutes where I stand with my ear pressed to the door, convinced she is checking Alice's cupboard for any missing items – I hear her pass by my room and go back downstairs.

Martha's presence in the house is a hindrance for the rest of the day. I want to continue searching Jack's bedroom, but I can't shake the feeling that she doesn't trust me, so I refrain. Instead, I spend an hour or two in the other bedroom and then – when that becomes too tedious to endure – venture downstairs in search of something to eat.

Martha is at work in the sitting room, so I tiptoe quietly past the door, and down the long corridor that leads to the kitchen. I'm surprised, yet again, when I see it. It's archaic in all the wrong ways. Where the rest of the house leans into its history – brooding oil paintings and antique furniture – this room is in serious need of modernisation. The ancient range in the corner pumps heat into the room, so it's just slightly too hot. The battered fridge in the corner could be a first edition, and not the valuable kind. It's small, poky, airless. A culinary prison cell.

Jack told me to help myself to anything I wanted, so I survey the contents of the fridge. It's all high-end stuff: glass bottles of milk from an upmarket dairy, cardboard punnets of strawberries. I'm simple in my food tastes, preferring plastic white bread to the seeded sourdough loaf that's been set on the side, but it's my only option, so I pop a piece in the toaster, and open a few drawers as I wait.

It's all pin neat. No mishmash of cooking utensils here. In the third drawer down, I find a stack of recipe cards. Handwritten, in a slightly jagged hand. I pull them out. They don't look particularly old. One, a recipe for cupcakes, still bears a smear of some floury mulch on the corner. Was this Alice's handwriting? These cards would fit with the holier-than-thou image I'm sure she went to painstaking ends to uphold.

The toaster pops. The only option for spread is fat-free plant-based 'butter'. I wrinkle my nose.

Martha comes to find me just as I've finished eating. 'I'm off now. Here's my number.' She holds out a piece of paper. 'If you ever need me.'

I don't know why she thinks I'll need it, or her for that matter, but I take it from her. There's a long pause where she stares at me, like she wants to say something else. I suppress a sigh. I hate hoverers. Just come out and say what you're thinking, rather than leaving the other person to deduce your meaning. 'Was there something else?'

'Can I have yours?'

I frown at her. 'What for?'

'Just in case I need to get in touch with you.'

I stare at her suspiciously. I don't hand my number out to just anyone. There are a lot of odd people out there, and you can never be too careful. But she's still hovering, and the sooner I can get her out the sooner I can return to my search. I sigh, then tap her number into my phone. I hear her bag vibrate.

She gives another curt nod, then turns on her heel.

'Bye then,' I mutter under my breath.

'I met Martha today,' I tell Jack when he returns from work later that evening.

Does his back stiffen as I say it? I'm not sure. When he turns to me, though, his face is impassive.

'Sorry. I should've mentioned she was coming. Hope she wasn't too frosty with you.'

'She was a bit. She seemed a little taken aback that I was here.'

'She's been with the family for years. A bit of a battle-axe, to be honest. Don't think she's ever really liked me, even when I was a child.' He pauses, then – with the air of someone getting something difficult off his chest – says, 'I struggled to connect with people back then. I was a pretty lonely kid at times.'

I can't imagine Jack – with all his charm and charisma – being lonely. That makes two of us. I love that he told me this. He's letting me in slowly, revealing a softer, more vulnerable side to himself. Allowing me to piece together the puzzle of his past. He takes a seat on the sofa, and I note how tired he looks. Different to the other night, when it was clearly the alcohol. Now, he looks as though he's slept badly, and I wonder if maybe he knew what he was doing when he put that arm round me last night. If perhaps he intended it to be as intimate as it felt. I sit next to him – too close to be platonic.

'I'm not sure she liked me much,' I say, and I smile in a self-deprecating sort of way. Cast my eyes to the floor.

'That makes two of us then.' And he grins at me through his tiredness. Like I am something *good* in his life, among all the bad.

I sit like that – arm brushing his – for a few more seconds, and then, when he makes no move towards me, I change tack. 'Jack,' I start slowly. 'Could I get a key?'

It's something that's been bothering me all day. Being here by his invitation only. I want the ability to let myself in and out, just as Alice would have done. I want access to all of it: his life, this house, its history. If I'd left today,

I'd have had no way of regaining entry. I want this house to feel like my own, just as it felt like hers.

At my question, there's another almost imperceptible shift in Jack's expression, but I'm not sure what it means. He's difficult to read sometimes. He clears his throat gruffly. 'Of course. There's one tucked away in the kitchen. I'll dig it out for you later.' Another tired smile, but this one is not quite as open – as honest, even – as the last. There's something almost forced about it. The pause between us somehow heavier. I wonder if perhaps he doesn't fully trust me yet.

'I was thinking,' I say, to break the silence, the sudden darkening of the atmosphere. 'I'd like to cook you dinner. Maybe tomorrow? To say thank you.'

And there it is. The return of that radiant grin. All because of me. *I* brought that out of him.

<h1 style="text-align:center">30</h1>

There was no grand finale. Not for Marcie anyway. She died as she lived: all at once, and then not at all. She didn't shout out as her foot slipped on that wet shingle. She was too surprised to scrabble for the sea grass that grew wild and unruly at the edge of the cliff. I stared at the spot she disappeared from and I didn't know how to feel.

There were no panicked shouts from below. No sirens. Just the whistling of the wind and the roar of the sea. I had to make sure. I had to see for myself. My own route to the beach was significantly slower than Marcie's. I scrambled down the cliff path, slipping on flat rocks, disturbing pebbles.

The rain had begun in earnest, driving holidaymakers back indoors. The beach was deserted. I saw her the minute I got to the bottom. The blood was almost unnecessary; I knew she was dead. Her eyes were open. A trickle of red ran from the corner of her mouth. Her arm was twisted away from her body at an awkward angle. I caught sight of the glint of silver at her wrist.

I dropped to my knees. Fumbled for it. The clasp was fiddly, and my hands were shaking. It took me three tries to release it. Then, it was in my hand. I held it up to the light. She'd collected several new charms in the years since she received it. A tiny pair of ballet pumps. A hairbrush. A small make-up palette. It hit me then: she was gone. She would never add another charm to this collection. I clenched the bracelet hard in my hand and felt the tears come. She and I had shared it all. A womb, a bedroom, a life. I felt very alone in the world all of a sudden.

At the sound of a shout behind me, I stowed the bracelet in my pocket. I wanted to keep this part of her for myself. A reminder that I'd once had a sister.

The boys found me hunched over her body, tears streaming down my face. Josh put his arm round me, helped me to my feet and, tucked under his arm, I allowed him to lead me away.

The next few hours passed in a blur. Josh, playing the hero, parked me in the hotel lobby and told the reception-ist what had happened. I listened to her on the phone with the ambulance. She sounded terrified.

When a primal, raw scream cut through the quiet of the lobby, I understood that someone must have told Mum what had happened. Seconds later, she rushed past me, out of the door. In the distance, the sound of sirens. Soon, paramedics and police were swarming the place like ants.

They asked to speak to me. They sat me on the edge of

my bed and placed a cup of tea in my hand. Two sugars, for the shock.

'What happened, Iris? Your mum said you'd been arguing,' they asked.

I could barely breathe, unable to shake the terror on Marcie's face as she realised she was falling. 'I don't know. The argument was silly. About something silly. She must have followed me when I left for the beach. I didn't realise what had happened until I saw her—' I broke off, took a deep, juddering breath. 'Her body.'

They handed me a tissue, but I thought I caught a glimpse of disbelief. If it was there, they had nothing on me. The hotel, as it turned out, had had complaints about the path before. They'd been planning to erect a fence the very next week.

They questioned me a couple more times after that, but it was inconclusive. The story went that Marcie had been upset by our argument. That she was not as careful as she should have been when approaching the cliff. That the rocks were slippery from the rain.

The journey back was silent. Dad's hands were white on the steering wheel. Silent tears ran down Mum's face. I looked out of the window. As we passed through the town, I caught sight of the boys piling into a car, a surfboard strapped to the top. They looked shaken and white. Josh and I never spoke again.

The fallout was even worse than I could have imagined. Mum and Dad walked the house like shells of their former selves. They stopped speaking to each other. They stopped speaking to me. Mum had to choose Marcie's clothes for her burial. She ripped Marcie's side of the room apart.

'Where's the bracelet? Where's her bracelet? She wasn't wearing it! Why wasn't she wearing it?'

I slipped it between the slats of my bed and the mattress after that.

We had a funeral. Billy came. I cried all the way through, and at the end he put his arm round me. It didn't feel like I'd imagined it to feel. He sent me a message afterwards, but I didn't reply.

I caught Mum looking at me during the funeral. She didn't cry, but her hands were trembling. She was frowning at me like my grandparents did: like I was a puzzle she didn't know how to solve. I stared at my feet and wished for it to be over.

Dad left three months later. It was the single most cowardly thing I've ever witnessed. They'd barely said three words to each other in that time, but suddenly their voices permeated the quiet mausoleum of our house.

'She had something to do with it. I know she did.'

'Listen to yourself. Do you know what you're suggesting?'

'I know exactly what I'm suggesting, Richard. And you do, too.'

'Don't be fucking ridiculous,' he snarled. 'You can't blame her for this. Do you know what that will do to her?'

'If they hadn't been fighting…' she moaned.

'Marcie could be difficult. You know that.'

He left that evening with a small overnight bag. He never came back to collect the rest of his things. A year later, he was married. A year after that, he had another baby on the way.

I tried with Mum. God knows I tried. For the first time, it was just the two of us. She'd started drinking heavily. Mostly, she barely seemed to notice I was there, but sometimes she'd look at me with something like fear in her eyes. I wanted to make her feel better. I thought I might be able to fill the void that Marcie had left behind. I was one half of her, after all. The only connection to her beloved daughter she had left.

One day, when the silence had stretched so tight it was stifling, I went to Marcie's side of the room. I opened her chest of drawers. I picked out the most Marcie-ish outfit I could find. Something unique, something special. I cut my hair. Coloured it blond. I barely recognised myself when I looked in the mirror. I liked it. And then I went to her.

Her reaction was not what I'd expected. I wanted her to take me in her arms, like she used to with Marcie. To kiss me on the crown of the head. To smooth my new, golden hair. Instead, she sat up and blinked at me, and her expression was one of abject terror.

I tempered it around the house, after that. But when I went out I noticed that people looked at me differently. And with their silent admiration, I felt a change occur within me. That confidence I'd always strived for seemed to flood my veins. I squared my shoulders, pressed my tongue to the roof of my mouth, and smiled at them as they passed me by, just like Marcie used to.

31

I set the stew down on the freshly laid table. I found a white tablecloth tucked away in one of the drawers. It really completes the scene. I've always had a good eye for design. I can thank my teenage artistic obsession for that. The candles – in the brass candlesticks I found – add a lovely, intimate glow. It's cosy. I've set two places next to each other at the end of the long table. I want it to feel romantic, close, familiar.

I'm not sure this sort of domesticity is for me, long term. I'm all for putting in the effort, but it must get monotonous after a while. Still, there's been a certain novelty to the whole experience: deciding on a recipe, buying the ingredients, pulling it all together. Jack forgot to find that key in the kitchen for me, so I borrowed one from Martha, edging into the room as she was dusting, clasping my hands in front of me, filled with meek apology for my request. She'd frowned at me when I said I did not have my own, then rummaged in her bag and handed me hers.

'I'll need it back, mind. When you're done.'

Despite her frostiness, I enjoyed picking out only the freshest ingredients from the little organic store round the corner (in keeping with Jack's preferences, of course), following one of those recipes I found in the drawer, laying the table with painstaking precision, all to show Jack that I, too, can be a homemaker. I deliberated for a long time over the recipe. I flicked through several online options that popped up when I typed in 'cosy dinner ideas', then 'nourishing dinner ideas', then simply 'dinner ideas', but felt overwhelmed by the choice. It was then I remembered the stack of handwritten recipe cards. I could hardly believe I'd forgotten. I liked the idea that I would be following the exact same process as Alice once did, in the exact same kitchen, wearing the exact same apron, which I'd found in the pantry.

I picked one that didn't seem overly complicated. It's important to acknowledge one's flaws, and cookery has never been my gift. It's never needed to be. When you're cooking for one, some of the joy does go out of the whole process. But this was simple and easy enough to follow. I'd have liked to have made my own chicken stock, too, as the recipe suggested, but time was not on my side, so I bought some from the shop. It all came together very nicely. It sits, now, steaming on the table, next to two bowls that I've laid out. The recipe called for it to be served with 'thick, crusty bread. Home-made if poss* *use recipe that J likes'. That, I decided, was beyond the realms of my capabilities, though I found the recipe she was talking about. She'd put a sentimental smiley face at the end, which only fed into the image I'd constructed of her. Sickeningly sweet, virtuous right to the end.

Though I didn't make the loaf that I now arrange on the chopping board at the end of the table, I'll pass it off as my own, obviously. A family recipe that's been passed down through the generations.

Jack got home five minutes ago, just as I was finishing up the stew with a dollop of sour cream. He stopped dead in his tracks as he entered the kitchen, his nose raised slightly like a fox that has caught scent on the wind. I was the picture of innocence, as though I wasn't fully aware of the link between smell and memory. As though this was not all part of the plan – using one of Alice's recipes to position myself even more firmly in the spot she so thoughtfully vacated for me.

'It smells amazing, Iris,' he said. 'I'll just go and change, then I'll be right down.'

And now, just before he arrives downstairs, the pièce de résistance. I uncork the bottle of wine I bought earlier. It's a good red – far out of my price range – but for Jack, I'd be willing to spend it all.

At the table, I pour two large glasses. I've weighed the risks of this move, and decided it was worth it. The wine will, I hope, lower his inhibitions. Loosen him up a bit. Chase any thoughts of her firmly from his mind. I'm not taking any chances. Not after our last disastrous dinner together.

Jack arrives downstairs two minutes later. He takes in the setup: the table, the stew steaming on the edge of the sideboard, the bread. Then, his gaze halts at the glasses on the table.

'Iris, I don't drink.'

'I know.' A breezy, insouciant voice. 'But I do enjoy a glass or two with supper and I don't like drinking alone. One can't make a difference, can it?'

He swallows again, eyes fixed on the glass. Finally, 'OK.' He doesn't sound completely sure, but the wine is poured and in front of him, and he is very recently back on the wagon. Too recently to have any real willpower.

We sit. I watch carefully as he takes a small sip, then – to distract him – I ask about his day. He shrugs, reaches for the glass again. A bigger sip this time, eyes closed in pleasure. 'It was fine. My bitch of a boss wanted me to stay later, but I told her I had to get back. Didn't want to be late. Not when supper's on the table.' He smiles, raises the glass in my direction. I'm surprised by the expletive. It jars, coming from his mouth, which is so often used to spill compliments and kind words.

'Well, let's hope it was worth it,' I say modestly, though I am very proud of my creation.

'It definitely was,' he says, chewing. 'Did you have a shift today?'

If he thinks I can whip up a feast like this around my day job, he is very much mistaken. 'I've taken some time off actually,' I say. 'After everything with Mum, I just felt like I needed to get my head together.'

In truth, the thought of cooking for Jack sent me into a total spin and, given I have now sorted my accommodation issue, the need for more shifts has diminished. I texted Mick, telling him about my falling-out with Mum, how it's brought back all sorts of difficult emotions for me. He replied, a little shortly, telling me to take whatever time I needed, though to please let him know further in advance next time. I refrained from a snippy retort. I'm learning.

'Have you spoken to your mum?' Jack asks.

I heave a long-suffering sigh. 'I've tried, but she doesn't pick up.' This is not true. Mum has been trying to call me almost incessantly since I left, no doubt with the intention of staining my name further, and I have no interest in speaking to her. She left a few messages that I haven't listened to. I blocked her number earlier today, fed up with the constant vibration. I lower my eyes sadly. 'I think I'll have to go over at some point. Just to check up on her.'

Jack reaches out across the table for my hand. His glass is empty already. 'You don't have to, Iris. You're not responsible for her decisions. You've done everything you can.'

'I know,' I say softly, employing one of Marcie's hard-done-by looks. They had great effect with Mum on several occasions. 'I just feel so guilty. She's the only parent I have left. I can't just leave her.'

Jack doesn't reply. He pours himself another glass of wine, then rolls his shoulders. He's loosening up already. I can tell from the slight flush travelling up his neck. I take a small sip from my own glass, curiosity clawing at me.

'What about you, tell me about your family,' I say.

He swallows another large gulp. 'What do you want to know?'

'Well, I got the sense that the house is a bit of a contentious issue.'

He sighs, nods, pours another glass. He wasn't lying: this man can drink. 'It is. I never wanted it. It was all my father ever thought about. He was obsessed with his "legacy", whatever that means. It came before everything else.' Another deep sigh. I love that he's trusting me with these snippets of his personal life. Giving me a glimpse beneath the veneer. The foundation for any good relationship.

'I didn't have the easiest relationship with my father,' he continues. 'He was... he could be a bit of a bully. He had a lot of power, and he knew it, particularly when we were growing up. Before I started challenging him.'

'Could you not just say no, to the house?' I have absolutely no idea why someone would *not* want to live here, but it feels like the right line of questioning.

He shakes his head. 'We have the good old British class system to thank for that. Firstborn son gets everything. Irrespective of what they really want. When he died, my sister and Mum got nothing.'

He tells me, then – with a bitterness in his voice that I have never heard there before – about his father. A cruel, domineering man who enjoyed wielding power over the whole family. He came down hardest on Jack, as the son and heir. His demands became so all-consuming that, when Jack was aged only eight, he nearly broke. He was shipped off to boarding school not long after, and there he experienced freedom for the first time. The shifting goalposts that his father put in place felt less imposing, and Jack stopped trying to be something he was not. He turned to drugs and alcohol instead and began to free-fall.

'He got off on it,' he says now. 'I guess he sort of loved and hated the fact that I was a failure. He told me about twenty times a day what a disappointment I'd been. Which just drove me towards the booze even more.'

'And Alice?' I ask now. Carefully. Don't want to spook him. 'What about her? Where does she fit in?'

'She saved me. Dad liked her, which helped. She had this way of making people like her. I always sort of envied her for it. Particularly because he just seemed to fucking *hate* me all the time. But Dad saw what she did for me, and things became a little better. She really took to this house, you know?' He's gone all misty-eyed, and I must resist the urge to stab him with my fork, bring him back to the room, remind him of who is sitting in front of him.

'I noticed—' I break off with a small, delicate cough. Getting to the crux of it all now. 'That there are no photos of her?'

'No.' He takes another large swig of wine. 'I couldn't bear to look at them. They're all in that chest in the sitting room. I just shoved them in there after she died. Can't bring myself to sort through them.'

Bingo. Chest. Sitting room. That's tomorrow's little job. I'm bored of talking about Alice, and Jack's family now. I must make my own position very clear. And so, I lean forward and place my hand oh so gently over Jack's and I curl my fingers round his, just as I did at the restaurant. My heart thuds in my chest. I watch his face carefully for any sign that he's going to pull away. Reject me again. Something *does* flash over his face. But it's not anger. It looks closer to guilt. That's to be expected: it's a complicated thing, falling in love after losing someone.

I don't remove my hand. Sometimes, all they need is a little push. He looks down, towards my chest, and I note him clock the necklace that shook free when I leaned forward. He doesn't say anything as he fingers it. The charm with the small 'A' inscribed on it.

For a second, I don't breathe. His face is very close to mine.

The kiss, when it comes, tastes like wine, just as my first with Freddie tasted like beer. Can't really fault him on that – I've barely touched mine and he's consumed most of the bottle. It doesn't matter. This is the outcome I hoped for, and I lean into it and flick my tongue against his. Another little tip I learned from one of Marcie's magazines. *Sometimes, they like it when you take the lead.*

And so, now, I do. I pull Jack to his feet. And we go upstairs to bed.

32

It was underwhelming in the end, as it so often is. Some drunken fumbling from Jack. Convincing sighs of pleasure from me; I discover it doesn't take a lot to convince a man of his competence in the bedroom. To his credit, Jack was tender. Afterwards, he asked if I was alright, and he smoothed the hair away from my face, looking at me with such intensity I wanted to bask in it.

Then, he ruined it. He went downstairs, ostensibly to check the door was locked, but when he didn't return I crept down and pressed my eye to the chink in the door to the sitting room. He was slumped on the sofa, tumbler in hand. I probably should have predicted that outcome. I crept back to bed, and now lie in the dark, stewing. I'm annoyed that he's downstairs. All I can think of is the chest, and how I am going to get to it.

I must fall asleep in the end, because when I wake – with the weak sunlight streaming through the curtains

– Jack is snoring next to me. I check the time. He's late for work.

I shake him gently by the shoulder – like a mother waking her slumbering child – and he jolts, eyes snapping open. I can smell him. That tang of sour alcohol. I don't know what time he came to bed, but it must have been late because I woke at one point in the early hours and the space next to me was still empty. Perhaps the glass of wine was a mistake – I should have known he'd struggle to stop at one – but hindsight's always twenty/twenty and it expedited the development of the relationship, so I can't say I regret it. He took me into his confidence last night in the same way Freddie did in those early days of our relationship: a slow baring of the soul, revealing the grittier, darker details of his life. Trusting me with those details. I want to harvest them all. I snuggle closer to Jack as he passes a hand across his face, reaches for his phone.

He swears when he sees the time.

'Fuck. Why didn't you wake me up?'

I pull away from him. His tone is so short, it extinguishes last night's glow instantly. I don't appreciate being spoken to like this – not when I went out of my way last night to cook him dinner. Not when I laid the table so beautifully and had to endure yet more eulogising about his dead wife. But I'm nothing if not adaptable. I widen my eyes in surprise and hurt. 'I only just woke up,' I say in a voice that is too high, too girlish, flecked with hurt. 'I'm so sorry.'

'Sorry's not going to help me now, is it?' he snaps, and pulls up his messages. He taps out a message – I read it over his shoulder. Hey, sorry, something's come up. Going to be half an hour late. Start the meeting without me.

Oops. If I'd known he had a meeting, perhaps I would have held off on the wine. Then again, maybe not.

He doesn't speak as he rises, pausing only to rub a hand over his face again, but I can sense his anger and I don't understand it. Not after how special last night was. That's worth being a few minutes late for a meeting, surely? I'd have quit my job at the magazine if Freddie had asked me to.

Jack's shower lasts only two minutes this morning, and does little to wash the hangover away. When he re-enters the bedroom, he clutches the doorframe, breathing heavily with his eyes closed.

'I'm sorry, Iris,' he says, grimacing as the sun breaks through a cloud, a beam catching the side of his face. He'd look angelic if he wasn't so obviously struggling. 'That was uncalled for.'

I'm still smarting, but I remind myself that *perfect* Alice had endless patience, endless forgiveness, and swallow. 'It's OK. I'm sorry you're late for your meeting.'

'They'll survive without me for a few minutes.' He smiles, wincing again, and his voice softens. 'Listen, last night was really nice. Thank you for making such an effort. I shouldn't have had the wine, though. I feel appalling.'

I do feel a little guilty for encouraging him to drink, but we might not have crossed that final barrier between us otherwise, so it fades. It's not lost on me that his relapse helps me to position myself as Alice did at the start of their relationship. And just like her, I can help him to get the help he needs. Maybe I'll message him later, suggest coming with him to AA. I bet that's what she would have done, and I do love a group setting.

Jack dresses fast today. Almost as soon as he puts his shirt on, it becomes damp with sweat. Before he leaves, he kisses me swiftly on the cheek, though I wish he hadn't; he's still damp from the shower and sweat drips from his forehead onto mine. As much as I love every part of him, even I have my limits.

He exits in a flurry of huffs and puffs. I get up as soon as he's left the room and take a long shower, scrubbing hard at my forehead, then dress quickly. The door slams downstairs, and I am finally alone.

I don't bother to clean up after Jack's bender last night, though bottles litter the living room. There are things to achieve today, and cleaning is not one of them. My eye is drawn to the chest in the corner of the room. I'd barely noticed it before, had assumed it was some priceless antique that looked pretty but held no function. Now I know it contains details of Alice's life, it takes on a whole new significance. Last night was only the first step. A necessary one, but men are fickle creatures. Once you've slept with them – given in to that primal urge to conquer – it's all about holding their attention. Keeping the excitement alive. Marcie knew that. That's why she never went past second base, despite the rumours that said otherwise. As a woman, you relinquish a portion of your power the moment you give in to sex. Last night, I wanted to sleep with Jack. It was important to me, to gauge how much he wanted me, but I'm aware of the power I need to reclaim.

I know I can't become complacent now that we have crossed this first hurdle. Not after what happened with Freddie. I always learn from my mistakes.

And that's why I need Alice. She'd played it right. She'd secured a proposal, after all, that ultimate promise of commitment. A trip down the aisle.

I try to raise the lid. It's so old that the wood groans with the pressure, but it doesn't give. Not an inch. It's then I see the old lock. Rusted with age, but still holding fast. I release a scream of frustration. She is so close I can almost touch her, and yet I'm being thwarted by an item that is at least a hundred years old.

I spend the rest of the morning searching for the key. I turn the house upside down and find a few more items that can only have belonged to Alice, but nothing that resembles what I'm looking for. In the bathroom, I find a pack of sertraline prescribed to an Alice Reynolds and a tube of Vagisil. I wrinkle my nose at that. A pack of hair ties – always useful. I keep the bottle of lime, basil and mandarin bath oil because it looks expensive, and I've never been one to turn down a freebie. If I can smell like her, too, Jack won't be able to resist me.

With nothing else to go on, I revert to my original plan. And for that, I will need to return to the dull domesticity of last night. I turn my attention to Jack's mess. There's no sign of Martha today, so clearly that particular job falls to me. Irritating on more than one level: aside from the cleaning, it means I don't have access to a key. Jack must have forgotten to dig out the one he promised me, and I keep an eye out on my search for the chest key, but there is no sign of either of them.

When I have finished cleaning, I turn my attention to the recipe cards. There must be at least fifty here, and some – crucially – bear helpful tips about Jack's predilections.

J likes this med. rare

J prefers this with brown rice

J LOVES this. Cook more often?

It's disgustingly thoughtful. But, if cooking was Alice's love language, then it's going to have to be mine as well. Dinner last night was a good starting point, but I cannot simply stick with stews for the rest of our courting period. This time, I'm going to attempt meat, and pudding as well.

Jack keeps up a steady stream of messages all day, evidently feeling guilty for his behaviour this morning. I stop what I'm doing each time to reply to him, but it does rather interrupt my flow. I remind myself that it's sweet he's so interested in my day. That not three days ago, I would have been thrilled at the constant contact.

Have you spoken to your mother?

I sigh when I read it. I wish he'd stop asking about her. His concern is touching, but every time he mentions her I remember her anger. The way her face twisted with something that looked almost like hatred.

But family is important, so I reply that I haven't. That I'm planning to reach out in the next few days. Then, to divert his attention away from things I'd rather not dwell on: Did you mention there was a key somewhere in the kitchen?

The reply comes instantly. Why? Do you need something? I can get it delivered? Don't want you to have to trek outside when you should be looking after yourself!

A tiny prickle of irritation. This is not the response I was looking for. I type back It's OK! I could do with the walk...

I wait, leg jigging, for half an hour, but my phone screen remains black and it is with resignation that I navigate to a delivery app and order duck breasts (the centrepiece for a recipe *J* supposedly loves) and cake mix. I don't feel that confident in my meat cookery, but I like the precision of baking. If you follow the recipe to the letter, nine times out of ten it's going to turn out alright.

When it arrives, I unpack the groceries on the counter and get to work. I marinate the duck breast, trying to touch the meat as little as possible. That slimy cool of flesh against my fingers turns my stomach. I mix the ingredients for the cake, pour the batter into a tin and put it in the oven to cook.

I'm prepared by the time I hear the door slam. The cake has turned out well. Beautifully risen with a nice golden crust. All that's left is to pan-fry the duck when Jack is ready to eat. I've put on Alice's apron and, as a final little touch, smeared my cheek with flour. It's the sort of sickeningly twee imperfection that I imagine made Alice so desirable.

But it's not Jack who enters the kitchen. I turn at the sound of the door, then freeze. The woman who enters is tall, middle-aged and austere. She has a haughty stare, the straight back of the English upper classes that probably goes some way to explaining the stick up the arse idiom. I recognise her instantly. It's Jack's mother, Catherine. When she sees me, she stops dead.

'Who are you?' The clipped, irritated tone is not lost on me.

I am ill-prepared for this stumbling block. This outfit – the apron, the flour – was not intended for a female gaze. Women are always so much better at seeing through a façade than men, who often only see what they want to. It's why Mum is always so difficult to dupe. I swipe at the flour on my cheek, but I can see from the way her perfectly plucked eyebrow lifts an inch that she has clocked the action. The apron will have to stay.

Never mind. I'll just have to make the best of it. I stride forward, wiping my hands, and take her icy-cold, thin fingers in mine.

'I'm Iris. So lovely to meet you.' I find myself mirroring her accent. Posh, lengthening my vowels, snipping the consonants. I've not had a lot of experience with people of this social stature, but I do know that – for them – like calls to like.

'Has Jack hired a cook?'

I feel my jaw set. Clearly, the accent needs work. 'No. I'm a…' I sense that I perhaps should *not* reveal the true nature of my relationship with Jack – not that I don't want to, but because Catherine could cause problems for us later down the line. She clearly remains a significant force in his life, and I'll need to get her onside. 'Friend of Jack's. We met at the grief group. And you must be his mum. You look so similar!'

The charm offensive seems to work. Or at the very least, to assuage her suspicions, because her shoulders drop. 'How is he? I haven't heard from him in two days.'

There's a chip of anxiety in her voice that I intend to exploit. I touch her lightly on the arm – to show that I'm not a threat, that I'm just as concerned for his wellbeing as she is. I lower my voice. 'Between you and me, I don't think he's doing that well,' I say. 'I suspect that he's drinking again, to be perfectly frank.'

She closes her eyes briefly, looking pained. 'I knew it,' she says. 'He always goes off grid when he drinks. It was just like this with Alice. We had to send him to rehab, you know. After Alice went into remission and she didn't need him so much any more.'

I drop the act instantly, hands falling to my sides. 'Remission?'

The word sticks in my throat. Remission is something Matt used to mention frequently, first with a hopeful inflection to his voice, and then, as the weeks passed, with increasing despondency. Finally, he stopped alluding to it at all. And yet I'm sure Jack said Alice *died* of cancer. She could have developed it again, but he's never mentioned anything about remission.

There is no time to probe further, however, because a distant echo in the hallway indicates that the man himself has come home. I check the clock on the wall. He's late. Nearly forty-five minutes late.

He comes straight through to the kitchen, and I stare at him, open-mouthed. I can't help it. He looks awful. Worse, somehow, than he did this morning. Rumpled and creased, grey-faced, years older. And there is something about his eyes: something wild and panicked. Like a deer that has spotted the rifle aimed at its heart.

He stops dead when he sees us, and doesn't speak for a moment, like he is trying to recalibrate. Seconds pass, and all he does is stare, that wild look still in his eye. I wonder if something happened to him on his commute home, and I'm about to ask when, with visible effort, he seems to gather himself. He clears his throat.

'What are you doing here?' he barks at his mother, who shrinks next to me.

'I haven't heard from you,' she says, almost tremulously. Entirely different to the woman who demanded to know who I was not five minutes ago. She sounds timid in his presence.

'What have I told you about just turning up out of the blue? If you can't respect my boundaries, I'm going to have to take the key back.' It's a tone I haven't heard from him before. Harder, more abrupt than it was even this morning.

'Jack,' she says, and there is a horrible, pleading note to the word. 'Darling. I think we need to talk about getting you back to rehab.'

'I'm fine, Mum,' he says, and he shoots a vicious glare in my direction that would shrink a lesser woman than me. I pretend it has had the desired effect. I back into the counter until I feel it press against my spine.

'We're just worried about you, Jack,' I say. I make my voice small and timid to match his mother's. Two women who only want what's best for him.

'Weren't very worried about me last night, were you?'

I falter. I'd hoped he wouldn't bring it up. I see Catherine shoot a quizzical glance in my direction. Time for damage control.

'I didn't… I didn't know how bad it was. I thought you could just have a glass. I'm sorry. That was my mistake.'

'Well, neither of you needs to worry. I'm going to a meeting this evening.'

'Do you think it's perhaps past that point, darling?' If I didn't know better, I'd say Catherine sounded scared.

'No. I can get a handle on this,' he says shortly. 'Without you two twittering in my ear.'

'OK.' She doesn't sound convinced. 'It's just, your father would have—'

'Don't talk to me about that man. Leave, please. Now.'

She doesn't need to be asked twice. She collects her bag, which she had set on the counter, and scurries out, leaving me and Jack staring at each other across the kitchen.

33

I manage to bring us back from the brink. Of course I do. I am demure, and so apologetic I almost believe it myself. It takes him a while to thaw. I cling to his arm and show him the cake, the marinated duck on the side. His face softens as he takes them in. He's quiet, pinching the bridge of his nose with his eyes closed before he opens them again, offers me a small smile.

'I've been a bit of a twat, haven't I? I'm sorry, it's been a long day.'

Understatement of the century, but I shake my head vigorously. I'd do anything to set him at ease, to show him how committed I am.

'Not at all. I shouldn't have given you the wine last night. That's on me. I'm sorry. Did work keep you late?'

'Work?' And there's that look again. That haunted, panicked expression.

'You said you had a long day?'

He coughs, looks at the floor. 'Work, yeah. I had something to take care of for them.'

He doesn't look at me, and I find I don't quite believe him.

But then, he comes to me, presses a kiss to my temple. I don't regret giving him the wine. Not at all. Not when it's led to this easy, casual intimacy between us.

We have a nice dinner. No wine. I avoid contentious subjects, like the wife, or the drinking, and generally just let him do the talking. Which he does. Almost like he's using his voice to resist the urge for a drink. On the table, his hand clenches and unclenches into a fist, and there's a tendon raised in his neck. I ask all the right questions and wait for him to relax. It takes a while – it was easier when he was lubricated last night – but eventually his breathing settles. I pounce on the moment.

'Sorry to bring it up again, but could I get that key?' Softly, casually. Like it's not a big deal. But the truth is, I will go stir crazy if I have to spend another whole day in this house. I don't like being cooped up. Not when there are things to do, items to purchase, people to watch.

I had far more autonomy in my relationship with Freddie, though – looking back – I wonder if it was perhaps too much. Too much time, during those long nights where I was not with him, to linger on details. To torture myself with thoughts of him with someone else.

I tried to convince myself the ring was for me. It worked for a while. Whenever my thoughts turned to the morbid, I'd imagine Freddie down on one knee. Somewhere public, where everyone turned to look as he proved his commitment to me with that ring. I tried to keep the fantasy going for as long as I could, but sometimes – in this dream – I'd turn, and there would be a face in the crowd. A woman who pushed through the throngs of people, walked towards us and threw her arms round Freddie's neck, right in front of me. Sometimes, she had Marcie's face.

I upped my efforts with Freddie. I employed all of Marcie's most successful tactics, but I couldn't help but feel he was still pulling away from me.

My work performance suffered as a result, but Freddie didn't bring it up, as though his guilt for what he'd done – for what he was *doing* – prevented him from admonishing me.

He was still solicitous, still caring, but there was something vacant about it. Something overly polite.

My suspicions were confirmed by Greg. One afternoon, I was watching Freddie from across the office, heart aching as he regaled some of our other colleagues with a story from his childhood. I didn't realise Greg was behind me until I felt his breath on the back of my neck.

He nodded towards Freddie, who was grinning as though his face would split with it. 'That's a sign of a man in love if I've ever seen one.'

I forced myself not to react. No one in the office knew about our relationship – Freddie would get in a lot of trouble if they found out – but I squeezed my hands into fists until I could feel the tendons screaming for release.

I had to find a way to bring him back to me. I messaged him later that afternoon. Hi Freddie, could we go for a drink this evening? There's something I'd like to chat to you about.

He didn't reply with his usual speed, but he accepted nonetheless. A tiny glimmer of hope.

We walked over together. As soon as we left the office, I noticed how he changed. Where he was loud and exuberant in the office, now he hunched in on himself, shooting anxious glances over his shoulder. I wondered if he was worried that our colleagues would see us together. It never seemed to bother him so much before.

And when we arrived, he ordered a pint and downed half of it immediately. He was acting almost afraid, glancing frequently towards the door.

I took a deep breath, tried to dredge up the speech I'd prepared, even in the face of this odd behaviour. I wasn't even sure if he was listening.

'Freddie, I wanted to talk to you because I feel like things between us have been a bit...' I searched for the word. 'Strained.'

If you have an issue, Marcie had said when she felt one of her many boyfriends wasn't providing her with her desired level of commitment, *ask them about it. Straight up. Know your worth. I'll never understand why women wait for men to read their minds.*

It took Freddie a moment to process what I'd said but, when he did, he sighed. 'I'm sorry, Iris. You're right. I haven't been myself recently.'

'Is there anything I can help with?' I'd do anything for this man.

Another long sigh. Another glance towards the door. He lowered his voice, and it felt – for the first time in weeks – as though he was taking me into his confidence. I relaxed, just a little. Perhaps there was still hope.

'Honestly…' He hesitated. 'You're going to think I'm mad, but I think I'm being followed. I keep catching sight of some guy behind me. Sometimes, I don't even see him. I just have a *sense* he's there. Greg thinks I'm being paranoid, but I don't know. Something just feels off.'

For the first time in weeks, I could breathe. *This* was the reason for his strange behaviour. His reluctance to engage with me. He was worried. Understandably so, given his concerns about being followed. I nodded sympathetically, chest loosening. 'That sounds terrifying. I'm here for you, Freddie. Whenever you want to talk.'

His smile was tight. 'Thanks. I'm grateful. Really.'

It was only afterwards that I remembered Greg's words. *That's a sign of a man in love.* My chest tightened once more. I checked Freddie's calendar for the fourth time that evening.

Now, Jack looks at me through bloodshot eyes, hand still clenching on the table. 'The key. Of course. I must have forgotten to reply to you. Sorry.' He stands and disappears into the other room. When he comes back, he hands me a key. My very own key. I stow it carefully in my bag.

We don't sleep together that night, though I crawl into Jack's bed without asking, and he doesn't comment. Only rolls over to kiss me goodnight and then withdraws to his side. I'm not complaining. I could do with the sleep, too. I wait for him to fall asleep first, but his breath doesn't even out, and we lie, side by side, awake for what feels like hours.

It occurs to me, as I'm drifting off, that he didn't go to the meeting he promised to.

The next morning, Jack is shaking. His hands tremble as he pulls on his shirt, and the bags under his eyes seem more pronounced.

'Have you got a busy day today?' I ask, less out of genuine curiosity and more because the silence has begun to feel oppressive.

'Probably. Someone's got to work to keep you fed and clothed here.' A nasty undertone to this comment that causes a flush of anger, which I dampen instantly, reminding myself that he is in the throes of withdrawal. That he is sleep deprived and probably still angry about his mother.

Even so, I can't quite keep the petulance from my tone. 'I do work.'

A huff of air through his nostrils. 'In a café,' he mutters.

I sit up, another spark of anger – bigger, this time – igniting. 'Sorry, is my job a problem for you? Somehow beneath you?' Careful, Iris. Don't allow the mask to slip.

'Not at all.' He straightens, then looks at me. 'By the way, since you're not going in at the moment, and now you've got a key, I'd really appreciate if you could grab my dry-cleaning from the shop down the road. Martha usually does it, but we've got to put you to work somehow, haven't we? I'll let her know.'

I wonder where this has come from. This sudden shift in him. This is not a request at all, but a demand. I want to hiss at him, cat-like, that I am not his servant. That I am the woman who can save him, just as his dead wife did. But, perhaps the dry-cleaning *was* one of Alice's jobs. I wrestle with the anger, remind myself of Alice's virtues, and nod meekly.

'Good girl,' he says.

It nearly tips me. I nearly release the full weight of my fury, but – once again – I force myself to remember where I am. Why this is important. I will help him through whatever this is, gently guide him back to becoming the charming man I met at the group that day. The one who thinks I am special. The one who bought me daffodils.

Jack doesn't improve much over the course of the week. If anything, his black mood seems to be getting worse. I put it down to the alcohol and the lack of sleep, but it doesn't make him any easier to deal with. The dry-cleaning that I begrudgingly collected was just the beginning. When he arrived home that evening, he asked me politely why I had not put it away, with a tightness to his voice that belied the simmering anger beneath. He begins to request things for dinner – complicated dishes that I'm sure are outside my limited capabilities, but which I attempt anyway, knowing that Alice would have excelled at them. One night, he merely wrinkles his nose at my offering, lays his napkin down on the table and exits the room. I don't see him again for the rest of the evening.

And while Alice might have put up with this childish behaviour, it begins to grate on me. Jack hasn't made me feel special, or appreciated, or *loved*, since our first dinner together.

By the following Tuesday afternoon, I am crawling the walls. When I receive a message with yet another unreasonable demand: Could you change the sheets in our room? They should be in the airing cupboard – no kiss, no thoughtful appendix – I decide enough is enough. I realise that the group meets this evening, and I could use it tonight more than ever.

Jack isn't back when I don my coat, and I'm glad for it. I'm not in the mood to navigate yet another of his stormy shifts in personality. I don't bother writing a note. Let him wonder where his new lackey has got to.

I'm early to the community hall, so I make small talk with Fiona as the others trickle in. Something stops me from telling her about Jack – she no longer waits for him at the start of each session – and, as much as I would like to boast about my new relationship, Jack's behaviour recently has left a funny taste in my mouth. I doubt I could muster the enthusiasm anyway. I've been feeling flat recently, which is unlike me.

What I really need is validation. Some confirmation that I still exist. The feel of all the eyes in the room turning towards me. And so, when the session begins, I am the first to speak. My hand is in the air before Fiona has even finished asking if anyone would like to kick off today's session.

'I would,' I say, and I like the feeling of being in control again. Of commanding the attention of the room. The familiar thrill begins to build. God, I've missed it. I summon tears. I don't even need to use *the* memory. They've been threatening to spill over all week: tears of anger and frustration and disappointment.

Fiona pats me on my shoulder, and I even manage not to flinch. 'My mum and I had a huge argument. She blamed me for the death of my twin sister,' I say, and I pause to allow the words to settle.

It's the first time I've said it aloud. It doesn't hurt as much as I'd thought it would. Talking about Marcie is easier now that I'm no longer moulding myself from her. It creates some much-needed distance, and the words are looser and more forthcoming. 'It was an *accident*. She slipped. We were only seventeen, but I do feel responsible, in a way. We'd argued that morning, like you, Hannah, and your mum.'

Hannah dips her head as though she understands. I love her for it. This tiny gesture of acknowledgement makes me feel seen for the first time in days.

'Perhaps if we hadn't argued, she'd have taken more care. But I know it's not helpful to dwell on questions like that.'

'I didn't know you'd lost your sister, too, Iris. I'm sorry,' Fiona says, and she begins rubbing circles on my back. I shift slightly out of her reach. She's a heavy smoker, and I don't want the smell of stale ash to transfer to my clothes.

'Yes, well. It was a long time ago, but obviously, with losing Freddie, too. It hasn't been easy.'

'Your mum sounds like she was out of line, blaming you like that,' Matt interjects, and I give him a gracious, albeit watery smile. He's right: she was out of line.

'We don't always say what we mean when we're suffering a loss,' Fiona reprimands gently, but she looks like she agrees with him.

'Oh, I think she meant it,' I say darkly, remembering her twisted features.

'Well, do try not to take it personally, Iris. Am I right in thinking that your mother' – she clears her throat delicately – '*struggles* with certain issues?'

I nod. I mentioned Mum's problem with alcohol early on. It came after a particularly hazardous conversation about Freddie, where Mum had probed about our relationship, asking for detail after detail, almost like she didn't believe he was real. There was something purgative about revealing this darker, dirtier side to her in front of a group of strangers.

'It sounds like she has a few demons to exorcise, too. You've been very brave sharing with us today.'

'Thank you,' I say, one ear straining for the murmurs of sympathy filtering through the room. I *have* had a tough deal. It hasn't been easy for me, and it took coming here to remind me of that fact. A cathartic exercise. A form of self-care, even.

When I make it clear that I have said all I want to on the matter, Fiona turns her attention to Charlie and is met, unsurprisingly, with the sort of tortured silence that you usually find at funerals. Charlie lost his partner, Jeremy, to illness and has not been coping well. Given his lack of contributions, I don't know why he keeps coming, but perhaps it's less about airing his feelings and more about the fact that a regular date in his diary stops him from succumbing to wave after wave of grief and depression.

We get nothing out of him, and the session moves on.

At the end, Fiona claps her hands. 'I've been giving it some thought,' she says. 'And I think it might be fun for you to bring photographs with you to one of our upcoming sessions. What are your thoughts?' She asks the question as though she has just proposed a particularly exciting school trip. The response is less enthusiastic. There are some general, noncommittal murmurs, but nothing concrete.

'I'll send you all an email about it, shall I?'

34

There is an ominous ambience to the house as I step through the door. A bloated, expectant atmosphere that I can feel even in the hallway. Good. He's had three hours to stew over my absence, and I hope he felt every second of it.

I, on the other hand, am feeling excellent. Tonight has imbued me with a new vigour, a reminder of the reasons I am doing this. I've been feeling so out of sorts, I'd lost sight of my connection with Jack. The way he made me feel when we first met. How he seemed to pick me out of the crowd, focus his attentions on me and me alone. I felt a fraction of that this evening – those quiet, shocked murmurs of sympathy topping up a tank I didn't know had emptied. Now, I just need Jack to fill it to the brim.

Before I enter the sitting room, where I can hear the TV blaring, I take a moment to compose myself in the mirror. There's a flush to my cheeks – likely a product of my excitable mood. It is not quite the impression I want to give off, so I hunch to make myself look smaller, and hope he doesn't notice.

But Jack doesn't even look at me when I enter the room. I know he knows I'm there, because he leans forward and mutes the TV. Another episode of that awful reality programme plays on the screen. He really should be watching something educational. True crime is a personal favourite of mine.

'Where the *fuck* have you been?' His voice is so deathly quiet, I barely catch it.

I shift so I'm standing in front of the television. It's a bold move for a weak woman, but I want his full attention. Once I'm in position, I allow myself to cringe slightly away from him, like his tone is barbed enough to cause me physical pain. 'Jack. I'm sorry. I just– Things have been so odd between us. I just needed to get out for a few hours.'

'I'm so sorry that it's all become such an *inconvenience* to you. That my asking you to do a few things for me while you live here rent-free is such a problem. Do you know where I've been tonight? I went to an AA meeting, because I promised *you* I'd get sober, and this is how you repay me. Fucking disappearing. No note. No message. Have you even checked your phone? I must've called you twenty times.'

Truthfully, I did check my phone. I saw those missed calls, and I liked them. There is power in silence. I liked that he had cause to chase me for once.

Outwardly, I hold my hands up. 'I haven't checked my phone, I'm sorry. I'm grateful, I really am. It's just… all been a lot. With Mum, with—' I break off. I was about to say Freddie, but I sense now might not be the time.

'I asked you where you've been.' That quietness again. It would cause a feebler woman to quake, so that is exactly what I do. I don't want to tell him that I was at the group. It bolstered me so much that I fully intend to keep going, and I sense that revealing where I was tonight might cause him to do something rash, like forbid me from attending again. He's been so reactive recently, so on edge.

'I've been walking,' I say. 'Just trying to clear my head. Things between us have been so strained. I don't understand what I've done wrong. Everything was going so well, and now it's like you don't want to be around me any more.'

An echo from my conversation with Freddie. Jack stares at me like he's trying to read the veracity of this claim in my face, so I keep still. Utterly earnest: brows pulled together, eyes wide, not leaving his. Whatever he sees there must convince him, because he sags and the fight seems to leave him.

'You're right. I'm sorry, Iris. I don't know what's wrong with me. I always get like this at the beginning of a relationship. It's something I know I need to work on. I think, subconsciously, I'm trying to test how strong the connection is by pulling away. Seeing how much I can push you. Testing what it would take for you to leave.'

This confession feels like he is opening a door, allowing me in again. Granting me access to the inner workings of his mind. I rush towards him. 'I'm not going to leave you, Jack. I would never do that,' I say, and I mean every word. I love that he felt safe enough to admit to this darker portion of his personality. Darkness exists in everyone, after all. I know that, probably better than most.

He takes my hand, presses it hard to his lips. 'I do understand needing to walk. I'm sorry. I was just worried about you. But it makes sense why you'd need to get out. After Alice died, I walked for miles.'

The comment snags on something distant at the back of my mind. Something that recalls Matt, then Catherine, then Alice.

'Jack,' I say slowly, tentatively. I'd rather he didn't explode again, ruin our truce. 'Your mum. She mentioned something about Alice going into remission?'

His mouth opens, then closes again. His eyes snap quickly to the left, and then back to me. There is a long pause. 'She did,' he says quietly. 'And then' – he swallows – 'then the cancer came back.'

And though there is nothing about his tone to suggest he is *not* telling the truth, I log the way his eyes flickered. And I know that he is lying. I don't press the issue, because he comes towards me then, envelops me in a hug, and the smell of him is enough to chase such frivolous thoughts away. As his arms fold round me, I'm sure I catch the faint smell of whisky on his breath.

The next morning finds me standing in front of Alice's wardrobe again. It's the first time since Martha caught me snooping; until now, I haven't dared go back. I have tried to avoid Martha since our first encounter. As someone who is doing her very best to uphold an image of a submissive housewife, it makes sense that I shrink away from her whenever she enters a room. But working in my favour today is the fact that Martha is not coming in. Jack mentioned it this morning in bed as he stroked my cheek (in a blatant but welcome attempt to make up for last night). I saw my opportunity and snatched at it.

I was able to read between the lines last night. I have simply not been doing enough to prove to Jack that I am in this for the long run. He doesn't yet trust my feelings for him. That I'm not going to leave him like Alice did.

I run my hand across the clothes again. They're all so beautiful. I'll start with something simple, I think. I inhale the perfume that wafts from the cupboard and begin rummaging.

I settle on a pair of high-quality jeans and a cashmere, high-necked jumper. Thankfully, we're roughly the same size. When I pull the jumper over my head, the scent envelops me. I tuck the necklace – embossed with the A – beneath the collar, then, standing in front of the full-length mirror, pull on the jeans. They suit me. Amazing how something so simple can change an appearance so completely. They are the perfect accompaniment to my new persona. I twist in front of the mirror, liking the way the clothes hug my figure – thinner since Freddie died.

The buzz of my phone from the bed breaks me from my self-admiration. An unknown number. I don't answer.

It might be a scam caller, or – worse yet – Mum with a new number. The phone rings out, and a text pops up a few seconds later.

Please ring me back. I really need to talk to you.

Mum, then. While she might have forgotten the way she spoke to me, I certainly have not, and it will take more than a few feeble attempts at contact to get back into my good graces. I silence the phone.

I spend a few hours practising in front of the mirror. Perhaps I've been a little *too* meek. Rolled over too easily. Alice's clothes, in their brightness, are not suggestive of someone who shrank completely into the background. Kind, but with some steel in her backbone. I'm pleased with this deduction. The dull monotony of domestic chores has begun to grate on me.

35

I practise for the moment Jack gets home until I'm completely satisfied. I position myself on the stairs, trying out several different poses. I settle for one hand draped over the banister, neck long and erect – as though he has just caught me descending for the evening, dressed in Alice's exquisite clothes and looking forward to nothing more than spending an evening with him. When I enquire about his day, I will do so as though his response is the most important part of mine.

I'm so excited to help steer Jack back to the man he was at the beginning that I even allow myself the indulgence of reflection. This feels like a seminal moment of transition for us – a moment where Jack and I can take stock of everything that has brought us together and move forward in the knowledge that we are entirely committed to one another. It only seems right, now, to look back on everything that has led me to this moment. The learning curves, the setbacks, the deaths.

I go into the room Jack allocated to me on my first

night here and run my hand over the bracelet and the items I kept from Freddie's house. I press his pyjama bottoms to my nose again, but the smell is so faint now I can barely make it out. The truth is, Freddie and I were not perfect. No relationship is perfect. All we can do is try to be the best version of ourselves, even if that means going the extra mile and extinguishing the parts that are less desirable. I think, perhaps, that's where I slipped up. In fairness, he didn't make it easy for me. Not by the end.

I'd thought Freddie opening up to me in the pub would mark one of these moments of transition. Just as Jack and I have worked through our first disagreement, I'd thought his confession was a sign of his trust in me: a sign that I was more important to him than whoever this other woman was. I was wrong. If anything, in the days that followed, he seemed almost embarrassed by what he'd told me, like he regretted saying anything at all. When I tried to ask him about it, he brushed me off, mumbling something about having it under control. I tried to be there for him, but he threw my efforts back in my face at every turn. And still, he periodically disappeared at the end of the work day, leaving me to wonder where we stood. And I just *knew* that he was going to see her. For some reason, I wasn't enough for him.

It drove me a bit mad. I can admit it now. I did some things, then, that I am not proud of.

With Jack, it's different. If I can show him how much I care – how far I am willing to go – then we will have something very special indeed.

I fold the pyjamas and put them back in the drawer. As I am turning to leave, I catch sight of the daffodils he bought me on my first night here. Brown, crispy and drooping sadly, they are obviously dead. I'm hopeful he'll buy me some new ones soon.

Jack arrives home right on time, and when I hear his key in the door I am ready for him. My phone buzzes again as the door swings open – the same unknown number – and I fumble for it, switch it off. I will not allow anything to ruin this. I take up my position on the stairs, lengthen my spine, and adjust the jumper so that it falls in the most flattering way. Beneath, the lacy bra I found in a drawer itches. Alice's breasts were clearly bigger than mine, and the material rubs uncomfortably.

Jack doesn't see me immediately, which is a disappointment. I have to clear my throat awkwardly to catch his attention. But, oh, it's worth it when he does. Because, when he sees me, Jack looks at me in a way he never has before. I see the change – that slight widening of the eyes, the 'o' shape to his mouth – and I know I've finally got it right. No photograph needed. The answer has been sitting in the wardrobe all along.

He drops his bag on the floor, comes towards me quickly. And when he kisses me, it is with a hunger that I haven't experienced from him before. Like he is entirely consumed by me. 'God I've missed you,' he breathes into my neck – a neck I daubed with bath oil just before he arrived.

It's different, this time. This time, he is not tentative when he takes me up to bed. There is very little tenderness.

It's rougher, laced with an urgency and dominance that I didn't expect. I go along with it, obviously, but there is something jarring about it, and it's not just that he doesn't seem to care about my own pleasure. This feels like it is for him, and him alone. Still, I maintain the performance. I make all the right noises, but when it's finished – when he has rolled away panting – I feel like I need to shower.

I don't speak as I pad through to the bathroom and scrub at my skin. Afterwards, I pull on the same clothes and go downstairs to find Jack. I'd like him to hug me. To pull me to him and press a kiss to my forehead.

But he doesn't even look up as I enter the sitting room. He is setting a glass down on the table as I approach. A glass filled with amber liquid.

'I thought you'd given up?' I say, stupidly, too shocked to think about the reception these words might receive.

He whips round, eyes unfocused. 'Get off my fucking back, OK? You're always whining about something.'

And – for the first time in my life – I don't even consider arguing. Simply back out of the room, and up the stairs. I take off Alice's clothes, slip into my pyjamas. Then, I take one look at Jack's bed – still rumpled from the activity – and go into the other room. The room with the dead daffodils. I lie there for a very long time before I fall asleep.

Jack has already left by the time I wake the next morning. But when I poke my head into his bedroom, I see that he has laid an outfit on the bed. It's not one I've seen before, and it's far too smart to be worn around the house. When I lift it to my nose, her smell – that tuberose tang – still lingers around the collar.

36

I decide to give Jack the benefit of the doubt. We all have bad days – days when things aren't clicking as well as they should – and he's had a shock. I'd likely be confused – discombobulated, even – if he turned up wearing one of Freddie's novelty shirts. If he turned up smelling like Freddie. It's all part of the process. And although the sex needs considerable work, the way he looked at me when he saw me on the stairs, that hunger in his eyes? Well, that's what I've been searching for. I felt special again.

So, I put on the clothes he laid out on the bed.

I won't mention the drinking again. He's worse when he's sober, and, if it helps bridge the gap between Alice and me further, then it might even be useful. I've had to block that number that keeps calling. It's been incessant – at least once every two hours. Whatever it is, Mum is not giving up easily.

Once I've decided what I'm going to cook for dinner and been to the shops and done all the necessary prep,

I pass the time until Jack gets home on my laptop in the sitting room. I'm firing off a message to Tilly when I catch sight of the folder of photos I keep of Freddie. My chest pangs as I click on it. As hundreds of images of him fill the screen. I scroll through them, wondering if this is a strange sort of self-sabotage, yet I'm unable to stop looking.

There are a few of Freddie and me together: in a pub, his hand resting on my shoulder, heads tilted slightly towards one another, as though there were an electro-magnetic field between us. We could barely keep away from each other in those days. Before everything started going wrong. I scroll again. One of him in a towel in his bedroom, hair wet, looking slightly away from the lens. One of him at his cousin's wedding, giving a speech that made everyone laugh. It's hard to believe this is the same man who gave away everything we had so easily.

'What the hell do you think you're doing?'

I jolt back to the present and twist in my seat to see Jack in the doorway. In full view of the screen. He looks furious.

Fuck. I was doing so well. This will be a tricky one to navigate my way out of. Feminine wiles? Grief-stricken girlfriend? I can't decide how to play it. So, I go with the safer option. Meek and weak. Because – when all else fails – men do like to be reminded that they could overpower us, should the mood strike them. I discovered that little nugget from a Reddit thread that started with a man going on about why *men love feminine women*. It descended, quickly, into something far darker.

I make a show of pressing a delicate hand to my chest, because my feminine constitution can hardly take the surprise. Victorian women had it right: if it weren't a little overdramatic, I might even consider fainting.

'Jack,' I say breathlessly. 'I didn't know you were home.'

I have no idea exactly what the time is, but from the light outside he must be back earlier than usual.

'Well. I am. I got sent home. My meeting went badly.'

I stand from the sofa, still with my hand pressed to my chest, and approach him. 'I'm sorry to hear that.'

'And then I come back here, and you're looking at pictures of your ex?'

'I can explain.' The tremor to my voice is entirely real. 'I remembered that I still had photos of him. And it didn't feel right to have them. Not when what we have is so good. I was about to delete them.'

It is a flimsy lie, but the words trip over themselves in their haste to leave my mouth, which adds a nice legitimacy to what I am saying. He's doing that thing again; his eyes dart over me as though he is trying to read the lie on my face, but I don't make amateur mistakes. Not any more. I keep my eyes fixed on his, reach out, interlace our fingers. 'You know it's you, Jack,' I say, voice low and earnest. 'It's always been you.'

And when he doesn't resist, I stretch onto my tiptoes and give him a swift kiss on the cheek. He nods his acceptance when I lower back down. Like – once again – he was only searching for confirmation of my dedication to him.

'Just get rid of them,' he says roughly, and I am so pleased to have avoided another meltdown, I nod vigorously. I won't, though. I need to keep these photos as a reminder of how wrong a relationship can go. 'After dinner, OK?'

My cooking skills have improved dramatically already. Turns out, practice really does make perfect. I do, admittedly, try extra hard for dinner that night, to make up for my faux pas, and, as I pull the chicken out of the oven, I congratulate myself on my versatility. I am excelling at the parochial gender roles of a half-century ago, though I'm not entirely sure that's something to boast about.

After dinner, Jack reminds me to delete the photographs of Freddie, and I make a show of collecting my laptop, tilting the screen slightly away from him so he can't see that I'm simply moving them into another folder.

It does strike me that now would be a good opportunity to ask to see a photograph of Alice – quid pro quo and all that – but there is still a faint crackle of tension in the air, and I don't want to rock the boat. We sit on the sofa and the chest seems to wink at me from the corner. I've had no luck getting into it, despite renewed efforts to find the key and – when that failed – pick the lock. It's a skill I realise I should really have taught myself earlier. It would have saved me a whole lot of trouble.

I haven't forgotten Jack's reaction when I asked about Alice being in remission. The way his eyes shot to the left. And I can't help but feel that the answers may be contained in that chest. I don't like the idea that he might still be hiding something from me. Honesty and trust form the foundation for any good relationship, after all. And, while I am going to great lengths to prove my dedication to him, he seems to have forgotten that it's a two-way street.

37

The next afternoon a woman approaches me. Another slow morning with nothing to do except plan the next meal, and I was itching to leave the house. I don't know how Alice endured it: the monotony. The endless hours that yawned and stretched and languished. *I am languishing.* I tell myself I don't mind, that this is all part of the plan. I remind myself how special our bond is, that this – the clothes, the adopted traits – is a way of proving to him that I care. Sometimes, though, it's not quite enough. Sometimes, it all feels a little boring.

I'm sure it's the reason I've become so caught up by the past in recent days, craving that excitement again. That sense of drive and perseverance. Of finally getting what you want.

Conscious that I was descending into self-pity – always dangerous for someone of my constitution – I left the house. I had a vague plan to stop by the café, anticipating the onslaught of sympathy that Mick would provide, but

I don't get that far. Because there is a shout from behind me as I turn off Jack's road, and I swing round to see a woman marching towards me.

'Has he got you wearing her clothes?' She delivers this with so much anger and aggression, I take an involuntary step backwards.

This woman is blond, red-lipped and furious. Her face is twisted with it. And I realise I'm glad of it. I'd take anything at this point. Anything to shatter the boredom.

'I asked you a question.' Her jaw is set, eyes narrowed. Her accent bears the distinct trace of money and good breeding: clipped consonants, rounded vowels.

'I'm sorry,' I say, calmly. 'I have absolutely no idea who you are.' And I don't.

'Well, why would you? You're just the stranger who jumped into her bed when it was barely cold.'

I think we can safely assume she is talking about Alice. People always get so tedious about honouring memories, like the deceased are sentient, not decaying corpses that are currently six feet under and riddled with worms or burned to a cinder and scattered to the wind. Like they are beings that continue to live and breathe among us. It's all bollocks. That's the point of death. They're gone, and any claim they hold over those they've left behind should have evaporated with them.

But I'm not one to miss an opportunity to take the moral high ground when it's presented to me. 'I'm sorry,' I say in a dignified manner. 'Are you talking about Alice Reynolds?'

'Yes, I'm talking about Alice Reynolds,' she spits.

'Hasn't she been dead for, what – six, seven months now?'

I know the exact date, of course – it's the same as Freddie's unfortunate departure from this world – but I'm enjoying how her face is reddening.

'Which,' she says, 'is absolutely no time at all. So, I'll ask you again: has he got you wearing her clothes?'

Truth be told, I am in Alice's clothes again, and Jack did pick them for me. They were laid out on the bed, like yesterday, but this time he'd placed some underwear on top. Not my usual choice: comfort is key, and thongs always make me feel like I'm being split in half; but I sighed and put on the lacy garment anyway.

'Yes,' I say. No acting necessary. It's the truth, which makes a nice change.

'That sick fuck,' she says, and she takes a step away from me. 'Do you know what you're getting yourself into?'

The hysteria is starting to get dull. 'Look,' I say, holding out a conciliatory palm. 'I can see you're upset and I'm not trying to step on anyone's toes. But Alice is *dead*. She's not coming back. And the way I see it, better for me to be wearing her things than them rotting in a cupboard. No need for clothes where she's gone.'

She stares at me, eyes wide, then takes a step backwards and begins shaking her head. 'You're just like him. I've been trying to call you – to warn you – but clearly you don't need my help.'

'No,' I say, and I shrug. 'I don't.'

'He makes me sick. And so do you.' And then she does something that I would never have expected from someone of her girls' school training. She spits on the pavement in front of me, turns on her heel and walks away.

It is the sort of gesture that once would have called forth a spew of vicious words. But they don't come. I stare at her retreating back with my mouth open, indignation pulsing through my veins.

I walk to Mum's, unsettled. I had assumed that my phone ringing off the hook was her trying to get through to me but now that woman has put paid to that theory, it feels, suddenly, important to check she's alright. We may be in the midst of our worst argument to date, but usually we'd have patched things up by now, begun a tentative reconciliation. I unblock her number and try to call her as I walk, but it goes straight to voicemail. I have no leverage with her any more. Perhaps she meant it when she said she never wanted to see me again. The thought makes me feel inexplicably sad.

When I get to the house, there is no twitch of the curtain on my approach, and when I ring the bell nobody comes to the door. Perhaps Tilly changed her mind, and really did call the police.

When Jack gets home that evening, I wait until he is seated at the table before I broach the subject of the woman.

'Blond, red lipstick. Tall, about five-eight. Do you know her?'

I watch his reaction carefully, and – yes – there it is. Once again, his eyes flick to the left. He takes a careful sip of wine. I log it, but don't react. Just continue to spoon pasta onto his plate. A simple dinner this evening; I wasn't in the mood to slave away in the kitchen all afternoon. Not when Mum's phone continues to go to voicemail. Not when I'm still fizzing from my encounter with that woman.

'It must have been Serena,' he says eventually.

'Serena?' Voice nice and light. Even though the bitch spat at my feet like I was nothing. Like I meant nothing. 'She was... very angry to see me.'

He clears his throat. 'Yes. I'm not surprised. Serena was...' A slight pause – slightly too long. I pause too, as I'm spooning pasta onto my own plate. 'An ex of mine.'

An ex. It would explain the vitriol. It would explain the fury. It wouldn't explain why she knew exactly what Alice's clothes looked like. Unless he did the same to her: dressed her up like a child's doll just to stopper the chasm Alice's absence left behind? Maybe I misjudged Serena. Maybe she was playing the exact same role I am. It's not beyond the realms of possibility that Jack had an affair before me: he's famously cagey about his past. But what doesn't make sense is how concerned she seemed about Alice. Too concerned for some jilted ex.

I decide to let it lie. Jack doesn't like it when I press. But I mull over the problem in my head as I shovel pasta into my mouth.

It's a few seconds later that I realise Jack's looking at me. His brows are pulled together as he watches the fork travel to my mouth.

'Everything OK?' Sweet, light, girlish. Even as the problem of Serena churns over and over in my mind.

'All fine,' he says, but I don't believe him. 'It's just – you've got quite a big portion there. That's a lot of unnecessary calories.'

I place my fork – still full of spaghetti – back onto my plate. He did not just say that. The fury is so intense, I'm sure there's a flicker of it on my face. I shut it down: force myself to breathe. This isn't him. He's pushing me away, testing my loyalty.

'Of course,' I say. 'You're right. I wasn't thinking.'

But later, in bed, his words come back to me and the fury rises again, and I release it on him. I take control, tighten my fingers round his throat until he is gasping for breath. He is stronger than me. And it's not long before he is on top of me, and his hand is tangled in my hair, and his breath is hot on my face as he pulls my head back by my scalp.

'Good girl. Good girl, Alice,' he says, as he finishes.

38

I smear another piece of white bread with butter. The full-fat stuff. Not that 'naturally light' bollocks he has in the fridge. Fuck the diet. Fuck this new version of Jack. Fuck it all. Today, I'm going to eat what I like. I cram the piece of bread into my mouth until it is bulging. A globule of jam lands on my chin, but I don't wipe it away. I swallow, take another bite. The waistband of my – Alice's – jeans is cutting into my stomach, but still I stuff in more and more and more.

'Am I interrupting?'

I look up. Martha is standing in the doorway, a bulging plastic bag clutched in her fist. The bread is still claggy in my mouth, so at first I can only chew at her. Then – with a not inconsiderable amount of effort – I swallow, and wave my hand across the kitchen.

'Not at all. Go ahead.'

'I came to see you, actually,' she says.

I blink at her. This is unexpected. I have gone out of my way to avoid Martha since our first unfortunate encounter, and I can't help but feel she has been doing the same to me.

'Why?' Brazen, bold. Entirely unlike the image I've been going to great lengths to portray to her.

She's quiet for a moment. 'I thought you might be hungry. He told me to bring some food.'

'Well, as you can see, I'm fine. So, he doesn't need to worry.'

'I can see that,' she says, raising an eyebrow. 'I'd better put all this away just in case.'

'I'm perfectly capable of buying my own food.' I don't bother to bury my irritation beneath civility. I am tired of being civil.

She shrugs. 'I'm sure you are. I'm just doing what I've been told.'

I watch her unpack the items onto the counter. Fruit, 0% yoghurt, nuts, vegetables, wholegrain rice cakes. I wrinkle my nose, aware that the disgust is written on my face.

'Was this your choice, or did it come from Jack?'

'Jack sent me a list. But' – she reaches into the bag, pulls out a packet of chocolate biscuits – 'these weren't on it.' She pushes them towards me. I'm so touched by this act of kindness that I feel my edges soften. Suddenly embarrassed by my behaviour, I swipe at the jam on my chin.

'I really appreciate it, Martha. Thank you. Jack's right. I can be so forgetful. That's why I'm eating this... not exactly nutritious.' I grimace, gesturing to the plate, feeling suddenly disgusted with myself. This is not who I am now.

She presses her lips together and continues to unload items from the bag.

'Here, let me help you,' I say. Earnest, *likeable*. The woman from two minutes ago wiped clean away.

I transfer the yoghurt to the fridge, and she stands back to allow me to move past her. It's not an entirely selfless act. I feel like I'm coming apart at the seams, unable to stop the darkness in me seeping through. Jack's behaviour recently is bringing out the worst in me. Nothing I do is right any more, and I can't help but feel that there's something I'm missing. That he isn't being honest with me. Martha just might be the key.

'I was talking to Jack about this place the other day. He mentioned it's become a bit of a burden.'

Her hand stills in the bag.

'Yes,' she says stiffly. 'I imagine it's not easy to keep it up.'

'Hard. That he didn't really have a choice in the matter, I mean. It's a big responsibility to take on. Whole family reputation resting on him.' I keep my back to her, one hand still in the fridge like I'm searching for something, not wanting to spook her.

'Well,' she says slowly. 'I'm not sure that's entirely true. Jack didn't have to take the whole house on. He chose that. His father gave him a choice.'

This is new. Jack implied the house was a poisoned chalice, one that tied him to this life of privilege he resented. This life he did not want. Choice certainly never featured in our discussion.

'But Jack's father pressed him into it, didn't he? Made him feel like he didn't have a real say in the matter,' I say.

She's silent for a long time, considering me. Finally, she sighs. 'Jack's father could be difficult, yes. But his heart was in the right place. He would never have forced Jack into something if he really didn't want it. They always had a complicated relationship, but he cared about him.'

Jack told a bald-faced lie then. I do not like being lied to. I do not like being deceived. And it seems Jack is skilled in both departments. I wish he'd see that he could tell me anything and I'd still love him. That's what love is all about. Accepting the good with the bad. The ugly with the beautiful.

'Complicated how?'

'I really shouldn't be telling you this.' Martha closes her eyes briefly, as though waging some internal war with herself. Something gives, and – after a moment – she carries on, 'Jack wasn't the easiest child, truth be told. In fact, he was incredibly difficult. His parents didn't know what to do with him. They sent him to a day school in London, and he was kicked out for bullying. Jack could be incredibly charming and he could generally talk himself out of any trouble, but it got so bad the school were eventually forced to make a decision. So, they sent him to another school, and the same thing happened. Eventually, they sent him to boarding school. I don't think they knew what else to do with him. The problem there was drugs.

That lasted for a while. Drove his parents nearly spare. The arguments that Jack and his father would have...’ She shudders. ‘They were horrible. He’d threaten to kick him out, but he was too soft to actually go through with it. Then Jack met Alice, and everything changed.’ She breaks off.

I press: ‘*How*? How did everything change?’

But Martha seems to gain control of herself. Perhaps I seemed overly eager, because she clamps a hand to her mouth. ‘I shouldn’t’ve said any of that. I’m sorry. Please don’t mention it...’

‘Of course I won’t, Martha, but I want to know. I *deserve* to know, don’t you think?’

But she’s shaking her head in something that looks like fear. ‘No. I’ve said too much. I’m sorry.’

I conceal my irritation behind a mask of calm understanding. She’s given me a lot to think about. Clearly, I can’t trust anything that Jack has told me of his past. He’s been lying from the start, and it hurts to know how little he trusts me. My job, now, is to sift through everything he gave me as decree, and piece together the real truth. Only then can we really move forward, united.

I look at Martha, who is clearly panicked. Her hand shakes as she puts away the final few items. Usually, I love it when people talk out of turn, enjoying the transference of power. Now, I just feel sorry for her.

I’m about to promise her that I will say nothing to Jack about what she’s told me, press her on the issue of Alice, when her phone, which she has set down on the counter next to the shopping bag, begins to vibrate with a call.

She isn't quick enough to silence it, and I see what's on the screen. Serena – the red-lipped woman who spat at my feet – is trying to call her.

And the anger returns in a flood.

'It was you,' I whisper. It makes sense now. Her insistence that she took my number, her faux concern for my wellbeing. Now I know where Serena's conviction that Jack and I were sleeping together came from. Martha's been feeding her information about me all along. I thought I might have made a friend here. The rejection is painful, and I want to lash out. To hurt her in the way she has hurt me.

Martha's eyes are wide. 'Please – please don't tell Jack. I can explain.'

'Get out,' I say quietly, and, for the first time in a long while, I feel the power in being entirely myself. Cold, hard, unforgiving. 'Right. Now.' I bare my teeth in a snarl.

'Please, Iris.'

'Out!' I roar. Her face flushes red and she looks like she wants to say more, but her shoulders sag. She collects her bag and scurries out of the door, leaving me alone with my thoughts.

39

I regret it the moment I hear the door close. Kicking her out like that. An unattractive loss of control that compromises me and everything I have been working towards. I shouldn't have revealed that side to myself. I should've at least mined her for the information she does have before kicking her out so definitively. I can't believe she played me like that. Reeled me in with biscuits, kept me sweet by feeding me details of Jack's past, all so she could report back to Serena. Now, I don't know who to trust.

I feel as though I am going mad. So many moving parts, so many different accounts. And even if Martha was lying, I am sure that Jack is, too, about something. I've become very good at sniffing out lies since Freddie.

For lack of any other leads, I try the chest again, but it's still locked, and all the frustration that I have suppressed erupts. I aim a kick at the old wood, but only succeed in stubbing my toe so hard I grit my teeth in pain. I need air. I need to get out of this house.

But when I go through to the hallway to collect my key, I find it's not there. I'm always so careful about where I leave it – in the little bowl atop the radiator cover as you walk in. I always like to have an exit strategy, just in case things go wrong. You can never be too careful. But it's gone. And I have a very good idea of who has taken it.

He *still* does not quite trust me. That much is clear. I don't know what more I can do to convince him. Trust is a difficult thing. Once it's gone, it's nearly impossible to rebuild. It was just the same with Freddie. That lack of trust drove me to depths I did not think myself capable of.

Now, the plan comes to me fully formed. A risk, but the time for caution has passed. I must get to the truth. I still have my phone, so I log in to my own Facebook profile: the one that bears my own picture. There are limited details about my life on there. I've never had friends to tag me in pictures, but I prefer it that way. That way, I can control the narrative.

I find Catherine's Facebook profile and tap out my message.

Hi Catherine, it's Iris (staying with Jack). I'm sorry to get in touch out of the blue, but I'm worried about him. His drinking is getting out of control again. Is there a time you could meet today? At the house? He's out until 7.

It's not a complete lie. Jack's promise to go to AA was evidently a platitude. I can smell him when he comes home at night. That stench of alcohol that I associate with my mother.

The reply comes ten minutes later.

I'll get a train up this afternoon. Be with you at 5.

I have the whole day to perfect my persona, and it is so effective – that look of calm concern, when underneath I am still reeling – that, when Catherine enters the house, she takes one look at me and pats me gently on the arm.

'Thank you so much for getting in touch. I can't tell you how nice it is to know that someone is looking out for him.'

I nod reverentially. 'Of course. I'd do anything for him – Jack.' And I would. I really would. She gives me a strange look. A cross between pity and alarm.

'Come through,' I say, and I lead the way to the kitchen. I bustle around, making a show of my familiarity with my surroundings. Allow silence to settle between us, so that – when I break it – she will hang on my every word. I take my time – asking only if she takes milk and sugar – and I am sure I succeed in appearing like the perfect hostess.

Finally, I set the tea down between us and take a deep breath.

'I think it's all getting to him,' I say. 'He's been drinking earlier and earlier. I suspect it's because of her. Alice, I mean.' I pause, allow this to sink in. Cracking the door open, so that when my questions come there will be nothing suspicious about them.

She nods slowly. 'Well, yes. That makes sense. It was all so sudden. I thought he was doing better – he was going to work at least – but I suppose grief does hit you when you least expect it.'

'Yes. I have to confess' – I lean forward as though I am taking her into my confidence. Confessing some innate failing of mine in that way that people do when they are trying to form a connection – 'I'm not entirely clear on what happened to Alice. Jack mentioned something about cancer, but I was under the impression that she went into remission. Is that right?'

'Is that what he told you?' Her voice is sharp. 'That she died of the cancer?'

'Well.' I look down. 'He implied it, yes.'

She's shaking her head, face very white. 'Alice didn't die of the cancer. That's just what he'd like to believe,' she says quietly. 'She committed suicide. It rocked the whole family to the core, as you can imagine. I don't think any of us saw it coming.'

'God, I am so sorry, Catherine. I had no idea.' The news rocks me, too. Jack's web spans before me, endless mistruths, misrepresentations. This woman has no reason to lie to me. Jack's been playing me. The real question is why he would lie about something so import- ant? Particularly to me?

'It was terribly sad, yes,' Catherine is saying. 'I'm not surprised Jack turned back to drink. I tried to get him to come and live with me in Dorset, but he insisted he'd be OK.'

I bite my lip, adopt that confessional tone once again. 'I've been trying to move any alcohol I find out of the house. But there always seems to be more. There's a chest in the sitting room. Do you know it?'

'The old antique? In the corner?'

I nod, heart skipping. 'Yes. I think he's hiding his booze in there, and I've looked, but I can't seem to find the key. I don't suppose you have any idea where it might be?'

She looks at me blankly. 'God, I didn't even realise we had a key to that. Did you check the drawer in here?' She nods to an old drawer that contains an assortment of odds and ends, and I do my very best not to roll my eyes. It was – obviously – the first place I looked.

'I have, yes,' I say, regretful. 'Not there.'

'Well, I'll have a think and let you know. And perhaps you can have a think about ways to get him back to rehab.'

'Of course.' I have no intention of doing anything of the sort. 'Oh,' I say lightly. As though the thought has only just occurred to me. 'I don't suppose I could borrow your key to the house? Just for the next couple of days. I think I've misplaced mine.'

'Misplaced it?' Again, there's that slightly sharp edge to her tone. If I didn't know better, I'd say it was almost panicked.

'Yes' I say. 'Frustrating, but I've always been a bit of a

scatterbrain, and I'm sure I just put it down somewhere and forgot where it was.' Silly, ditsy me.

'Of course,' she says, and she rummages in her bag. 'I've got a spare at home anyway.'

'Thank you, Catherine. I really appreciate it.'

She checks her watch. 'I'd better be getting off. Jack will be home soon, and I doubt he'd be pleased if he knew we were talking.' She's right. He'll be home in half an hour.

When she gets to the door, she pauses, gives me a long, searching look. 'Don't think too badly of him, please. He's had a very difficult year. And I know he can be tricky, but his heart's in the right place. When Alice was ill, he spent every moment he could with her. Between him and Alice's friend, Serena, she was barely ever alone.'

The mention of that name very nearly blows my cover, but I wrestle with my face, keep it neutral. 'I know that,' I say. 'He's a kind soul underneath it all.'

I truly believe it. Jack showed me that kindness all those weeks ago, when he recognised that I was someone worth talking to. 'Do let me know about the key to the chest,' I call after her. 'I want to give Jack every possible chance of fighting this.'

She turns in the road. 'Of course I will.'

Jack gets home twenty minutes later. Not everything I said to Catherine was a lie. When he kisses me, in that hungry, possessive way of his, I can taste whisky on his breath.

It is later that night – when Jack is still downstairs, drinking himself into a stupor – that the email from Fiona comes in.

Hi all, as I mentioned briefly last time, please do bring photos with you to the next session. It will be a fun experiment! F x

40

A small bunch of carnations have been placed on top of the blue chair right across the circle from me. Wrapped in clear plastic, so I can only assume Fiona stopped at her local petrol station in a last-ditch attempt at compassion. I suppose it's the thought that counts, but, if *my* entire life was reduced to a bunch of half-dead flowers that still had the price tag attached, I wouldn't be best pleased.

'I know losing Matt might give rise to some complicated emotions in all of you,' Fiona is saying, and, while she is doing her best to sound sincere, there is a definite note of glee to her tone. For a bereavement group leader, presumably a death among your attendees is like Christmas come early. 'He was a big part of this group, and I know that he appreciated the support you gave to him. Each and every one of you. Hopefully, he can find some peace now.'

A ridiculous statement. Matt went to the grave furious, and – if such a thing as the afterlife does exist – I have no doubt he is currently in the process of killing his brother once and for all.

The rest of the group are still in silent shock. I don't know why. It's not like we didn't expect it, and I liked Matt, but you'd think we'd be better equipped to deal with news like this.

I shift my weight and feel Freddie's photo crinkle in my pocket. I'd have liked to have spent longer choosing the perfect one – considered, in fine detail, how best to present him to the rest of the group – but Jack was hovering around and the last time he caught me looking at photos of Freddie retribution had been swift. I had to pick one at random, slamming the laptop closed with my heart hammering when I heard Jack's footsteps in the corridor.

The one I've chosen is fine but doesn't show him at his very best. Gregarious, funny, charming. It's a pretty bog-standard image of a white, middle-class male drinking a pint, but I'm just pleased I was able to get one printed at all.

Jack seems to have sensed a shift in me since his mother came over, like the urge that is building in my chest – that drive to find out everything I can about him – is a living, pulsating thing in the room between us. He's clung ever closer as a result. I never mentioned that I suspect he took my key. So as far as he knows, I'm still confined to the house when he leaves each morning. I slipped out yesterday to get this photo printed, and drew the fresh air into my lungs with a renewed sense of vigour. I'm getting closer to the truth, I can sense it.

And Jack and I will finally have an open, honest relationship. Essential for any healthy union, according to Google. There are things I will never be able to tell him, of course. Things about Freddie, Marcie. But if one half of us lays all their cards on the table, then perhaps it negates the need for the other to do the same.

He'll be furious when he discovers me gone, and, while I don't like to make him angry, it seems he's always hovering at the brink these days. Perhaps all those lies are catching up with him.

We spend some time reminiscing about Matt, before it becomes painfully clear that we knew very little about his personal life. That's the problem with these things – we tend to define someone by their loss, and everything else falls to the wayside. Once that's gone, you realise you never really knew them at all.

After an awkward pause, Fiona clears her throat.

'Right. Shall we push on then?'

There is a general murmur of assent, at the same time as the swing door behind me bangs open. It's such an aggressive noise amidst the solemn silence that I twist in my seat with a thrill of horror. Because there is only one person who would be angry enough to open the door with such force. And there he is.

Jack strides right through the centre of the circle, hands clenched into fists. He moves Matt's flowers with so little ceremony, I hear Fiona tut. Then he sits heavily and stares at me with such intensity that I look at my feet. I suppose it doesn't take a genius to figure out where I might be disappearing to each Tuesday. Probably should've seen this one coming. But Jack is impossible to read, and I was sure he believed me last time I said I was just walking to clear my head.

Perhaps I'm not as convincing as I thought. Maybe he's suspected all along.

'Jack!' Fiona says. 'We didn't think you'd be joining us any more.'

'I'm so sorry for my absence,' he says with such candour I almost believe him. 'I've found recent weeks difficult, but I'm back now.'

'Well, we're glad to see you.'

This is an understatement. Rita's hand has flown to her hair. She stopped with the excessive make-up after Jack's absence continued, and now her face is filled with regret. Even Hannah has sat up straighter in her seat. Only Charlie hasn't reacted. He's still staring, unseeing, at the centre of the circle.

'Right.' Fiona's face is an unsightly pink colour. 'Well, Jack, I'm afraid the format is a little different this week. We've all brought photos of those we've lost. We're going to share them with the rest of the group.'

Jack's eyes flick to mine. Shit. He's going to know that I didn't delete all of Freddie's photos.

'That's fine,' he says, and he reaches into his pocket and pulls out his phone. For all my planning, for all my desperation to get into that chest, I realise now that he's been keeping a digital record of Alice's life that I could have accessed at any time. Rookie mistake – I've been making a lot of those lately. It's easy to break into a phone, if only you know how. I've been sharing a bed with this man who is passed out drunk most nights. It would have been easy to swipe it from his bedside table.

He's scrolling through it now, and, despite my discomfort at his sudden appearance, I experience a swell of excitement too. Finally, I am going to see the woman I have been basing myself on. I will see how she compares to me, what I could do differently with my hair and my posture.

I pull Freddie from my own pocket. If I'd known that Jack was going to be here, I would've found time to pick the very best picture I could. Because Freddie is a reflection of me, even in death.

'Could everyone pass their photographs to the left please?' Fiona jigs her leg with nervous excitement.

Jack hands his phone over to Hannah, and I swallow. I would like to go and snatch it from her hands, but I must practise patience, keep my face neutral. It would be unseemly to be too keen. Morbid, even.

Rita hands me her photograph and I give a cursory glance towards her father. He looks much as you'd expect from a man who celebrated his retirement with a private cruise around the Caribbean. Bullish in stature, with the pinched, wily features of a rodent. He stares defiantly at the camera, wine-stained teeth bared in a smile. I can barely compute that this is the man deserving of those long, tedious Facebook posts. What is it about fathers being so unbelievably disappointing?

Freddie's not getting the reaction I hoped for. I wanted glances in my direction – faces filled with sympathy as they took in this man who was taken from me too soon. But – after superficial glances – he is passed unceremoniously to the left again. I knew I should have taken longer over my selection. It's Jack's fault he's not getting the attention he deserves. If only I'd been allowed to ponder my choice, pick one that truly reflected Freddie and everything he stood for…

It doesn't help that Alice, by comparison, seems to draw sharp intakes of breath from whomever she is passed to. Even Fiona – hardened harridan that she is – puts a hand to her mouth. When she looks up, I'm sure I see tears in her eyes.

It's not fair on Freddie. It's not fair on any of the other people who are being handed round the circle, and I can't fathom what is drawing such sadness from all of them.

I'm so distracted by the progress of Alice round the circle, I can barely bring myself to look at Hannah's mother: a kind, if fragile-looking woman. I wonder what picture I'd use of Mum. What people would assume about her.

And then, finally, it's time. Rita hands me Jack's phone and, the moment I catch sight of the image there, I very nearly drop it. I don't want to look, but at the same time I can't look away. That direct gaze, levelled at the camera, so different to how I initially imagined her. This is not the meek woman I'd pictured. This is someone very different altogether. Staggeringly beautiful, an ethereal, unpinpointable essence that rocks me to my very core. And even when I close my eyes, I can still see her, like an echo that will not stop reverberating. She stares right into the lens, right into me, and there is something accusatory about her gaze. Like she knows exactly who I am. Exactly what I have done.

The nausea comes on quickly. I'm suddenly clammy with it, the phone slippery in my hand. I know I need to keep it together, but she is lodged firmly in my head now, and I can't focus. All I can see is her. I don't even care that Jack is still staring at me, a muscle tic-ing in his jaw. I need to get out. I need the fresh air.

I'm brought back to myself by a buzzing in my pocket, and I pull out my phone like it is a beacon in the darkness. Another unknown number, but at this point I don't care. It gives me the excuse I need to exit this hot, airless room, where it feels like I can't breathe. So I can no longer see those blue, haunting eyes.

I push Jack's phone into Charlie's hand and stumble to my feet, glancing across the circle at Jack. Freddie has reached him now. He is looking down at the photograph with pure, unadulterated hatred stamped across his features, but I can't worry about that now. I stagger to the door and wrench it open, aware that I have drawn every eye in the room, and, for the first time, I wish they wouldn't look at me.

In the corridor, I lift the phone to my ear, still shaking. 'H-hello?'

'Is that Iris Jones?' A man's voice. I don't recognise it.

'Yes.'

'Hello. My name is Brian. I'm calling from the coroner's office. Is there somewhere quiet you can talk?'

'Yes. I can speak now.'

'Are you by yourself?'

'Yes.'

'Is there someone you can ask to be with you?'

Not Jack. Not after I caught that expression on his face. 'No.'

'OK.' An uncomfortable pause. 'Well, I'm calling about your mother, Sarah Jones?'

My heartbeat suddenly feels very faint. 'I'm sorry to have to give you this news over the phone. Your mother was found dead earlier this afternoon. We're yet to do a post-mortem, but it looks as though she's been dead for quite some time.'

Dimly, I'm aware that I have slumped against the wall, gasping for oxygen that doesn't seem to be there.

'How?' I whisper.

'I can't say with any certainty, but it looks as though she might have fallen down the stairs.'

I try to focus on his voice, but I zone in and out and the questions pound every inch of me. When? How long after I left? Was she alone? Did she think of me at all? Was she there when I rang the bell the other day? I disliked her, hated her even, by the end, but I didn't want this. Brian's voice seems like it's coming from a long way away.

He is saying something else about the timing of the post-mortem, and asking if I would like to come and see the body, and, vaguely, I hear myself saying no. I can't think of anything worse than seeing the body of the woman who never loved me like she loved her other daughter. I've outlived both of them now.

'Who found her?' I whisper.

'It was a…' The sound of rustling paper. 'Richard Jones. Her ex-husband, I believe.' After all this time, he went to see her.

'Well, if there's nothing else you need to ask…' Brian trails off. When I don't speak, he mumbles a sorry and says goodbye, and the line goes dead.

And all I can think is that Mum went to her grave and she never knew the truth. She never found out what happened to Marcie. I wonder if I should have told her.

41

I went back to school a month after Marcie's death. A month of tiptoeing the house, listening to my mother's grief, my father's flat monotone. I was nervous about returning. That I'd go back to being branded strange and withdrawn. I didn't even have my connection with Marcie to draw from any more.

That morning, I dressed in my school uniform, then paused by the mirror. I should, I realised, pay tribute to Marcie in some way. I fished the bracelet out from under the bed and fastened it round my wrist.

I heard the whispers as soon as I stepped into the playground. I noticed heads turn to look at me, and eyes widen. I even heard a gasp. I ignored them all. I walked straight through to the classroom. Billy smiled at me, but I ignored him. I noticed several people half rise in their seats when I arrived, as though they wanted to speak to me but didn't know how to begin. I realised that I was in a unique position. I was the only person who could shed light on the tragedy that had befallen Marcie Jones.

I stood taller with the knowledge and waited for them to come to me.

No one wanted to approach me at first. I spent my first morning alone as usual, staring at the front of the class-room. I enjoyed how kind the teachers were. They pulled me back at the end of lessons and told me I didn't need to do the homework, that I could stay inside at lunchtime, that I could go home whenever I wanted. Eyes followed me wherever I went.

A pack of three approached me first. Olivia, Jessica and Helena. Marcie's three best friends. They made their move at lunchtime, dragging their feet, arranging their faces into sad expressions that didn't quite hide the hunger in their eyes. I pretended not to notice their approach. 'Iris,' Olivia whispered. I jerked my head up. 'Are you OK? We heard what happened.'

I stifled a sob, and she put her arm round me. With this first contact came more. Soon, I was swarmed with people. It was the first time I had ever been the subject of such intense scrutiny. They clamoured for answers like starving dogs, feeding off whatever scraps I threw for them.

'It was awful,' I said over and over again. 'Just awful. She was just there one moment and gone the next.' I pictured Marcie's face as I said it: the surprise, the shock, the horror, the fear.

'We're so sorry for your loss, Iris.' Again, and again, and again. Whispered like a prayer.

The feeling was electric. I've craved it ever since.

42

Vaguely, I hear the door bang open behind me. Jack's thunderous face softens as he sees me slumped on the floor. I feel his hands – his warm hands – on the tops of my arms, heaving me up, shaking me gently by the shoulders, asking what's wrong. What's happened? Who was it? And I hear my voice reply as though I am speaking from a long way away. As though I am underwater. Somehow separated from reality. I tell him it's Mum. She's dead.

'I'm so sorry. I'm so sorry for your loss,' he repeats over and over. It doesn't feel like it usually does. There's no thrill attached to the words now. Only a dull, throbbing emptiness.

I don't remember most of the journey home. Jack gets us a taxi, and I watch the tree-shaped air freshener swing with the movement of the car. I barely even register the offensive smell of it: artificial pine, something like bleach.

She's gone. Just like that, snuffed from the world as though she barely existed at all. She didn't exist, though.

Not really. Marcie's death, Dad's departure. They ruined her. Ruined her for me. She still had one living, breathing child, but she chose to mourn the one she always loved more. And it's not so much sadness that settles in me, but a gaping emptiness. My one final, true tie to family gone for ever.

Jack helps me through the front door. He runs a bath, helps me into it. I'm not self-conscious about my nakedness and he doesn't seem to care. He washes my hair, then finds the lime, basil and mandarin bath oil and pours a liberal amount into the water until it turns cloudy.

Another death to take responsibility for. If I hadn't lied about the divorce, would she still be here? I don't know. I picture it. The moment of the fall. I imagine her drunk – drunker than she's ever been before – stumbling against the railing on the landing, mistiming her step. The tumble down the stairs. Her decomposing at the bottom. The smell that must have hit Dad when he entered the house. She was stingy about the heating, so I suppose – with the cool weather we've been having – it probably wasn't as bad as it could have been. A sad, banal way to end a sad, banal life.

Jack wraps a towel round me, steers me through to the bedroom, where he has laid another outfit on the bed. A thin, lacy camisole, which he dresses me in. He pulls back the covers, helps me into bed.

All I can see is Mum's face as she screamed those accusations at me. She took her suspicions to the grave. And then – in among that yawning absence – a distant weight lifts from my shoulders.

It doesn't feel like I expected it to. Over the coming days, I don't wail my pain, because there is none. There's only quiet. My head – for the first time in years – is quiet.

Through it all – the waves of shock and dawning comprehension – Jack is there. Like a solid, steady heartbeat. Just as he was before. He asks few questions. Sometimes, after my bath, he puts his nose to my neck and inhales the scent of the bath oil. I rarely wear the same thing twice, but whatever he pulls down over my head always bears that faint, distinct smell of tuberose. I imagine our skin cells – mine and Alice's – binding together on the material and wonder if my transformation is finally complete.

I'm aware of Martha, too. Like a silent ghost in the corner of rooms: dusting, tidying around me. Sometimes, I catch her throwing an anxious glance in my direction, and I wonder if she is still worried that I will tell Jack what she revealed to me. I won't. Somewhere, vaguely, like a distant reverberation, I remember that what she told me was important.

I have never been entirely reliant on another human being before. I'm not sure I like it. It goes against every instinct I have. I feel horribly vulnerable in Jack's hands, and, though he is nothing but the sweet, solicitous man that I first fell in love with, the memory of those tempestuous moods means I can't settle under his care. He insists I stay in bed, recover. And, when I insist on leaving the bedroom, that I stay confined to the living room, lying on the sofa. He insists on dressing me, bringing me meals – all healthy, of course. Green salads, pulses, grains, rice cakes.

Sometimes he will bring me a whisky, and pull me into him, so that I'm resting against his shoulder. It's too hot when he does this, but he tightens his hand whenever I try to move away. He insists my phone is bad for my recovery – 'you don't need to be inundated with all those updates when you're feeling like this' – and takes it away with him, 'to charge'. When I ask for it, he watches carefully over my shoulder, and – unable to use any of my other accounts under his observation – I tire of it quickly. I swipe the missed calls from unknown numbers away, the memory of Brian and the news he imparted still horribly sharp.

For the first two weeks, Jack works from home. He 'takes care' of every tiny aspect of my life. And then, the Monday after a stiflingly boring weekend in which we complete an entire series on Netflix and I stare unseeingly just to the right of the screen, he announces he's going to have to go into work. I try not to show my delight.

'Are you going to be alright today?' he asks, hovering by the wardrobe. 'Remember, I'm just at the end of the phone. Anything you need… You've had some really bad luck, Iris, but don't blame yourself. What happened to your mother was a terrible, terrible accident.'

I wonder when I mentioned the accident to him: I don't remember doing so, but the whole day was a blur.

'If you're going, I need my phone. To call you, in case I need you,' I say blankly.

'Ah yes. Sorry, I was charging it.' He hesitates before returning with my phone. It feels like freedom when he hands it over, though I work to keep my face impassive, neutral. I sense he wouldn't take kindly to how pleased I am that he is finally leaving me alone to my thoughts.

Before he goes, he lays out another set of clothes on the bed. A cashmere jumper. The same pair of jeans I wore that first day. Then he kisses me on the forehead and leaves. Even his sympathy, the sympathy I loved so much at the beginning, has begun to lose its lustre.

The moment I hear the door close, I rise. It's the first time in weeks that my time is entirely my own, and I shower rather than bathe. Jack insisted on depositing me in the bath every morning, even when I protested. He didn't seem to understand that I hated the idea that I was sitting in my own dirt. Not in the mood to conform to his whims, I choose something different from among Alice's clothing.

After I've dressed, I go downstairs. I think about going out, but, when I look for my secret key that I borrowed from Martha and never gave back, which I'd hidden in my bag, it's gone. I barely have the energy to care. I go through to the kitchen instead. I haven't eaten proper food since Jack took charge of my 'recovery'. There's barely anything in the fridge that isn't horribly healthy, but in the freezer I find an old pizza that I scorch in the oven and then eat, hot grease dripping down my hand.

Jack messages to check how I am – his third this morning already – but I ignore him, log in to my social media profiles and scroll through updates, finally feeling as though I can breathe again.

There's a message from Tilly.

You'll never guess what's happened. The ex is dead!
She fell down the stairs drunk. It's actually quite sad –
Rich found her. He said it was horrible. She was at this
weird angle, and her neck was clearly broken. After
everything that happened, he went over to talk to her.
I think he wanted to try and make things alright, now
so many years have passed, and I think – between you
and me – he's feeling a bit guilty about his daughter.
Not speaking to her for all these years, etc.

In another message directly under this one, she continues:

ANYWAY, get this. Apparently, it's not quite as cut
and dried as they thought. Something to do with the
angle she fell at. I'm sure they'll get to the bottom of it
though, and I guess they've just got to cover all bases.
Hope you're well. xx

I've come to expect this sort of wanton flippancy from Tilly, but it still irks me that she is speaking about my mother with so little respect. Like she's nothing more than an anecdote to entertain her online friend.

I fight the urge to send a snappy reply. She really is an incontestably awful woman, but she's my only link to Dad. My one and only tether to my past. And, as such, I need her. Particularly if Dad wants to put right all he did wrong.

Yes, I can see myself as a daddy's girl. He always made me feel so special. I could play up to it, become overly reliant to the point of idiocy, desperate to please. Without Mum there to pour poison into his ear, and the many years that have passed since Marcie died, I've little doubt I could worm my way back in. Just in case things with Jack don't turn out the way I hope. A blasphemous thought, but it's good to have a back-up plan.

I'm unsettled by the way he's been acting recently. It is not just the over-solicitousness. It's the sense that, when he looks at me now, it is not really me that he sees. And I have my own qualities that should be recognised. That I will make him recognise.

I tap out a reply to Tilly.

That's awful! I know you didn't like her, but that's a horrible way to go. Hope you're all holding up OK. Perhaps speaking to the daughter would be a good idea. She must be upset if her mother has died. I know that's what I'd do.

She doesn't reply, but that's alright. I've planted the seed, and now I can only hope that it blossoms into something productive. I need some good news. It's my turn to be in the limelight now.

I'm not so proud I can't admit when I've made a mistake, and I'm beginning to wonder – particularly after the last two weeks – if my strategy with Jack *has* been a mistake. If turning myself into his wife has perhaps unlocked something in him that he would rather keep buried. It wouldn't be my first mistake. The last time I slipped up, the consequences were fatal. Following Freddie into that alleyway, the argument.

It will be impossible for Jack and me to move forward unless I have all the facts. Unless I understand the reasons behind his ever-changing moods. The Jack I'm living with is so different to the man I fell in love with that, sometimes, I wonder if they're the same person at all.

43

It's not hard to find Serena's number. It's in my call list, and she was tenacious about trying to get in touch before she ambushed me on the street. All I have to do is scroll back a few weeks to find it. I'm conscious, as I tap the message out, that I'm going to have to do a significant amount of grovelling. I allowed the mask to slip too much during our last encounter. I'll have to find a way of spinning it to work in my favour.

The one thing I cling to is Serena's obvious revulsion towards Jack. If she dislikes him that much, I'm hopeful she won't think twice about spilling his secrets.

Now, I just need to find a way to draw her in.

Hi Serena, it's Iris. We met the other day on the street. I know you probably don't want to hear from me, but there are some things I want to discuss with you. Could you give me a ring at some point? Or come over? It's just… I'm finding things with Jack quite tricky at the moment. Thanks, I x

There is a long, long wait until three dots start bouncing at the bottom of the screen. They stop, start again, stop. And then, the message comes through. Short, to the point. Not at all warranting the length of time she took to tap it out.

I'll be there in 10.

This doesn't give me much time to prepare. I can't come across as I did the other day. Clearly, Serena still harbours complex emotions around Alice's death, and that tends to come from a place of love. I would know. It seems, with her, I'll have to align myself with Alice again.

She turns up bang on time. She looks more collected this time – the smear of red lipstick less angry – though her mouth is still set into a hard line. I meet her at the door with a flurry of gratitude, a slightly nervous smile pinned to my face.

'Thank you *so* much for coming,' I say as I usher her into the house. Before I close the door, I check both ways up and down the street. Just in case Jack is lurking somewhere. When I turn round, I see Serena has clocked the action. Her face is softer, a small crease between her brows. I take her through to the kitchen.

Serena knows her way around this house. I have to stop myself from bristling as – in the kitchen – she takes over, flicking on the kettle, taking two mugs from the cupboard. I take a few deep breaths, and seat myself at the breakfast bar as she fusses around.

'It's really kind of you to come,' I say as she pours the water into the mugs.

She turns, gives me a long, searching look. 'I nearly didn't.'

A straight talker. That bodes well.

'Well, I'm grateful you did. I didn't have anyone else to turn to and things have been so... odd recently.'

She doesn't respond – doesn't ask how, or why – just gives a small, jerky nod as though this confirms some internal suspicion of hers.

When she sets the tea down in front of me, she takes a moment to arrange herself on the chair, then fixes me with a piercing look. I hunch my shoulders – a far cry from the woman she met on the street the other day.

Just as I intended, this seems to thaw her slightly. She releases a long sigh. 'I'm not entirely surprised you called. Martha mentioned things have become quite bad recently.'

I send a silent prayer of thanks to Martha as I give a tiny nod.

'Did you tell him we ran into each other the other day?' she asks.

'Yes. He told me you were his ex.'

She looks first surprised, then sickened. 'What? Even for him, that's quite low. I'm not into men, but if I were I still wouldn't go near him even if we were the last two people on earth.'

This is good. She *hates* him, and that is exactly what I was counting on. People are far more likely to reveal secrets about those they dislike. Just look at what I told Dad about Marcie.

'I'm sorry for the way I acted. When we bumped into each other. I was way out of line. He'd been feeding me all these lies. I thought you were… bad news. I see now that I was wrong, but it still doesn't excuse the things I said.'

She nods again – the same jerky movement. 'I could see you were well wrapped up in him. He's good at doing that to people.' She gives a mirthless laugh, then breaks off as she eyes me. 'I still can't believe he's dressing you up in her clothes. I knew he was psychotic, but *fuck*.'

Necessary to feed into her revulsion, befriend her. Suggest we have a common goal. 'I hate it. He lays them out every morning. Gets so, so angry if I say I don't want to wear them.'

Another firm jerk of her head that suggests she has been expecting this, too.

'How did you know Alice?' Timid, tremulous.

She takes a deep breath, closes her eyes for a second. 'I am – I was – Alice's best friend,' she says. 'I asked Martha to get your number. When I heard he'd moved some other woman in… God, I was so angry. I was a bit hot-headed that day. I should've been more understanding. I'm sorry, too.'

'It's fine,' I say quickly. 'You were defending your friend.'

'The reason I wanted to speak to you was to tell you what sort of man you're living with. You need all the facts. But I'll leave you to make your own decision. I just ask that you listen.'

'Of course,' I say, and my heart starts to pump with excitement. This is it.

Like she has been waiting a lifetime for this moment, Serena plunges straight into the story.

She tells me that she met Alice at a bar, on the first night of their freshers' week at uni. They were both nervous, both out of their depth, and they gravitated towards each other.

'We got chatting. She was just impossible not to like, you know? I couldn't believe that anyone could be that nice, but she genuinely was. Didn't have a bad word to say about anyone.'

I stop myself from rolling my eyes. Call me sceptical, but I simply do not believe that anyone could actually be that nice. I wonder what was going on underneath that perfect smokescreen. What dark thoughts she was harbouring, roiling just beneath her surface.

'But that quality made her trust people too easily,' Serena continues. 'We were friends all the way through uni, and I mean *best* friends. We were so close, then. I helped her through everything: bad breakups, bad flatmates. We both moved to London after we gradu-ated, and, not long after, she met Jack. And everything changed.' She sighs.

'Notwithstanding the fact he was a mess – clearly into some quite heavy stuff – he was awful at the dinner where she introduced me to him. It was just the three of us, but he kept making these inside jokes that only the two of them would understand. It sounds ridiculous, but I felt really left out.

'Then, Alice helped him get sober, and if anything he got worse. He acted like he couldn't give less of a shit about her wider circle. He never asked any questions about me, always acted like he thought he was too good for us. I didn't know whether to tell her or not. She was so obviously in love with him, but he was just wrong for her.' She wipes a tear away.

'I wish I *had* said something now. I don't know if it would have made a difference, but at least I could say I'd tried. Anyway, I started to see less of her. At first, she just cancelled on small things, like drinks or a film. But then she cancelled on my birthday. I asked her about it. I told her I felt she was avoiding me. Do you know what she said?'

Serena laughs bitterly.

'She said, "Jack doesn't feel very comfortable around you. He doesn't feel that you like him very much." I'm not going to lie, I was pissed off that she was throwing away a friendship that she'd had for nearly five years for a man she'd known for six months. We stopped speaking so much after that. Whenever I did see them, Jack would make this point of saying how everyone he knew was impressed by her… Like she was some trophy to show off or something. It was bizarre.'

She takes another breath.

'About a year later, he proposed, and she said yes. Do you know how I found out? Fucking Instagram,' she spits.

'I thought the friendship was well and truly over, but she invited me to her engagement drinks. That was something at least. But it was then that she told me that Jack wanted to keep the wedding "in the family", so she'd asked his cousin to be the maid of honour. She said she hoped I didn't mind.

'I couldn't really say anything, could I? A few months went by, and I saw basically nothing of her. It was at the hen party that I noticed she had a bruise on her arm. I asked her about it, and she went red, and snapped at me to mind my own business. It was the most venomous thing I think I'd ever heard come out of her mouth.

'Anyway, they got married, obviously,' Serena continues, 'and at the wedding both of them basically ignored me. I'm not trying to make this about me, I'm really not, but we were so close, and now she was acting like we were distant acquaintances.' She clears her throat again and presses her lips together.

'There was one moment, during the wedding, where it felt like everything was normal again. We were all quite pissed, and she came over and hugged me, and we danced together. Jack must have seen us, because within two minutes he was between us, dragging her away from me. And he just had this look in his eyes as he pulled her away, you know. It was almost mocking. Like he'd got the prize, and he knew there was nothing I could do about it.

'After they got married, I just got on with my life. I stopped hearing from her entirely, and I stopped trying to get in contact with her. And then out of the blue, about two years into the marriage, she called me hysterically crying down the phone. I'm talking like *sobbing*. I'm not going to lie, I was angry. There'd been some huge changes in my life – I'd come out, and she didn't even know about it – but I obviously didn't like to hear her upset. She told me that she'd been diagnosed with breast cancer.

'Well, you can't be angry with someone who's got cancer, so I talked it through with her, and she apologised and said she knew that she'd been a bad friend, and it all felt alright again.

'I went with her to every appointment after that. Jack couldn't do anything about that, of course, because her family were around a lot as well, and he didn't like to be seen as "controlling".' She makes quotation marks with her fingers.

'He was all charm. Then she got really sick while she was going through the chemo, and I think he was grateful for the help.'

Serena dabs her eyes with the heel of her hand. I take a large sip of tea. 'Alice and I got to spend some time together for the first time in years. And she was so supportive of everything I'd been through, and she apologised again. And after a while, she started talking about the marriage, and what it had been like. She said that mostly, it was amazing, but she confided in me that Jack had this domineering streak. He wanted to be with her the whole time, and wanted to know where she was whenever she went out. Her social life had begun to fizzle out by then, and he didn't like her talking to me.'

She coughs. 'Well, I told her to leave him.' Another bitter laugh. 'She didn't, obviously. But after she went into remission, I think she started standing up to him a bit more. I began to see a bit more of her.' Remission. That word again. I press my hands between my thighs so Serena does not notice them shaking.

'Once she was a bit stronger, she became more like her old self. Happy, not as self-conscious as she'd seemed since she was with Jack. It was like the old days. She would sneak out for our lunches so he wouldn't know she'd left.

'We got really close again, and I kept trying to get her to leave him, but she'd always shut down. Then, one day, she confided in me that she'd met someone at the gym. That she thought she was in love. She was planning on leaving Jack for him, but she was scared about how Jack was going to react.

'I was thrilled. I thought she'd finally be able to live a normal life. Then' – Serena's voice cracks – 'she called me crying again. Said she thought Jack might have found out. She told me that she was scared. I offered to have her come and stay with me, but she said she knew Jack would come after her. Said she needed to collect evidence of his abuse that would support her divorce claim, maybe even a restraining order.

'On the night she died she sent me a picture of herself. Jack was working late, and she was going to see her new man. She was *excited*. Hopeful, even.' Snot is trickling down Serena's face. I watch its progress, but I don't go for my sanitiser. I already feel dirty. 'The coroner recorded it as an open verdict. But I know she didn't do it, despite what everyone thinks. I know she didn't kill herself.'

I take a deep breath. 'Jack told me that she died of the cancer.'

Her eyes widen. 'Fuck me. He really is the worst human being. Listen, I don't know how to say this, but I don't think you're safe here. I've always thought there was something more to her death than they made out, and due to a lack of evidence or – God I don't know – they never did anything about it. She "fell" off a footbridge. How easy would it have been for him to push her? She was still weak from the cancer.'

I picture it. Jack, hiding in the shadows, waiting for the right moment. A chilling theory, to think this man who has shared my bed, my life, might be capable of that.

Serena composes herself. 'So, I'm here to warn you. You're living with a dangerous man, Iris. I don't know for sure what happened, but I do know that Alice was scared of him when she died. Really scared. She didn't know what he was going to do to her if he found out about the affair. So yeah,' she finishes, an anticlimax after that explosive reveal. 'I just came here to say that. If he could do it to her, then I have no doubt he could do it to you, too.'

The implication that I'm somehow lesser than Alice isn't lost on me, and, even despite everything she has just told me, I feel a prickle of anger. To disguise my irritation, I lean forward so my hair falls in front of my face, and as I do so the necklace becomes dislodged from the neck of my sweater.

Serena sits up straighter. 'What's that?' Urgent, scared even. 'Is that Alice's? Her necklace with the A on it?' She grabs for it. I hate it when people get into my personal space without asking, but I'll allow it. Just this once.

'Is this hers?' she says loudly. Too loudly.

I nod. 'Yes.'

'Where did you get it?' She's practically hyperventilating now.

I stare at her. 'Jack gave it to me.'

'Fucking hell,' she whispers. 'I knew it. He was fucking there. I've looked at that picture she sent me a million times, and she was definitely wearing it. I just thought it had come free in the water. She was wearing that on the day she died.'

44

Serena paces up and down until I'm sure she is going to carve a path in the kitchen flagstones. Her mind is running at a million miles an hour. She throws out theory after theory, forcing the pieces of the puzzle together until – half an hour later – she has a complete story. Jack found out that Alice was going to leave him and tracked her down. In his rage he confronted her, and, when she didn't deny that there was someone else, he pushed her. 'It would be just like him,' she muses frantically. 'There's no way he'd let her get away with it.'

I half-listen. She's becoming hysterical, and this is all moving too fast for me. I need time. If Jack is who she says he is – a controlling abuser – then she's right. I am in danger. Yet still I grapple with the idea. He thinks I'm special. He has his flaws, but don't we all? Haven't we all been driven to the brink by love? Forced to do things we didn't previously think ourselves capable of? But – a tiny, insistent voice at the back of my mind – *does* he think I'm special? Have I not been modelling myself on others for years? Would he think I was special, I wonder, if I showed him the real me?

'We need to take it to the police.' Serena sits, takes my hands in hers. 'This is the evidence we need.'

Her theory has holes. I need to be sure, so I urge caution. 'Didn't Alice die late at night?' I ask. 'Is it possible that she took the necklace off? What time did she send the photo?'

'She sent it in the early afternoon, but she always wore it. It was a present…' She tails off and bites her lip. 'It was a present from Jack.'

'OK,' I say gently. 'Do you think that maybe, if she was planning on leaving him, she might have taken it off if she was going to meet the man she was having an affair with?'

Serena is quiet for a long time. I've stumped her.

'We need more than this, Serena. The police aren't going to reopen a case for a necklace. I'll have to stay here. See if I can find something else. Then we can go to the police.'

Reluctantly, she agrees. 'Will you be safe here?' she says, and I nod.

'I've got my ways,' I tell her.

She tells me to take the necklace off. She offers to take it with her and, reluctantly, I agree. She tucks it into her purse. Just before she leaves, she drains her tea, throws an anxious glance around the room, and shudders.

'God, she's everywhere here. Don't you feel it? Be careful, Iris.'

And she goes, in a cloud of expensive perfume. The second she is gone, I pull out my phone. Three hours until Jack gets back. Time to get moving.

When Jack arrives later that evening, I am up and ready for him.

He comes straight to me, presses his lips to my temple, and my traitorous body leans into it for a second before I remember.

He steps back, appraises me, and a small line appears between his brows. I've changed. I'm not wearing Alice's clothes tonight. I've gone for something I feel comfortable in, not the tight, tight jeans, the figure-hugging tops. These clothes are my own. Clothes I wear when I'm not modelling myself on someone else. They're not from a boutique brand, but they are mine.

Jack looks confused – not only are these not the clothes he laid out for me this morning, they're not Alice's at all – and he falters, nose raised as though he's testing the air for scents of food.

I haven't cooked tonight. On the counter in the kitchen, I've laid out a tin of baked beans, a packet of white, plastic bread. It was a welcome respite from cooking, truth be told, and it gave me the time to take care of some other errands.

I meet Jack's gaze dead on. It's something I used to get vilified for. *She* stares *a lot, doesn't she?* my university cohort used to whisper when they thought I wasn't listening. But I was always listening.

And, once again, Jack falters. He takes a tiny step backwards, confusion still stamped across his face. It is such a diversion from his usual self-assuredness that I want to laugh. So, I do.

The sound is too loud. It shatters the shocked silence that's settled between us – not the pretty giggle he's become accustomed to, but a harsher, bigger noise. It's this that seems to bring Jack to his senses.

'What the fuck is going on?'

'I don't know what you mean.' I don't allow my gaze to drop. There's no bashful look at the floor now.

'I *mean* why are you dressed in clothes that look like they've come from the charity shop? Why haven't you made dinner? Why are you *staring* at me like that? It's giving me the creeps.' He shudders visibly, and I feel my jaw set. 'I don't have time for this, whatever it is. Go and get changed. We can order something for dinner.'

He walks through to the kitchen, but I don't go upstairs like a pliant little wife. I follow him.

He moves towards the fridge, grabs a bottle of wine by the neck, pulls down a glass. I watch him, heart aching, silently begging him to take back what he just said. Wanting him, desperately, to take a sip of his wine and then come to me. Prove me wrong. Take me in his arms and tell me I'm beautiful. Special just as I am. Instead – as though sensing my eyes on him – he swings round again.

'Why are you still standing there? I told you to go and change. And I hope you didn't expect us to eat this *crap* for dinner?' He nods towards the baked beans. 'Stop staring at me. You're being so fucking weird.'

I feel something inside of me snap, as Jack's eyes move to the countertop. To the two mugs that I have forgotten to put away. To the one smeared with red lipstick. Serena's lipstick.

His hand tightens round the stem of his glass. 'What's that?' he says softly. I would have preferred if he had shouted. 'Don't...' he whispers. 'Do *not* tell me that you had that woman over?'

I'm normally quite good at thinking on my feet, but I find myself frozen in fear. No mask to hide behind now.

'She came over today.' A croak. I sound as scared as I am.

'You invited her in?' he growls.

Every instinct is telling me I am in terrible danger now – and as though my body can sense the precariousness of the situation, my brain kicks in just in time. It can sense how much rests on this answer, and it's telling me – screaming at me – to lie. I'm good at lying. It feels more natural to me than the truth, these days. I've already deleted my call to Serena from my phone, in case Jack should go snooping. For that, I thank my foresight.

'I swear I didn't. She just turned up.'

He leans forward with a long, intense look that rivals the one I was giving him earlier, as though he is trying to see right through the lies. I've put my mask back on just in time.

'What did she say?' That soft, low voice again that sends a shiver scuttling up my spine.

'Nothing. She just said she'd heard I was living here. She told me... well, she told me that she was Alice's friend.'

'She was spreading lies about me, wasn't she? And you believed her.'

I shake my head. Sharp and vehement. The frightened movement of a child. Of a woman who realises she is utterly at the mercy of a man's whims. Just as Alice was. He must take pity on me.

But the action doesn't work. Or perhaps he is just so far beyond reason, he doesn't see it. 'I know you're lying to me, Iris.' He lunges for me, grabbing the top of my arm so tight my hand throbs, blood pulsing under the skin. He drags me from the room, right up the stairs, and into the bedroom he allocated to me at the beginning. I struggle against him, but it's futile.

'Please. Jack. I didn't... she didn't say anything. I'll go back to Mum's. I need to sort through her things anyway, figure out what to do with the house. I won't tell anyone what Serena told me.' The desperate plea of a woman condemned. He twists my arm hard. So hard I cry out.

'I'm not going to let you go running back to your mum's, Iris. Not now. Do you not understand the things I've *done* for you? The lengths I've gone to? All for you to fuck me over like this? Your mum was quite the character, wasn't she? Screaming like a banshee, telling me to leave you alone.'

The words land like a dead weight in my stomach. I stop struggling against him, the shock so heavy, so complete that I no longer have control over my limbs. If he is saying what I think he is saying, he's far more dangerous than even Serena suggested. I can't breathe, can't even think.

He pushes me inside the room, and the fear of being trapped in here by this man sends adrenaline shooting through me. I turn, scramble desperately for the handle, but I'm too late. I hear the old lock turn in the door. 'Stay. There,' he says through the wood, and then his footsteps fade away.

This was not how it was supposed to end. There were two possible outcomes to this evening, and this was neither of them. This room is two storeys up, and, when I rush to look out of the window, I realise I wouldn't survive the jump. Not without breaking bones, and, if I misjudged the angle, perhaps my skull. There's nothing I can use to escape in here. Nothing I can fashion into a weapon. I don't even have my phone – I left it on the counter downstairs. The door, when I bash against it again and again with my shoulder, doesn't give an inch.

I slide down it, suddenly spent. What a fucking awful way to die. No glory, no big final moment. Apart from Mick, no one who cares about me knows I'm here. Mick only cares about the person I've presented to him, anyway. Just like Jack. Jack has shown his true colours now. And it has become ever clearer that, whatever he felt towards Alice, it wasn't love. Not even close. The things he's done… the things he's capable of doing. *Mum.* And suddenly, the image of Jack coming home that day when his mother was here comes to me. The panicked, haunted, wild look in his eye, as though he'd just done something terrible. Something he couldn't take back. I feel sick.

It's as I turn to bang the heel of my hand against the door once more – knowing even as I do that it is useless – that I see them. The marks, right at the very bottom.

And my blood freezes. Because gouged into the wood, splinters still splayed horribly, are four perfect lines. As though someone else has tried to scratch their way out of this room.

45

What becomes clear, as the night deepens, is that Jack has no intention of letting me out today. He's passed the door several times – presumably to check that I am still incarcerated – but, though his footsteps have slowed on his approach, he doesn't speak. Not even when I plead with him: my voice a genuine stutter of fear, of *desperation*. I hate how pathetic it makes me sound. I hate that he has so much power. More than anything, I hate that I made such a monumental mistake. That I believed he could love me for who I am.

I have laid out the contents of my pockets on the floor, my sanitiser and my wallet, in case there was anything I could use to make my escape. I even retrieved the old key to Freddie's flat from his box that I'd left here on my first night, and tried to jam it into the lock. It's far too small.

I can't stop thinking about what he said. *Mum.* Why her, of all people? Because he wanted to own me so completely that when I lied – told him she was the most important person in my life – he decided she was a threat?

As much as I don't want to believe that the man I have been sharing a bed with could be capable of such depravity, it's the only conclusion that makes sense.

Any love I felt for that man has evaporated. I'm filled only with a burning hatred so strong I could – and do – scream. For everything he has put me through. For making me believe that I could be someone worthy of his time. His attention. His love. But it wasn't me he wanted. It's never me they want.

It was exactly the same with Freddie. When it became too difficult to ignore his blatant disregard of our relationship, when I'd tried and failed to bring him back to me, ramping up my performance, acting as Marcie would have done, all to no avail, I decided the time had come to confront him. I was out of all other options. I waited until he left the office. Then, I followed him.

I just wanted to find a quiet place. A place far from the prying ears of our colleagues, so that we could talk. Properly, this time. When he hurried down an alleyway, I waited ten seconds, then followed. He was on the phone – leaving a voicemail, from the sounds of it. And I knew, just by his tone, that it was a message for *her*. I drew closer, hoping to hear more, throwing caution to the wind in a way I never will again. And what I heard was horrible. It confirmed my worst suspicions. There was someone else. I was not enough for him.

Ten minutes later, Freddie was dead.

Now, suddenly, the answer comes to me. While Freddie's great love was at least alive, Jack is still caught up with the love he lost. And, in order to escape, I realise I will have to slip into the role she vacated, turn myself into her one last time. The stakes are higher than ever. Any slip-ups could be fatal.

I'm going to have to put on the performance of a lifetime, pretend I'm still utterly, irreversibly in love with this man who I feel only revulsion for. I've done it before. I can do it again.

He's gone to bed. About an hour ago he hovered by the door, and I cried, screamed, begged for release. There was no answer.

At some point – I'm not sure what time – I drag myself away from the door, over to the bed, and collapse into it. I must fall into an uneasy sleep, because when I wake the key is rattling in the lock, and I only have time to sit up, clutching the blankets to my chest, as Jack enters the room. I'm sleep-fuddled, but not enough to forget my plan. The new plan. Jack stands in the doorway, staring at me, and I'm off the bed in a second, rushing over to him and clutching at his arm.

'I'm *so* pleased you're here, Jack. I need to explain. Please will you listen? It's not what it seems. I *love* you, Jack.' Voice low, earnest, intense, I don't move my eyes from his. 'I don't care about Mum. I never have. She treated me terribly after Marcie. She never cared about me. I see it now. No one cares about me like you do. I love you.'

This final declaration gives him pause. Once again, he searches my face for the lie and finds only desolation. Devotion. Predictable, the way his eyes soften. He is arrogant enough to believe that I could possibly still love him after everything he has done.

'I understand why you're so angry, Jack. It makes total sense. I'd be angry, too. But I *promise* you I didn't invite that woman over. If I'd believed *half* of what she was saying, would I still be here? She was jealous. Of you, of the life you gave to Alice. It was so obvious.'

Jack looks like shit. Haggard from whatever he indulged in last night. He rubs his hand over his face as though trying to make sense of what I'm saying. Because it does make sense. He knows my argument is solid. Of course it is. I came up with it.

'I'm so confused, Iris. You're driving me crazy. I don't know what to do.'

I tighten my grip on his arm. 'Let me out. Let's go back to the way things were. She's *nothing*. She's so unimport-ant. What matters is you and me.'

Nothing for a second. Then, a slow nod. I reach up on my tiptoes to give him the softest kiss on the cheek. He doesn't pull away, so I plough on. It's working. Just a little further now.

'You're a good person, Jack. You care about people. That much is obvious. Just look at how much you've looked after me for the last few weeks. You deserve to be happy. You've been through so much, it's time to let me look after you.'

And, because he is an idiot, he believes me. I can tell from the way he draws me into him, presses a kiss to my temple that I must fight the urge to wipe away. The door stands open behind us.

Timorously, tremulously, I ask the question: 'Can I come out?'

He sighs, long and low, and then nods. 'I'm sorry.' His voice is choked. 'I'm so, so sorry.'

'It's OK,' I croon, though of course it is nothing of the sort. I fight the urge to run down the corridor as we exit. But Jack's hand is still on my arm, and there's a warning in the tightness of his grip. We don't go downstairs. Instead, he leads me through to his bedroom.

I have to endure sex with him. I'd half-expected it, but it doesn't make the experience any more pleasant. He's domineering again, and I allow it. A perfect, submissive doll who doesn't ask questions, who pretends he is a master of pleasure, when in actuality his violent thrusting is giving me carpet burn.

It's only when I rise, announce that I am getting in the shower, that I realise he doesn't intend to leave me alone for one second.

'I'll come with you,' he says, and he rises too.

I turn away from him and roll my eyes. Showering – particularly for someone with my standards – is a very personal experience, but I grit my teeth and acquiesce once more.

In the shower, while I am pretending to enjoy the way Jack rubs soap into my shoulder – about as unpleasurable as the sex – I plot my escape.

I broach the subject when we are dressing.

'Jack.' That slow, timorous voice that I have grown to hate. I can't believe I've been reduced to this weak, snivelling little girl who bows to his every whim. 'I've been thinking. It's the group tonight. The first one since I had my little… moment about Mum. I think it might be useful for me to go. Only if that's OK with you, of course. I just feel that it might help me process it all a little better than I have been?' I raise the pitch of my voice at the end of the sentence so that it sounds like a question. A servant seeking approval from her master. To remind him of how much power he has over me.

I can practically see the cogs whirring in his brain as he computes this question. I know what he's thinking: it's a risk – a big one – to allow me to go; but I assured him of my feelings, didn't I? I made a point of drawing attention to what a good, good person he was. One who has simply lost his way in the world. One who I'm willing to help back onto the right path, if only he'll let me. If only he'll grant me this one, small favour.

A slow, glorious nod, and I turn away to hide my smile.

'But I'll come with you,' he says, and his smile doesn't reach his eyes. Annoying, but again not entirely unexpected.

'Great!'

Jack calls in sick to work and forces me to watch yet more drivel on TV. For someone I assumed was fairly cultured, he does watch the most unbelievable crap. But I interject at all the right moments, follow the lead on the canned laughter, and feel him loosen beside me as he takes in this relaxed, giggly woman. The one who laughs at the same jokes as him, and likes the same shows as him, and has sex with him whenever he so desires it.

The hours tick down. Jack follows me to the loo, and I let him. At lunchtime, we go through to the kitchen – together, of course – and I see my phone isn't where I left it. I make us lunch as he sits at the breakfast bar, conscious of his eyes on me. I don't break character. Not once.

After lunch, we go back to the sitting room. Watch a film. And then, the sky is darkening, and the session is almost upon us.

I stand, stretch, note the way his hand hovers midway towards me, as though to grab for my wrist should I try to run. 'We should think about heading off,' I say. *We.* There has never been a *we.* I see that now. Now, there is only him, and only me, coming at this from opposite ends of the playing field.

And then, he is unlatching the door, still holding me firmly by the arm, and we step out into the night.

I clutch him and give him a bright, sunny smile. 'I'm so pleased we're doing this together,' I say.

The community centre has never looked drabber, and I've never been more pleased to see it. Jack steers me towards two available seats and we sit. Rita's eyes follow us across the room. Her lipsticked mouth purses as she takes in the intimacy between us. Frankly, she can have him. I'm done, dusted, fed up. If she wants locked doors, mediocre skills in the bedroom and shit TV, she can be my guest. He does have a big house, so I suppose that's his one redeeming feature.

I turn to give Jack a small, encouraging smile, and he leans gently against me in response.

He has no idea what's coming. What I'm about to reveal about him, in this forum where he will not be able to retaliate. My smile grows wider.

And then, from behind, there is the unmistakable sound of the vacuum of air created by the swing door. I frown, do a quick count. Everyone's here. Well, Matt isn't, obviously. Surely Fiona hasn't had the audacity to fill his seat already.

But, sure enough, she's turning, fixing her welcoming smile to her face, and spreading her arms. I turn too. And the world stops turning for a second.

Because, walking into the room, is Greg. Freddie's Greg. The Greg who figured me out, who outed me to Freddie. The Greg who disliked me the moment he laid eyes on me. The Greg who suspected everything.

My heart gives a nasty little skip and I sink into my chair, ducking my head. I should stand, leave, but Jack – as if sensing this sudden urge to bolt – wraps his fingers round my arm again. And then it's too late. Because Fiona has pointed to the chair, and Greg has sat down, and he has noticed me.

His eyes widen with shock, then darken with dislike, and I can't breathe.

Fiona's prattling on about the type of group we are – her usual introductory crap – and doesn't notice how the atmosphere has soured.

'And could you tell us what brings you to the group today, Greg?'

'That's a good question,' he says, in that deep, gravelly voice. He looks at me, and I know then what's coming, with a certainty that sends bile rising in my throat. 'I lost a colleague – a good friend – a few months ago. I've been OK, generally, but I saw the advert for this group, and I thought I'd come. I've found things hard without him.'

Fuck Fiona, and her fucking marketing strategy. The leaflets and the online adverts and the book she wrote. Causing problems left, right and centre.

'Freddie didn't have a very good end to his life. He was terrified, actually. It's a hard thing to come to terms with: that someone was so unhappy just before they died. So, I think I came to try and get closure.' And the way he looks at me then... as though he is about to get his wish.

'Thank you, Greg. Right,' Fiona says briskly. 'Introductions!'

He hasn't acknowledged the connection yet, and I can only hope that he doesn't intend to. I'll have to navigate this very carefully. Jack's looking at me, as though he can sense my discomfort. Which he probably can. My whole body is vibrating as I wait to speak with a tongue that feels suddenly too heavy for my mouth.

We go through Rita, and Jack, and even Charlie speaks, and then it's my turn.

I swallow, hard. 'I'm Iris. I lost my mum a couple of weeks ago.' I try to leave it there. Try not to look at anyone, but I see in my peripheral that Fiona has raised her eyebrows.

'Anything else to add, Iris?' she says eventually.

'And' – a deep, steadying breath. 'I lost my fiancé. A few months ago.'

'And *his* name was also Freddie, wasn't it?'

I want to stuff every page of Fiona's stupid book into her stupid mouth to shut her up, but it's too late. The damage is done. I raise my eyes to Greg's and see understanding dawning there.

And his voice cuts across the circle like a machete. 'What's your rule on someone pretending that they had a closer relationship with the person they lost than they actually did?'

Fiona's eyebrows rise an inch. 'I'm not sure I follow, Greg. Are you saying you didn't lose your friend?'

He clears his throat, and, though I can't look at him, I can feel his stare burning through the side of my face. 'No. That's not what I'm saying at all. I'm saying that there's someone here who is pretending they were in a relationship with someone when they weren't.' He points at me. 'She barely knew Freddie at all.'

46

Greg makes it sound bad. Worse than it was. He misses out the *romance* of the whole thing. He frames it as something entirely different. 'He said it all started with a kiss,' he tells the group, who seem to lean forward as one. To hang from his every word. Already, Greg is wrong, but I find I can't voice my rebuttal. My throat feels like it's closed up.

That's not where it started at all. It all started when he paid for my coffee that day. When he recognised something in me – a sadness, perhaps, that I saw reflected in him. He wouldn't have paid for my coffee otherwise. And then again, when I saw him in the office. In London, the chances of bumping into the same person are minuscule in a *year*, but the very same day? That's got to be something close to fate.

When he told me that he, too, had lost a sibling, it was confirmed. Something had brought us together, and I was not going to let it get away from me. He seemed to *like* me, with some persuasion from Marcie's repertoire of moves, of course. He asked me out. Our first date, at the pub. We bonded over our shared loss, and I was so sure that he was the one. The person who would make me feel less alone in this world.

'He said he felt bad about it – that he thought he'd maybe encouraged her a bit,' Greg is saying. 'They'd both lost siblings, and I think he felt protective over her. But she was always so weird towards him. At the first office drinks she came to, she made a beeline straight for him. Barely spoke to anyone else.'

Why does he have to make it sound so seedy? I didn't know the rest of the office was coming, and, besides, Freddie didn't seem interested in any of them. Not once Greg had moved away, anyway.

And then there was the second date. Just the two of us. When he bought me lunch and asked me all about myself. And the way he brushed against my leg under the table: I wasn't imagining that. I *couldn't* imagine the spark of attraction that ran between us in that moment.

'He said he took her for lunch one day, just to check in. See how she was getting on. He was her manager, so it was his responsibility to make sure everything was going OK, but he said she didn't want to talk about work at all. Kept evading the questions about work and staring at him in a really intense way. Eventually, he thought she might want to talk about losing her sister, so he tried to pave the way for that conversation.'

He's wrong. Freddie encouraged it. He was interested in getting to know me, too. He opened up to me that day, told me personal details that I was sure he'd never revealed to anyone else. Greg doesn't have the whole picture. He doesn't know about our secret meetings, where it was just the two of us. Like when we were in the kitchen together, and the air crackled with electricity. Like in meetings when our legs would meet under the table. The way it always took him a little too long to move away.

'She kept cornering him, so they'd be alone together. Finding little ways to talk to him. Insisted on sitting next to him in meetings. There was one point, in the pub, where we all got together for a photo. Iris practically pushed me out of the way so that she could be next to him in it. I think he found it funny, to begin with. Shrugged it off as a schoolgirl crush.'

I loathe Greg. I hate that he has reduced what we had to something as minor – as inconsequential – as a crush. I glare at him with as much hatred as I can muster, but it doesn't deter him. He ploughs on. Spreading lies, falsehoods.

'He made a bit of a twat of himself after that. I think he'd been having girl trouble, not that he was ever particularly open about it with me, and he was definitely drinking too much. We had another work night out, and most people had gone home by the time Iris arrived. I left the two of them alone together, and the next morning he came to me and told me he'd done something stupid. That he'd kissed Iris, and he was worried that he'd overstepped. Said it was a drunken thing, but he was concerned that our boss would find out.'

No, no, no. The kiss was genuine. I felt it. I *knew* it.

'I encouraged him to speak to her the next day. Play it down. But I think he felt so embarrassed by what he'd done, he just ignored it and hoped she wouldn't say anything.'

Greg doesn't know the half of it.

'That's when things started to get really bad. Freddie started getting the sense that someone was following him. He thought it was a bloke at first, but I've always wondered if it was her.' He tips his head in my direction, and all eyes turn towards me, like he's broken the spell he was binding them with. 'I thought he was being paranoid at first. He kept going on about feeling watched. Thought there was someone in his flat. I'll regret that I didn't do more for a long time.'

Well, on that point he's got me. I did mention love pushed me to lengths I didn't think myself capable of. Even before I suspected there was another woman, I'd found ways to get into Freddie's flat. He was never particularly security conscious, and occasionally he left a window unlocked. But when I began to suspect his infidelity after Greg – *fucking* Greg – planted that seed of the other woman in my head, I went further. I began following Freddie. I stole his keys so I could access his flat whenever I wanted.

It was easy enough to do. He always left them on his desk, and I waited until he was in a meeting, then swiped them. I had them copied at the key-cutting place down the road, and they were back on his desk before he even missed them.

I sent him a few messages, just to gauge his feelings towards me, but he was unresponsive, clipped. And so I decided to use them. I let myself into his flat and I began to look for evidence. I didn't find anything that first time. It was a thrill just to know I was there: in this intimate space of his. I lay on his lumpy mattress, and inhaled the smell of him from the pillow. I even took a pair of pyjama bottoms, savouring the fact that they had pressed against his skin.

As time passed and I wasn't caught, I grew bolder. Sometimes I'd wait until he was asleep, then let myself in and watch him breathe from the corner of his bedroom.

I grew bolder in my search, too: looking in places I hadn't previously dared to go lest he notice a difference. It was in Freddie's sock drawer that I found the ring, buried in among his underwear. It was exactly the sort of ring I'd have wanted. It broke me a little seeing it there, so incongruous in its tiny velvet box. Something inside me gave.

'I put two and two together a few weeks later,' says Greg now. 'I watched Iris staring at Freddie across the office, and something just slotted into place. I warned him that it could be her, tried to get him to go to our boss, but he was worried he'd be in trouble for encouraging her. Weirdly, I think he was quite pleased that it was only Iris. That it wasn't something more sinister than a crush.'

I fucking *hate* Greg.

After I found the ring, I decided to confront Freddie. I would lay my cards out on the table. Tell him I loved him. *Prove* to him that I was the one he wanted.

Wanting to get him alone, I waited for him to leave the office, and then followed him into that alleyway. He had his phone to his ear, speaking in the continuous stream that indicates a voice note. His tone was soft, crooning, sickening. When I heard what he was saying, it was like a physical pain. I staggered, and the noise of my soles on the concrete caused Freddie to swing round towards me.

He hung up and was on me in seconds. He grabbed me by the arm so hard I could feel the tendons twisting.

'It's been you all along, hasn't it? Fucking hell. Greg was right. You've been following me for weeks, letting me think I had some sort of *stalker*.' He was so, so angry. He didn't understand that it came from a place of love. 'I'm sorry if I gave you the wrong impression with the kiss. That should never have happened. But you have *got* to stop texting me, and messaging me, and staring at me. You're freaking me out, Iris. You're being so fucking *weird*.' It was the shudder he gave that made something in me snap. The utter revulsion it contained.

He didn't know what he was talking about. He was wrong. We *were* right for each other. Just as soon as he forgot about this other woman, we would be together.

'Please, Freddie.' I hated the note of desperation in my voice. He heard it too, because his lip curled.

'Never contact me again, Iris.' And he dropped my arm with a final sneer and marched away. Towards the main road. Towards his end.

The call came early the next morning: an accident, my boss said. A lorry. I couldn't breathe. 'Take all the time you need,' he said as he ended the call, in a tone of voice that suggested he meant the exact opposite. 'I know you two were close.'

The days that followed were awful. I could barely keep my head above water, the grief, the tragedy of losing Freddie was so strong. I didn't go into the office the day after he died. I couldn't face the thought of his empty desk.

When I finally mustered the strength to go back, Greg was in our boss's office, shouting. I could hear him through the glass. 'He was *sure* he was being followed. She's had this weird obsession with him for weeks.'

Not long after that, I was called in by stony-faced HR.

'We're letting you go. Don't make this harder, Iris. You're lucky that we haven't got the police involved.'

So, I left – with no references; nothing to show for the months and months of work I had given to them. They let me go like I was nothing. I couldn't find another job after that. Not until Mick took me on. Greg made me lose everything: my job, my flat. Now, he's going to take this from me, too. The group. My safe haven.

I don't look at Jack, but I can sense his gaze boring into the side of my face. Judgement rolls from every corner of the room in thick, black waves. I am so blindsided by this turn of events, I can't even think of a way to worm myself out of it, cast aspersions on Greg's testimony, twist the narrative so that *I* am the wronged party here. I can only sit there.

'I always just had this *sense* about her,' he finishes. 'Like she was acting. Like she was an empty shell and there was nothing underneath.' He shudders. Just as Jack did earlier today. Just as Freddie did minutes before he died.

The silence stretches. No one moves. Somewhere in the distance, a siren screams. I could say he's delusional. That Freddie and I decided to keep our relationship a secret, even from him. But they won't believe me. Greg pitched it perfectly: his voice low yet angry, imbued with just the right amount of righteous injustice to add veracity to his claims.

I can't out Jack now. I can't do anything now. How has everything gone so spectacularly wrong?

Even Charlie has deigned to lift his head. Above, one of the strip lights flickers.

After a long, long pause in which I can only stare at a patch of chewing gum on the floor, Fiona speaks. 'I think, Iris, it's probably best if you leave us.'

No anger. Just deep, deep disappointment. I'm used to it. I disappointed Mum the moment I was born, and every day after that.

It's a bad situation, but – as I always do – I intend to make the best of it. Because, unknowingly, Fiona has provided me with an escape. I may not be able to out Jack as the controlling abuser he is, but I have been afforded an option Alice never had. The option to leave.

So, I do. If I'm quick, I can slip out before he has a chance to raise the alarm. He wouldn't want to grab me in here: too many witnesses. If I can get through the door to the lobby, I might just be safe. I dread to think what would happen if he caught me. Now that I know what he did to Mum, what he's capable of. This is my one chance to get out, start over. I could move abroad. I've always liked the sound of Italy. Over there, fall in with the right people and law and order are more guidelines than decree.

I give myself a dignified departure. I'm owed that, at least. I've given a lot to this group. I stand, make sure I stare each person – even Jack – right in the eyes, and then, with my back perfectly straight, I walk right through the centre of the circle. Back to being myself.

47

Once I am in the lobby, I break into a run. I need to be quick now. Jack is not the type of person to allow such deceit to slide. But even as I think it, I hear the door go behind me – know instinctively that it is him. And I run harder, into the street, zigzagging left and right. I'm horribly unfit. Those days that Jack forced me to stay in bed are catching up with me, and my breathing becomes ragged and painful too soon.

He's getting closer. I can hear his own breath labouring in his lungs, his footsteps heavy. This must be what it feels like to be hunted. Which instinct is stronger? The hunter's, with the promise of a reward at the end? Or the prey's, whose only reward is their life?

My answer comes quicker than I expected. Embarrassingly quickly, truth be told. Jack's fingers close round my arm as I'm about to dart round the side of the community hall. His fingers are so tight, my whole arm starts to tingle.

He wrenches me round to face him, and when I see his face I realise that he is going to kill me. I can see it in his eyes: fury, disdain, hatred. And beneath that, emptiness. A blank space where the soul should be. I've been dancing with the devil, and this is my prize.

'Make one fucking noise, and I will slam you so hard into the pavement you'll never make a sound again.'

God, he's vile. I can't believe I ever felt a modicum of affection for this man. But I do as I'm told, and I'm not acting. The fear is genuine. The pliancy is genuine. When the chips are down, it seems I am just as helpless as every other woman who has been in a scenario like this.

He keeps his arm tight round mine as we walk towards his house. To anyone else, we'd look like a happy couple, leaning against one another as we made the journey home. We pass three people on the way, and with each one, I try to catch their eye, hoping my face – twisted in fear – will give them pause, but they don't lift their heads. Welcome to London, where the weather is shit, and the people even worse.

With one hand still wrapped round my arm, Jack fumbles for his keys. He is so much stronger than me, I don't struggle. Inside, he pulls me roughly through to the kitchen, keeps his hand on me as he reaches into a cupboard for a bottle of whisky. He unscrews it one-handed, then lifts it to his mouth to drink straight from the bottle. I watch his Adam's apple bob up and down, up and down, and wonder if I would be strong enough to push the bottle into his open mouth, smash out his teeth, buy myself some time to get out. To get away. But then the moment has passed, and he is dragging me towards the table. Unsteady on his feet. On the way, he pulls a knife from the block. It's huge – one I've used several times when prostrating myself making dinner for Jack's pleasure. To align myself with a woman he was clearly abusing. What a fucking fool I've been.

He sits me down in front of him so that his knees are clamped tight round my own, so that any sudden movement from me will alert him to my intentions. He sets the knife down on the table in front of us. The blade glints in the dim lights. Could he do it? Could he push it into my flesh as though I was nothing more than a piece of meat? It'd be fitting considering that's what I've made myself to him.

Could *I* do it to *him* though? I think so. Should the need arise.

'So.' His voice is quiet, yet seems too loud at the same time. 'You've been lying to me. All this time.' His top lip retracts so that he is baring his teeth at me, and it is so inhuman that I shudder. Yes. He could push the knife in.

I don't bother with the Alice act. There's no point now, not when I've been exposed. He's going to kill me either way. I can see it in his eyes. And so, I straighten my shoulders and stare right at him. My jaw juts.

'That makes two of us.'

'We'll start with you, shall we? I'm sure a clever girl like you has got her story all lined up, all her ducks in a little row. Isn't that right, Iris?'

'There is no story. That man was wrong. Freddie and I did have a relationship. Greg just never understood it.'

'It sounded to me as though that *relationship* was a little one-sided.'

'Not true. Freddie liked spending time with me. He kissed me.'

'Oh, he *kissed* you. Why didn't you mention it before? He must have been in love then.'

The sarcasm makes my fury bubble. 'This is all a bit rich coming from you, isn't it, Jack? Alice was going to leave you, wasn't she?'

His legs tighten on my own and he grabs for my wrist. 'Why don't you shut the fuck up about things you don't understand, you little bitch?' I twist away from him, and he composes himself, closing his eyes and taking a deep breath, as though to recalibrate.

'And the engagement?'

Ah. This one will be difficult to wriggle out of. 'That didn't happen. No.'

There's something quite satisfying about finally telling the truth. Maybe I should do it more often. Assuming I get out of here. Assuming I have the grit to take that knife and stick it in whatever part of him I can reach. I've never killed anyone that way. Too messy. Now, I'm so angry I can practically feel the handle in my hand already. I should have known he wouldn't understand.

'Let me get this straight,' Jack is saying. 'You barely knew the man – no, sorry, you'd *kissed* him, and you thought that was enough to warrant going to a grief group, did you? Under some misguided notion that you were in a relationship with him. And then, to top it all off, you pretend that he proposed? Do you know how mental that sounds? Do you know how mental you *are*?'

Fucking outrageous, coming from him. I clench my hand until I feel the nail cut into the skin on my palm. 'I did know him.' Teeth gritted. 'We were good friends. And more. Greg's only telling one side. But I'm not sure I owe you the full story, Jack. Not when you've been telling so many lies yourself. Poor, poor Alice. You made her life a misery, didn't you?'

'I gave her *everything*.'

'You isolated her from everyone she knew. You locked her in that bedroom – I've seen the scratch marks. She was never more than a trophy for you, was she? Someone to keep locked up until you wanted to wheel her out.'

He looks as though he's choking. I hope he is. It would save me a lot of trouble later on. 'That's not true.' But the words are staccato and forced. He knows I'm right. *I* know I'm right.

'Then tell me,' I say, voice hard, unforgiving, so unlike that stupid, girlish lilt I've been putting on. 'What *is* the truth?'

I don't really expect him to answer me. I expect us to do this dance for a few more minutes before we both lunge for the knife. Before fate decides which of us will walk away from this. It's closer to him. I'll have to wrench my legs away, half-stand to reach it.

But – amazingly – he starts to speak. In the tone of someone confessing their deepest, darkest secret. And in a way I wish I hadn't asked. Because I come to understand that now that the floodgates have opened – now that he is finally telling the truth – he expects me to take this knowledge with me to the grave.

'She was the best thing that ever happened to me. She really was. Everyone loved her. I've never really had that, you know? I managed to make people like me by changing parts of myself, but she just had this natural way about her. And I think people liked me more just because I was with her. I finally felt like I'd achieved something, you know? I don't know where it all started going wrong. I've always been quite jealous, but with Alice it was… well, it was worse than it had ever been. I think I knew she was better than me underneath it all, and it terrified me that she'd work it out. But she was always so patient with me.'

For a moment, he looks genuinely vulnerable. A look I've never seen him wear before. It's disconcerting – until I remember who he is. *What* he is.

'When I proposed, I thought that everything would be better. I thought that knowing she was mine – that she was going to be tied to me – was going to make me feel more secure. My parents were thrilled. They helped plan this huge wedding. And Alice was so lovely through all of it. She tried her best; I know she did. But I made mistakes. And after her treatment, I could sense she was pulling away. I hated it. I think that must have been around the time she met him.'

I lean forward. I have no idea who he's talking about. 'Who?'

Jack ignores my question.

'I knew something had changed straight away. She was different. Secretive. I was convinced she was having an affair. It drove me mad. I locked her in the spare bedroom, and went through her things, her phone. And I was right. She'd tried to hide his name, but I found the messages. It wasn't hard to find out who he was. That's how I came to find you, Iris.'

'What?'

He gives an insane smile. 'You didn't think we met by accident, did you?'

48

Once again, I am on the back foot. Unaware of where this story is going. And it is this – more than the knife, more than the blankness in Jack's eyes – that makes me feel incredibly, horribly vulnerable. Jack is looking at me as though I have been very stupid indeed. As though I have missed some essential piece of the puzzle. A piece he is about to slot into place. I've lost control of this situation, and he knows it.

Jack smiles – a chilling baring of teeth that repulses me, fascinates me. 'I really thought you'd got it all figured out. Clearly, I gave you too much credit.

'I came to the group because of you, Iris. Not because of some coincidence. Not because it was ordained. I knew you'd been going to the group before I decided to join, too.'

'What?' I hate the way my voice trembles. How frightened I sound.

'I followed you for weeks, Iris. This whole fucking mess has been created by you. Don't you see that? I stood outside that stupid little café for weeks. I waited outside your flat.'

I hear his words, but they don't make sense. 'Why?'

'Because of Freddie,' he says simply. Dispassionately.

'What does Freddie have to do with anything?'

Jack exhales slowly, closes his eyes as though I'm a child testing his already limited patience. 'He was fucking my wife, that's what! Behind my back. They were going to run away together. She was going to leave me. She was going to go and live with him in his disgusting flat. Over *this*.' He gestures to the room we are sitting in. 'He'd proposed to her – I saw it in the messages. She couldn't wear the ring, obviously. But they knew I wouldn't make it easy for them. I wasn't going to give her up – not the best thing that's ever happened to me – without a fight. So, she kept coming back to me. Every night, even though she was plotting her escape. Pretending everything was fine. Makes me sick.'

The air feels very, very thin.

'I'd been following him for a while. Trying to figure out what was so special about this man that had stolen my wife. Trying to see what qualities he had that I didn't. He was so fucking disappointing, it was almost insulting. I saw him with you at the pub. I saw you letting yourself into his flat, and I thought that he was in a serious relationship. He was fucking my wife, but he also had this little bitch on the side. I think Alice suspected I knew something. She broke it off with him for a while, even told him she felt guilty. Not guilty enough to go running back to him, though. That's when I caught Freddie kissing you.

'When they got back together not long after that, my wife told him she'd leave me for him. I simply couldn't let that happen.'

His tone is flat. Expressionless. 'It's my fault she died. She was scared of me. No wonder she felt she had to escape the way she did. I'd made her life miserable. I'll have to live with that for the rest of my life, my punishment for the way I'd treated her. But when she died, I realised I was still angry. So fucking angry. I couldn't let it go. I went a bit mad when the police told me what had happened. If Freddie hadn't come along, she would never have been walking back home – back to me – stinking of him. She wouldn't have died. We'd have made it work, I know it.' His gaze snaps back to mine.

I'm not sure what frightens me more: the mad smile he gives me, or the fact that I am suddenly aware he is about to confess something terrible. Something that will make it impossible for him to let me go.

'Jack, I don't need to know this,' I say, voice trembling again. I mean it. I don't want to know whatever he is about to tell me. 'I'll go. I'll leave the country. You haven't told me anything yet.' When did I become so *weak*?

But Jack continues as though I haven't spoken. He tightens his legs round mine. 'The day after Alice killed herself – well, I suppose it was the same day, given she died in the early hours of June sixth – I waited for Freddie outside his office. Your office, too.'

I want to stop him from speaking any more. Every word feels like another nail in my coffin. I place my hand on the table while his eyes are still fixed to mine. As though I am leaning against it for support. And I begin to inch towards the knife.

'I followed him,' Jack continues. 'I blamed him for everything: for Alice dying, for ruining my marriage, for taking what was mine by law. I saw you arguing in some disgusting alleyway, and I realised that he must not know yet that Alice had died. Who would think to tell him? He had no claim over her, nothing linking him to her. He was still planning to meet her that evening. I saw red. He left you in that alley, walked out onto the street and stopped at a traffic light. I saw my opportunity, and I took it.'

My hand is mere inches from the knife now, but Jack leans forward and grasps my forearms with his hands. I pull back. Force myself to meet his eye. His breath – hot with whisky and rancour – heats my face, and I turn away from him, gritting my teeth.

'I pushed him. Straight into the middle of the road. And do you know what? It was the easiest thing I've ever done. There was a lorry. And suddenly, my issue was just... gone.

'I thought I'd feel better, after that. I'd rid myself of the problem. But I realised I was still coming home to an empty house, and it was all my fault. I realised I was still so angry. And I thought: who's the only other person who might understand even an iota of what I'm going through?'

He leans forward so that his face is now only a centimetre from mine. I push my hand forward again, so that I can feel – against the tips of my fingers – the handle. 'You, Iris,' he whispers.

'I started following you, then. I saw you were going to this stupid group, and I thought: why not? It would be a good way of getting to know you. I originally planned to tell you the truth at the end of the first session. To tell you how the man you were so in love with was fucking you over – but then you threw a curveball. You told everyone he'd proposed. When he'd also proposed to my *wife*.' He shouts the word, and I jump.

I'm so close now. I inch my middle finger over the handle.

He pauses for a moment and cocks his head as though listening for something. I've been so focused on my task of inching closer to the knife that I didn't hear anything, but now, a knock. Coming from the front door. There's a pause, and then the bell goes, loud, long, insistent. A tiny spark of hope. If Jack goes to answer the door, I can grab the knife, hide, make a break for it when his back is turned. Ask whoever it is to run for help.

But Jack has other ideas. 'Don't fucking move,' he says quietly.

There's a long, painful pause. They must have gone. It's totally silent aside from Jack's slightly laboured breathing. And then he continues as though we weren't just interrupted.

'The anger, Iris. You've never felt anything like it, I guarantee you. He was dead, and yet I still wanted to hurt him. I wished then that I'd kept him alive. So that I could inflict more pain on him, by stealing you out from under him. I wanted something of his, like he'd taken something of mine. It didn't take long. I realised you were practically gagging for it, so lost and lonely and pathetic. I knew you'd been following me around like a pathetic puppy. Sitting outside my house night after night. And it was nice, to have someone else around for a while. I actually started to think we might be able to make a go of it. But then you kept going on about going to see your mother, and I thought you were planning to leave me, like Alice left me. So, I took care of that problem, too.

'You started to change. Confusing me. Dressing like her. For a while, it felt like those early days with Alice all over again, when she couldn't do enough to please me. I thought I could find a way of making amends for what I did to her through you. And now, this. You've been lying to me for so long.

'And I really hate being lied to. Did you really think you stood a chance against her? *You?*'

It is this that makes me finally go for the knife. The implication that I am not as good as Alice. I lunge forward, tearing my legs out of his, just as a crash comes from the front hall. Jack is quicker than me, though. He grabs the handle, waves it wildly around, then takes a haphazard stab at me.

I feel the flesh of my arm tear as the blade meets the skin. The white-hot, searing pain that makes me stagger backwards, clutching at my blood-soaked sleeve. And then Jack makes the mistake that will cost him dearly. He should have killed me. But his shock at the knife meeting my skin buys me a second.

A second where the kitchen door slams open, and the police burst through it. The last thing I remember, before I black out, is Jack being tackled to the floor. The sound of the knife skittering across flagstones.

Epilogue

Six months later

The table is heaving with food. A juicy roast chicken has been placed towards one end of the table, ready for carving. Smaller plates are dotted on every available surface: there are potatoes, and carrots, and cauliflower cheese and peas and broccoli. I've never seen such a spread.

The house is a hub of activity. It's nicer on the inside than I'd originally thought – less beige, more cream. There is a flurry of movement as the final plate – stuffing – is set down on the table, then Dad stands and begins to carve. It's a singularly masculine role, and he takes it up with relish. The two girls – I always struggle to know which is which – squabble over something inane, and Tilly scolds them before heaping food onto their plates, and throws a small glance in my direction. She doesn't like me being here. I get the sense she still doesn't quite trust me. She tells Sally all about it: *There's just something odd about her. Like there's nothing going on underneath. She treats her father like he's God's gift. I don't know, maybe I'm being unfair.*

Tilly is, by far, the worst part about this new arrangement, though I know I have her to thank for my newly reinstated relationship with my father. He's a lot kinder than my mother, and we've had many talks where he's opened up and apologised about his behaviour over the years. 'I'm so sorry, Iris. I think after Marcie... well, I think I just needed to get away. And your mother... you know what she was like. She was *convinced* you had something to do with her death. And I'm sorry to say, I almost believed her. I shouldn't have left you behind after everything. You were so young.'

It didn't take much to convince him of Mum's madness. Of the way she pined for him when he left, the way she made me the scapegoat for everything. 'I was unfair on you,' he admitted finally. 'I know you only ever had her best interests at heart.'

I reach for the peas, allowing my sleeve to fall back and reveal the long, jagged scar left by Jack's knife. Out of the corner of my eye, I catch Tilly grimacing at it. I'm enjoying the sensation of being part of a proper family for once. I've been invited to stay in the spare bedroom for as long as I need, and I've been preparing all week, practising my indulgent smile, my laugh in anticipation of Dad's frankly terrible jokes. These days, I'm the picture of the dutiful daughter.

Dad's sympathetic about what I've been through in

the past year. It's part of the reason he won't allow Tilly to say anything about my presence in the house, though I've heard them whispering together sometimes, with her asking when I'm going to leave. Dad shuts her down immediately, tells her he's lost me once and he's not going to do it again. 'Think about everything that's happened to her, Till.'

He is referring, of course, to Jack. The aftermath of his horrific attack is still a little hazy, though I do recall the way Plan B fell into place at exactly the right moment. Plan A was always a long shot. A final, desperate attempt to see if Jack could ever love me for me. The shudder confirmed it: he could not. I'd suspected that would be the case all along. That's why I laid the foundations for Plan B.

After Serena left with the necklace, I messaged Catherine. I told her that Jack's drinking was getting out of control. Had she had any more thoughts about the location of the key to the chest? She replied, listing a few hiding spots, and, lo and behold, I found it. Buried beneath the recipe cards. Heart hammering, I'd unlocked the chest. Jack – as it turns out – was not quite as clever as he'd thought. Because in among the wedding photos, the sickeningly happy pictures of him and Alice in the early stages of their courtship, there were others. Pictures of bruises, black eyes, red welts. She'd been documenting her abuse as she prepared to leave him. Jack must not have known they were there.

With my doubt about Plan A and the memory of Jack's

behaviour towards me over the last few weeks reverberating around my head, I went to the police, met Serena
there. She brought the necklace with her, and one final
nail in Jack's coffin: Martha.

Martha, who had witnessed the horrific abuse that
Jack subjected Alice to. Who had noted the scratches on
the back of the door. She was tired of sticking up for a
man who was capable of that, family loyalty or no. While
Alice was alive, he'd threatened her in no uncertain terms:
if she said anything, he'd ruin her. Perhaps worst of all,
she'd provided Jack with an alibi on the night of Alice's
death. He'd known he would be the prime suspect. This
time, he'd threatened her with her life. The guilt had been
eating her up ever since, and, when she saw that he'd
invited another woman to live with him, she knew she
needed to do something. She'd hated him for a very long
time, was willing to accept whatever punishment came
her way, for the chance at redemption.

And so, the three of us presented what we knew to the
police. And in typical British fashion, it was logged into
a system, and we had to wait. I convinced Serena and
Martha to let me go back there afterwards. Told them
that we didn't want Jack to get wind of what was going
on and bolt. Told them that we must nail him for what he
did to that poor, poor woman. Reluctantly, they agreed.

I had to try. I had to see. I'm not sure what I would
have done if he'd taken me in his arms, confirmed he'd
known who I was underneath all along – that he saw in
me the same darkness that he harboured within him.

Perhaps suggested we move abroad together. Start afresh. But like I say, I knew the odds were slim. Nobody ever seems to like what they find underneath my veneer. That's why I've gone back to acting now. I grin at Dad across the table, tuck in to the food. It's delicious. Tilly, for all her many faults, is a good cook.

After Serena lost contact with me for a day and then the night too, she panicked. Suspected it was happening again. And so she went back to the police and emphasised the urgency of the whole situation. Just in time, as it turns out. That cut could have been fatal. I lost a lot of blood in those few seconds it took for the police to restrain Jack. The hospital was nice though. Dad came to visit. His sympathy was a balm for both the physical and the mental scars.

On my direction, the police found the scratches on the back of the door, had them tested and discovered Alice's DNA. It wasn't long before everyone was doubting whether Alice really did kill herself. It had never been conclusive. It was looking very bad for Jack indeed.

And now, he is awaiting trial for the murder of not two, but three people.

Alice, Freddie and Mum. It's Mum's death that hits the hardest. I can almost understand why he felt compelled to kill Freddie: jealousy can do funny things to a person, after all. But Mum was needless. I feel partially responsible, but how was I supposed to know the lengths Jack would go to?

In prison, Jack began to talk. He knew his goose was

cooked. He said he hadn't intended to kill Mum: his intention was to warn her to stay away from me, but she'd confronted him outside the house as he was watching it one evening, and he'd pushed her inside in case the neighbours heard. She was screaming at him, telling him to stay away from me. She'd seen him come to collect me. She wanted to warn me, after everything. She managed to break free from him once inside, and ran upstairs to grab her mobile, call the police. She didn't get that far, apparently. He'd grabbed the back of one of those ratty old tops of hers, and she'd toppled backwards, right past him. Rumour has it he's aiming for a manslaughter charge for Mum's death, but I don't think he'll get it. Not in light of Freddie and Alice.

A nice upside to all this tragedy is that Mum left me the house. Well, it wasn't an active decision on her part, but, without a will, her whole estate passed to me. I don't want it, of course. I'm doing it up to sell. Too many memories, and I'd rather not be reminded of Marcie at every turn. Dad's helping me with the DIY that I don't outsource to contractors. He's surprisingly handy.

He did try to get in touch with me after Mum's death, as it turns out, but he didn't have my number. He's apologised profusely for that, too. 'Your mother was...' He sighed, scraping at the back of his neck. 'Complicated. I got in the habit of changing my number, and I must've lost yours in the process.'

But he was still my next of kin, and the hospital tracked him down. He turned up looking sheepish. After numerous apologies, during which I assumed a stately, aloof silence, I finally caved. It was nice that he cared enough to grovel. He told me how special I was. How special I'd always been to him. When I smiled at him, I pressed my tongue to the roof of my mouth.

I would never, of course, reveal that Mum was right in her suspicions. That I felt something in me snap when Marcie and I had that final blowout, where she told me that Billy thought I was weird. It was easy, after that, to find the strength to push her, just as she'd pushed me all those years ago at our grandparents' farm. She was gone in an instant. She'd taken and taken and taken from me. And now, it was time for me to take from her. To instate myself as a full member of this family.

Dad looks over at me now and pats my hand. Tilly's lips tighten. 'All OK?' he asks, and I beam at him, nod.

'More than OK. This is delicious, Tilly.'

Tilly replies with a thin-lipped smile. One of the children – I suppose they're my sisters, though they don't feel like it – looks up at me with wide eyes. 'I heard that you were going out with someone who killed his wife, is that right?'

Tilly splutters across the table. 'Where did you hear that?'

But I put on my best child-facing smile, roll back my sleeve further and show her the scar. Still angry and red, after all this time. 'Yes. He was a very bad man. But – fingers crossed – he's going to go to prison for a very, *very* long time.'

Jack is a bad man. There's no doubt in my mind about that. That's why I don't have an issue with pinning Alice's murder on him. When Jack said it was his fault that she died, I can only assume he meant figuratively.

Because I was very much there when she went over the edge of that bridge and plunged into the water below. Like Jack, I've also found pushing to be an effective way of killing someone.

Freddie always left his phone on the desk when he went into meetings. I knew his passcode; he'd never made any effort to hide it, and one afternoon I slipped it away and took it to the loo with me. I only wanted to see why he hadn't been replying to my messages. I wanted to get a steer on how he was feeling. But what I discovered made me feel sick. Hundreds of messages in his phone from a woman named 'A', talking about plans, recent meet-ups, proposed hotel visits. It felt seedy. Some of them were quite explicit. I continued to scroll, and my nausea built.

All I had to do was wait on his street on the date of their next proposed meet-up. I'd been doing it enough that by now it felt like second nature to me. I watched them enter the flat that felt like mine. They were all over each other before they were even through the door. An hour later, she came out again, fixing her hair. Freddie stood in the doorway, watching her leave. He blew a kiss and shouted at her retreating back: 'Only a couple more days and you'll be able to stay for good. I love you.'

She laughed, gave him one final wave and started to walk down the dark street. I hated her. This woman who had taken Freddie's love and made it her own. She was very elegant, I realised, as I followed her. A willowy grace about her. Perhaps it was that she was so thin. So thin that when she turned onto a badly lit bridge, when I made my move, rushing up behind her and shoving her hard, she barely made a splash. When I brought my hands back, I realised that the chain of her necklace had become tangled in my fingers. I got the clasp fixed at a tiny repair shop that only took cash. I kept it in the box of Freddie's things as a reminder of why I was better off without him.

Imagine my surprise, then, when I saw Alice's picture at the grief group, and I realised what the 'A' stood for. When I realised that she was the person who, not six months before, I had watched struggle against the current. Naively, I'd chalked it up to coincidence. Some cosmic joke. Another mistake. But coincidences like that, I've learned, are rare.

It was almost like I'd known it was hers, though, when I'd paired it with Alice's clothes. I pretended to Serena that it was another item Jack had thrust on me. I couldn't have foreseen how it would ultimately save me from him.

In a way, I suppose it was a kindness. Jack would never have let her leave that house alive. And they do say that drowning is a nice way to go.

I'm seeing someone new now. He's a policeman – one of the men who helped me into the ambulance once I came round after Jack's brutal attack. Men do love to play the hero. His name is Will, and he is utterly in awe of me. I've started popping in with little updates for the police, ostensibly so I can keep track of Jack's case, but mainly so I can see him. I've already learned his shift patterns.

I'm back working with Mick, too. He was so glad to see me – he'd heard about everything I'd gone through and is deliciously understanding about it. I'll look for something new as soon as the sympathy dries up, but for now I'm enjoying it.

I help myself to another portion of roast potatoes and reach for the gravy, but not before one of the children knocks my hand, and the contents of the jug spill everywhere. It burns me, and I snatch my hand back as Tilly apologises, though I can tell it's not genuine.

I fake my own smile, and assure them it's fine, but it's really not.

Dad chuckles at their antics, and my thoughts stiffen into something darker. I've only just got him back, and I want him all to myself. Tilly and the children are mere distractions. I smile sweetly at the three of them, though inside I harden.

I've never been very good at sharing.

Acknowledgements

Writing a book is a crash course in self-doubt, and there is no way I would be writing these acknowledgements without the legion of incredible people who have helped me get to this point.

Firstly, the most enormous thanks to my extraordinary agent at Janklow & Nesbit, Hayley Steed. I have been lucky enough to work with you as a colleague, where I saw how you fought for your clients every day. To be able to call you my agent now, on the receiving end of your tireless advocacy, is the most enormous privilege. To Stefanie Lieberman at Janklow & Nesbit US for your incredible vision and strategy for the novel stateside, thank you. To the wider team: Nathaniel and Mairi, Mina, Adam and Molly and everyone else at Janklow & Nesbit UK and US, I am so grateful for everything you do.

To my amazing editors and the teams working with you: Cassidy Sachs at Dutton, and Rachel Imrie at Corvus, you have made this process an utter pleasure.

Your incredible notes and exceptionally astute revisions have improved this novel tenfold, and I have been blown away by your collective vision for it.

To Sarah May at the Faber Academy for setting me off on the right path and all the infinite wisdom you shared when this novel was still embryonic. I come back to your advice daily and have absolutely no doubt I would have given up long ago were it not for you!

Mum, when you said you felt as though you'd written this book with me, you weren't lying! Thank you for taking endless tearful phone calls, reading early snippets, the countless cups of tea and for always pushing me forward. You are my absolute rock – and I promise Iris' Mum isn't based on you!

To Dad, for all the questions ('does writing a novel normally take *this* long?') as well as for your unshakeable belief that I could do it. Your innate optimism has always been, and continues to be, such a source of inspiration to me.

To the wider McVeigh family: I'd namecheck all of you, but there are just too many and I've got limited space as it is. Thank you!

To my amazing friends for your endless patience, humour and support as I cancelled and rearranged over and over again.

To Basil, for providing comic relief, clawing at my ankles when I got ahead of myself, and for keeping me company every day, often to the detriment of my wordcount.

And finally, to Dom. Thank you for your unwavering support and belief in me, for making me laugh, for keeping me calm and for putting up with the many ups and downs. From the bottom of my heart, thank you.